2008

JOIN IN ON THE HIGH JINX

PEARL

"A hysterical, fast-mov[...] between Caleb and Clair[...]
—Roun[...]

"4½ Stars! Hill's books [are] inventive and heart-tugging. They are guaranteed mood boosters!"
—*Romantic Times BOOKreviews Magazine*

"Hilarious . . . The characters are colorful and vibrant, coming alive with every turn of the page . . . Packed full of humor and adventure, sizzling SEAL sex, and enough romance to touch even the coldest heart . . . A real pearl."
—ARomanceReview.com

"[Hill is} the queen of humorous contemporary romance . . . The laughs keep coming . . . The audience will appreciate this zany Keystone State caper."
—*Midwest Book Review*

✦

"For a hilarious good time, readers can't go wrong with a Sandra Hill book. *Pearl Jinx* is loaded with charm, smart-alecky dialogue, adventure, and an endearing set of characters . . . rollicking . . . Hill's signature style shines through."
—SuspenseRomanceWriters.com

more . . .

PINK JINX

THE CAJUN COWBOY

"Hill will tickle readers' funny bones yet again as she writes in her trademark sexy style. A real crowd-pleaser, guar-an-teed."
—*Booklist* (starred review)

✦

"A pure delight. One terrific read!"
—*Romantic Times BOOKreviews Magazine* (four stars)

TALL, DARK, AND CAJUN

"If you like your romances hot and spicy and your men the same way, then you will like *Tall, Dark, and Cajun*...Eccentric characters, witty dialogue, humorous situations...and hot romance...[Hill] perfectly captures the bayou's mystique and makes it come to life."
—RomRevToday.com

Also by Sandra Hill

Tall, Dark, and Cajun

The Cajun Cowboy

The Red-Hot Cajun

Pink Jinx

Pearl Jinx

Wild Jinx

Sandra Hill

GRAND CENTRAL
PUBLISHING

NEW YORK   BOSTON

This book is a work of fiction. Names, characters, places, and incidents are the product of the author's imagination or are used fictitiously. Any resemblance to actual events, locales, or persons, living or dead, is coincidental.

If you purchase this book without a cover you should be aware that this book may have been stolen property and reported as "unsold and destroyed" to the publisher. In such case neither the author nor the publisher has received any payment for this "stripped book."

Copyright © 2008 by Sandra Hill
All rights reserved. Except as permitted under the U.S. Copyright Act of 1976, no part of this publication may be reproduced, distributed, or transmitted in any form or by any means, or stored in a database or retrieval system, without the prior written permission of the publisher.

Cover design by Diane Luger
Cover illustration by Tom Hallman
Typography by Jon Valk

Grand Central Publishing
Hachette Book Group USA
237 Park Avenue
New York, NY 10017
Visit our Web site at www.HachetteBookGroupUSA.com

Grand Central Publishing is a division of Hachette Book Group USA, Inc. The Grand Central Publishing name and logo is a trademark of Hachette Book Group USA, Inc.

Printed in the United States of America

First Printing: March 2008

10 9 8 7 6 5 4 3 2 1

This book is dedicated with much love to the women
in my family...strong women, all of them,
in the tradition of my mother, Veronica Cluston.
My sister Flora, my nieces Lori, Amy, and Julie,
my granddaughter Jaden, and my two
daughters-in-law, Bethany and Kim.
They've all had to suffer a bit (well, not Jaden),
but always proven they carry the strong women gene.
They've been able to buck up and face whatever
comes their way, including the sometimes clueless,
hardheaded men in their lives.
They are like the heroines in my books. Survivors,
all of them. And they've got great senses of
humor, the best survival tool of all.
Here's to all women who can laugh at life...and survive.

Wild Jinx

Chapter
1

Home, home on the...bayou...

It was dawn on Bayou Black, and its inhabitants were about to launch their daily musical extravaganza, a performance as beautiful and ancient as time.

The various sounds melded: a dozen different frogs, the splash of a sac-à-lait or bream rising for a tasty insect, the whisper of a humid breeze among the moss-draped oaks, the flap of an egret's wings as it soared out from a bald cypress branch. Even the silence had a sound. The only one not making any noise was its lone human inhabitant, John LeDeux.

But not for long.

"Yoo-hoo!"

About five hundred birds took flight at that shrill greeting, not to mention every snake, rabbit, raccoon, or gator within a one-mile radius.

John jackknifed up in bed and quickly pulled the sheet up to the waist of his naked body. He was in the single bedroom of his fishing camp, another name for a cabin on the bayou. He knew exactly who was yoo-hooing him. His ninety-two-year-old great aunt, Louise Rivard, better known as Tante Lulu. *Who else in the world says "Yoo-hoo"?*

He should have known better than to buy a place within a "hoot 'n' a holler" of his aunt's little cottage. She took neighborliness to new heights. *And "hoot 'n' a holler"? Mon Dieu! I'm turning into Tante Lulu.*

By the time the wooden screen door slammed, putting an exclamation mark on her entry, he'd already pulled on a pair of running shorts. He yawned widely as he walked into the living room, where his aunt was carrying two shopping bags of what appeared to be food. Not a good sign.

But this was his beloved aunt, the only one who'd been there for him and his brothers during some hard times. He'd never say or do anything to hurt her feelings. "What're you doin' here, *chère?* It's only six-thirty, and I don't have to report for work 'til ten." John was a detective with the police department in Fontaine, a sister city to Baton Rouge. It was a two-hour drive, and most nights he stayed in an efficiency apartment he rented in Baton Rouge, but some nights, like last night, he just wanted to be home, here in his raised cottage with its stilts half-submerged in the bayou stream he loved. It was located on Bayou Black, far enough away from Houma to still feel private but way too close to Tante Lulu.

"You gots bags under yer eyes, Tee-John," his aunt said, totally ignoring his question. Tee-John...Little John...was a nickname that had been given to him as a kid, way before he hit his six-foot-two.

She went into his small kitchen and was unloading her goodies. French bread, boudin sausage, eggs, beignets, red and green tomatoes, garlic, okra, butter, Tabasco sauce, and the holy trinity of southern cooking: celery, onions, and bell peppers. That was just from one bag. His small fridge would never hold all this crap.

"Yeah, I've got bags. I didn't get to bed 'til three."

"Tsk, tsk, tsk! Thass one of the reasons I'm here."

"Huh?"

"Come sit you pretty self down, honey."

He sank down into a chair, breathing in deeply of the strong chicory coffee, which she'd already set to brewing.

Now she was whipping up what appeared to be an omelette with sides of sausage and fried green tomatoes. It would do no good to argue that he rarely ate before noon.

"I may be old, but I ain't dumb. Even here in the bayou, we hear 'bout all yer hanky-panky."

He grinned. "Do you see any hot babes here?"

"Hah! Thass jist 'cause I walked in on you las' month with that Morrison tart, buck naked and her squealin' like a pig. Ya prob'ly do yer hanky-panky elsewheres now."

"You got that right," he murmured.

"Why cain't ya find yerself a nice Cajun girl, Tee-John?"

Like they don't like hanky-panky as much as the next girl! " 'Cause I'm not lookin', that's why. Besides, Jenny Morrison is not a tart."

His aunt put her hands on her tiny hips...she was only five-foot-zero and ninety pounds sopping wet. "Does she have yer ring on her finger?"

His eyes went wide. "Are you kidding? Hell, no!"

"Ya gonna marry up with the girl?"

"Hell, no!" he repeated.

She shrugged. "Well, then, yer a hound dog and she's a tart. Hanky-panky is only fer people in love who's gonna get married someday."

That was the Bible, according to Tante Lulu.

"Best I bring ya some more St. Jude statues."

"No!"

She raised her eyebrows at his sharp tone.

"Sorry, but, come on, Auntie. I've got a St. Jude statue in my bedroom, bathroom, kitchen, porch, car, and office. There's St. Jude napkins and salt and pepper shakers here on the table, St. Jude pot holders by the stove, St. Jude wind chimes outside, a St. Jude birdbath, and God only knows what else."

"A person cain't have too many St. Judes."

St. Jude was the patron saint of hopeless causes and his aunt's favorite. She was going to heaven someday on St. Jude brownie points, if nothing else.

"I'm not that hopeless."

She patted his shoulder as she put a steaming mug of coffee in front of him on the table. "I know that, sweetie. Thass one of the reasons I'm here. I had a vision las' night."

He rolled his eyes. *Here it comes.*

"It mighta been a dream, but it felt like a vision. Charmaine says I should go ta one of those psychos." Charmaine was his half-sister and as psycho as they came.

"Psychics," he corrected.

"Thass what I said. Anyways, back ta my vision. Guess who's gettin' married this year?"

"Who?" He asked the question before he had a chance to bite his tongue.

"You," she chirped brightly.

He choked on his coffee and sprayed droplets all over the table.

She mopped it up with a St. Jude napkin.

"I'm too young, only twenty-eight," he protested. "Luc and Remy were thirty-three when they got married, and René was thirty-five. I got lots of time. What's the hurry?"

"The time is right fer different folks at different times."

"Any clue who the lucky lady will be?" he asked, deciding to go along with the nonsense. He wasn't even dating anyone steadily, and he for damn sure didn't know one single woman he wanted to spend the rest of his life with.

She shook her head. "That wasn't clear, but it's gonna happen. The thunderbolt, she's a-comin'. Best ya be prepared." The thunderbolt she referred to was some screwball thunderbolt of love that she claimed hit the LeDeux men just before they met the loves of their lives.

"No way! And just to make sure, I'm buyin' a lightning rod before I go in to work today. Speaking of which, I've gotta take a shower. Can you put a hold on that breakfast for about fifteen minutes?"

"*Oui,* but first I gots ta tell ya my news."

"Oh?" The hairs stood up on the back of his neck. The last time she had news to announce, she'd popped a surprise wedding on his brother René. Or maybe it was the time she and Charmaine had entered a belly dancing contest. "I thought the vision was your news," he teased.

She smacked his arm with a wooden spoon. "Stop yer sass, boy. My news is that I hired Jinx, Inc. ta come ta Loo-zee-anna."

"The treasure hunting company? They're coming here?" John had worked twice for the New Jersey operation, which hired out to find lost treasures of any kind... sunken shipwrecks, cave pearls, buried gold, lost objects, just about anything.

She nodded. "We's gonna hunt fer pirate treasure."

"Where?"

"On Bayou Black."

"Auntie." He sighed loudly. "There's no treasure here on Bayou Black."

"Well, not right here. Out past René's fishing camp. In fact, we's gonna use his camp fer our headquarters."

His jaw dropped. It wasn't the first time she'd mentioned this idea, but it boggled the mind that his aunt had convinced a reputable treasure salvaging company that there was pirate gold on Bayou Black.

"Too bad ya gots ta work. It should be fun."

"You're talkin' about Jean Lafitte, I suppose. Don't you know that treasure legend is bullsh...uh, just that...a legend?"

"We'll see. I gots clues what no one else has."

That is just great! Probably another vision. "How are you involved?"

"I put up two hundred thousand dollars fer half the profits."

He inhaled sharply. "That's a lot of money."

His alarm must have shown because she shot back, "It's *my* money ta spend anyways I want."

He put up his hands in surrender. "Absolutely. When is this venture gonna start?"

"Next month."

"Okay. That's great, really. I wish you all the luck." That's what he said, but what he thought, standing under the shower a short time later, was, *The bayou is never gonna be the same again, guaranteed!* Immediately followed by, *Treasure hunting is never gonna be the same after bein' hit by Tante Lulu. Talk about!*

The menu at this nightclub was edible...uh, incredible...

Celine Arseneaux took a deep breath, then started across the crowded parking lot of the Playpen in suburban Baton Rouge, Louisiana, trying to ignore the fact that she was all tarted up like a high class call girl.

The get-up had been the bright idea of Bruce Cavanaugh, her editor at the *New Orleans Times-Tribune*, designed so that Celine would meld in the crowd at this upscale club, which provided sexual favors to both men and women, all run by the Lorenzo branch of the Dixie Mafia. Thus the black stiletto sling-backs, the sheer black silk hose, the black slip dress with red lace edging the bodice and hem, not to mention the flame red lipstick. Her shoulder-length boring brown hair had been blown and twisted into a wild curly mane. Normally, her idea of dressing up was new jeans, lip gloss, and a ponytail.

No way would she ever be confused for the award-winning journalist she was. Nor would she be taken for the mother of a five-year-old child. Nope. She was a woman on the make for a little action...illegal, paid-for action.

"I look like a Bourbon Street hooker," she'd complained to her fellow reporter, Jade Lewis, just a half hour ago as she'd helped plant the tape recorder inside her push-up bra and adjusted the tiny camera into the gold and rhinestone, rose-shaped brooch at the deep vee of her front. "I didn't even know I could have cleavage."

Jade had laughed. "Not a hooker. You look too high class for that. With the diamond post earrings and that brooch, you look like a bored, upper class gal with a wad of dough looking for Mister Studmuffin."

"A desperate housewife?"

"Something like that."

So now Celine walked up to the doorman, who resembled a pro-wrestler in a tux, and flashed the small card she'd been given for admission. Apparently, no one could enter the private premises unless they were with a member, or had obtained one of the cards...cards which were impossible to obtain without careful vetting. How Bruce had obtained hers she didn't want to know.

The big bruiser studied the card, then stepped aside and held the door open for her. She could hear soft music up ahead...no bump and grind sordid business here. A hostess, who could have passed for a runway model in a trendy culottes outfit, inquired, "Black, white, or blue?"

"Huh?"

A light smile tugged at the hostess's lips. "First time here?"

Celine nodded.

"The black room is for men wanting to hook up with a woman. The white room is for women wanting to hook up with a man. And the blue room is for men and women, together, wanting to hook up with...whatever."

At Celine's confused look, she elaborated, "*Ménage à trois,* honey."

Oh, good grief! Celine hoped she wasn't blushing. "White, please."

She wondered with a suppressed giggle how another reporter, Dane Jessup, was going to handle this situation when he did his part of the story tomorrow night. The gay male angle. Besides that, if Celine was a geek, Dane was dweeb to the max.

Soon she was seated at a small round table in the back of the room with an empty chair across from her. An in-house phone sat in the center. There was subtle lighting and the atmosphere of an upscale bar, that image heightened by the soft rock being played by a two-piece band. No Chippendale style dancers here or bare-chested waiters. A female waitress in a perfectly respectable black uniform asked if she wanted a beverage. They only cost ten dollars a pop... and that was for pop.

The ratio of men to women in the room was about five to one, with about two dozen women sitting at the various tables. Several were on the small dance floor with attractive men. Most of the men wore suits, or sport coats over khakis, or golf shirts tucked into pleated slacks. A few wore jeans, but they were combined with tucked-in, button-down dress shirts. No cowboys or construction workers. Subtlety again. Those men not partnered on the dance floor or at tables leaned against the two bars, nursing drinks. Or leaned against a far wall. A few glanced her way with interest.

It looked like a singles club. Maybe this wouldn't be so bad.

But then she opened the "menu" in front of her... and felt like crawling under the table.

Welcome to the Playpen. We are here for your enjoyment. Please study the menu below. Then look around the room. If you see anyone you like, pick up the phone and indicate your choice. Only then will you be approached. If after talking to one of our men you change your mind, you can make another choice. Accommodations are upstairs, or off-site arrangements can be made. Good luck!

This was followed by a menu of services that were available... very detailed descriptions... with prices. She wasn't sure she even knew what some of these things were, and for sure there were some she'd never done or had any desire to do. Eeew!

After the waitress plopped her whiskey sour down on the table, and Celine had taken a big gulp, she braced herself. It was only pretend on her part. It was just a story. She'd done worse things to get a scoop. Well, no, she hadn't, but it was important that these outrageous activities be exposed. Especially since the Dixie Mafia was rumored to be involved.

Morphing into professional mode, she made mental notes of what she'd seen so far and decided she would "interview" three different men before making her escape following a trip to the ladies' room. Bruce might want her to take one of them upstairs, to see how it was done, but no way was she going that far. Pressing one of the roses in her brooch to launch the zoom lenses, she began a slow scan of the men from right to left.

Some of the prostitutes looked downright dangerous. Way too blatantly sexual for her tastes.

Okay, the young blond man would be her first. Extra long hair in a low ponytail. Clean cut. Wearing a light blue Oxford-collared shirt, tucked into dark blue chinos. He looked like a college student.

Then maybe the older gentleman with salt and pepper hair. Fiftyish. Well-built. Designer suit.

Third...hmmm, she couldn't decide. She should probably invite the guy who looked like Tony from *The Sopranos,* if she had the nerve. Or the scowling man who was both homely and tempting as hell; rough sex, for sure.

She had her hand on the phone, about to request her first "date," when she noticed two men amble into the room laughing at some private joke. Her survey started to swing on a return scan, then doubled back.

Oh. My. God!

Could it be...? No, it's impossible.

The tall man with dark hair, late twenties, wearing a black suit over a tight white silk T-shirt, stopped dead and was staring at her, too. Her camera took him in, which she intended to erase the moment she got home. Or maybe not.

This was an absolute nightmare. The worst possible thing that could have happened.

It was that slimebucket, oversexed, full-of-himself Cajun jerk. John LeDeux.

Whom she'd had a crush on as a girl and been hopelessly attracted to as a woman, despite her seeming intelligence. What was it about men like John LeDeux that caused women's IQs to nosedive? She had successfully avoided him for five long years. Why else would she have stayed in Texas for so long? What irony, to finally run into him, after being back here for only six months, in a…a sex club.

If some higher power would just let a crack open in the floor, she would gladly jump in, assignment be damned.

He'd like to be on her menu, guar-an-teed!…

John LeDeux ambled into the Playpen for his night shift.

The idea of him selling sex, or buying it for that matter, was ludicrous, but the dickhead managers of this place couldn't see past their cash registers. *One hundred dollars for a blow job? I don't think so! I'm worth way more than that.*

He scanned the room, looking for potential "customers." Then went stone cold still.

Well, well, well, lookee here. Celine Arseneaux, out to buy herself some action.

Was she that hard up? She always was a stick-up-the-ass prudish geek, too smart for her own good. Thought she was better than the rest of stupid mankind. Except for that one time that he barely recalled. She'd been hot damn non-geeky that night if his fuzzy recollection was accurate.

But wait, wasn't she supposed to be some hotshot newspaper reporter in Dallas? No, wait, someone mentioned recently that she'd moved to the *New Orleans Times-Tribune*. Why would she be here…?

Oh, good Lord. She's here on assignment. Man, this is a FUBAR waiting to happen.

He whispered to Tank Woodrow...Police Lieutenant Clifford "Tank" Woodrow...at his side, "Nine o'clock. Lady in black and red dress. Reporter."

"The one with the flame-colored mouth that looks like it could melt salt off a pretzel stick?"

He laughed, just knowing how much Celine would appreciate that description. Not! "That would be the one."

"Shiiit! She's gonna blow our cover."

He and Tank had been undercover at the Playpen for the past week. The Fontaine police department, in conjunction with the special state organized crime unit, were about to bust this and other operations of the Dixie Mafia wide open. This woman would ruin it all.

Not if he could help it.

The instant she saw him, she recognized him, her eyes going wide as saucers.

"Watch my back," he told Tank.

Against Playpen rules, he approached the table, amused to see Celine averting her face, hoping she could escape his notice. Fat chance!

He yanked a chair around and sat down close to her, with his back to the bar, where the client facilitator stood watching. Yeah, that's what the pompous pimp called himself.

"Hey, darlin', lookin' fer a date?" he asked with the lazy southern drawl he had perfected over the years.

She mumbled something, her face still averted. He was pretty sure she'd told him to do something to himself that was anatomically impossible.

"Nah, I'd rather do you, sweetheart."

She turned and stared him straight in the face. "Get lost, LeDeux."

"Now, now. Is that any way to treat the man who's gonna show you a good time?" He picked up the menu of services that was sitting on the table, opened it and pointed to one particular line. "I'm really good at *that*."

Her face flushed. "You are such a pig."

"Compliments will get you everywhere, sugar."

"What are you doing here?"

"The better question is, what're you doin' here? Oooh, is that a camera in here?" He flicked the rose brooch on her chest, and felt an odd zing where the back of his fingers touched her warm skin.

He could tell by the look of horror on her face that she'd felt the zing, too. Or maybe it was because she realized that her hidden techie camera hadn't been as hidden as she'd hoped.

"Go away," she said with a groan. "I've got a job here."

"So do I, and it's not to dole out sexual favors. This operation is about to be busted, and we are not gonna let you jam up the works."

"We? Who is we? Fontaine police? State police? Feds?"

"All of the above. You're not gonna screw up this operation, babe."

"Oh, yeah, how you gonna stop me, *babe?*"

"Just watch me." He picked up the phone. "The lady, she wants numbers five, six, and seven. She's too shy to tell y'all herself. Two hours. Upstairs. A rodeo, a dirty bath, and a missionary. You got her credit card number on file? Okay."

Celine was too busy gawking at the description of five, six, and seven to notice him standing and pulling her up with him. Wrapping an arm around her shoulder, tucking her tightly to his side, he prevented her from bolting, trying his best to ignore her light floral perfume and the softness of her skin. "Let's get outta here," he said. "Maybe if you're lucky, I'll show you how well I can perform."

She squirmed out of his hold and glared at him. "I'm not going anywhere with you." She looked as if she might be about to belt him a good one.

But then all hell broke loose.

Police in SWAT uniforms rushing in all the entries and blocking all the exits. Bullhorns blaring out, "Stay where you are, people. This is a raid." Women were screaming. Men were cursing. The band stopped dead in the middle of "Love Shack." It was a full-blown police operation. At least fifty armed local, state, and federal law enforcement officers in the three rooms on this floor, he would estimate.

A pigload of people were going to be arrested, including himself, since his identity had to be protected. Ms. Hot Shot Reporter was not going to be able to fast talk herself out of this mess 'til later.

She was flashing her chest all over the place, taking pictures, he presumed, not showing off her assets. Maybe she wouldn't be so mad at him now.

No, that was not to be the case.

Turning swiftly, she windmilled her arm back, then clipped him on the chin with her fist.

"What was that for?"

"Everything."

A cop he didn't recognize was approaching, already reading them their rights, flex-cuffs dangling from his fingertips. But first John had to do something. He grabbed Celine, tugged her flush against his body, and kissed her, long and hard. He might have even used his tongue, but who knew! He was as dazed as she was when he broke off the kiss. "Which one of you is the hooker?" the amused cop asked.

"Him," she said.

"Her," he said at the same time.

Smoke practically blew from her ears as she glowered at him. Wait 'til she found out that the mind-blowing kiss had been a ruse to allow himself the opportunity to slip off her brooch and the tiny mike inside her bra. They were now in his suit pocket.

"*Laissez les bons temps rouler*," he murmured as they walked off together, in custody. "Let the good times roll."

She gave him the finger.

Chapter
2

Advice to women: When rogues grin, run like crazy...

Celine was sitting on a bench seat in the paddy wagon, hands cuffed, ankles shackled, with the bayou bad boy on her left and Hal "I could make you scream, baby" Hopkins on her right. If Hal made another lewd suggestion to her or if John continued to chuckle, she was going to put a curse on the two of them...one that would impair their precious scream-maker parts for life, and she knew a French Quarter voodoo priestess who could do it, too.

There were three female and two male prostitutes and one trick, or sex club client, or date, or customer, or whatever they wanted to call them, on one of the benches, along with her and John, and on the other facing bench were a "client facilitator," one alleged Playpen owner...i.e. Mafia guy named Emile Lorenzo, a male prostitute, and three more tricks or clients. Apparently, there were other members of the Lorenzo family—an

Italian-Creole unit of the Dixie mob—in the other emergency police vans. A black police officer stood near the back door with a rifle in one hand and a tear gas canister in the other. Like any one of them was in a position to bolt! Another cop—red-haired, Irish-looking, also armed—stood near her and John, with his back to the metal grill that separated them from the driver in front.

They had all been Mirandized back at the club. Not a pleasant experience, even when a person was innocent, as she was. Apparently, there was a sitting grand jury just waiting for them to be hauled in. The police would want immediate indictments for some of the flight risks.

"I was not a customer," she told the black cop, who was closest to her, now that the hubbub had died down. "Actually, I'm a reporter. I was there to do a story." They had all been protesting their innocence, but her claim to being a journalist caused the heads of the club owner and three clients on the other side to shoot up with interest. Emile Lorenzo glared at her with a silent warning that she would be swimming with the fishes, or rather the bayou gators, if she wrote anything about him. But the interesting thing was the way the three clients averted their faces in a panicked fashion.

Well, she supposed she would be embarrassed to be found hanging out in such a place, too. Still…hmmm. Celine's journalistic instincts went on red alert, and she studied them a little closer. "Oh, no!" She *did* recognize the three of them.

"Shhh," John murmured.

Jeesh, he was a good-looking man. He was twenty-eight to her twenty-six; she knew because she'd been two years behind him in Houma High School and then Tulane University. Tall…maybe six-two…he had dark

Cajun hair and eyes. He'd probably shaved that morning, but now a dark, not unattractive, stubble covered his face. He had a smile that would melt most women's hearts...and morals, truth be told. Not hers.

Well, once. Until today she'd considered that one-night stand an aberration. A blip on her intelligence radar. This rogue had a reputation throughout southern Louisiana as a world class womanizer, and any woman with a grain of good sense would steer clear of his magnetism.

After all she'd suffered...waitressing and attending college classes 'til her labor pains started, the embarrassment of welfare aid, the ego blaster of single motherhood, the constant financial hardships, despite her grandfather's help...she had survived and thought herself stronger for the struggle. Then an hour in John's presence, and she was right back to step one, virtually drooling over the hottest guy in town.

She was not a bad-looking woman these days, but still, she felt like Ugly Betty to John's Hugh Jackman.

But none of that mattered. What did matter was that she get away from John as soon as possible. He could not find out about Etienne. Not after all this time. Not ever.

Even that was irrelevant now. What *was* important was that she'd just stumbled onto an even better story than the Playpen operation. These three well-known Louisianans were going to grace the centerfold of page one tomorrow. She chuckled and was about to "interview" them. Not many reporters could claim to have interviewed some prostitutes and their clients in a paddy wagon. It would be a feather in her cap at her new paper.

"*Mon Dieu!*" Leaning into her ear, he said, "Now's not the time to out these folks, darlin'." So, he recognized the three clients, too. And, yeah, he was right. She should wait to confront the three dodo birds back at the station. Maybe in a holding cell.

John had a heavy southern accent, which many women found attractive. Sort of a lazy, sexy drawl. She was Cajun, too, well, three-quarters Cajun, but she'd only moved to Houma to live with her grandfather at age fifteen when her mother died of cancer and her father committed suicide. Bad times then!

Trying her best to ignore the faint scent of mint, probably soap, as he continued to lean close, she nodded hesitantly. "Is that Pastor Leroy Evington? The bigshot TV evangelist from Shreveport?"

"Looks like," he whispered. "And beside him is Ted Warner. The owner of that chain of TV stations?"

John had just confirmed what she'd already suspected. Holy moly! This was turning into the scoop of the decade, even better than her exposé of Katrina corruption while still working in Dallas. She was so excited she could barely restrain herself from letting loose with a whoop of joy.

"Oh, yeah! This raid is haulin' in some big fish."

She studied the trio again. They weren't able to hide their faces completely, restrained as they were. But the woman...a sleek, expensively dressed blonde in her late forties, she would guess...looked familiar. Her heart rate accelerated with sudden understanding. "Do you know who that woman is?" she said against John's ear, her voice no doubt giving away her excitement.

"No, but I like the way you keep blowin' in my ear."

She made a sound of disgust.

"Just in case I didn't mention it before, you look hot tonight, Celine." His compliment was particularly compelling with his mouth so close to her face.

"Like I care!" She moaned inwardly, not wanting to care.

He winked at her.

"Be serious." *Oh, God! Another inward moan.*

"Okay, I give up. Who is she?"

"Callie Martinez."

His neck practically got whiplash swinging to look at the woman in question. "Congressman Martinez's wife?" he mouthed silently to her.

She nodded.

"You can't report this."

"Report what? The bust? You better believe I'm going to report that."

"Shhh. Keep your voice down. Not that. The names of those three dingbats over there. If you do, all hell is gonna break loose."

She smiled widely. "Yeah."

"You're gonna have a boatload of Rolex lawyers swarming around the police station before they're even arraigned. They might even find a loophole to dismiss this whole bust."

"This is a big story...as big as the sex club and the Mafia connection, the focus of my original story. I can see the headline: 'Sex for Sale: Even the High and Mighty Are Buying.'" The whole time she talked in a side-of-the-mouth undertone, she studied the two Johns and a Jane, who continued to duck their heads, taking mental notes of their appearance and demeanor.

He groaned.

"I need to call my editor. You're a cop. Why don't you get us out of here?"

"Not yet. Can't blow my cover. Besides, I don't know these guys. They're staties ... state troopers. Don't worry. You'll get your call soon. Besides, your crime reporter will have already heard about tonight's operation on the police radio."

"Hey, you two," the Irish cop by the door said. "Enough chitchat. Set up a date later."

She raised her chin at the grinning officer. "I work for the *New Orleans Times-Tribune,* and you're going to be the star of my exposé if you're not careful."

"Yeah, yeah, yeah. And I'm the king of Mardi Gras."

"Listen, lady, give it up." The black cop leaned down and picked up her purse at her feet. Opening it, he took out the Playpen admission card and waved it in her face. "Enough said."

It was while the cop was picking up her purse that she noticed her brooch was missing. She raised her cuffed hands and felt against the place where the mike should be planted inside her bra. It was missing, too.

"That'll be enough of that, sweet cakes," Irish said, using a billy club to steer her hands downward, away from her chest. "No feelin' yerself up. You can do that once you've bought one of these honeys here." He glanced pointedly at John and Hal bracketing her.

"I was not—"

"Lady, give it up," Irish said tiredly. When she opened her mouth, about to plead her case some more, the cop waved the Playpen card in front of her.

"I can explain that." Her face was probably beet red.

The cop held up a halting hand. "Save it fer the judge, honey."

Something occurred to her then. Turning to John, she asked with forced softness, "Did you steal my camera and mike?"

"You had a camera and mike? Tsk-tsk-tsk!"

"I want them back."

"You do, huh? How bad?"

She narrowed her eyes at him. "What do you mean?"

He shrugged.

"Are you trying to sell my equipment back to me? That's illegal."

"How legal is it to tape people without their permission?"

"That's different."

"Oh?"

"Journalistic exception."

"Bull!"

"I could make you return them."

He just laughed.

"You're a pig."

"You said that before."

Both cops walked up to stand before them. "You two are really startin' to piss me off," the Irish cop said. "Enough with the whispering!"

"Should I Taser them?" the black cop inquired of his pal. He was probably kidding. She hoped.

"Only if you want to lose your badges," John told them. And he cited some police code guideline number that made both cops raise their eyebrows and back off. They kept eyeing John strangely after that.

Finally, the rat did something about their situation. Already her brain was at work, putting together the story and sidebar she would be writing later tonight. It would help to have the photos and tapes, though. "What exactly do you want in return for my camera and mike?" she gritted out.

"A number six."

Whoever said "Any publicity is good publicity" wasn't a cop...

It was a large conference room in police headquarters where the debriefing was held early the next morning, but still it was crowded with all personnel who had been involved, directly or indirectly, with the Playpen bust.

There were more than forty men and women from the Fontaine police and district attorney departments, FBI, ATF, state troopers, and State Organized Crime Commission—and that didn't include uniformed arresting officers—sitting on folding chairs arranged in rows throughout the room, most of them holding Styrofoam cups of black Creole coffee. No whipped-cream-covered lattes here.

In another conference room across the hall, reporters from various media, local and nationwide, waited to get the full scoop. Separate interrogation rooms held Congressman and Mrs. Martinez, TV mogul Ted Warner, and evangelist Leroy Evington with teams of high-priced lawyers driving cars worth more than the entire Katrina Disaster Relief Fund. They would probably get off with hefty out-of-court settlements. Clients and customers who could afford the bail had been released last night.

Not so the Dixie Mafia, fifteen of whom were already in custody and more to come. Not the big boss or godfather, but two of his sons, one counselor or consigliere, three lieutenants, and nine soldiers, several with the Lorenzo name. This bust wouldn't break the mob in Louisiana, which included prostitution, drugs, extortion, illegal gun sales, theft, murder, and various other sundry crimes, but it would curtail it substantially. Anti-Mafia operations way back to Eliot Ness had learned that getting the bad guys often meant back-door arrests for lesser crimes with maximum punishments.

"Okay, listen up, everyone," Captain Samuel Pinot said, stepping up to the podium. Captain Sam was head of the Fontaine police department but a Cajun, like himself, from Terrebonne Parish. John had known him since he was knee-high to a crawfish. In fact, Sam had once had the hots for his half-sister Charmaine, but a whole hell of a lot of southern Louisiana men had been bird dogging Charmaine's tail at one time or another. "Good job!" Captain Sam yelled, pumping a fist into the air, which was met with cheers from throughout the room.

Next, the captain introduced Gil Tremaine, head of the crime commission and number one on the Dixie Mafia's hit list. He and his team had been pursuing the mob here in Louisiana for years.

"The DA's office will want to talk separately with each of you to prepare the case against the perps." Tremaine motioned over to Dean Avery and his squad of assistant DAs leaning against the wall. "I don't need to tell you to keep a low profile. The Dixie Mafia is still out there, alive and well. We don't want any potential witnesses, meaning some of you, found at the bottom of some bayou swamp wearing a concrete suit."

A titter of laugher rippled through the room, but every one of them understood that this was a serious threat.

He and Tank and the other undercover cops would be small cogs in this prosecution, but that didn't mean they were unimportant. Especially once the prosecution witness list was given to the defense. Yeah, Tremaine and his boys were highest on the Mafia's enemy totem pole, but everyone was at risk.

"Detectives have already taken witness statements and will expect to follow up with more," Tremaine continued. "That means you folks in here who were undercover, as well as club employees, hookers, male and female, and customers."

"Hey, Lacy," yelled Tank, who sat beside him. "I hear you got propositioned twenty-seven times in one night, working the Playpen's black room...or was it the blue room?"

Lt. Lacy Jessup glared at Tank. They had a running hate/love relationship going for the past year. "Actually, Tank, it was thirty-two, and all men." She gave emphasis to *all men*, as if Tank did not fall into that category of manliness. Tank's face flushed, but luckily he kept his mouth shut, especially since the chief was not too happy at the interruption.

"Which brings us to the three high profile 'tricks' caught with their pants down, so to speak," Tremaine said, turning the podium over to Avery.

"Their embarrassment is going to be punishment enough, but they'll be given substantial fines and community service," the DA explained. "All hush-hush, which means you'll read about it in the newspaper before the ink is dry on the documents." Avery went on to detail what they had found and what needed to be done yet, including more arrests. He then discussed the schedule for handling the case; they hoped to bring the case to trial ASAP. Tank and John were expected to give their initial depositions after this meeting.

The FBI, ATF, and crime commission reps discussed their involvement in the case. Then the mike was turned back to Captain Sam. "I don't need to tell you all to keep your mouths shut with the press. Let our media relations personnel be the only contact persons, unless given permission otherwise. Which leads me to this…" The captain held up what looked like a copy of the *New Orleans Times-Tribune*. "It appears there was a reporter in the Playpen last night. Celine Arseneaux."

"Uh-oh," Tank said at his side.

"The main front page article isn't too bad," the chief said, "though we would have preferred that we put our own spin on the story. Nope, what has my temper about to boil over is this sidebar titled, 'Fontaine Cop Was One Hot Prostitute.' The first sentence reads: 'Fontaine has its very own sex cop, and he is hot, hot, hot.' No name. No photos. Just a cutesy little article poking fun at the department." The chief leaned both elbows on the podium and asked in a way too sweet voice, "I wonder who it could be?"

The eyes of the chief and about thirty-nine other people turned to him.

John slid down in his seat, to no avail.

Laughter exploded throughout the room.

The general public wouldn't know it was him, but his fellow cops and his family? Yeah, they would guess.

John would never live this down.

Two can play this game, sweet thing...

"What the hell is this all about?"

John, blood-curdling mad, stormed into the newspaper office the next day, waving yesterday's issue of the *New Orleans Times-Tribune* at Celine Arseneaux, who had the good sense to put her desk between them.

The witch flashed him an evil smile. "What? You don't like my story on the Playpen bust?" She batted her eyelashes with exaggerated innocence.

Man, she had the prettiest, unique pale blue eyes he'd ever seen, especially on a dark-haired Cajun. Must be a mutant gene, or else she wasn't pure Cajun.

And, oh, yeah, she was as innocent as a cobra at a tea party. He growled and fisted his hands to prevent himself from leaping over the desk and throttling the infuriating pain-in-the-ass idiot.

Her newspaper had run not just a front page article, but also a full-page inside spread on a history of the Playpen, sordid details of exactly what was offered and for what price, the Dixie Mafia involvement, the arrests made, including the three public figures who were surely threatening to sue, bios of the various prostitutes, some of whom were college students working there part-time... a real tabloid style exposé that could very well earn Celine and her colleagues who'd collaborated on the assignment some major newspaper awards. For the rest of them... law enforcement and the arrestees... what they would earn was quite different.

The three "celebrity" clients were out on bail, their high-priced lawyers having indeed negotiated plea deals to keep them out of the courtroom and further notoriety. The prostitutes and other clients were slapped with hefty fines. Not so lucky the fifteen various-level Mafia guys for whom no bail was allowed. They were headed for a long stay in Angola if the eventual trial was successful. Unless they were willing to squeal on some of their buddies up higher in the food chain, which they would not do, having been sworn to *omertà,* a code of silence which pretty much said, "You talk, you die."

But that was all out of John's hands now...till the trial, when he would have to testify. Which led him right to Ms. Celine von Lois Lane here.

It wasn't the main articles, front and inside, that had pissed off John, although he thought it was ruthless of the newspaper to use the names of people who had not yet been found guilty. No, what had his head about to explode was the sidebar Celine had done on the opposite inside page. *About him!* The headline read: "Fontaine Cop Was One Hot Prostitute."

"I didn't use your name or photograph."

"Thanks a bunch."

"No one would know it was about you unless you told them."

"You can't be that clueless. This was revenge, pure and simple, Celine, and I wanna know why."

She shrugged. "Stealing my camera and mike. Being an asshole. One small step for womankind. Whatever."

"Is this about that one-night stand when we were in college?"

Her face turned a mottled beet red, and it wasn't attractive, either. Unlike her slutty appearance the other night, she wore jeans, a Tulane T-shirt, and no makeup. Her shoulder-length hair was scrunched up on top of her head with one of those comb claw thingees. Her pale blue eyes peered up at him over a pair of half-circle, wire-rimmed reading glasses perched near the tip of her nose. "You remember that?" she squeaked out.

"Hell, yes. Why would you think I didn't?"

"Well...uh..."

"Get your hand bag. We're goin' outside where we can talk in private." He could see a number of her office mates eavesdropping on their conversation.

"In your dreams, bozo."

He could flash evil smiles, too. Taking an envelope out of his sport coat pocket, he pulled out several photos and dropped them on the desk in front of her.

She gasped.

There were a half-dozen photos of her on the night of the Playpen bust. And she sure as hell didn't look like any hoity-toity I-am-so-pure newspaper journalist. Nope, she looked like a high class slut on the hunt for what his great aunt would call hanky-panky. She hadn't been the only one with a hidden camera.

"Where did you get these?" she gritted out.

Gritting is good. Turning the tables when attacked is good. Rule number one of police training. What is that old saying? "You can be the hammer or the nail." Well, I pick hammer. "You weren't the only one wired, baby."

Setting her glasses on the desk, she exhaled on a loud whoosh which caused her breasts to move under her T-shirt. Which he was not noticing.

"Can I assume there are copies?"

"What do you think? Frankly, you look pretty good, sugar. Betcha *Penthouse* would offer you a mint to pose, based on these pictures alone. It could have the headline: 'New Orleans Reporter Was One Hot Sex Mole.' "

She said something under her breath that most refined

southern belles didn't. Not that she was a belle. Nope, she was more like that other B-word.

"Tsk-tsk. 'Ya gotta wash the okra if ya want a good gumbo,' as my Tante Lulu would say. You better wash your okra, Celine." He used an exaggerated Cajun accent, then drawled out her name so it sounded like saaay-lean.

"Screw you!"

"No thanks."

She picked her purse up off the floor. "Let's go."

As he followed her swinging hips through the cube farm to the elevator, heads were popping out of office cubicles, like gophers in a Bill Murray movie. A few of the men flashed him surreptitious high fives.

When they were enclosed in the elevator, she glared at him, then hit the down button so hard it was a wonder it didn't fall off.

"You don't really think I'm going to be intimidated by a sissy glare, do you?"

She pressed her lips together—*very nice lips, even without lipstick, dammit!*—forcibly preventing herself from reacting to his comment. *Smart girl!*

There were about six feet between them. No way was he getting within smacking distance

Into the silence, he grinned at her. Why? Because she hated his grinning at her. "Ain't payback sweet, *chère?*"

Chapter
3

He...rather, the food...was yummy...

A short time later, they were in the Oyster Bar of the Red Fish Grill on Bourbon Street, feasting on barbecued oyster po'-boys...a Louisiana specialty served on loaves of French bread overflowing with red onions, lettuce, tomatoes, and homemade blue cheese dressing. If that wasn't enough, there were sides of Creole potato salad and tall glasses of sweet tea.

She demurred on a dessert after the huge meal, but then found herself picking at John's double chocolate bread pudding. An oddly intimate and strange thing for her to do. But everything about the angry sparks that flew between the two of them was strange.

They were seated before a long bar, on sculpted metal sea creature barstools. The atmosphere was heightened by the giant oyster mirrors on the ancient brick wall behind the bar and by the black and white photographs of Louisiana bayous and residents taken in the 1940s. The artwork had been part of a dissertation at Newcomb

College of Tulane by Claire Brennan, mother of Ralph Brennan, the original owner. Those who had grown up in southern Louisiana, like her and John, knew this establishment and frequented it often.

Many restaurants and businesses in the quarter had suffered and still suffered from Katrina. But New Orleaners were survivors, as evidenced by how busy the streets were this afternoon.

She turned her stool to face him, even as she continued nibbling at his sinfully delicious dessert. As she ate, he watched her closely in a disturbing way she didn't want to analyze.

"Okay, you made me come—"

"Hardly."

"You are so crude."

"Thank you."

"I'm trying to say, you made me come *with you*. So, spill."

He used his thumb to sweep some chocolate off her bottom lip, then sucked on his thumb. He honest-to-God didn't seem to have done it for sexual reasons, but she felt his action all the way to her curling toes. Whoo-boy, he was one potent male. Especially clean-shaven today, wearing jeans, a black T-shirt, and a blue linen sport coat with the sleeves pushed up, *Miami Vice* style.

She could not get close to this man. She could not lower her defenses. One one-night stand was enough. And she, for sure, could not tell him he had a son. When her grandfather had emptied his meager bank account so that she could finish college—she'd been a junior and John a recent graduate by then—she'd made a promise to him that she would keep the paternity secret. She'd lost her scholarship because she had to drop out for a semester after the birth. And now that she'd moved back to Houma, her grandfather was Etienne's primary caregiver while she worked erratic hours. Even before that, her grandfather had been her rock, especially after her father's suicide, when it had been brought home dramatically to a fifteen-year-old girl that her father chose death over a life with just her. Yep, she owed her grandfather so much! Gramps had a long-running feud with Valcour LeDeux, John's notorious alcoholic father, and if he chose to pretend that Etienne had no LeDeux blood, well, so had she.

And, frankly, she didn't feel guilty over her secret, or not very much. John had a reputation from his early teens of being wild, moving from woman to woman. That's not what she wanted as a father for Etienne. She doubted he'd have any interest in having a son, anyway. It would interfere with his lifestyle.

But what about Etienne? her conscience sometimes nagged at her. *Doesn't he have a right to a father?*

"Earth to Celine. You ask me a question, and then tune me out."

"Oh. What did you say?"

"I said that, as a result of your article, I've been given a leave of absence."

"A suspension?"

"More like a request to request."

"Why? You didn't do anything wrong. Did you?"

He shook his head. "Police do not want publicity, especially undercover detectives, even when their identities aren't specifically spelled out."

She flushed. She had wanted to embarrass John, in a private way, not make him lose his job. "What will you do?"

He shrugged. "Out of sight, out of mind."

"Paid?"

"Yes, but I've got to disappear for a while. Until after the trial. I have an idea for some work I can do in the short term. After that..." He shrugged. "I'm not sure I can go back to the force in Fontaine. They'd probably assign me to office work."

"I'm sorry, John. I never intended for this kind of thing to happen." She put her hand on his forearm without thinking.

He stared down at her hand, then glanced up at her face.

She removed her hand, which sort of tingled. *No, no, no! No tingling. Last time I tingled around this bundle of sexual magnetism I ended up pregnant.*

"Actually, my suspension is due to some other things, too," he admitted.

She smacked him on the arm. "You rat! You deliberately tried to make me feel bad."

"Just deserts, baby." He smiled at her.

Damn, she hated it when he smiled at her.

"Congressman Martinez is threatening to cut state funding to our police department for embarrassing his wife. Ted Warner is running editorials non-stop on his TV stations about police brutality. And that bogus evangelist did a public confession in which he managed to make law enforcement Satan's disciples and him the repentant sinner."

"Well, I'm not surprised. As you can imagine, they've been lobbing volleys at the newspaper, too."

"My biggest beef, though, is what you did to me. I'm this close..." He held a thumb and forefinger about two inches apart. "...to gettin' calls from *Cosmo* magazine,

Entertainment Tonight, Matt Laurer, *Star Magazine,* and every other media outlet in the world, wanting an interview with the general theme bein' 'The Very Virile Cop.' "

She couldn't help but giggle.

"You think that's funny, do you? There's even a dingbat who wants to set up a fan club Web site for the anonymous hot cop."

"So, what does this have to do with me? That horse is already out of the barn, no putting it back now."

He nodded. "You're gonna pay, that's what I've decided."

She narrowed her eyes at him. "How?"

"What have you got to offer?"

"For you? Nothing."

"Tsk-tsk-tsk! So much hostility. One can only wonder how you would put that hostility to work for you in certain situations."

She could feel herself blush, which was probably what he intended. "What do you want for the pictures?"

"Hmmm." He leaned back on his barstool and surveyed her slowly from head to foot. "I'm thinkin' I'd like a weekend of hot screaming can't-get-enough sex at a place of my choice."

Oh. My. God! "You can't possibly mean that."

"I was just wonderin', *chère,* are you a faker or a quaker?"

"Huh?"

"In the sack."

"How immature!" she said, when she finally understood, even knowing he was just needling her. Then, "Look at me. I am the farthest thing from your usual sex toy."

"My reputation is vastly inflated, sweetheart. And if you're implying that I don't find you attractive, you're so far off base it's laughable."

"I don't even like you."

"I don't give a rat's ass what you think of me." He pulled another photo from an inside pocket of his jacket. "Oops, it looks like there's a photo I forgot to show you. You can thank Tank for these."

She took it from him, then wished she hadn't. It was the kiss between her and John at the Playpen. While one of his hands held her nape, the other was inside the front of her dress. It must have been when he filched her mike from inside her bra and unclipped the brooch. They both had their eyes closed. The kiss was open-mouthed. The worst thing was, she didn't appear to be struggling.

This is bad. Really bad. "This is blackmail."

"And your point is?" Slapping some bills on the bar, he stood and took the photo out of her hands, tucking it back in his pocket. Before he left, he said, ominously, "I'll be in *touch.* Be ready."

I hear spirits...or something...

You ought to be ashamed of yourself, John told himself when he was back at his Baton Rouge apartment, packing. He often heard voices in his head, which he identified as his conscience, but Tante Lulu would probably attribute to St. Jude.

Hah! Did you see the look on her face when I mentioned wild sex? said his darker side, his non-conscience.

Her idea of wild sex is probably a vibrator and a George Clooney movie.

He zipped up a duffel bag and continued to fill a small, wheeled overnighter. No way was he going to sit around this small efficiency twiddling his thumbs while the department decided what to do with him. He was off to Bayou Black, where he could think more clearly . . . make some decisions.

Meanwhile, the voices in his head were waging a bloody battle.

Yeah, but the blackmail . . . the sexual barter. You didn't really mean that.

Didn't I?

She's a good girl.

One, she's a woman, not a girl. Two, she wasn't all that good when she hit the sack with me six years ago. Three, Celine in that hooker dress and bed-mussed hair did not spell "good girl."

You're a pig.

So I've been told, but kiss me hard enough and I stop squealing.

Very funny. She has a secret.

Huh? That thought caught him up short. Where did that come from? What did it mean?

He frowned. He did sense something that Celine was withholding. But a secret? He didn't know about that.

You'll see.

Her secrets have nothing to do with me.

There was laughter in his head now.

He was going to have a talk with Tante Lulu about this mind message crap she was planting in his head.

The laughter continued.

He inherited the mischief gene...

John LeDeux was the father of her five-year-old son Etienne.

But he didn't know it.

He never would.

Her grandfather was waiting for her when she got to their Houma home later that day, a glass of iced lemonade sitting on the kitchen counter in welcome.

She took a long drink, then asked, "Where's Etienne?"

"The rascal, he is in his room havin' quiet time."

She arched her eyebrows.

"He painted Mrs. Thibodeaux's cat. Purple."

She put a hand over her mouth to stifle a giggle. Mrs. T's cat Wiener was the ugliest creature, with mottled white fur and pinkish-gray eyes that tended to cross.

"Gramps, I was thinking today...maybe I should tell John LeDeux about his son. Now, now, don't go getting excited. Hear me out."

Her grandfather's face was florid with outrage.

"Not for John's benefit," she went on quickly, "but doesn't Etienne have a right to a father? And, really, John isn't that bad. I had lunch with him today, and—"

Her grandfather stood and literally growled. "Not so bad? He's a LeDeux, ain't he? Girl, ya cain't be thinkin' straight. That boy has a reputation as wild as a peach orchard hog."

"He's not a boy anymore, Gramps," she told him. "He's twenty-eight years old."

"That doan make no difference. He's a wild *man*, too. Besides, have ya thought on what you'd do if he wanted to take Etienne away from you? That whiz-bang lawyer brother of his would be on ya like white on rice."

That was a concern...a remote one, but a concern nonetheless. She relented then, recognizing the worry in his eyes, and patted him on the arm. "It was just a thought."

He appeared mollified, but still grumbled. "I doan like ya breakin' bread with no LeDeux."

"More like bread pudding," she muttered.

"What?"

"Nothing. I'll talk to you when I come down." She was already heading toward the stairs, but she turned around and backtracked to give her grandfather a quick hug, whispering in his ear. "Don't be worrying about the LeDeuxs."

"But John LeDeux...you were with him."

"I am not involved with John LeDeux, and I never will be. Okay?" In the back of her mind was John's ominous threat about the kiss photograph and a wild weekend of sex. *He can't possibly be serious. I can't stand to be around him for five minutes, let alone forty-eight hours.*

Her grandfather nodded at her reassurance.

"Let me go talk with our little Van Gogh," she said with a smile, heading for the stairs again. "What's for dinner?"

"Crab soup."

"Yum! It'll go great with the fresh bread I bought down at the French Quarter Market today."

She entered Etienne's pint-sized bedroom with its alligator wallpaper, goldfish aquarium, plastic baseball bat, kiddie-sized fishing rod, and Hot Wheels and pirate collections. Not to mention that jar of worms which Gramps had failed to throw out when Etienne took his nap this afternoon. They probably stank by now.

He launched himself at her so his arms were wrapped around her neck and his skinny legs straddling her waist. She practically fell backward, but then sank down on the bed with him in her lap.

All in one breath, he told her, "I dint hurt Wiener. I jist put some purple dots on him with my paint markers, and he liked 'em. He really did. He licked my face. And then Grampa said I did a nasty and made me go ta my room. And it's so boooring. I wouldn't hafta play with Wiener if I had a dog. A big dog." Etienne had a playmate, Pete Doucet, who had a German Shepherd. Ever since Etienne had seen it, a puppy had been his constant request.

"Listen, honey, you mustn't do anything to anyone else's property. Not their animals. Not their houses. Not their toys. Anything. It's not right. Do you understand?"

He nodded. "I want a dog."

So much for remorse. "I know you do, sweetie, but not yet. Gramps doesn't get around as good as he used to. Let's wait 'til you're old enough to care for a dog yourself."

"I'm old enough now."

"Not quite." She lay down on his bed and motioned for him to lie beside her, his face pressed against her chest. She kissed the top of his head and murmured, "Tell me about your day, honey."

"You and Me time" was a tradition with them. Even when she was working two jobs and attending classes, the first thing she did when she got home was lie down with her baby and chat about little nothings. On more than one occasion, she'd fallen asleep along with her baby. "It's just you and me, kiddo," she'd repeated often, especially when the loneliness became almost overwhelming.

Now, her "baby" blathered on about worms and butterflies and dogs and swing sets and birthday parties. She told him about the bread pudding she'd had for lunch, though no mention of his father, and the peacock feathers she'd seen in a French Quarter shop, and how they needed to go to the mall soon to buy him some new athletic shoes, and, yes, he could get the light-up ones.

Giving him one final hug, she said, "Now take off those dirty clothes so we can go downstairs and eat dinner. I bought some praline ice cream for dessert."

He brightened at a combination of his punishment being over and his favorite ice cream. While he changed his clothes, chattering the whole time, she watched him closely. Something became apparent...something she had tried her best to avoid seeing in the past but being so close to John today made it impossible to ignore.

Except for his pale blue eyes, he looked just like John. Even worse, she suspected he'd inherited his father's rascal gene.

He was the target...of teasing...

John was sitting on Tante Lulu's back porch with his three half-brothers waiting for the first meeting of the Pirate Project team to start. The out-of-town folks were down at the banks of Bayou Black admiring Useless, René's pet alligator.

For all of them, the bayou was a touchstone. They could leave for short periods, but the swamp mud in their blood drew them back every time.

Tante Lulu's cottage was built in the old Cajun style...an exterior of *bousillage,* or fuzzy mud mixed with Spanish moss and crushed clam shells...but in this case, the stucco had been covered with half-logs and white chinking. There was a stretch of lawn that led down to the water's edge, centered by a spreading fig tree heavy with fruit. Rock-edged flower beds surrounded the house, and a wire-mesh fence enclosed neat rows of her vegetable garden. John and his brothers took turns helping to keep the place in shape, a real pain in the ass since everything grew at warp speed in the bayou, but this place had been a refuge to each of them at one time or another from their father's alcoholic binges. Besides, how could anyone say no to Tante Lulu?

Since he was on "suspension," John had decided to join the Jinx team once again, but he had to do it surreptitiously, especially since the witness list had been given to the defense this morning. Once the project started, he would stay at René's remote cabin. Luckily, the project site was located at a spot not too far from his brother's property. In the meantime, he wore disguises whenever he was out in public and drove his sister-in-law's puke green VW bug, a comedown from his red Impala convertible, that was for sure. He hadn't been specifically identified in the article, and Tante Lulu was only a silent partner; so, he should be safe here. Still, he was taking no chances.

"You look ridiculous," remarked René from where he

was sitting on a rocker next to his. René, who used to be an environmental lobbyist, ought to know; some of his tree hugger friends were the most ridiculous-looking in the world. In fact, they ate so much twigs and bark, aka granola, that John once told René that they looked like bushes themselves. Not René, of course; he had to be a good-looking dude to get a babe like *Trial TV* lawyer Valerie Breaux for his bride. René was going to act as part-time consultant on the job. Nothing visible. Ever since Hurricane Katrina, folks in Louisiana were more concerned about protecting the coastal wetlands and the bayous which fed into the Gulf of Mexico. René would make sure the Jinx team toed the environmental line.

"What? You doan lak me in blond hair, *cher?*" He touched the blond wig he was wearing under a baseball cap—borrowed from Tante Lulu—and removed the black frame glasses.

"You look like a dork. And you talk like a dork when you use that fake Cajun drawl."

"That's the point."

"Bet it cramps your style with women."

"What women?"

René's left eyebrow rose just a fraction, a trick he'd never learned himself. "Not getting any action lately, bro? Tsk, tsk, tsk. You need some advice?"

"Not from you."

Remy and Luc, sitting on the remaining rockers, laughed at the verbal sparring. They were going to help but not actively participate in the Pirate Project. Remy would be taking lots of equipment along with the project members out to the remote site in his hydroplane, in several different trips.

His brothers were here today for no reason other than

to be pains in his ass, enjoying his most recent notoriety. All of them were draining cold Dixie longnecks, the best thing on a warm Louisiana day.

Luc pulled out the newspaper again, pointing to the infamous article. They'd been razzing him about it for the past hour. "Me, I'm just a dumb ol' Cajun, but is this article really sayin' you're a cop whose job it was to have sex for money?"

"My name wasn't in that article. How do you know it referred to me?"

"Puh-leeze! Man, you've been in some scrapes before, but this one beats them all. Talk about!" Luc, one of Louisiana's most successful lawyers, was anything but dumb, and he was enjoying the hell out of what he called John's latest "scrape."

"Scrape? Shit! You guys act as if I'm ten years old and still gettin' into *scrapes*."

"Earth to Tee-John. Ten-year-olds don't sell their bodies for money. At least, most of them don't. Did you?" Luc blinked at him, as if his question was serious.

"Get real! And stop callin' me Tee-John. I'm not little anymore." He inhaled deeply for patience, a lost cause with these three. "Not that I'm admitting that article was about me, but the undercover cops didn't actually have sex with anyone at that club."

"Oh, great! Ruin a married man's fantasy." René pretended that he lived vicariously through John's life, but it wasn't true. Although he and Val, who used to be a *Trial TV* lawyer, had two preteens, Jude and Louise, and they'd been married for almost twelve years, a person only had to be in their company for a minute to see that they still had a hot sex life.

"*Mon Dieu!* I couldn't believe it when I saw the newspaper," Remy added. "In fact, I was still in bed when Rachel brought the paper up to me. She was laughin' so hard she practically peed her pants."

"I live to make women pee their pants."

No one paid any attention to him.

"I for one would be really pissed if I was sent undercover and didn't get any of the *undercover* benefits," Luc said.

"I'd like to hear you repeat that in front of Sylvie. She'd roast your balls over one of her bunson burners and serve them to you in a hot gumbo." Sylvie was a chemist, and the love of Luc's life. About fifty, they'd been married forever, but were devoted to each other, like all the LeDeux men were once they settled down with their women, except for their father.

"Ouch." Luc pretended to hold his crotch.

"Well, I've had enough of bein' your joke pin cushion." John got up from the rocking chair and walked down to help Tante Lulu and Charmaine set out some food. To his back, one of his brothers muttered, "Spoilsport."

Charmaine was arranging food on the folding tables set about the back lawn. Every couple minutes she swiveled her hips and sang along in Cajun French to the zydeco music playing softly from the boom box near her feet. It was René's band The Swamp Rats singing on a CD demo they'd made several years back.

He smacked Charmaine on the butt.

She yelped and jumped back. "Well, if it isn't Mr. Sex-for-hire, bless his heart. Tell me, sweetie, what did you charge for…" Charmaine mentioned something so explicit she almost made him blush. Almost. Then she wagged a long-nailed, red-enameled forefinger at him. "Tsk, tsk, tsk! Y'all better stay away from Tante

Lulu. She's been rehearsin' a few words for you on the subject."

"She already told me what she thinks."

She smiled, knowing exactly what he meant.

"My name was never mentioned in that article, ya know."

"Puh-leeze!"

"Why does everyone keep sayin' that?" he complained.

Charmaine wouldn't be working on this treasure hunt; she had more than enough to do with her dude ranch/beauty spas, and her three-year-old Mary Lou, who was a female clone of her daddy, Raoul Lanier. Everyone said that Rusty...or Raoul...was so good-looking women stopped on the street to gawk at him. He couldn't see it himself, but then he was a guy. It was probably because he was a cowboy; women went apeshit over cowboys.

"You oughta let me dye your hair blond and stop wearin' that silly wig," Charmaine offered. "Where'd you buy it? Wal-Mart?"

"No way! You are not touchin' my hair. No offense, but you'd probably throw in a perm or dreadlocks."

"You need long hair for dreadlocks."

"See, you would've actually considered it."

She slapped his arm. Then she turned serious. "Are you really in enough danger that you need a disguise?"

He shrugged. "These are bad guys."

She squeezed his shoulder. "You be careful, hear?"

Charmaine wasn't really a blood relative of Tante Lulu; nor was John, but they were both children of Valcour LeDeux, as were Tante Lulu's three natural great-nephews, Luc, Remy, and René. To Tante Lulu they were all kin, blood or not.

Watching Charmaine and Tante Lulu bustle around the tables, he had to smile. In some ways, Charmaine, a former Miss Louisiana, could have been her daughter, so much alike were they in attitude. With big black Texas hair, tall as a model, and stacked like Pamela Anderson, she wore tight white capri pants, a leopard print halter top, and high-heeled wedgies.

This was probably the way Tante Lulu had dressed when she was young. Even though she was only five-foot tall and ninety-two years old, the old lady still dressed outrageously. Today she'd dyed her short, curly hair red, and she wore her favorite purple shorts with its matching lavender tank top with a built-in bra. Grandma Moses with cleavage! Her only concession to her age was the orthopedic shoes, but she'd painted red polka dots on them. Lots of people didn't look past Tante Lulu's appearance, but those here in the bayou knew her for the accomplished *traiteur,* or healer, that she was.

"Another great adventure, Auntie?" He gave her a hug.

She didn't push him away, but she didn't answer him either.

"Givin' me the silent treatment, *chère?*"

Turning, she glared at him.

"My name wasn't in that article. It might've been anyone."

She gave him one of her looks. At least she didn't say "Puh-leeze!" Then she sighed deeply. "How am I ever gonna find you a gal when yer gallavantin' around with scarlet wimmen?"

Only Tante Lulu would refer to whores by that old-fashioned term.

"I don't want you findin' me a *gal*. I can take care of that myself."

"Doan look ta me like yer doin' such a good job. Gumbo doan make itself, ya know."

Whatever the hell that means.

"By the way, I like that hair color on you. Sorta like Tab Hunter."

"Who's Tab Hunter?"

Ignoring his question, she went on, "Mebbe ya oughta let Charmaine do yer hair up proper."

Yep, the two of them are clones.

"And now ya lost yer job," she said with disgust.

"I didn't lose my job. It's just suspended for a while, 'til things die down. Besides, aren't you glad I'm here to help on the Pirate Project?"

"Well, there is that." Slowly, a smile broke the wrinkles on her aged face. "But I still say the thunderbolt is headin' yer way."

After another hug, he went down to the stream where the other members of the Jinx team were still gazing at Useless, tossing him the occasional gingersnap or cheese doodle. To Yankees, gators were a marvel; to those living on the bayou, they were just everyday pests.

"Hey, John. I'm so glad you'll be able to join us." That from Veronica Jinkowsky, owner of Jinx, Inc., the treasure hunting company she inherited a few years back from her grandfather Frank Jinkowsky. Ronnie was fascinated by, but keeping her distance from, Useless, even though the old gator was harmless. Well, fairly harmless, as long as he got his daily allotment of cheese doodles or gingersnaps.

"Hey, it should be fun. Thanks for lettin' me jump in this late in the game." *And for givin' me a hidin' place.*

"Not so late. We haven't started yet. Besides, having a local diver will be helpful."

"You again?" said Caleb Peachey, extending a hand to shake. He knew Caleb from two previous Jinx projects he'd been on. Caleb was an ex-Amish Navy SEAL. Talk about oxymorons!

"You can't get rid of me that easily. Where's Claire?" Claire was Caleb's wife.

"She's back in Pennsylvania, about to run her outdoor farm camp for children." He rolled his eyes. Caleb had an aversion to farm life, thanks to his early years of hard work in a large Amish family, but Claire, some kind of fancy pancy historical archaeologist (which meant she obsessed over Indians), loved farms. Needless to say, they lived on a farm.

Adam Famosa, a Cuban professor of oceanography at Rutgers University and a diving expert, was on his cell phone, probably talking to some woman. You could say that John and Adam had a little friendly personality conflict. The numbnuts was gonna love John's discomfort over the Playpen incident.

While Peach managed to overlook his appearance, Famosa glanced up at him and smirked. "LeDeux," he said, shaking his head. That's all he said, but he continued to smirk. A big ol' Yankee jerk of a smirk.

John shrugged and turned to Brenda Caslow, a former NASCAR mechanic, who had just arrived with her husband, Lance Caslow, a NASCAR driver. Lance would be leaving Brenda behind when he caught a plane later today for trial runs in Tennessee. NASCAR racing was big in the South. If Tante Lulu's neighbors found out Lance Caslow was here, they would be mobbed.

"Hey, buddy, I know what bad press is like," Lance

said, patting him on the shoulder. "Just lay low for a while."

John opened his mouth to protest, but gave up trying to convince them that the article wasn't about him.

"Hah! The difference in your bad publicity, dear," Brenda told her husband, not so sweetly, "is it usually involved a front page photo of a bimbo sitting on your lap looking at you as if she'd like to lube your engine."

John laughed and Lance did his best not to laugh.

"Not anymore, honey." Lance pulled Brenda into his arms, giving her a big wet kiss. When he was done, Brenda looked a little dazed.

Tante Lulu called everyone to the tables. "Come 'n eat, ever'one."

They all dished up gumbo, Lazy Bread, sliced tomatoes warm from the garden, red beans and rice, corn on the cob, and a bushel of crawfish set by itself on a plastic cloth-covered table. On another table, she had arranged dishes, cutlery, napkins, glasses, a pitcher of iced sweet tea, and two Peachy Praline Cobbler cakes. There was also a cooler filled with ice and bottles of Dixie beer. An everyday Cajun feast.

"Everything looks wonderful," Ronnie observed. "Should I wake up Jake?"

"Nah, let him and the little one sleep. Food will keep."

Jake Jensen, Ronnie's four-times ex-husband, was asleep on a nearby hammock with their three-year-old daughter Julie Ann sprawled over his chest. Jake was a professional poker player, taking a break from the circuit for a few weeks. Ronnie kept glancing his way, her eyes filled with love for the two of them. If Tante Lulu had her way, with a little help from St. Jude, Ronnie and Jake would be marrying again.

"You didn't have to do this, Tante Lulu," Ronnie said, even as she piled her plate with the delicious food. "Just because you're an investor in the Pirate Project doesn't mean you have to open your home to us rowdy folks."

"Feedin' my family and friends is a joy, dearie. Food, she is an important part of Cajun life. And I have plenty experience with rowdy folks, believe you me."

"Ain't that the truth?" He sneaked a peach off her cake and popped it into his mouth.

She smacked his hand away.

A companionable silence followed then as people dug in . . . until Tante Lulu made an offhand remark. "That newspaper story . . . it was written by Celine Arseneaux, weren't it? I know her paw-paw, James Arseneaux. Her maw-maw died years ago."

"Yeah," he said hesitantly, not sure what direction his aunt was headed, but she had that wily gleam in her eyes which set up the red alert hairs on the back of his neck.

"She's a good Cajun girl, ain't she?"

John choked on his beer. "Part-Cajun, I think. She has blue eyes."

His brothers and Charmaine burst out laughing.

"What's up?" Famosa wanted to know.

"Yeah, share the joke," Caleb added.

"No, no, no," he said, but it was too late.

Tante Lulu grinned. "Me, I think I smell thunder."

Chapter
4

Did anyone hear thunder?...

Tante Lulu gaped at her rascal nephew whose face was flushed with pure panic.

"What's goin' on? I was jist teasin'," she whispered to Charmaine.

"Tee-John *is* a bit flustered. I wonder why," Charmaine whispered back.

"I heard that," Tee-John said. "Don't get any ideas about me and Celine Arseneaux, either one of you. Celine hates my guts."

"How do you feel about *her* guts?" Luc asked. He had come up behind Tee-John without his noticing.

Tee-John flashed him a look of disgust.

"Mebbe St. Jude sent you and Celine ta that hanky-panky club t'gether fer a purpose. Mebbe she jist needs a thunderbolt ta jump-start her heart."

"St. Jude and a sex club? I don't think so," Tee-John scoffed.

"Stranger things have happened," Luc pointed out.

"The ol' guy got me with a love potion Sylvie concocted in her lab."

"I got feng shued." Remy winked at Tee-John, who still wore a frowny face.

"Val got kidnapped and dropped in my lap." You could tell how pleased René was to tell them about that.

"I've got you all beat. I had to become a born-again virgin before I landed Rusty." Charmaine's announcement was met with stone-cold silence.

The Yankee gang was staring at them all, open-mouthed. That was Yankees for you. No sense of humor.

"Listen to me, Tante Lulu. I want nothin' to do with Celine Arseneaux. Not now. Not ever. Did you hear me?"

"Holy crawfish! They heard you in Biloxi."

"I'm too young ta settle down," the boy continued, looking around him for support.

No one agreed with him.

He glared at each of his brothers and Charmaine, in turn, then muttered, "Traitors," and walked away, down toward the bayou.

"Deader 'n a doornail," Luc remarked to Remy, who nodded.

"Best I be warmin' up my frottir fer the weddin' celebration," René said.

"Me, I'm gonna get Tee-John's hope chest started, right quick," Tante Lulu decided.

Tee-John screamed. Which was really funny. Tante Lulu couldn't recall ever hearing a man scream before, except maybe Valcour LeDeux the time she hit him in the privates with a baseball bat.

Just call me...

Celine got a call later that night, from John LeDeux, of all people. Good thing her grandfather hadn't answered the phone.

"What do you want?" she snapped.

"Hello to you, too, darlin'."

"I don't have time for your nonsense, John. I'm in bed." *With a book. Darn it!*

"Alone?"

Are you kidding? I haven't had sex for so long I probably forgot how. "That's none of your business."

"Jeez, Louise! I was just askin'. I figured we're sorta friends now that we both hang out at sex clubs. Do you have a boyfriend, Celine?"

"A boyfriend? What, are we in high school again?"

"Okay, a lover?"

"That is definitely none of your business. I repeat, what do you want? Talking to you twice in one day is more than my system can digest." *Actually, it's kinda nice. Darn it!*

"I *am* yummy."

She rolled her eyes. "Why are you whispering?"

"Because I'm callin' from my aunt's bedroom. I don't want her to overhear me."

"Are you afraid of your aunt?"

"Damn straight!" He paused, then asked, "What're you readin'?"

"What makes you think I'm reading?"

"Because if I was in bed with you, I wouldn't be lettin' you talk to some other guy. Wanna know what I'd be doin'?"

Yes. "No."

"So what're you readin'?"

"*The Red-Hot Cajun*."

"I'm a red-hot cajun."

"How did I know you would say that? It's a romantic humor novel."

"Actually, I know that. One of the lieutenants on the force, Mollie Andrews, was readin' it last week. Couldn't stop laughin'."

She yawned loudly. "Look, this is real pleasant and all, but why are you calling?"

"I just wanted ta warn you. If any of my family members approach you, run."

"Huh?"

"Don't pay any attention if someone mentions thunderbolts or St. Jude or a hope chest."

"A hope chest? For who? Me?"

"Hell, no. For me. My great-aunt makes hope chests for all the men in our family."

Celine couldn't stop herself from laughing.

"It's not funny."

"Yes, it is. I never heard of a hope chest for a man."

"It's a LeDeux thing. Anyhow, just ignore anything they might say."

"John, I haven't seen any of the LeDeuxs, except for you, in years. And even with you, it's been years."

"Believe you me, baby, you're probably gonna be seein' a whole hell of a lot of them now. Just ignore the whole crazy bunch."

With those words, he hung up.

Celine stared at the phone, and wondered if John had

gone off the deep end. Maybe his job suspension was hitting him harder than expected. Or maybe he was just drunk.

But then an alarming thought occurred to Celine. She couldn't have the LeDeuxs coming around here. For one important reason. Etienne.

Tomorrow she was going to send her grandfather and Etienne on a vacation to her cousin Julian's ranch in Texas. They'd been talking about such a trip for ages. Now was definitely the time.

Damn those LeDeuxs.

Damn John LeDeux.

Avast, me maties...

Veronica was impressed with the work René LeDeux had done for them thus far on the Pirate Project. Too bad the bayou ecologist, who taught school, didn't want a full-time job.

They were all crammed around the table in Tante Lu-lu's kitchen, except for Luc, Remy, and Lance, who'd already left. She and Jake would leave with Julie Ann after the project was launched, passing the reins to Adam. Project heads changed regularly so that eventually all team members got a shot at director. Jake had a poker tournament in Atlantic City, and she had work to do back in the Barnegat, New Jersey, office of Jinx, Inc.

Tante Lulu's kitchen was a charming room with cypress cabinets, an old white porcelain sink, red and white checkered curtains, and a matching tablecloth over a 1940s style enamel table. Off the kitchen was a large pantry holding all of Tante Lulu's *traiteur* remedies. Through the single pantry window, dust motes danced off the butcher block work table. The pantry's pungent scents wafted into the kitchen and beyond: hanging dried herbs and shelves loaded with floor-to-ceiling glass containers, some of them antiques, with everything from chicken hearts to alligator tongues, along with normal herbs like basil and mint. Very, very impressive. The eccentric old lady was definitely more than she appeared to be.

But Veronica's mind had been wandering. She picked up on René's words.

"See here, the bottom transparency is the way the network of bayou streams looked two hundred years ago before erosion and dozens of hurricanes," René explained.

"It looks like a spider web," Veronica observed.

"Or a lace doily," Tante Lulu added. "Actually, Remy says that from the air it looks like a sheet of glass what's been shattered."

"But see how it changed over a hundred years." René laid a second transparency on top of the first. Then he laid a third on top of those, from fifty years ago; a fourth from just before Hurricane Katrina; and finally one done last month. René was an expert on the environment, but also highly informed on the history and geography of southern Louisiana. Not to mention being a very handsome man. Not as handsome as Jake, of course, but still attractive.

"Holy shit!" Caleb noted. "Many of the streams have disappeared altogether and new ones have appeared. There's almost no comparison, except for the major waterways, like Bayou Teche, and even those are different than they used to be."

"Yep, the Louisiana coastline has been sinking for years, giving way to the sea at an alarming rate. Experts have known for decades that a Hurricane Katrina–type devastation was in the works. It was inevitable. And, believe me, there will be more of the same, not just here in Louisiana but coastal lands across the country." He pulled out a large map of the Gulf Coast and told them, "Anything that happens on the coastline has a rippling effect here on the bayou. Loss of the barrier islands, oil drillin', man-made canals, levees, all of it combined is killin' what some people consider just a swamp, but we Cajuns consider paradise. The bayou, she is a dyin' thing."

"René could go on fer hours 'bout the bayous and how us folks are destroyin' 'em, but we's here ta find some treasure," Tante Lulu said.

"Point taken." René laughed. "Okay, here's the deal. See this old map that Tante Lulu claims is the site of the Lafitte treasure."

Everyone leaned forward to study the crackly paper that Tante Lulu said she had received from a descendent of one of the pirates who had served under Lafitte.

"This whole venture could be a wild-goose chase," John cautioned. "Most people think that if there was any treasure, it would have been on Barataria Island, Lafitte's main stomping grounds."

"It's a risk we take every time we start a new treasure hunt," Adam pointed out. "That's partly what makes it so much fun."

"Hey, maybe there's a little bit of the gambler in all of us." That was Jake, of course, standing in the doorway leading to the living room, their daughter Julie Ann in his arms sucking on a lollipop. That remark was a jab at Veronica because she had always been critical of his gambling.

She stuck her tongue out at him to show she'd gotten the message...and wasn't offended.

He just grinned.

"This project, she is a gamble, yes," John said then, "but there's evidence that Loo-zee-anna does have buried treasure. Some of it is legend, yes, but it's also part of our history going back to the days of Spanish galleons."

"Good God! The redneck sex cop is giving us a history lesson," Adam teased.

His back to Tante Lulu, John mouthed a foul word at Adam, then continued, "There've been many discoveries of buried and sunken treasures over the past two hundred years right here in southern Loo-zee-anna, but mostly explorers have learned to keep their discoveries secret, to avoid the inevitable pile-on."

René nodded, then put a forefinger on the old map. "The treasure, according to this old map, would have been located deep in the swamps of Bayou Black, about a quarter-mile from René's fishing camp, right about here. But based on what I've just shown you with the overlays, that spot was once on land, but is now underwater."

"So, we're talking about a dive and a dig, both, right?" Veronica asked.

René shrugged. "Assuming there ever was a treasure. Assuming the treasure hasn't moved with the current and various hurricanes over the years. Assuming what was buried wasn't biodegradable."

"Gold coins ain't biode...bio-whatever-you-said,"

Tante Lulu insisted. "And doan you be such a balloon pricker, René LeDeux."

"A prick? Yer callin' me a prick." He grinned at his aunt, then ducked when she swung an arm to slap him a good one.

"A party pooper who's allus prickin' ever'one's balloons," she explained. "Behave yerself, boy, or I'll whup ya so hard you'll be burpin' the first milk ya drunk as a baby."

They all raised their eyebrows at that one.

"Listen, I know I've already said this, but I have real reservations about the effect on the bayou of a half-dozen adults trampin' around the streams, cartin' machinery. The least little thing can affect the balance of the ecosystem. And I'm not just sayin' this because it's my lodge."

"We're aware of your concerns," Veronica said. "Please know we'll do everything, and I mean everything, to leave that section of the bayou the way we find it."

"Where did you get this old map?" Adam asked Tante Lulu.

"Lefty Delacroix from over Lafayette way."

"*Mon Dieu!* Crazy Lefty...who claims he was once a pirate?" René was staring at his aunt with disbelief. To the others, he explained, "He even has an eye patch and a peg leg. Refused to get a prosthetic after the Korean War. Then, he lost his eye wrestlin' an alligator during a drunken binge."

"Thass prejudice," Tante Lulu chastised René. "Makin' fun of the handy-capped. Tsk, tsk, tsk."

"That's all we need. Two crazies on this project. The Dingbat Duo. Oh, wait, that would be three crazies."

Adam gave John a smirk. "I forgot about the crazy red-neck sex cop."

John mouthed another foul word at Adam, which his aunt couldn't see.

But Tante Lulu wasn't paying attention to them. She was still glaring at René. "Doan ya be puttin' down ol' Lefty. He knows stuff. And ya cain't say there ain't no treasures in Loo-zee-anna, boy. Men layin' pipelines through the bayou fer the oil companies find pirate gold all the time."

"I'll give you that," René conceded, "although it's not all the time. Occasionally."

"And there's lots of buried treasure on those old plantations, too. Hidden when the damn Yankees was comin'. My apologies to you damn Yankees."

The damn Yankees present took no offense.

Veronica hoped the old lady wasn't thinking that Jinx would be digging on those plantations. She had jobs lined up for the next two years. Besides that, she'd only been here one day and already she'd seen enough gators to last her a lifetime. And Caleb, who had an aversion to snakes, claimed to have seen thirty-seven today alone, some of them hanging from trees. She hoped he was exaggerating.

"Okay, we got a bit off course. Do you have a time-table for us, Caleb?" Veronica asked.

Caleb had been with Jinx since she took over six years ago. Although it had been a while since he'd been a Navy SEAL, he still wore his hair military short. She laughed to herself as she mused that at least he wasn't growing a long Amish-style beard like his twin brother Jonas.

Caleb pulled out a clipboard. "Adam and I have already been out at the site, scouting the terrain. René has agreed to rent us his fishing camp, which is actually more like a lodge. The original camp burned down a few years ago, and he built this bigger place as a vacation home. Anyhow, even though it's in a remote area, there's electricity, thanks to a generator, and running water from a cistern. The lodge has two bedrooms which can sleep five, a pull-out sofa in the living room, and we have some high–grade tents that will keep out mosquitoes, snakes and other small animals."

"Snakes?" Caleb looked a little bit green.

"Ya cain't come into the bayou without seein' snakes," John told him, adding a little too gleefully, "Actually, there are three hundred species of snakes here. After all, it is a tropical setting, *cher*, but not to worry, most of them are non-poisonous. Except for the water moccasin, of course. And the Slim Jim Viper and the Crimson Slitherer and—"

"Shush, yerself, Tee-John," Tante Lulu said. "I been livin' on the bayou all my life and never been bit."

"Actually, most snakes avoid people, and most snake bites take place when alcohol is involved," René informed them. "Usually preceded by the dumbass statement, 'Betcha I could...'"

"Stupid rednecks," Adam muttered.

"Rusty says poisonous snakes can only strike their body length. So, you're safe at five or six feet away," Charmaine pronounced, as if that was good news.

"Not to worry. We have a fully-stocked first-aid kit, including snake bite antidotes," Brenda told them.

"That makes me feel better," Caleb said. "Not!"

"Now, all the legal details, permits, are taken care of, right?" Veronica asked.

Tante Lulu waved a hand dismissively. "I called my friend Easy Gaudet. Piece 'a cake."

"She means Congressman Edward Gaudet," René elaborated, obviously not happy that laws could be bent so easily.

"Thass what I said. Besides, finders keepers is what I allus say."

"Oh, God!" Veronica murmured.

"I checked on all the environmental and historical requirements," René elaborated, passing out some sheets detailing the dos and don'ts of their project.

"Who owns the property where we'll be digging?" Caleb asked.

"No one," Tante Lulu replied.

Several eyebrows rose at that.

"It probably belongs to the state. It's hard to tell with some of these old deeds," René told them.

"And that won't be a problem?" Veronica was genuinely concerned. What they didn't need was to find the treasure, then have someone file suit, claiming ownership.

"I tol' ya. I got all the legal permissions ya need. Jist take my word on it." Tante Lulu certainly looked confident.

Veronica glanced at John and René, both of whom nodded, apparently satisfied that the legal permits were in order.

They all agreed to meet at Remy's the following day at eight A.M. Remy was a licensed pilot, a veteran of Desert Storm. He had a small hydroplane on the water and an honest-to-God copter on a helipad on his multiacre property farther down the bayou. The hydroplane was one of those small Piper vehicles with floats or pontoons on each side, allowing it to land even on small bayou streams, provided there was tree clearance. He would be transporting the machinery and some of the team tomorrow, in two or three trips. Other than the hydroplane, the only way to reach René's cabin was by pirogue, flat-bottomed canoes that could ride even in shallow waters, but that would take days.

After that, they toasted the new venture with Tante Lulu's dandelion wine.

"Here's to the Pirate Project, maties." Veronica raised a St. Jude glass.

"Aye, aye, cap'n," Jake said, winking at Veronica. "Want me to show you how I bury *my* treasure, lass?"

"Behave, you scallywag." Veronica winked back.

"*Merci.*" Tante Lulu bowed, thinking he had meant her when he referred to "cap'n."

"God help us all," John murmured.

"St. Jude help us all," Tante Lulu corrected. "God, too, of course."

Note to self: Make sure Tante Lulu doesn't put St. Jude figureheads on the prows on the pirogues.

And then the other shoe dropped...

John stood at Tante Lulu's kitchen sink, his arms in soap suds up to his elbows, washing dishes. How he got stuck hanging around was a puzzle. He'd gone into the bedroom to make a phone call, and when he came out, everyone had left. Oh, it wasn't that they hadn't offered to help clean up, but Tante Lulu, bless her heart, had volunteered him.

She was setting him up.

"Tee-John," she said in that honey-sweet voice that had every fine hair standing to attention on his body.

"What?" he asked, even though his common sense told him to run.

"I mighta done sumpin' today that yer not gonna like." She had this mock sorrowful look on her face, like she wasn't at all sorry about whatever she had done.

Uh-oh. "Mighta?"

"Sorta?"

"Exactly what did you mighta sorta do today, Auntie?"

"Doan be mad."

This is gonna be bad. Real bad. That look on her face...reminds me of the time she nominated me for People Magazine*'s Sexiest Man of the Year...and I wasn't even a finalist.* He took his hands out of the soap suds, dried them on a St. Jude dish towel, then placed his hands squarely on his hips. "Okay, spill."

"I jist happened ta be talkin' ta my ol' friend Cletus 'the snake' LaFonte. He's called 'the snake' 'cause of the way he kin flick his tongue. Whooee! The stories I could tell ya."

Oh, please don't.

"Cletus usta be an editor. Actually, I was over Houma way healin' his grandson's colic, which was the worstest case I ever—"

"Aaarrgh! An editor of what?"

Her face flushed. It took a lot to make his aunt be flushed. "A newspaper."

Oh, this was not good. "Did you mention the Pirate Project?"

"Of course not. Whatcha think I am? Stoopid?"

That question did not warrant an answer.

"I was jist askin' Cletus if he knew any reporters on the *Times-Tribune*."

"Like Celine Arseneaux?" He groaned.

"*Oui*. See, that wasn't so bad." She beamed. "And the best part is that I found out she ain't married, but—"

"I already knew that."

"Doan be interruptin' me. She ain't married, but yer gonna have a real uphill battle with that gal."

"Tante Lulu," he said on a long sigh, "there is not going to be a battle with me and Celine of any kind. Would you get that out of your head?"

"Will ya let me finish? Cletus tol' me that Celine moved back ta Houma a few months back ta live with her grandfather James Arseneaux after he had a stroke. What I learned from Cletus is that James Arseneaux hates all the LeDeuxs 'cause of somethin' yer daddy done to James's cousin Josie Lynn."

John's eyes about rolled up in his head. "Just about everyone in southern Louisiana has a gripe against my father. What else is new? Besides, what does any of this have to do with me?"

"Doan be dense, boy. I gotta find out if she's *the one*."

"She's not."

"We'll see."

"We will not see. Forget about it. I mean it."

She must have sensed his fraying temper. "Doan go gettin' yer skivvies in a twist. What will be will be."

That's what he was afraid of.

Chapter
5

He made her an offer she couldn't refuse...

"A treasure hunt? You want me to spend days, maybe weeks, covering some screwball search for Jean Lafitte's buried treasure?"

"It'll be fun," her editor, Bruce Cavanaugh, told Celine as they sat in his office.

She said a foul word under her breath, something about what he could do with his fun. "Don't you think my talents are best utilized on something more...serious?" Celine gritted her teeth. It was a constant struggle for women in journalism. They were assigned the fluff pieces while men got the Pulitzer Prize–worthy stories.

"C'mon, Celine, you've worked nonstop on hard news the past few months. There's nothing wrong with lightening up on occasion. Besides, you'll find a way of making it a good in-depth piece. Hell, you could make a PTA meeting newsworthy."

"Bruce," she said tiredly, "another Jean Lafitte treasure hunt? Do you realize how many of these half-brained schemes there have been over the years? They're scams."

He shook his head. "Not all of them. One of his stashes was found on Jefferson Island. There are authenticated letters from Lafitte saying that he hid $240,000 in gold somewhere on Catouche Bayou."

"Who's the contact person?"

"Veronica Jinkowsky from New Jersey. It's a legitimate business." He shoved a folder across her desk, which she flipped through. It did appear to be a bona fide treasure hunting company, with some impressive finds under its belt. "Look, you can go along with them to Bayou Black. That's in your home turf, Terrebonne Parish, right? All you would have to do is watch and see how they go about retrieving the treasure. Get some historical background on Jean Lafitte; there are plenty of his descendents around and enough historical data to fill a library. What do you say?"

"Maybe."

"What's your problem?"

"My problem is that I should be past fluff pieces."

"That's your opinion...that it's a fluff story. C'mon, Celine, you're a professional. Act like one."

That hurt, and was totally unwarranted. "If I do this, Bruce, you are going to owe me big-time."

"Agreed," he said, reaching across to shake her hand.

She'd have liked to bite his toady hand, but she didn't.

"Uh, there is one thing...or two."

She stiffened.

"You would have to get permission from the Jinx people to observe their operation."

"You didn't get permission?"

"Not yet. We just heard about this last night. There shouldn't be a problem. This organization has to have dealt with the media before."

"Where did you hear about this project?"

"Someone who works over at Terrebonne Airport heard secondhand about a pilot who was going to be transporting a team over to some remote region on Bayou Black."

"And based on that flimsy report, you think there's a legitimate story here?"

Bruce's jaw visibly tightened. "You've got your assignment, Celine. Take it or leave it."

Okay, he was drawing a line in the sand. Over such a piddly story?

Was she ready to cross the line? Could she afford to lose her job? What was it Harry Olsen, her old journalism professor, used to say, "Pick your battles, whether they be in war or the newsroom."

"Okay, I'll do it."

"You'll probably need to go out on site with them for ... I don't know ... maybe a week."

This got worse and worse. Celine was glad she'd sent her grandfather and Etienne away for two weeks. Hopefully, they wouldn't be back 'til she was done with this rinky-dink story.

Bruce made a big mistake then. He said, "Hey, maybe you and this team of treasure hunters could dress up like pirates for a photo shoot if they find the pirate loot. One of them could be a Johnny Depp version of Jean Lafitte, and you could be his pirate wench, like Anne Bonny. Ha, ha, ha."

The sound of his office door slamming after her could probably be heard all the way to Lake Pontchartrain.

Is there an antidote for a love bug bite?...

John was helping to load equipment onto the hydroplane for its second run to René's cabin. It would probably take two more trips to get them all there. But it was a balmy day...well, balmy for southern Louisiana, only eighty today...and no one was in a rush.

The water plane was parked in the stream fronting Remy's ten-acre property, some distance from the huge house he'd built to accommodate his family that included his wife Rachel and seven...*seven*...kids, both biological and adopted. He also had a houseboat down on the bayou which he used for guests.

Everyone was steering clear of Brenda, who was doing a final check of the supplies. She was in one snarky mood, probably missing her husband. Hey, if he was a woman, he would probably miss Lance Caslow, too, not because he was so good-looking, but because there'd be NASCAR tickets for life.

He and Famosa and Peach had thoroughly checked over the diving gear. The depth of the water at the spot they hoped to search was roughly fifteen feet, not so deep for free diving in short spurts, but they needed tanks to stay down for any length of time.

Tante Lulu would probably have lunch prepared by the time everyone arrived. He'd helped tote a half dozen grocery bags of food in the little VW this morning.

Jake was carrying Julie Ann back and forth across an

open area, trying to soothe the fussy child, who was getting a cold and was not a happy camper. Who knew a body that small had lungs the size of a Goodyear blimp? There probably wasn't a gator or egret left within a mile of the kid's last bellow.

Ronnie was coming out of the house, heading this way, but she'd stopped to talk to... He squinted, then groaned. "No, no, no, no!"

"What's the matter?" Famosa asked, coming up beside him.

John pointed. "Trouble. Celine Arseneaux." Quickly, he reached for his athletic bag and pulled out the wig, jamming it on his head. Maybe she wouldn't recognize him from there.

Celine was wearing white running shorts, a purple Mardi Gras T-shirt, sneakers with no socks, and a Saints baseball cap with her ponytail sticking out of the back. Nothing seductive. Certainly a far cry from her tart outfit. A laptop case was slung over one shoulder, and a camera case and a canvas carryall over the other.

"Is she married?"

John flashed Famosa a disgusted look. "You've got a one-track mind."

"Like you don't."

"Not where Celine Arseneaux is concerned. She's a newspaper reporter."

"Uh-oh." The two of them watched Ronnie and Celine; they appeared to be arguing. Jake, with Julie Ann thankfully asleep on his shoulder, finally, headed toward Ronnie's side, sensing trouble.

"So, is she married?" Famosa persisted.

"No. But she's not for you."

"You want her for yourself, don't you?"

"Hardly. You're welcome to her. Not here on this project, though. You can call her later." *In fact, I dare you, bozo. Go ahead. Pull one of your loser moves. I can't wait to see Celine kick you in the nuts.*

"Why?"

"Why what?"

"Why are you being so generous?"

"She's too hot for me." *Ha, ha, ha.*

Famosa was eyeing him suspiciously. "What's wrong with her?"

"Nothing. Honest. She was the reporter who was at the Playpen the night we did the raid. Man, you should have seen her in a push-up bra, stiletto heels, and screw-me red lipstick. I don't know this for certain, but I think she was wearing a thong." *If he repeats this to Celine, I am dead meat.*

Famosa was practically salivating now as he gazed at Celine, picturing her in the killer bra and thong, no doubt.

Time to stick it to Famosa. "She's kinda shy, Celine is. Likes guys that come on strong."

Famosa nodded, using the fingers of both hands to comb his hair off his face and tidy the long swath he had clubbed at the neck with a rubber band. A Cuban Fabio.

John mentally wrung his hands with anticipation.

Ronnie was walking toward them now, leaving Celine talking to Jake. Ronnie motioned for them all to follow her over to a picnic table under an enormous live oak tree with its dripping Spanish moss. Once seated, Ronnie said, "That's Celine Arseneaux. A reporter for the *Times-Tribune*. She wants to do a story on our project."

"Celine Arseneaux?" Tante Lulu asked with surprise.

She'd been sitting on a folding chair, taking a rest. Her surprise soon turned to glee. She whispered, "St. Jude."

John put his face in his hands for a moment.

"I don't see any problem if she does the article after we're done," Famosa said.

Ronnie shook her head. "She wants to accompany us. She has up to two weeks free from regular assignments."

"Two weeks! Do you think we'll be out there two weeks?" This was from an alarmed Brenda, even though two weeks wasn't all that long for a Jinx project.

"She's promised not to run any stories 'til after the search is completed," Ronnie continued.

"How did she find out about the project?"

"Someone from the private airport in Houma that Remy sometimes uses," Ronnie told them.

Something occurred to John then. "Whoa, whoa, whoa! Does she know I'm part of this project?"

Ronnie frowned. "No. I don't think so. Why?"

"Because she's the reporter who did the no-name hatchet job on me."

"Oh. Well, that settles it then. We can't let her participate."

"There's somethin' more important here. My whereabouts has to be secret 'til after the trial. Maybe I should just drop out."

"No!" they all said.

Their loyalty touched him.

"I'll tell her that she can't participate, but we'll give her an exclusive afterward," Ronnie said.

"She's a pit bull. Her reporter antennae are gonna shoot up instantly. Nope, Celine is not gonna give up," John told them.

"So you don't trust her?" Ronnie asked him.

"Hell, no."

"I mean, if I tell her that we have someone on board whose identity *must* be kept secret for high security reasons...if I can get her to promise she won't reveal that this person is here, would her word be good?"

John was uneasy.

"If there's one thing I learned as a SEAL," Peach said, "it's better to keep the enemy in your crosshairs."

"She ain't Tee-John's enemy," his aunt protested.

"She could be, Tante Lulu. Whether intentionally or not, she could put my life in danger."

His aunt's face went white, and she sank back down to her chair.

He squeezed her hand, wishing he hadn't mentioned danger. He didn't want to scare her. Turning to Peach, he said, "So, you think we should invite her to come along?"

Peach nodded hesitantly. "As long as you set ironclad conditions. And watch her ass."

Now, that shouldn't be a problem.

No, no, no. I did not think that.

"Let me go talk to her," he said. "If I don't feel comfortable, I'll drop out."

He approached the place where Celine still stood talking to Jake, who caught his silent signal and walked off toward his wife.

Celine didn't recognize him...at first. When she did, her eyes went wide. "You!" she accused, then she burst out laughing. "You look like that guy from *Dumb and Dumber.*"

"Jim Carrey?"

"No. The other one. The big blond no-brain." She went suddenly serious. "You're part of this Pirate Project?"

He nodded.

"And you're going to blackball me?"

"That depends."

"On what?"

"How willing you are to adhere to some conditions?"

Her body bristled with suspicion. "Like?"

"Like you cannot reveal in your article...or to anybody *at all* that I'm here. At least not 'til after the Mafia trial."

"And that would be when?"

"Three weeks, or longer. Both sides are lookin' for a speedy trial date."

"Impossible. I can't wait three weeks to write an article on the Pirate Project."

"And you keep my name out of any articles you write."

"Why should I?"

"You owe me."

She raised her chin in disagreement.

"Celine, I have to go in hiding because you outed me." *Not quite true, but, hey, a little guilt never hurt anyone.*

"Will you give me an exclusive interview during the trial?"

He cocked his head in an inquiring fashion. "Double rewards, huh? An exclusive on the Pirate Project and the trial?"

"Yep."

"You are not interviewing me on this project, though, not even as an anonymous person."

"That's unreasonable."

"That's the deal."

"And if I refuse?"

"Then I drop out of the Pirate Project, and you get neither story. There's one more thing, and this is non-negotiable. If we agree to let you follow us on this project, you have to stay here the entire time. No going home at night. We can't risk someone following you out here, for my sake and the sake of our prosecution, but also to preserve the viability of this project."

She gasped, as if he'd asked something horrifying, like nude treasure hunting.

Now, there's a thought.

"Stay... stay here? With you?"

"Not me, precisely. You can sleep in the lodge, or in one of the tents." He frowned. "What? Do you need to go home every night?"

"Why do you ask that?" Her voice was shrill and panicky.

What the hell is going on? "Your grandfather... I understand he had a stroke. Does he need you home every night?"

Her shoulders sagged with relief.

Which was really odd.

"No. I mean, he's better now. Still, I like to be home at night. However, they... I mean, he is out of town for two weeks." She was stammering.

He affected women that way sometimes. "Then it should be no problem."

He could tell she wasn't happy, but she agreed to the terms, all of them, and he was soon helping her carry the laptop and camera case, leaving her with the carryall. He gave Ronnie a silent signal that she had agreed to the terms.

Ronnie introduced her, "I want you guys to meet Celine Arseneaux. She's a reporter from the *New Orleans Times-Tribune*. She'll be here for the duration. So, behave yourselves."

John spoke up first, as if he hadn't just talked to her, "Hiii, Celine. Welcome to the Pirate Project."

"Drop dead," she said.

He chuckled.

"I'm Adam Famosa. Anything you need, just come to me, baby." Apparently, he was taking John's ill-advice that Celine liked men who came on strong. For a college professor, Famosa had the brains of a bayou gnat. But then, he was a Yankee. They didn't know jack about women.

Not surprisingly, Celine gave Famosa the same message she'd given him. *Drop dead, baby.* Except in Famosa's case it was an unspoken message contained in a disapproving glower.

Famosa glared at him.

He shrugged his innocence.

Famosa stomped off, mumbling something about redneck pricks.

As Ronnie led Celine to meet the other team members, John found himself watching Celine's back view. She was tall, maybe five-nine, kind of slim, but he noticed the rounded cheeks of her ass moving, first one, then the other, alternating up and down. A real nice rhythm she had going there. Hot-cha-cha. He supposed it was what they called a heart-shaped bootie.

And her legs. Man, she had nice, long, tanned legs, with the most intriguing dips behind her knees. Dips he suddenly envisioned himself licking. Slowly. Long, long laps like a cat. Would she taste sweet, like cream, or tangy with sweat from a bout of hard, energetic sex?

A jolt at his crotch called him up short. *Holy crawfish! I'm getting a hard-on over Celine the Geek's knees.* That's what she had been known as in high school, and even college when she'd blossomed a bit. A true blue high IQ, high achiever who looked down on those less intelligent or prone to unimportant things, like fun. God only knew why she'd deigned to go to bed with him that one time. Well, yes, he did know. They'd both been wasted, celebrating the end of exams just before spring break. *But knees? Who knows what I'll do when I get a gander at her breasts?* Another jolt of his you-know-what was his answer. Despite his reputation, it had been a long time since John had a steady lover, or even a one-night stand. Yep, that must be it. It wasn't Celine. He just needed to get laid.

But then she turned, and while she was talking to Brenda, she casually whipped out a tube of chapstick, a protection against the fierce sun. She was running it over her mouth. The top lip, right to left. The same for the bottom lip. She filled in the fullness of both lips. Then pressed her lips together.

The blood drained from his head and passed through his body in waves, making him feel faint, all over. His jockeys suddenly got tighter.

This was unbelievable. Totally unbelievable.

Could it be...?

He gasped, spun on his heels, and practically ran over to his aunt. "Tante Lulu, did you put some kind of voodoo aphrodisiac love spell crap on me?"

She was trying to find something in her purse, which was big enough to give a grown man carrying it a hernia... "What you talkin' 'bout, boy?"

"Celine Arseneaux. That's what I'm talkin' about.

Did you put some kind of love potion in my coffee this morning?"

It wasn't as outrageous a suggestion as it might seem. His sister-in-law Sylvie was a chemist who'd once invented a dingbat love potion that she put in jelly beans. His aunt was big on juju tea. And practically every woman in Louisiana, the birthplace of that celebrated priestess Marie Laveau, knew about voodoo spells.

His aunt just stared at him, for once in her life at a loss for words. Then she grinned, slowly, and did a little Snoopy dance, waving a handkerchief like the marchers in a Bourbon Street funeral. "Praise the Lord and pass the gumbo. The thunderbolt done struck again."

He made a screensaver of WHAT?...

Celine made her way over to the picnic table where John was chewing on a mechanical pencil, staring with much concentration at a laptop screen, occasionally typing in some data.

"What are you doing?"

He jumped, not having heard her approach, then turned back to the computer, ignoring her.

Okay. So, that's the way he's going to play it. Yeah, I agreed not to interview him, but this is taking things too far. "Don't you think you're being a little immature?"

Without looking her way, he replied, "Says she of 'Drop Dead' and 'Sex Cop' fame."

"You annoy me."

Silence.

"I didn't want this assignment."

Silence.

"My editor forced me to come."

Silence.

"What do you think of my belly button ring?"

His head jerked toward her. "Very funny!" He turned away and resumed his silence.

Remy LeDeux, his brother and a pilot, had already taken half the Jinx team in his hydroplane to the project site. She, John, and the rest would go next. That Remy, he was one drop-dead gorgeous LeDeux, but only from one side. Apparently one side of his body, including his face, had been burned in an explosion in Iraq some time ago.

She stared at John in frustration. He was wearing a pair of tan cargo shorts today with a drab green "Bite Me Bayou Bait Company" T-shirt, and flip-flops. His tanned arms and long legs showed muscle definition of either an athlete or guy who worked out regularly. She assumed the latter in his case, probably jogging. His dark brown, almost black hair was a little long, halfway down his neck, now that he'd removed the ridiculous wig.

No doubt about it, John was a good looker, like all the LeDeux men. Even better than he'd been in college when she'd made one of the biggest mistakes of her life. Well, not a mistake when she considered the result...Etienne.

Meanwhile, John continued to ignore her.

"I had a double major in college. Journalism and computer science," she told him. In fact, for many years she'd earned the tag of computer geek. "I could help with that computer work."

Silence.

She was seriously contemplating whacking him over

the head with that oar propped again a pirogue sitting on the bank. That would get his attention. "So what's with Adam?"

He chuckled. "What? Our Cuban Lothario been hittin' on you, *chère?*"

"Constantly. And I've only been here an hour. Is he perpetually horny?"

"Nah. He's just hardwired to make a move on any beautiful woman." He shook his head, as if disgusted, whether with himself for talking to her, or with Adam for hitting on her, or for his referring to her as beautiful, she wasn't sure.

And, no, she was not going to let that back-handed compliment please her in any way, even though she couldn't recall the last time anyone had called her beautiful.

"Sort of like a dog that rushes in to mark his territory before another dog can get there first," he elaborated.

Okay, so I'm not complimented. "Are you comparing me to a dog?"

He grinned. "No. The hydrant."

She laughed. "I stepped into that one."

"Anyhow, Famosa comes on strong, but he's a good guy." He paused, then made a snorting sound. "I cain't believe I'm defendin' that Yankee brick-for-brains." Celine had been living around southern drawls most of her life, but John's was particularly attractive...slow and sexy, even when he was discussing fire hydrants.

Then, the lout went back to ignoring her.

She started to flick through some laminated maps spread out next to him.

"Don't touch those," he snapped, leaning over and

slapping the maps out of her hands. Then he went back to his keyboard tapping.

"Touchy, touchy!"

He turned around, flashing her a glower, before his gaze lowered.

"Why are you staring at my knees?"

"You doan wanna know, baby." His voice had dropped again into a lazy Cajun drawl.

"Huh?"

"Listen, if ya gotta interview someone, go pester Ronnie."

"Pester? Do you try hard to be obnoxious?"

"No, it comes naturally."

"Can't we call a truce here?"

"Hell, no. You are not gonna make me the star of any more of your fantasies."

"I beg your pardon. I have never had any sexual fantasies about you."

He grinned. "I wasn't referrin' to sexual fantasies. Talk about! I meant you makin' me out to be some sex cop in a newspaper article, even if you didn't name me. A fantasy, guar-an-teed."

"It wasn't that bad."

His eyebrows shot up in disbelief, highlighting dark brown eyes that were beyond pretty. For a man. Like rich chocolate. "I was so embarrassed. So, do me a favor, baby, and take your sweet ass somewhere else. Like Alaska."

Celine had been feeling guilty over that sidebar, but she did not like his attitude. Not one bit. So, instead of apologizing, she said, "I didn't think there was anything that could embarrass you."

He swung around in his chair and gave her his full

attention. "You know what's embarrassing? As repulsed as I am by what you've done to me, I have the strangest compulsion to lick the back of your knees. Now, that's embarrassing."

"You're kidding."

"Wanna bet?"

"My knees?"

"The back of your knees."

She felt the most delicious sensation behind her knees...and up higher. As if he could turn her on by touching her knees! Her knees were not erotic spots for her. Besides, she wouldn't let John LeDeux within a bayou mile of her body, in the sexual sense. Not again. "This is a joke, right?"

"I wish! Not to worry, though. I think it's some love spell nonsense my aunt is pullin' on me. It'll pass. Either that, or I'm gonna kill myself."

"It's that unpalatable that you would be attracted to me?" she asked before she had a chance to bite her tongue.

"Not unpalatable. After all, I sure as sin didn't find you unpalatable that one time." His lips parted, and his dark eyes went half-shuttered at mention of her one and only fall from grace. The man was a menace to womankind.

"Never mind."

"No, no, no! You can't say somethin' like that and then just drop it. I don't find you unpalatable, Celine. Just dangerous."

Now, that she could not ignore. "Dangerous how?"

"Do you really want to know?"

Yes. "No."

As if she hadn't spoken at all, he went on, "One, next

time you might use my name and that could ruin my career. Two, you hate my guts, which would be a challenge to any red-blooded male, but especially to this Cajun hot-blooded male, to seduce you into ... well, the opposite of hate. Three, I haven't been laid in a month, and I've got testosterone oozing out my pores. Four, I am not in the market for a bride, no matter what my aunt says. Five, this is a serious venture, and you are a distraction ... to everyone." He turned back to the computer.

Celine's anger rose higher and higher with each of his numbered remarks. She'd like to answer, one by one, his outrageous assessments of her. But she knew that's what he intended ... to bait her into an outburst of temper. Instead, she plunked herself down on the bench beside him and said, "So, what are we working on here, John? It looks like a grid. Is it the project site?"

"That does it," he said. "Don't say I didn't warn you." With a couple of quick clicks, he exited the program, logged off, then asked her in an sickly sweet southern drawl, "Would ya lak ta see mah new screen saver, sweet thang?"

Without waiting for her reply, he pulled up what appeared to be the beginning of a puzzle. The first piece was the back of a neck. Then the back of another neck ... a woman's neck, with male fingers cupping the nape. Dark hair, on two different people. A diamond post earring. Then red lips. *Yikes!* It was her red lips. Being kissed by John LeDeux. And it looked as if she was kissing him back. The jerk had blown up the photo of the kiss he'd given her at the Playpen into a seventeen-inch head shot. The kiss that had been a ruse to filch her camera and mike, but you'd never know it by this piece of carnal photography.

Stunned, she couldn't speak, at first. His mouth was open over hers. And her mouth was open, too. Probably in outrage, about to protest, but no one looking would know that. Both of their eyes were closed, long lashes like sensuous fans against his dark and her lighter face. It was just a kiss, but if she hadn't known better, she would have considered it a highly erotic bit of foreplay.

"You had no right—"

"Is my tongue in your mouth there? I don't remember, but hot damn, it sure looks like it."

She sputtered. A mistake. It gave him an opportunity to continue.

"Every time I look at this picture, I get turned on. How 'bout you, Celine? Do you get turned on lookin' at our kiss?"

Actually, yes. "You are such a toad." She stood, uncaring that John had accomplished his goal . . . getting rid of her.

He said the oddest thing then when she was about to stomp away.

"If I were you, I'd steer clear of Tante Lulu. I suspect she'll be sprinkling juju dust all over you."

Chapter
6

Talk about being blindsided!...

The day had been a bust.

Well, not entirely.

John and all the others had worked steadily once they arrived at René's cabin. First, on orders from Tante Lulu, they'd carted in supplies to the state-of-the-art kitchen, started the generator, turned on the air conditioner, and cleared the pipes to the cistern. No cooking over the campfire here. They were about to sit down to the feast Tante Lulu had spent the past few hours preparing.

They'd also brought in laptop computers which were set up in one corner of the great room, another word for a frickin' big living room. They still called René's place here a cabin, or fishing camp, even though the original fishing camp had been replaced with this Better Homes and Bayou Lodge. Donald Trump would be comfortable here.

John hadn't participated in a Jinx treasure hunt for two years, before he'd joined the police force. But he had done some diving in the interim and kept up his licenses. It would be a different kind of diving in the bayou waters which were pure but the color of well-steeped tea. Plus, the depth was nowhere near like their ocean dives. They probably wouldn't need more than one tank each. And wet suits, not dry suits.

Using a fifty-by-sixty-foot grid system with twenty-five cubes, they would begin their dives tomorrow morning. One cube of bayou waters at a time, like a lawn mower. Bayou streams varied vastly in width, in some places so narrow a person standing in the middle could extend arms and touch each bank, but in others as wide as the Mississippi. At the project site, the bayou was about sixty feet wide.

Celine, as excited as a kid with a new video game, was fiddling around at the end of the porch, by herself, with a backup sonar scanner, after some sickeningly cozy shoulder-to-shoulder instructions from Famosa. No one had paid any attention to John when he'd warned the team to be careful in how much they let a newspaper reporter participate in the project. Ronnie had taken Celine at her word, that she could be trusted.

John didn't trust her any farther than he could throw her.

Waiting for dinner, he leaned against the porch rail, drinking a longneck Dixie, keeping an eye on Ms. Tabloid...which wasn't a burden; she had changed to a red tank top and scrunched her hair on top of her head, exposing her neck and shoulders. Now he had fantasies not only about the back of her knees, but her neck and shoulders, too, and especially her ears. In fact, he'd been playing a game with himself. Counting up all the different things he could do to her ears. Seventeen so far.

He was pretty sure she wasn't wearing a bra, but he was saving that fantasy feast for later.

Famosa and Peachey were down at the stream attempting to catch some fish. He could show them how it was done here on the bayou. Maybe later. Ronnie and Brenda were inside helping Tante Lulu. Remy had left, but would return occasionally with René who would no doubt want to make sure the team was doing everything in an environmentally friendly manner, not to mention checking up on his property.

They'd all worked hard this afternoon taking supplies to the project site by pirogues. Then they'd had to build a raft to carry the heavier equipment...the primary sonar scanner to take pictures of the bayou floor; the magnetometer to detect iron and steel, even when well buried in the muddy bottom; shovels, pickaxes, vacuum pumps, and blowing devices. Regular and underwater cameras. Diving suits and oxygen tanks.

"How about a drink?" Celine asked.

He'd been lost in his own thoughts and hadn't realized she'd come up to him and was reaching for his beer, which was half empty.

She tipped her head back and he watched, mesmerized, as her throat worked. Chug, chug, chug. And, yep, he'd been right. No bra. Raising her arms caused her chest to arc out, giving him a really good idea of just how her breasts would look uncovered. A nice handful, in his estimation, but would they be pink-tipped or dark rose? He couldn't recall from that one time they'd been together. Hell, he couldn't even recall if they'd taken their clothes off.

"Stop it!"

His eyes shot up. "What?"

"You know what. First my knees, now my boobs."

"Sorry. You planted them right in my face. What was I supposed to do?"

"Look the other way."

"Yeah, right."

"This place is really nice," she commented, bracing her hands on the rail beside him.

He turned to stare in the same direction as she was. "It *is* a pretty spot...René calls it his paradise." The cabin faced a wide section of Bayou Black. Off on the right, the water veered into a fork, the center of which was a small island, about half the size of a football field.

"Do you ever go over to the island?"

"Sure. Sometimes during storms, it gets covered by water, but mostly it stays above ground. It's the natural habitat of a zillion birds and animals. A microcosm of its own. *National Geographic* filmed here one time as a segment of its 'Hidden Treasures of Nature' TV special. I'll take you over sometime this week, if we have time."

She nodded, but she did it reluctantly, which really pissed him off. Even when he was being nice, she couldn't bend a little. "What is it with you and that chip on your shoulder with my name on it? What did I ever do to you?"

Her face went stiff and closed in, as if she was trying to hide something.

This was getting weirder and weirder.

He cocked his head to the side. "Surely, you don't hold it against me that we did the dirty that one time. It was consensual, babe. I didn't force you into anything you didn't want to do."

"I never said you did, and I don't appreciate talking about it, if you don't mind."

"Why?"

"Why what?"

"Why don't you want to talk about it? Are you ashamed?"

"Of course not. Well, yes, I am. I was never in your league, and I feel foolish that I put myself in that position."

"League? What league?"

"I was invisible to you, before and after the...uh, incident."

Incident? That's what they're calling the deed today? "What a crock!"

"Don't try to say you ever noticed me in high school or in college before that party. And you sure as Satan ignored me afterward."

Now we're getting somewhere. "I did not ignore you. You walked by me with your nose so high in the air that, if we'd had a rain storm, you would have drowned."

"I only ignored you because you ignored me. This is a pointless discussion. You asked me what I have against you. Well, you treat women as sex objects, bouncing from one to the other as if life is a sexual trampoline. You're too frivolous. You think you're hot stuff. How's that for a start?"

"You do not know me. At all. Yeah, I like women, but my reputation is vastly exaggerated. And I like havin' a good time. Why not? My life at home was hell, if you must know, an abusive alcoholic father and a clueless mother who cared more about shopping than any bruises on my body. I work hard at a job that provides a service, and I'm a good cop, too, despite your friggin' article. As for hot stuff..." He shrugged. "Yeah, I am pretty hot."

They both glared at each other, then burst out laughing at the same time. He reached over and gave her a quick hug, just to show there were no hard feelings.

"Come eat," Tante Lulu yelled from the doorway which was only about three feet from where they were standing.

Startled, he and Celine jerked apart. The gleam in his aunt's eye told him that she interpreted the hug as another spark from the thunderbolt. He would have to set her straight later.

Before they went into the house, he reminded Celine, "I still intend to collect on my payback."

She ignored his threat, but he could tell that she knew what he meant. Just in case, he said, "A weekend of hot screaming can't-get-enough sex at a place of my choice."

"Moron," she muttered. But she was smiling.

Soon they were all seated at a long, rustic pine table with benches on either side and armed chairs at either end. He made sure he was at the opposite end of the table from Celine, not chancing any further conversation that would give her more ammunition to use against him.

But he wasn't the only one with trust issues.

Despite her best intentions, she glanced at John more times than she should. She didn't trust the Cajun rogue any more than she would trust that friendly alligator Useless. He was a devil, that's what he was, just waiting for the opportunity to jab her with his pitchfork, in one way or another. She felt like she was fifteen again, the Plain Jane Geek watching the Cool Guy stroll by, never sure if he was going to cut her dead by ignoring her or do something to humiliate her...like smile...or wink.

Aaarrgh! This assignment was going to be the death of her.

Meanwhile, various conversations were taking place around the table, and she had to admit it was an interesting group of people. They would make a colorful feature story, in themselves.

"How long have you been a newspaper reporter?" asked Brenda Caslow, who was seated on her right. And, boy, talk about interesting! She was a former race car mechanic and was married to superstar NASCAR driver Lance Caslow. The sports editor at the *Times-Tribune* was going to have a bird when he found out she'd gotten a promise of a personal interview with Lance and an exclusive on some yet-to-be-disclosed future plans.

"Since I graduated from college. I started out with a Houston weekly, went to the *Dallas Morning Call*, and then six months ago moved to the New Orleans paper."

Adam Famosa, the Cuban professor, turned to her, from her other side. He was about forty, with silver-threaded black hair tied at his nape with a leather thong. Not unattractive when he wasn't aggressively hitting on her. She suspected there was a human interest story in him, too. Just how did he arrive in this country at age eleven? "John says you've had lots of awards...for someone so young."

Celine's gaze shot to John with surprise.

"What?" said John. "You didn't think I knew anything about you, *chère?*"

Now, that is an alarming idea. "Why would you care to know anything about me?"

"Darlin'," he chided her, "you're a good-lookin' woman. I'm a Cajun man. Enough said."

"Bull! I don't want you checking out anything about me."

He waggled his eyebrows at her, as if to show he was definitely checking her out. "What? It's okay for you to dig into my past, but reciprocation is taboo?"

He had a point there. She crinkled her nose at him.

"What's with you two sniping at each other all the time?" asked Caleb Peachey, an ex-Amish Navy SEAL, of all things. Caleb was overly serious and rarely spoke about anything personal, Celine had noticed. Getting his life story wouldn't be easy. "You two got a thing goin' on?"

"No!" she and John said as one.

"Mebbe," Tante Lulu interjected.

Celine's head swiveled on her neck to stare with shock at the old lady behind her at the stove. She hated to admit it, but Tante Lulu was the most interesting of them all. Outrageous in appearance and the things she said, the old lady had a reputation throughout the bayou as a respected healer. "Where would you get such a ludicrous idea?"

John laughed and put his hands up in a "Not me!" fashion.

"Doan go gettin' yer thong all bunched up, Celine. I jist said mebbe."

"There is no maybe," Celine insisted, her face flaming at the mention of her wearing a thong. She never wore thongs, but they were all probably picturing her in one.

"Methinks the chick doth protest too much," Adam murmured.

The *chick?* With still heated face, she decided to ignore the bunch of them and resumed eating the shrimp étouffée which Tante Lulu had placed before them along with warm French bread and a crisp green salad smothered in vinaigrette dressing. "The food is delicious," she remarked. "As good as any meal in a French Quarter restaurant. I expected to see cold sandwiches and bottled water."

"Not with my aunt," John pointed out. He and Tante Lulu exchanged warm smiles. It was obvious that they were really close.

"Thank ya very much, sweetie," Tante Lulu said to her. "We's havin' okra ice cream fer dessert."

Celine's head shot up, along with a few others at the table.

"Jist kiddin'. There's beignets and coffee comin' up."

"I hate okra," Celine said with a shiver of distaste.

"Ya cain't be Cajun and hate okra," Tante Lulu contended. "How come ya doan have a Cajun accent? And what's with them blue eyes?"

"I was born in Houma but moved away with my parents when I was six. My mother was half Cajun. I didn't come back 'til I was in high school to live with my grandfather. My mother died of cancer when I was fifteen, and my father..." She paused, not wanting to mention her father's suicide, "He died soon after. I guess I moved here too late to take on Cajun traits."

Tante Lulu squeezed her shoulder, obviously aware of her father's suicide, and the gesture touched Celine in the oddest way. In that instant, she realized how much she missed a woman's touch...a mother's touch, actually. She blinked back tears.

Ronnie, Jake, John, Adam, Caleb, and Brenda began talking about what they hoped to accomplish the next day. Apparently, they would be working from dawn 'til dusk, if necessary. Celine was glad to have the attention diverted away from her.

They really were professionals, which was enlightening to her. In the past, she'd viewed treasure hunters as delusional crackpots out for a quick buck. But these people, even Ronnie, who had been a corporate lawyer, took treasure hunting seriously. Trained divers. Computer savvy. Mechanically proficient. Able to work as a team. All these things, along with their research talents, impressed her more than she'd expected.

Everyone in southern Louisiana knew about the pirate Jean Lafitte. He was part of their heritage. Both the good and the bad. Yes, he had been an out-and-out pirate, even involved in the slave trade at one point, but he had also been a hero. Never attacking an American ship...in fact, aiding the Americans in the war against the British. Giving to the poor. Not to mention having a reputation as a great lover.

If by some remote possibility the Jinx team was successful in recovering any of the Lafitte treasure, it would be making history as well as a financial boon. One thing puzzled her, though. "Tante Lulu...John...how did you get involved with Jinx? They're based in New Jersey."

"Six years back, I went ta Atlantic City ta bring my nephew home," Tante Lulu said. "He was strippin'."

Why am I not surprised. Celine raised her eyebrows at John.

"Hey, I like ta dance."

"Well, ya doan hafta be showin' yer hiney to dance."

"It was only two weeks, and I did it on a dare," John told Celine.

Everyone at the table was chuckling and shaking their heads at John. Apparently they knew him and his antics well.

Yep, great father material. "I saw you dance one time. At a high school dance marathon for some charity." Why she'd felt the need to impart that news to John was probably an indication of her nervousness.

"Really? Was I good?"

"Very good. You won, as I recall."

"Did I dance with you?"

"No." Good grief! She would have had a heart attack in those days if he had even asked. To her chagrin, she felt herself blushing.

"Tsk-tsk-tsk! Even I know better than to tell a woman I don't remember her," Adam said to John.

"I didn't say I didn't remember Celine. I didn't remember *dancing* with her."

"Same thing." Adam smirked at John. "Maybe I could teach you something about Yankee finesse."

John told Adam what he could do with his finesse.

Tante Lulu smacked John lightly on the shoulder with a wire whisk.

Then John frowned, no doubt taking in her heated face. "Did I hurt your feelin's by not askin' you to dance, *chère?*"

Yes! "Hardly!"

He was still frowning.

"That's like not remembering a woman after you've nailed her," Adam went on.

"Adam!" Tante Lulu, Ronnie, and Brenda all said regarding his crudity. Tante Lulu gave Adam a whack with the whisk, too.

But that remark caused John's face to flush, and hers to turn even redder, for different reasons, obviously.

Beside her, she heard Caleb chuckle.

Enough! "Brenda, did you say something about having a little girl?" Celine asked, opting for a change of subject.

Brenda began a story about her eleven-year-old daughter Patti that soon had everyone laughing. The little girl was obsessed with *American Idol* and had talked her father into getting tickets for the finals last year, which proved to be an embarrassing mistake when Ryan Seacrest shamed Lance, who was tone deaf, into coming up onstage and doing a short duet with Paula Abdul to "I've Got You, Babe."

"Speakin' of *American Idol,* how's yer sister Lizzie doin'?" Tante Lulu asked Caleb. Tante Lulu looked at Celine and explained, "Caleb's sister is a wonderful singer. She wants ta be on *American Idol.*"

Celine flashed Caleb a sideways glance of surprise. "Isn't she Amish?"

He nodded with a grimace. "Lizzie made it through the first round two years ago, but then she got mono and couldn't continue."

"She called herself an Amish J-Lo," Tante Lulu elaborated.

"Now, she calls herself an Amish Carrie Underwood." Caleb smiled, and, whoo-boy, a smile from this taciturn man was unexpected and dazzling. He was a testosterone-oozing hunk, for sure. "Actually, she's gonna participate in the tryouts in New Orleans next month."

"Ooooh, thass nice. Mebbe we kin all go support her."

"Well, she and Patti should get along," Brenda said. "She'll go nuts when I tell her. I'll mark the date on my calendar."

"Do ya think Patti will like havin' a baby sister or brother?" Tante Lulu asked Brenda.

Brenda gasped.

Uh-oh! Good old tactless Tante Lulu.

"What makes you think I'm pregnant?"

Tante Lulu waved a hand dismissively. "It's not 'cause yer gettin' fat, if thass what ya think." Celine had only been here a few hours, and already she knew about Brenda's constant and unusual diets, even though she had a Marilyn Monroe–style figure that men loved. "Brenda, honey, I'm a *traiteur.* I can sense these things."

Brenda's face flushed with embarrassment.

"Are you happy about this pregnancy?" Ronnie asked after giving Brenda a hug.

"Yes. And no. I would like another baby. Of course, I would. But I'm thirty-nine years old."

"I was almost thirty-five when I had Julie Ann," Ronnie pointed out. "Does this mean you'll stop working with Jinx?"

"Just for a few months. Maybe a year, but I want to come back eventually. My mother lives with us. She'll help with the baby, just like she did with Patti. Lance will help, too."

Now, that would be a story. Lance Caslow. Mr. Mom.

Tante Lulu patted Brenda's hand. "Not ta worry. Wimmen have babies much older t'day, even when their boobs are saggin' and their bottoms have gone all mushy."

The old lady was outrageous.

"Babies are a blessin', no matter when they come," Tante Lulu concluded.

Maybe not so outrageous.

"Do you have any children?" Ronnie asked Celine, out of the blue.

"Yes," she replied, taking herself and everyone else by surprise. *Oh, my God! Oh, my God!*

Why did I admit that?

Because it would be like slamming my own son, that's why.

Do I subconsciously want John to find out?

Of course not. I'm just an idiot.

She could tell that her slip shocked John. He leaned forward and turned his head to the right so he could see her better. "I didn't know you were married," he said, frowning. He was probably trying to remember if she'd ever said that precisely.

Her heart was beating so fast she feared everyone could see it through her T-shirt. "I'm not married," she replied without looking his way. "But I'm engaged." *I've never been embarrassed about being a single parent... at least not in the past. What's going on here?*

And I never lie, either.

Oooh, what is it they say about lies and how they always come back to bite you in the butt? Any more of this and I'm going to have to wear armor on my behind.

"Oh, no!" Tante Lulu said. "Tee-John, how could this be? Ya know what I thought... about Celine and the thunderbolt and such?"

"What thunderbolt?" Celine asked.

"Don't ask," John advised her, then stood and hugged his aunt. "I told you it wasn't the right time, Auntie."

"Is yer fiancé the baby's daddy?" Tante Lulu asked.

That was really intrusive, but Celine didn't think she could back down now. In fact, she felt as if she'd stepped into quicksand of her own making. "Uh, no."

"When's the weddin'?" John asked in an oddly grim voice.

"Uh, not for a while. Darryl is…uh…in Afghanistan. A war correspondent." *Quicksand, quicksand, quicksand.*

"No kidding? What's his last name? What squad is he embedded with? Maybe I know him?" This from Caleb, who probably still had lots of contacts in the military.

The situation was spiralling out of hand. She needed to get the focus off her and the blasted fiancé.

"Boy or a girl?" Brenda asked. "Your child, I mean?"

Thank you, God! "Boy. His name is Etienne," she said, pronouncing it with a drawn-out A-T-N, like ATM. "He's…uhm, four years old." That must be about her sixth lie in less than five minutes. She was going to confession first thing when she got back home. But, no, maybe not. In order to get absolution, she would have to promise to correct the lies.

Meanwhile, John was studying her way too closely.

Something was wrong here. John wasn't sure what it was, but his antennae were on red alert. He'd taken a class in college on body language—one of those easy-credit courses—and he would bet his badge that Celine was lying about something. In addition, he'd had a few conversations with Jake about "tells," the little body giveaways that experienced poker players knew how to hide, but not the average person.

Celine was lying through her teeth about something.

But what?

And why?

Hmmm. She must have been a junior or senior in college when she got pregnant, after he'd graduated. He wondered who the father was, whether she had ever been married, and how she'd managed to complete her education while caring for a newborn. But he could see how uncomfortable she was discussing her private life, even about her fiancé, who would no doubt adopt her son.

Tante Lulu was still shaking her head with disbelief. "I jist doan understand," she muttered. "St. Jude never gets it wrong."

Well, at least this development would take Celine out of his aunt's crosshairs in the bride hunt.

"Etienne is a rascal, all right. An adorable rascal." Celine must have been talking while he'd succumbed to his shell shock. "Practically from the moment he was born, he's been driving me nuts with his antics. And then, when he's caught, he just flashes one of those irresistible grins, and I cave. He's got the mischief/charm thing down pat." She seemed to be babbling. With nervousness. How odd!

"Sounds jist like Tee-John," Tante Lulu said.

Celine flinched, as if his aunt had made a derogatory remark.

Now, that was insulting...that she didn't want any kid of hers being at all like him. *What am I? Slime?*

"Should you be diving if you're pregnant?" Celine asked Brenda, clearly wanting to change the subject.

"I'm only two months along, and this isn't a particularly deep dive."

"Do ya have a picture of yer boy?" Tante Lulu wasn't about to let Celine off the hook so fast.

"No!" she said, way too vehemently for such an innocuous question. They were drowning in oddness here. "I mean, not with me." She glanced his way and blushed.

This was getting curiouser and curiouser.

And he could tell that Tante Lulu's antennae were up, too.

Celine was hiding something.

Maybe it was about the father. Could it be someone he knew? Yep, that must be it.

But she was uncomfortable with Tante Lulu, too. That narrowed the field down a lot. Someone he and his aunt both knew. Hmmm.

Was there anything lower than a man who made babies, then disappeared from the scene? That's probably why Celine was so skittish. She'd been dumped by some two-bit piece of crap and left with a bun in the oven.

He shrugged. It was none of his business.

Chapter
7

Beware of ladies with funny tea...

Tante Lulu took a break after cleaning up from dinner. And, yes, she thought of herself as Tante Lulu, like everyone else, instead of Louise Rivard.

She was out on the porch, listening as Tee-John teased Brenda, trying to draw the young woman out of her obvious blues. Now that she was pregnant, she probably wanted to be home with her husband and little girl. Cajun music played softly in the background...a song by a band named BeauSoleil, she thought.

The boy—and yes she thought of Tee-John as a boy, even though he was twenty-eight—was good at heart, and she loved him almost more than all the others. He'd had to live with that devil Valcour LeDeux longest. Lots of people thought he was wild and worthless, even though he'd settled down when he took that cop job a few years back. She knew better. All his running around and joking was like a mask he put on. Inside he was still the little boy who came running to her cottage with welt marks from his hiney to his shoulders. And it wasn't only one time, either. To this day, she got tears in her eyes thinking about the things she'd seen done to this child. Luc, Remy, and René had had each other, and her of course, when Valcour LeDeux had gone off on one of his rages; Tee-John mostly only had her.

At her request...okay, demand...Tee-John was pruning the climbing roses that were growing every which way almost as high as the roof. She'd given René cuttings from her own garden to plant here years ago when he rebuilt the cabin, but then everything grew like wildfire in this tropical heat. "So, what do you say to a NASCAR driver when you're about to make love? Va-va-voom?" Tee-John continued to tease Brenda.

Brenda, who was painting her toenails with first one foot, then the other, propped on the porch rail, smiled at him and said, "No. I say, 'Gentleman, start your engine.'"

"Good one! Hey, I could paint your toenails for you? I'm real good at it."

"I'll bet you are," Celine muttered behind Tante Lulu.

"You mean like the movie *Bull Durham*?" Brenda asked.

"Yeah, but better."

Celine snorted. "You're no Kevin Costner," she teased.

"Yeah, but better," Tee-John repeated, this time to Celine with a waggle of his eyebrows. Tante Lulu would have to talk with the girl later; she needed to know snorting was not ladylike. On the other hand, that rascal Tee-John did tend to bring out the snort in a lady.

"Lance would kill you," Brenda told him. Now that

she was finished, she put the cap on the nail polish and put both feet on the rail to dry.

"He could try," Tee-John said, over-confident, as usual. Then, craning his neck to the side so he could see Celine, he offered, "I could do you, Celine."

Celine made a choking sound, and everyone on the porch or in the front yard smiled. Tante Lulu smiled, too. These two put off more sparks than a Fourth of July sparkler.

Done with his pruning, Tee-John came up onto the porch and tugged on one of Brenda's blonde curls. "Did you hear about the blonde who thought General Motors was in the Army?"

Brenda shot right back with: "Mental anxiety. Mental dysfunction. Menopause. Menstrual Cramps. Notice how all women's problems begin with men?"

Adam, who'd been sitting on the front steps with Caleb, jumped in with, "Did you hear about the redneck who thought Taco Bell was a Mexican phone company?"

"No, but do you know what to do if you see a dumb Yankee throw a pin?" Tee-John batted his long eyelashes at Adam. "Run. He's probably got a grenade in his mouth."

"Are you people nuts?" Celine asked.

Tee-John winked at Celine, and even Tante Lulu could see that the boy did have a sexy wink. Those long black eyelashes, no doubt. "Didja hear 'bout the half-Cajun gal who confused her Prozac with her birth control pills? No? Well, she had a dozen kids, but she doesn't give a damn."

Celine tried but couldn't stop herself from smiling.

Tee-John had that effect on women, bless his heart.

Which was puzzling. Tante Lulu could swear she had seen thunderbolts zig-zagging between these two. Even when the girl had written that newspaper article about him, even if it didn't mention him by name, Tante Lulu had sensed that Celine had done it to get his attention. How could she have been so sure that Celine was the one for Tee-John if she was already taken? Could she be losing her matchmaking instincts? Was she getting so old that her powers were weakening? If that was so, would she be losing other talents as well? Like healing? Or heading the family? Or being a hottie?

"Are ya sure yer engaged?"

Celine's face got all pink and splotchy. "Um... why?"

"I was so sure."

Celine frowned in confusion.

"Best ya doan frown so much. Girl yer age could get wrinkles."

The frown disappeared, but the pink splotches remained.

"Yer glistenin', Celine. You want I should get you a wet wipe?"

"Glistening?"

"Yep. Dint ya ever hear it said here in the South that pigs sweat, men perspire, and women glisten?"

Celine just shook her head as if Tante Lulu was hopeless. Hah! She wasn't the one hopeless on this porch. *Which reminds me. I best pull out that St. Jude birdbath from the storage shed tomorrow.* The girl was wiping off her face now with a tea towel that a laughing Tee-John had thrown her way.

"Ya ever wear makeup, honey? My niece Charmaine has a beauty spa in Houma. She could give ya tips. She could help ya get rid of those splotches, too, lickety-split."

"Of course I wear makeup sometimes, but why would I wear makeup here in the boonies?"

"Hah! I know some wimmen who wear makeup jist ta take the garbage out. But then, they probably have hunky garbage men."

"Aaarrgh!"

Lots of people said that around her.

"What were you sure of?" Celine asked Tante Lulu testily.

"I was sure the thunderbolt had finally come fer Tee-John."

"What thunderbolt?"

"The thunderbolt of love."

"I'm probably going to regret asking, but what has this thunderbolt of love to do with...oh, no! You couldn't possibly have thought...? Me and John LeDeux?"

"Are ya sure yer engaged?"

"Yes."

"When're ya gettin' hitched?"

"Um, when Duane gets home."

"I thought his name was Darryl."

"Um...Darryl is his first name, but he prefers to use his middle name."

"His name is Darryl Duane?"

"Um, yes."

"Whass his last name?"

"Um...Dalton."

Tante Lulu arched her eyebrows. "Darryl Duane Dalton?"

"Um...yes."

Tee-John snickered.

Celine glowered at him.

There are a bunch of ums comin' outta that girl's mouth. Hmmmm. "When'll it be?"

"What?"

"The weddin'."

"Um…next year."

"Next year? Holy moly, there's lotsa time yet."

"Time for what?"

"Fer the thunderbolt ta work…and St. Jude, of course. Do ya have a St. Jude statue, honey?"

Celine just stared at her, like she was dumb…or dumbfounded. Same thing.

"Why dontcha come into the kitchen with me, sweetie. I'm thinkin' what a gal like you needs is…" She beamed with inspiration, "…a cup of my famous juju tea."

Everyone else on the porch said, "Uh-oh."

You're out in the bayou with WHO?…

"Holy shit! Only you would go into hiding with the enemy."

"She's not the enemy, Chief."

"She sure as hell isn't your friend…or that of the department."

"I've told you that she promises—"

"Screw promises. Get the hell out of there. I'll call the FBI. We'll have you set up in a safe place by tomorrow."

"No!" he barked, then softened, "I mean, let me case the situation out. There's no way to leave here unless

Remy comes in by hydroplane, or someone spends days traveling by pirogue."

"What happens if this project ends in a week or two? She'll be coming back then."

"She promises that my name won't be mentioned."

"LeDeux, LeDeux, LeDeux. Even now, she could call her newspaper."

"No, she can't. Cell phones don't work here. I'm calling on a secure satellite phone. So, there's no way she's chit-chatting with anyone."

"I don't know."

"Trust me. You won't find a safer place than this remote cabin. But if you still insist, I can go to my brother Luc's fishing camp. It's even more remote."

"Is being on this treasure hunt that important to you?"

He hesitated. "Yeah, it is."

"Let me talk to the DA tomorrow morning. See what he thinks."

"Remy's flyin' in about noon to take the owners of Jinx, Inc. back. So, try to make a decision by then."

"Okay."

"Boss, I can handle Celine Arseneaux."

"That's what I'm afraid of."

Hit me with your best shot...in the WHAT?...

The old lady was giving her the heebie-jeebies, one of Etienne's favorite words.

All evening long Tante Lulu had been pushing some

pungent-tasting herbal tea on her...that was when she wasn't hinting about some thunderbolt nonsense...or when she wasn't giving her a mini plastic St. Jude statue or a St. Jude key chain or a St. Jude medal.

The senior citizen dingbat thinks I'm hopeless.

I'm not hopeless.

I'm hopeful.

Well, okay, a little bit hopeless, but only in certain areas.

Aaarrgh!

So far, she, the old lady, and the pregnant Brenda had to go pee ten times.

Meanwhile, she was having the strangest, most unwelcome thoughts about John LeDeux. Way more than her knees were involved.

Now, she was lying in one of the three single beds in the second of two loft bedrooms, pretending she was asleep so that Tante Lulu would finally shut up. The old lady, who was in the middle bed, with Brenda on the far bed, had an opinion on everything in the world, and asked the most intimate questions.

"Do ya wear a thong, dearie?"

"Are ya on the pill?"

"Didja ever wear fishnet stockings?"

"I wonder if Richard Simmons wears boxers or briefs." Tante Lulu had a crush on the exercise guru. Celine didn't know what was more unbelievable: that a ninety-two-year-old woman still got crushes, or who the object of that attraction was.

Celine really didn't mind the old woman. In fact, overall, she was kind of charming. And her family certainly loved her, and vice versa.

To her surprise, Celine had enjoyed her first day on

the Pirate Project. They hadn't discovered any treasure yet; they hadn't even tried, for that matter. It had all been set-up and planning.

"Clark Gable kissed my knee one time," Tante Lulu said out of the blue.

Celine turned on her pillow to stare at Tante Lulu. By the moonlight streaming through two large windows, Celine could see that Tante Lulu was lying flat on her back with a sheet pulled up to her neck. Pink foam curlers adorned her hair which she'd dyed blonde earlier that night. On the other side, Brenda was staring at the old lady, too.

"What is it with you LeDeuxs and knees?" Celine exclaimed.

"Huh?" Tante Lulu said.

"Oh, nothing."

"Ya cain't stop there."

"It's just that John said something to me about licking the back of my knees. He was just teasing."

Tante Lulu murmured something that sounded like "*Merci*, St. Jude," while Brenda started to giggle.

"So, what were you saying about Clark Gable?" Brenda asked.

"Jist that he kissed my knee one time. I was visitin' the set fer *Gone With the Wind* when I tripped and fell. He came over and kissed the boo-boo. Whoo-ee, did that mustache tickle! Talk about! I dint wash my leg fer a week."

Celine thought a moment. "That movie was made in 1939." She knew because it was one of her favorites on DVD.

"So?"

"You must have been some hot chick at one time,"

Brenda observed while both of them made mental calculations of how old she must have been in 1939. About twenty-five.

"I'm still a hot chick."

Celine didn't need to glance over at Brenda to know she was smiling, just like her.

"Ya know the one thing I'll regret when I die?"

Celine was becoming used to the sudden bends and twists in the old lady's conversations. "What?"

"I never found my G-spot."

Oh. My. God!

Brenda made a choking sound, probably trying to suppress laughter.

"Ya found *yer* G-spot yet, Brenda?"

Zap!

"Lance found it for me." There was outright laughter in Brenda's voice.

Celine knew what was coming next but didn't know how to deflect it.

"Ya found *yer* G-spot yet, Celine?"

"I'm still looking." She thought that would be the end of it. *Foolish me!*

"Maybe Tee—"

"We had an interesting article in the paper last week," Celine interrupted before the old lady could suggest what she was sure to do. "Doctors can give women a shot so their G-spots are more prominent."

"I read that article," Brenda said. "Something about how the injection causes that area to plump up."

"Sounds painful to me," Celine said.

"Hey, women stick needles in their lips to attract men," Brenda pointed out. "Why not needles in their va-gee-gee?"

"It's a little bit different. Ouch!"

"Charmaine was gonna have her thingamajig sewed up one time," Tante Lulu told them.

Celine couldn't not ask. "What thingamajig?"

"You know, the virginity membrane whatchamacallit. That was when she was gonna become a born again virgin. But then Rusty got outta jail, and that idea went out the window, kapooee. He had her in bed faster'n she could say 'Your bed or mine, sugar?'"

"This is the most bizarre conversation I've ever had," Celine commented.

"Ain't this nice, though? Jist like a sleepover them teenage girls has. If it was earlier, we could put makeup on each other and practice dance moves. Or watch Richard Simmons tapes and do jumpin' jacks. Mebbe tomorrow."

Not if I can help it.

"Well, best I be goin' to sleep. Tee-John'll be leavin' early, and I wants ta give him a good breakfast before he's gone."

Celine went on red alert. "Where's he going?"

"I doan know. It's a secret, I suppose." The old lady yawned loudly and rolled over.

"Is he leaving because of me being here?"

"Prob'ly."

Celine lay awake pondering, even after soft snores came from Tante Lulu's mouth. Finally, she got up and pulled on her sandals. She didn't bother changing her clothes since she was decent in the fake-silk tank top and tap pants she slept in, or fairly decent.

"Where you going?" Brenda asked sleepily.

"To knock some sense into an idiot."

Chapter
8

When dumb chicks stroll into the fox's den...

She crept through the living room, not wanting to disturb Jake, Ronnie, and their little girl who were sleeping on a pull-out sofa. The three of them planned to leave tomorrow after the project was officially launched; Remy would be coming for them in his hydroplane. That's probably how John intended to leave.

Caleb and Adam slept in bunk beds in the second bedroom upstairs. John had told them over dinner that he planned to sleep in a self-enclosed tent outside, nature's way.

"You'll be covered with mosquito bites by morning, Nature Boy," Adam had scoffed.

"Not inside my tent," Tee-John had insisted.

"Hope an alligator doesn't chomp you for a tasty snack." Adam had clearly meant the opposite.

Tee-John had gotten the last word in. "Me, I'm too sweet for any ol' gator. They prefer tougher meat...Yankee meat. Yep, Yankees make good gator kibbles."

Luckily, the loud whirring of the ceiling fan covered the sound of Celine opening and closing the screen door. She had thought he would be on the porch, but a quick survey under the light of a full moon showed that instead he had put up his small tent down near the stream, across from the island.

Although Celine hadn't moved to southern Louisiana 'til she was in tenth grade, she had a strong appreciation for the bayous. Probably the Cajun in her blood. Even when dark, like it was now, there was a beauty in the silence, which wasn't really silence at all. And the sense of mystery! Surely there were ghosts lurking about...the spirits of southern belles and their handsome gentlemen, escaped slaves, and, yes, pirates like Lafitte. Even outlaws, like Bonnie and Clyde, who were rumored to have met their death here in Cajun Louisiana.

A sturdy affair, the tent appeared to have thick screening on three sides and fabric on the fourth side and the roof. When she got closer, she hissed, "John! Wake up!"

Nothing. He slept soundly on his side, his back to her. It appeared as if he was wearing boxers and nothing else. That was okay. It wasn't his body she was after.

"John!" she whispered again.

Nothing.

She went to nudge her shoe against his behind which was backed up against the tent screening, but she slipped and instead kicked him.

"Hey!" He shot to a sitting position. Then, peering outside, he said, "Celine?"

"Yes, let me in. I'm being eaten alive by mosquitoes."

"You want to share a tent with me?" His incredulity was rather insulting.

"Just let me in, dammit, or I'll really kick you this time."

"I'm the fool, I reckon." Swearing under his breath, he unzipped the tent and moved over to make room for her. It was a tight squeeze.

Lying on his back, propped on his elbows, he grinned at her.

She smacked his chest.

"Ouch!"

"I didn't hurt you. Yet."

"First a kick, now a slap. You into S and M or somethin', *chère?*"

"You wish!" She managed to lie down beside him by shoving her hip against his. He was still grinning. Braced on her elbows now, too, she turned and asked him, "Are you quitting this project?"

"Yeah. Probably."

"Because of me?"

"Mostly."

"You are not quitting this project." She smacked his chest again.

"Are you sure about the S and M?"

"Just be glad it's not your head. Then again, I suspect you've got a concrete brain."

"You're orderin' me around like a dominatrix. And those sexy slaps? Oooh, baby!"

"Like I would even know what a dominatrix does!"

"Really, Celine, you're way too uptight. How about releasing your inner sex kitten? You're halfway there in that screw-me red outfit."

She gritted her teeth, then released the breath she hadn't realized she'd inhaled. "This is perfectly respectable sleepwear."

He shrugged, as if that was debatable.

"Furthermore, I have not ever been or want to be a sex kitten."

"Your loss, baby."

The jerk really, really annoyed her. Which had probably been his goal. Yep, he lay back, his arms folded under his neck, a silly grin on his mouth.

Glancing over, she saw his eyes glued to her breasts.

Even worse, she noticed some movement in his shorts.

She did blush then.

He chuckled. "What're you doin' here, Celine?"

"I told you that I wouldn't write any more articles about you. And I promised Ronnie I wouldn't print a story on the project 'til after it was completed. So, what's the problem?" When he didn't immediately answer, she exhaled with disgust. "You don't trust me." It wasn't a question.

"Not just me. My boss says we can't take a chance. I either drop out, or they'll force me into a boring as hell witness protection kind of set-up...probably in some seedy motel in Bodunk, Mississippi."

"And your boss reacted this way all because of me?"

"Bingo!"

"They don't trust me?"

"Pfff! Why should they? The press and police are rarely bedfellows these days, although..." He waggled his eyebrows at her.

She ignored his suggestive eyebrow waggling. "Do *you* trust me?"

"Hell, no!"

For some reason, his lack of trust hurt. "When I give

my word, I keep it, and, frankly, I'm insulted that you would think otherwise."

"Celine, I don't know you. Until last week, I hadn't seen you since college. Even then, we didn't hang with the same crowd."

"You mean, you were with the in-crowd, and I was with the losers."

"Give me a break. I meant that you were two years behind me."

"Oh."

"You've got one serious bug up your butt where I'm concerned. What's with that?"

"That's your imagination."

"I don't think so."

"Call your boss in the morning and let me talk to him."

"Are you nuts? Why would I do that?"

"Maybe I can convince him that you're safe here."

"Why would you care one way or the other if I stay?"

"Because I feel responsible."

"I'm a big boy. I don't need a woman to cover my ass." He grinned. "Unless you're offering...?"

"Get serious."

"I don't know, babe. You on my ass would be seriously tempting."

"Are you trying to say you would stay if I offered you sex?"

John went stiff with surprise, and, well, stiff for other reasons, too. About two feet of space separated them, and he could swear he felt her body heat...her female body heat. He tried not to show his shock to Celine. "Uh...well...is sex on the table?"

"John! You and I know that I'm not your type."

"Are you kidding? Red silk. No bra. Wide-legged tap pants. Probably no panties. Sex heaven, as far as I'm concerned."

Her lips parted and her eyes went wide.

John had been around the block too many times not to recognize that Celine was turned on by his words. He faced her now, so close he could smell the mint of her toothpaste. "Wanna make out?"

"No."

"Liar. I've learned stuff since we were together that one time."

"I would hope so."

"Hey, I was drinkin'."

"Give it up, John. You and I are not going to happen."

He trailed the back of his fingers down one bare arm, shoulder to wrist.

Goose bumps rose on her skin, and her nipples peaked under her shirt, giving lie to her words.

Oooh, boy! John was on a slippery slope here. Still time to jump off, but maybe he could slide a little bit longer. It could be a hell of a ride. No, no, no. Celine was not the type a guy fooled around with, then jumped off the happy train. Sucking in a deep breath, he encouraged, "Tell me about your son."

"Why?"

"Why not?"

"He's beautiful and fun and I love him to pieces."

"Is the guy in Afghanistan his father?"

"No."

"Does his father share custody? Ever see the kid?"

"No!" There was horror in her voice.

"The bastard! Ya want me to kick his ass, *chère?*"

A chortle of amusement escaped her lips. "That would be interesting. But, no thanks. And, really, I would rather change the subject."

"Ya wanna make out?"

Celine was tramping up the incline to the cabin a short time later.

The good thing was that she was smiling.

The bad thing was that she was tempted.

I can float your boat, honey...

By seven A.M., there was a chain of pirogues... well, four of them... headed upstream toward the project site. The flat-bottomed, dugout-style canoes were indispensable here in the often shallow waters of the bayou.

Famosa and Caleb led the parade with Jake, Ronnie, and their kid in second place. Then came Brenda and Tante Lulu, and finally John and Celine.

Although they'd already transported most of the equipment and supplies the day before, the pirogues were well-stocked again today. For example, Tante Lulu, declining efforts to get her to stay back at the cabin, insisted on bringing a small camp stove for what would no doubt be a gourmet lunch, Cajun style.

Despite his words to Celine last night, John was still here, obviously, with no immediate plans to return to Houma with Remy this afternoon. He'd promised the Chief in a post-dawn phone call that he would stick to Celine like Krazy Glue, even when they were sleeping, the last of which had not amused his boss. When he'd informed she-of-the-red-hootchie-mama-nightwear, he'd made sure he was outside of slapping distance. In the end, she agreed, reluctantly, although she probably didn't think he was serious about the sleeping arrangement. He was. Oh, yeah, he hot damn was. He had plans.

For now, heat shimmered above the tannin-stained waters with the sun already beating down on them, but in a pleasant way. It was going to be in the eighties today, which was balmy for the bayous where temps often rose over a hundred. Plus, the radio weather station predicted low humidity; so, hopefully no rain, at least not while they were away from the cabin.

"Do you spend much time in the bayous, *chère*?" He was speaking to Celine's back as she was on the shelf seat in front of him, doing the right-hand rowing, while he handled the left rear. They made a good team...for canoeing anyway.

"Not much anymore. My grandfather used to take me crabbing on the bayou outside Houma when I first moved in with him. But then, I turned sixteen and had other interests."

"Boys?"

"No, tree stumps."

He grimaced. Her sarcasm had a bite to it. But then, he was getting his own back at her, in a more silent way. Every time she leaned forward to dip her paddle into the water, her butt lifted up slightly off the seat, straining the fabric of her shorts so that he got an up close and personal view of two perfect half moons. Even better, the whole rhythm thing...dip, stroke, lift, dip, stroke, lift, over and over, reminded him a little bit of another exercise. Okay, maybe his mind was working overtime, seeing as how he'd been celibate for a long time...one whole month.

But then, he noticed something. Tapping her on the shoulder, he indicated that she should put down her oar and look to the left bank. He moved forward carefully so that he knelt behind her, banking the pirogue slightly in the muddy edge of the stream so it wouldn't move. She turned in her seat; they were shoulder to shoulder.

"Isn't that amazing?" he whispered.

A huge mama alligator, at least eight feet and ugly as sin, was ambling along the muddy bank with three of her young'uns riding her back. They were probably headed toward their nest, a raised platform of mud and sticks.

"They are so cute," Celine whispered back.

"Oh, yeah, cute as a chain saw in a kindergarten. Even those babies have teeth that could chomp off a finger."

"I know, but they're still cute."

"Speaking of cute, you're lookin' pretty cute yourself today," he remarked, knowing full well that it would annoy her.

She was wearing sunglasses, a pink baseball cap, probably one of those breast cancer awareness things, a pink short-sleeved T-shirt proclaiming "I'm a Saint," in honor of the beloved New Orleans Saints football team, black thigh-length, spandex running shorts, along with hiking boots, a necessity when bee-bopping through the swamps, as they would be today. "Enough with the fake compliments! Do you see me making personal remarks about your appearance?"

"You can if you want to."

She removed her sunglasses and gave him a full-body survey, then said succinctly, "Cute," and not as a compliment.

Okay, he would let that semi-insult ride. "Anyhow, that's not what I wanted to show you. Look up there." He removed his sunglasses, as well, and pointed to a half-submerged bald cypress limb rising out of the waters, the knobs of its roots rising up here and there like knees. On one of its limbs, faintly obscured by the hanging moss of a nearby live oak, sat two herons, their necks intertwined, like a braid. They stayed unmoving in that intimate position for a long time, then unwound themselves and just stared ahead. Soon, the male was wrapping himself around the unprotesting female again. "The male is trying to seduce the female into mating," he told Celine.

Instead of her making her usual sarcastic reply, she sighed. "They're beautiful. Thank you for showing me."

He and Celine remained still, watching, she half-turned on the low seat, he on his knees. The bayou surrounded them, like a cocoon. The silence, the lush beauty, the rich scents of a hundred different flowers and plants, the warmth of the sun.

John couldn't help himself then. With the fingertips of his left hand, he coaxed her chin a little more so that she was facing him. Now would be the time for her to tell him to buzz off or for her to shove him overboard, but instead her eyelids were already drifting closed and her lips parting.

Oh, man, this is so not a good idea.

His kiss was gentle but open-mouthed, wanting to take all of her in, laving her lips to wetness with his tongue. Then, still gentle, he moved his mouth back and forth over hers in changing patterns, learning the shape of her lips. And, worst of all, or best of all, she allowed him to coax her into pliancy and began to kiss him back.

Other than the kiss, the only place they touched was where his fingertips touched her jaw. Which was amazing because it felt like a hot, wild, devouring exercise in sensuality, not this tender, smoldering exploration. Blood seemed to surge from his fingertips to his toes and a few important spots along the way.

A moan, so low he barely heard it, started deep in her throat, an erotic vibration against his tongue, already buried deep inside her hot-hot mouth.

Note to me: moaning vibrates the tongue.

A hair-trigger arousal hit him like a sexual sledgehammer to the groin. If he weren't already on his knees, he would have probably been knocked there.

They broke apart at the same time and stared at each other, frozen in a mixture of confusion and horror, as if neither knew how they had come to be kissing. Something intense flared, and it scared the crap out of him. Surely, this wasn't Tante Lulu's famous thunderbolt.

"Sorry," he mumbled, hoping she wouldn't look down. "I didn't mean to do that."

Their eyes caught and held. The air practically sizzled.

She nodded, a rush of pink staining her cheeks.

And he soon knew why she was embarrassed when his eyes strayed to "I'm a Saint," where two hard points were dotting the m and the i.

With a huff of disgust, Celine put her sunglasses back on and folded her arms over her chest. "We better get a move on. The other pirogues are out of sight." She said pirogue as pee-row, which was the correct pronun-

ciation; lots of people thought it was like those doughy
things filled with cheesy mashed potatoes.

This time he changed positions with her, took both
paddles and gave her a pole to use, if necessary. He figured she was probably admiring *his* ass now, just as he
had done hers, but the difference was, he didn't care. In
fact, he welcomed a little hottie-watching, both ways.

"How'd you ever get all these pirogues out here anyhow?" she asked, probably figuring a change of subject
would cool them down.

Fat chance! "My brothers and I spent five days here
two years ago, building the things. It was great fun. The
usual chaos with all the wives and kids and Tante Lulu,
of course, but still fun."

"Wow! I'm impressed."

"Don't be. It's not that hard to make a pirogue. In
fact, they sell kits on the Internet that promise they can
be made over a weekend."

"Still, they appear to be well made."

"They are. So, wanna make out?"

Chapter
9

Just another day, down on the bayou...

The project site, about one mile from the cabin, was situated on a wide bend in the bayou. The stream here was about sixty feet wide and fifteen feet deep.

Celine took personal notes for her story by speaking into a small tape recorder, but she'd more than willingly agreed to help with the photography work on the project, chronicling every step of the venture, except for the underwater exercises which would be done by the divers.

"Over the years, the network of bayous changed constantly, due to storms and flooding," Celine said into the recorder. "Land existing today might disappear underwater in five years, and vice versa. Thus, according to the treasure map, the pirate Lafitte's booty had been buried on dry land, but that spot is now underwater. See written notes on history of the map. And check photos of map on digital chip A, numbers 17, 18, and 19." She scribbled a few lines in a small notebook, then set both the camera and notebook aside, gazing about at the flurry of activity preparing for the first dive.

In the small clearing up about twenty feet from the water, two open-sided tents had been erected, one for Tante Lulu's cooking and the other with folding tables set up for maps and computer equipment. In the event of a sudden rainstorm, the side flaps could be put down for protection.

She had some questions to ask about today's schedule, but there was no way she was going within spitting distance of the Bayou Bad Boy who was discussing the upcoming operation with Ronnie and Caleb. After that killer kiss, he could very well turn her into the Bayou Bad Girl. Even though both of them had been playing an avoidance game for the past hour, there was no question they were acutely conscious of each other.

"Doan ya be worryin' none, sweetie," Tante Lulu said, patting her on the behind as she lugged a big bag of rice past her.

"Huh? What makes you think I'm worrying?" She followed the old lady into the cooking tent and helped her lift the bag of rice onto a folding table.

"Mebbe it's the furrows in yer forehead. Toss in some dirt and a fella could plant corn."

"Thanks a bunch." Without thinking, she swiped a hand across her forehead to smooth it out.

Tante Lulu glanced up and grinned, but it wasn't her forehead she was looking at. It was her mouth. Reaching down to a styrofoam chest, she got an ice cube and handed it to her.

"What's this for?"

"To soothe them sore lips. They be swollen from a whole lot of kissin', I reckon. I wonder who?" Tante

Lulu smiled from ear to ear, knowing full well who had been kissing her. "Iffen that weren't clue enough, Tee-John, bless his heart, keeps givin' ya hot looks."

She glanced over to John, who was pulling a diving suit out of a special chest, along with Brenda, Caleb, and Adam, who would also be diving. And, yeah, he gave her a hot look, followed by a wink when he caught her staring at him.

She groaned.

Tante Lulu chuckled. "Best ya be sendin' a Dear John letter ta Darnell."

"Darnell?"

"Yer fiancé."

"Oh. Why would I do that?"

"Ya thick or sumpin', girl? The thunderbolt, she is aworkin' overtime here. I gotta tell ya, I been lookin' forward ta this day fer a long time. Tee-John gettin' married. Whoo-boy! They's gonna be a boatload of wimmen cryin' on the bayou."

"John is getting married?" This was news to her, especially since he'd been practically licking her tonsils a short time ago. But then an alarming thought occurred to her. "You can't possibly mean me."

"Cain't I?"

"There is nothing like that between me and John."

"There will be, honey. St. Jude is in the buildin', so ta speak, and yer fate is sealed."

She thought about arguing, but knew it would be like throwing Jell-O against a glass wall. Nothing would stick with this matchmaking bulldozer. "What's in that juju tea you keep plying me with?"

Tante Lulu fluttered her sparse eyelashes with as

much innocence as a cat with a cream mustache. "Whatcha mean, honey? Ya feelin' a little feisty?"

Celine narrowed her eyes. "Was there some kind of aphrodisiac in there?"

"Do ya believe in aphro...aphro...uh, love potions, sweetie?"

"No."

"Then ya gots nothin' ta worry 'bout, I reckon." Under her breath, Celine could swear the old biddy said something about thanking St. Jude. Then she added, aloud, "I got lots ta do when I get home. The bride quilt. Tee-John's hope chest, which is almost full, thanks be ta God. Monogrammed tea towels and doilies. We could get Charmaine's little Mary Lou ta be a flower girl; she's more than three now, and cute as a June bug, 'specially with all those corkscrew curls that Charmaine gives her. Do ya think yer little boy could be a ring bearer? Betcha they'd look cute together."

Celine could ignore some of the things Tante Lulu said, but not when it came to her son. "No!" she said with more vehemence than she intended.

The old lady's gray eyebrows—a sharp contrast to her blonde curly hair—shot up with surprise. "Why not?" she demanded. "Girl, surely yer not implyin' that Tee-John couldn't be a father ta the boy?"

Her only response was a choked out, "No, of course not."

"Well then?" Tante Lulu had her hands on her little hips, encased in Mary Kate and Ashley hip-hugger jeans, and was tapping an orthopedic sneaker on the ground. She was like a pit bull protecting her young.

"I keep trying to tell you, there is not going to be

a wedding between me and your nephew. We have no relationship, at all."

"Did that boy kiss the daylights outta ya this mornin' or dint he?"

The daylights, the night-lights, the brain lights, the skylights, every which way kind of light. At Celine's presumably red face, Tante Lulu tossed her hands out in a "So there!" gesture.

It was no use arguin' with the old lady; so, Celine stomped off to confront John with the dilemma. Let him handle his aunt.

There were two problems with that. One, a section of the bayou banks between Tante Lulu's tent and where the dive was to take place was that pudding-like mud where tracks disappeared as soon as they were made. Which meant that she sank down to her ankles in the goop, some of it slopping up onto her legs, arms, shorts, and T-shirt. It . . . and now she . . . smelled like rotting vegetation and dead fish. Second, by the time she'd waded into the stream to wash the mess off, then approached John, he'd already shucked down to a brief bathing suit and was shimmying his too-buff body into a very tight, neoprene wet suit that was more revealing than if he were nude.

I am not looking at his groin.

I am not looking at his butt.

I am not looking at his wide shoulders and narrow waist.

Oh, God! Even his toes are sexy.

She was caught mid-gawk by John, who grinned and said, "Like what ya see, *chère?*" Then he used a forefinger to swipe a dirty spot on her cheek. At least he didn't attempt to remove the spot on her shirt, right above

"Saint," but he stared all right. "Ya look good in mud, sweet thang," he drawled, still ogling her chest. Then his eyes wandered. "I wonder...yep, ya do have some mud behind yer knees. Mercy!" He licked his lips, which—*be still my heart!*—reminded her of their kiss.

Shaking her head to clear it and hopefully shake him from the notion that she found him tempting as a beignet to a sweetaholic, she glared and said through gritted teeth, "I look like crap in mud. What's with you and this knee fetish? Stop staring at my boobs...and my knees. I am not your darlin'." She took a deep breath, then exhaled. "Furthermore, tell your aunt to back off."

"What's she doin' now?"

"Arranging our wedding."

The nitwit laughed.

"And one more thing."

"Uh-oh! When a woman says, 'One more thing,' that usually means a guy should duck."

"What's in that juju tea that your aunt keeps pushing on me?"

"Don't tell me...yer gettin' the hots fer me, baby?"

Like a furnace, sweetheart. Like a furnace.

John's teasing expression went suddenly serious. "Oh, Lord, the juju for you, and St. Jude novenas out the kazoo for me. We are dead ducks."

"What's that supposed to mean?"

"We should probably go have sex."

She had no chance to respond to that outlandish, but typical, remark from John because Adam—also wearing a wet suit, but not quite as gorgeous as the Cajun lunkhead, *darn it*—walked up and asked, "Who's having sex?"

"Nobody," she and John replied as one.

Adam's dark Cuban eyes widened with disbelief. "Clueless...the pair of them are clueless to the bone," he commented to the others. Then, "But, hey, Celine, if LeDeux's not up for the job, I'm available."

Choosing not to respond, she stomped off again, but this time avoided the mud pudding.

That's when she saw a snake the size of a fire hose.

And Caleb almost fainted.

And John pulled out a pistol—*Who knew he was carrying!*—and shot the reptile right between its beady eyes.

And Tante Lulu said, "Yippee, snake gumbo t'night."

It was as clear as mud ...

"Okay, guys, let's do a run-through of what we accomplished this morning and what we plan for the rest of the day...and week. Jake and I will be back in eight days, max, hopefully sooner."

Veronica was standing outside the work tent as she spoke, following a sumptuous lunch which had been prepared almost totally by that remarkable Cajun Energizer Bunny, Tante Lulu. The meal had not included snake, thank God, but not for the old lady's lack of trying. "Ever since we Cajuns was kicked out of Canada and France, and ever since all the upper crusts in Nawleans looked down their skinny noses at us, we Cajuns learned ta live off the land. We made a meal outta jist 'bout anythin'...squirrels, possums, snakes. Besides, it tastes jist like chicken."

"I don't care if it tastes like frickin' filet mignon, you

are not sneaking snake into my lunch, old lady. Don't think I won't be watching you," said the ex-Amish Navy SEAL, who had a huge aversion to snakes and was still looking a bit pale after the snake incident. Heck, Veronica was feeling a little shaky herself at the prospect of snakes that size slithering nearby, even if that particular one had been nonpoisonous.

"Anyhow, I'm sorry to have to abandon you all like this, but Jake and I have to be in Barnegat by this evening. My grandfather is being honored by the New Jersey Historical Preservation Society."

"Don't worry about taking off, Ronnie. We can handle things from this end," Adam assured her. At his side, Caleb nodded his agreement.

"Give him our congratulations," Brenda said, and the others concurred.

"Plus, I have to meet with three different prospective clients for upcoming projects. And Jake has to be in Atlantic City by tomorrow afternoon for his little poker tournament."

Jake chortled at her use of the word "little."

"Just kidding, sweetheart." To the others, she explained, "This is a million dollar grand slam thingee—"

"Thingee?" Jake inquired with mock affront.

"—and I wouldn't miss it for the world." She flashed Jake a "Gotcha!" look at her last remark. Then, back to the others, "Grandpa and Flossie are going to watch Julie Ann for us so we can spend two days down on the boardwalk."

She and Jake exchanged smiles . . . because there were several significant things in what she'd said, which only Jake would recognize. One, there was a time when she'd hated everything poker and wouldn't have willingly attended a poker event. Two, in the past her phobia about the ocean and the smell of saltwater would have made a stay at the seashore less than appealing. Three, thanks to her grandfather and his longtime girlfriend, she and Jake were going to be able to spend two full days of child-free time together.

While the others were wishing Jake good luck, John homed in on the latter. "Two days alone in A.C....whoo-ee! You guys wouldn't be thinkin' of gettin' married, wouldja?"

With heated face, Veronica replied, "Of course not."

With no heat on his face, Jake replied, "Maybe."

"They wouldn't do no such thing without invitin' all of us, 'specially me since I sicced the thunderbolt of love on 'em." This was from Tante Lulu, of course.

Celine muttered something like, "Thunderbolt *of love?* No way!"

"When Ronnie and I get married, you'll be the first one invited," Jake told Tante Lulu.

Veronica noticed that he said "when," not "if." But that was okay. It was inevitable that they try once again, despite having been married and divorced four times before, but it wouldn't be this week.

"I have a good idea," Tante Lulu mused, tapping her puckered lips thoughtfully. "How 'bout you two get hitched at the end of the Pirate Project. Sort of a double celebration. I throw a real good weddin', if I do say so myself. Jist ask René and Val. People in Houma is still talkin' 'bout the secret weddin' I threw fer those two."

John rolled his eyes and confirmed, "My aunt, she's not kiddin', no. René and Val weren't even speakin' to each other when they arrived at Tante Lulu's birthday bash, only to find it was really their weddin' she had planned. Talk about!"

Veronica had heard this story before, and it still boggled the mind. She was about to remind everyone that they had gotten off the subject when Jake came up beside her and put an arm around her shoulder, tugging her close to his side. Julie Ann was in the other tent, playing with her Barbie princess castle. "Let's do it, honey," he whispered in her ear.

"What?" She shivered. Even after more than fifteen years of being together, off and on, Jake could still make her insides melt with his breath in her ear, or even a look. She loved him so.

"Let's get married again."

She looked at him, full in the face to see if he was serious.

He was.

And suddenly she, too, knew the time was right.

They both turned to Tante Lulu and said, "Okay."

"But not during the Pirate Ball," Veronica was quick to add.

Tante Lulu's shoulders slumped.

"Ronnie's right," Jake said. "I want this to be private. Our wedding."

If she didn't already love this guy, she would now, for understanding. "I don't mind a bit of outrageousness, but let it be *our* outrageousness, okay?" she said to Tante Lulu.

The old lady nodded, but her brain was probably already in woo-woo land planning stuff. Veronica would worry about that later.

"Hey, we could call this the Pirate Marriage," she said to Jake. They'd given names to all their previous marriages: the Sappy Marriage, the Cowboy Marriage, the Tequila Marriage, and the Insanity Marriage.

"Nope. Remember, honey, I told you that the next time we get married, it was going to be called the Forever Marriage."

She kissed him then, despite their audience.

It was absolute chaos then as everyone had congratulations and opinions to offer.

From Caleb: "Hey, best of luck. Just don't let her talk you into a farm."

From Adam: "Hey, I have a cousin who plays in a Cuban salsa band. I could see if he's available to play at your wedding."

From Tante Lulu: "Salsa? I thought salsa was some kinda hot sauce. Nope, René's band will play Cajun music, and that's that."

From John: "You guys have been together a looong time. Betcha need to spice up the dirty. Not to worry. I can help with the honeymoon. I have a friend who owns a sex toy company, and—"

Celine snorted.

John winked at her and continued, "I could get you a special deal on some items which would juice up your sex life."

"Tee-John LeDeux! Shush yer mouth!" Tante Lulu reached over and swatted him on the head with a palmetto fan.

"Our sex life has plenty of juice, thank you very much," Jake told John.

From Brenda: "It better be soon. I'm not walking down the aisle wearing one of those god-awful bridesmaid gowns with a big belly. And, no, Tante Lulu, I'm not going to be a female pirate with a big belly, either."

Even when she wasn't pregnant, Brenda had an obsession with her weight and was always on a diet. She refused to believe that men loved her voluptuous figure. And, hey, who said anything about a big wedding that would require bridesmaids...or even an aisle, for heaven's sake?

From Celine: "I could do a nice write-up about the wedding for—"

"No!" every single other person yelled.

Veronica could only imagine what that article would involve. "Love: Better the Fifth Time Around."

But then Tante Lulu went off on a long-winded ramble, "I'm thinkin' a five-tiered cake. Do ya prefer lemon or raspberry or praline fillin'? We gotta move lickety-split if we's gonna reserve the hall fer another day that week. Okay, okay, mebbe not so soon. Still, we gotta plan. Mebbe I should call yer grandmother up in Boston and see if she wants ta help. When ya get a chance, Ronnie, could ya give me a guest list? 'Cause this is yer weddin'. I wouldn't wanna be takin' over or anythin'."

Veronica stopped listening after Tante Lulu mentioned her grandmother. The thought of the Cajun dingy and her uptight lawyer grandmother was enough to give Veronica a stroke. Jake winked at her, having experienced her grandmother's "help" in the past.

It was a half hour and three aspirins later before Veronica was able to pull the meeting back to order. Tante Lulu had gone into the cook tent to gather up her belongings for the return trip to the cabin. She wasn't going back to Houma, like she and Jake, but, instead, would remain at the cabin 'til the others came back this evening, probably preparing enough food for an army. Glancing at her wristwatch, she noticed that time was flying. Remy would be at the cabin in an hour, and they needed to be at the New Orleans Airport by four P.M. for their return flight to Jersey.

"Okay, let's discuss today's operations. We watched your progress on camera feed to the computers, of course, but that's not the same as firsthand experience," Veronica said. "You first, Adam."

"We used the magnetometer along with high–grade metal detectors over four grids, covering roughly five hundred square feet. All we've come up with so far are a fishing rod, two beer cans that probably came in from a more populated area, and a rustic skinning knife which might very well have some historic value. Houma Indian provenance, maybe."

"Diving in the bayou is totally different from our ocean dives," Caleb pointed out. "Here, depth and possible narcosis aren't issues, but visibility is. Man, it's like swimming through a cup of coffee."

"Yeah, but visibility is still possible in that kind of water, and it's pure water, too," John contended. "The problem isn't the clarity of the stream, but raking up mud at the bottom. Every time we even touch the bottom we ruin that site for at least a day 'til it settles down."

"If there's one thing my grandfather taught me, it's that every treasure hunt runs into unforeseen problems. You have to adapt as you go," Veronica said. "So we adapt. We'll look at the maps again. Instead of following consecutive grids...in the lawn mower pattern...we'll start with an X-pattern, bottom left to top right, then bottom right to top left. Only after we've completed those spots will we try the remaining squares. Do you follow me?"

Everyone agreed, some offering opinions.

"There's something else," John said, rubbing a hand over his mouth as if in deep thought. "I'm not so sure that the treasure is underwater. Yeah, I know Tante Lulu's map would indicate that it is, but who knows? If this water grid doesn't work out, I don't think we should enlarge it to encompass more of the stream. Nope, I think we should hit the land on either side."

"Do we have enough shovels for those kinds of digs?" Caleb asked.

"I think so," Veronica said, "but if we don't, we can order more through Remy."

After discussing other aspects of the day's search and what would be done that afternoon, she concluded, "That's it, then. Jake and I will be back soon. Call if you have any problems. Anything else?"

Caleb raised his hand. "Do we have enough snake antidote?"

Chapter
10

He sure knew how to muddy the waters...

John was dirty, exhausted and about to be reamed by Celine when she found out that she was going to be forced to stay here at the work site with him tonight. Alone.

Ronnie, Jake, Julie Ann, and Tante Lulu were long gone, and Peach, Famosa, and Brenda were preparing to return to the cabin in two pirogues. It would be a shorter trip back since they would be riding with the current. But someone needed to stay behind and guard the site and all the expensive equipment, which meant him. And Celine, according to Chief Pinot's orders.

At the last minute, he took Celine by the upper arm and drew her back. "What...what are you doing?" she asked as the two pirogues took off without her. "Let me go. That's the last of the pirogues." Jerking away from him, she ran several yards down the bank, slipping and sliding in the mud. "Hey! Wait for me!" she yelled.

No one bothered to stop. In fact, Famosa—ever Mr. Clueless—waved to her.

Sputtering with rage and tossing out a few expletives that would do a Bourbon Street pimp proud, she finally accepted that she was going to be staying here, unless she was up to a really long walk through what would soon be evening in the swampland. Slowly, she turned, inch by inch, to confront him. She was so angry she practically had smoke coming out of her blazing eyes.

He stood up by the cook tent, munching on an apple. His aunt had left them fresh fruit and vegetables, along with a large cooler full of perishables.

"I can explain," he said.

"I doubt it."

"There's a good reason for you to stay."

"I doubt it."

"Chief's orders."

"And you knew this...when?"

"This morning."

She made a low growling sound as her hands moved into claw formation, about to launch herself at him. The problem was, she had been standing in the mud pudding too long, and she'd sunk down to the tops of her leather boots. Launching herself was out of the question as moist sucking sounds filled the air with each of her plodding steps.

He thought about laughing, but then decided not to be totally stupid. Tossing the core of his apple aside, he walked over to the edge of the clearing, avoiding the mud. "Do you need my help?"

She gave him a killing glance.

Still, he held a hand out to her.

In her attempt to avoid contact with his hated self, she

backed up, slipped, and fell on her butt with a wet splatting noise. Mud spattered everywhere.

"You're a mess," he remarked idly.

"Bite me," she said.

"Okay," he replied and stepped into the mud. Picking her up by the waist, he walked over to the stream, with her kicking and screaming. Stepping carefully into the shallows 'til he was up to his knees, he dropped Celine. *Kerplunk!*

Surprised, she sank under the water, like a dead weight.

Grabbing her by the hair, he pulled her back up.

Sputtering and spitting out a combination of mud and water and various descriptions of his character in not-so-complimentary language, she staggered, trying to regain her balance. "Where are you going, you low-down, sneaky weasel?" she asked.

Okaaay. Friendly, I am not gonna get. "I'm gonna get some of that environmentally friendly soap that René sent. We both need a bath."

"Oh, great! Leave me to be eaten by an alligator or snake or something."

He laughed. "Honey, you've scared off every animal within a one-mile radius with all your squawking."

Oops, maybe squawk wasn't the right word.

She made a hissing noise.

Note to self: do not use the word squawk again.

She was dunking her body underwater, for the fourth time, when he returned. Placing two towels on a dry section of the bank, he shucked his shirt, shorts, boots, and socks, leaving only his black boxer briefs. If that offended her, so be it. Her bad mood was rubbing off on him. He smelled like sweat and mud and his skin itched. And she was annoying the hell out of him.

He sent the soap floating toward her, then dived underwater. The bottom had been stirred up here; so he swam underwater 'til the water was more clear. Crawfish scampered out of his way along with a sac-à-lait, three catfish, and a bream. He would try his hand at fishing later. The thought of fish cooked over an open fire caused his empty stomach to rumble.

Lungs bursting, he finally rose up straight out of the water with a big splash. Orca couldn't have done it better. He stood and combed his hair back off his face. She was about twenty feet away, shampooing her hair.

For one brief second he allowed himself the luxury of taking in a Celine like he'd never seen before. Her arms were raised as she combed her wet hair back off her face. Her posture caused her breasts and the hint of nipples to be prominent under the skin-hugging T-shirt.

He'd have to be made of stone not to react to the sensuality of her pose. Hard-core arousal shot through his body and lodged in lust central. Brain-dead under testosterone overload, he started to walk toward her in the thigh-deep water, but stopped abruptly, calling himself ten times a fool.

Then she raised her T-shirt over her head, and shimmied out of her shorts.

He went still, his heart thundering so hard he could barely breathe.

Oblivious, she used the bar of soap to wash her clothing. Was she crazy? He was a man, and they were alone. She had turned now, and all he could see was her back and the band of a flesh-colored bra.

"You don't have to wash those," he said weakly.

She swung around with surprise.

Despite using sunscreen, her face had a healthy glow, framed by hair that appeared black with wetness, accentuated by the incredible blue of her eyes. How could he not have seen how pretty she was before?

"You are a pig," she said, noticing the direction of his stare.

Maybe not so pretty. And certainly not friendly.

She resumed soaping up her shirt and shorts.

"Why are you doing that?" He wasn't sure if he was asking why she was washing her clothes or why she was standing there, practically naked, tantalizing him.

"I refuse to spend the night in filthy clothes." She slanted him a glance which told him loud and clear that she knew the effect she was having on him.

He dived underwater again, coming up about five feet in front of her. "There are clean, dry clothes in your duffel bag up in the equipment tent," he said, making sure he didn't look below her chin. "And you better get them on pretty damn quick before I do something really stupid."

"What?"

"Brenda packed up your stuff for you." He ignored her real question.

"And you waited 'til now to tell me?"

"When would I have had a chance? You were too busy squa...I mean, yelling at me." *And tempting the bejesus out of me.*

She threw the soap at him.

He caught it and began to soap up his chest, arms, underarms, hair, and then face, dipping himself under the water to wash off. Noticing that she was watching him, he slowed down, making sure she got a good show.

When she realized what he was doing, she snorted with disgust and continued to rinse off her clothing.

Once he was sufficiently clean, he glanced her way again, giving himself the treat of seeing a semi-clad Celine crawling up the bank. Whoo-boy! It was well worth the slap which was sure to come later if he was caught mid-ogle. The flesh-colored bra was pretty well transparent when wet, showcasing full breasts with up-tilted pink nipples, and the panties were outlined by two perfectly round buttocks. He whistled his appreciation.

She froze, half-turned, like a deer in the headlights, her nipples getting even harder and more visible as the seconds ticked by like hours. Shaking her head to clear it, she resumed climbing up the bank, saying, "We are not having sex," whether to him or herself, he wasn't sure.

"I never thought we were," he said to her back. *Liar!*

"Pfff! You didn't have to say it. It was in your eyes."

"I can't help what's in my eyes," he argued. *Or down below.*

But then she stepped onto the bank, and he got a full-blown view of her ass in low-riding, flesh colored panties, and of the backs of her knees—*What is it with me and knees lately? Jeesh!* —which were really, really...um, interesting, and the small of her back which was also...um, interesting. *Is that a tramp stamp there? Oh, God, I am lost, lost, lost if she has a tattoo almost riding her butt.* No, it was just a piece of grass.

Unapologetically, he watched her walk up the slight incline before the tents. Up, down, up, down, up, down, went her buttocks. She had the beat down pat. It was better than an X-rated video.

But he was a gentleman. *Most of the time.* He would

keep his mouth shut. *For now.* He would give Celine time to dress. *Five minutes max. Then, here I come, ready or not.* He would talk to her then, explain why the situation had to be this way, and everything would be peachy keen. *Ha, ha, ha.*

He decided it was better if he stayed in the water for a while longer. His brain, and that other organ, needed a good talking to.

Something fishy was going on with her...

Celine had refused to speak or listen to John for the past hour until her temper calmed down. Since that didn't appear to be on the horizon anytime soon, she walked downstream to where he was fishing with a makeshift pole.

"John...?"

Without turning to her, he snapped, "What?" Then, more softly, "Now you're gonna talk to me?" He actually had the nerve to sound hurt.

"Don't you think I have reason to be upset?"

He shrugged. "You knew comin' into this project, uninvited, that there might be problems."

"Problems, yeah. Kidnapping, no."

He turned. "Not kidnapping. Protective custody. Sort of."

"Bull!"

"Hey, it's either this or go back to Houma where you'll immediately be picked up by the authorities. The chief says you need to be watched 24/7 'til the trial is over. He's suspicious of your obsession with me and this project."

She inhaled sharply. "I am *not* obsessed with you."

"I'm just sayin', darlin'," he drawled.

She hated it when he drawled. Or was it that she hated it that she liked it when he drawled. *Aaarrgh!* "I've done nothing wrong."

"You are a major liability now, babe."

"Now?"

"Yeah. My partner, Tank Woodrow, was winged by a sniper, and he was five frickin' miles out on the Gulf in his boat. Right now, he's in temporary witness protection. Two other witnesses in the Playpen bust have been receiving death threats. And the word on the street is that the Lorenzo family has ordered a hit on me.

"Plus, the security alarm at my house has gone off six times since I've been gone. Vanguard is threatening to drop me as a customer."

"Oh, my God!"

"I don't think anyone can connect me with René or Luc's cabins, but it's a chance I can no longer take for me...or for you. Besides, it's out of my hands."

She let out a whooshy exhale. "I'm a mother, John. I can't cut myself off from Etienne and my grandfather."

"You told me they were out of town."

"They are, but I have to keep in touch. I call my son every night. My cell phone doesn't get a signal out here."

"It doesn't get a signal at René's cabin, either."

"John, I have to keep in touch. What if there were an emergency?" She gulped. "This is a nightmare."

"All we can do is make the best of it."

"I am not having sex with you."

He laughed. "I meant that we can agree to be amicable 'til this situation is resolved."

"Oooh, oooh, look. You have something on your line."

His rod was bent over in the middle with the force of his catch. With an expertise born no doubt of years on the bayou, he played the line...first tugging the fish in a bit, then giving it some lead, each time pulling it in a closer 'til finally he had it dangling over the water's surface.

He had nice hands, she thought. Long, thin fingers which would probably be just as expert at...*no, no, no, I am not going there.*

"Look at that sweetheart," John said, smiling at her.

Only belatedly did she realize he was referring to the fish as sweetheart, not her.

It was a big, ugly catfish with beady eyes and bristly whiskers. Frankly, she was more interested in his sexy smile. *What's happening to me? I must still be feeling the effects of that blasted juju tea.*

"Fish on the menu tonight, darlin'," he crooned.

In her hormone-warped brain, Celine thought at first that he had said, "Sex on the menu tonight, darlin'."

Could it possibly be wishful thinking on my part?

Impossible! It must be the Louisiana sun melting my brain.

Disgusted with herself, she sank down to a grassy spot and watched in silence as he continued to fish, sometimes wading carefully into the water. It was a companionable silence she felt no need to disturb.

Like the area surrounding René's cabin, it was beautiful here. Lush and serene. The air was heavy with floral scents, which could be almost anything in this tropical atmosphere; close by, she saw spider lilies, wild iris, and verbena. Birds chirped in the thick trees, one strain in particular sounded mournful, almost like a cat crying.

Noticing her head tilted in question, John told her, "Doves." Then added, with a wink, "Lovebirds."

Celine felt her cheeks burn, and not from the sun. How pathetic, that she was being turned on by a wink from that devil John LeDeux, who probably winked at grocery store baggers as easily as women he was attracted to. Not that she was in the latter category. He was just playing her... like the fish.

Resting her chin on her upraised knees, her hands folded in front of her calves, she continued to watch him, trying to figure out why she was suddenly attracted to such an unlikely man for her. Well, not so suddenly. She had always considered him good-looking from when she'd seen him on entering high school in Houma for the first time. He'd been surrounded by a group of equally good-looking girls.

In his defense... not that he needed her defending him... she had been pretty messed up at the time. Self-esteem hovering at zero. Ashamed that someone might learn about her father's suicide; at fifteen, a girl thought that reflected badly on her. She'd had no one but her grandfather to help her get ready for first day of high school, and the old man, bless his heart, had the fashion sense of Jed Clampett. So, getting a crush-at-first-sight on John LeDeux pretty much amounted to disappointment waiting to happen.

The one-night stand in college, she had been able to excuse away by the amount of alcohol they'd both consumed, but, really, the crush had still been there, beneath the surface, just waiting for the least attention from him to ignite. It was all well and good to explain her actions away, but the fact remained, she was stone cold sober now...and fighting an erotic fluttering in her tummy every time he looked at her. A ten-year crush? Pitiful, pitiful, pitiful!

"What's wrong?" John asked, easing down beside her in the grass. Two big catfish lay on the bank near his feet.

"What makes you think something's wrong?"

Jeesh! The guy threw off heat like a testosterone oven. She squirmed away from him a foot or two.

"Your frowny face." He leaned over and traced the furrows in her brow, for emphasis.

She flinched at that mere touch, her skin suddenly ultra sensitive. "I think your aunt drugged me."

"Huh?"

"She either slipped me a mickey, or rupie, or something powerful was in that juju tea."

He snickered.

"How else can you explain the fact that I want to have sex with you?"

She could almost hear the "thunk" as her blunt statement landed between them like a big fat pink elephant, impossible to take back, or ignore.

The expression on his face morphed from surprise, to amusement, to something hot and smoldering...a look he probably perfected by standing in front of a mirror, or practiced on a gazillion women. He licked his lips, still staring at her. He was probably laughing at her inside.

But then he said the most amazing thing.

"Back at you, babe."

And he didn't seem any happier than she was.

Chapter
11

Sliding head-first down the slippery slope of you-know-what...

There was a long-running dumb man joke on the Internet that said, when it came to sex, men are like microwaves and women are like crockpots. It was not a compliment.

Well, John knew for a fact that wasn't true. Ever since Celine had mentioned the word "sex," he'd been like a pressure cooker. From zero to hot damn in a nanosecond... and he'd been on a slow lust-boil ever since.

And he was starting to like her. Even worse, he suspected she was starting to like him, too. Like and lust: a prescription for disaster, where the two of them were concerned.

He cleaned the fish with the hunting knife Luc had given him when he was eight. And thought, *sex*.

He built a round fire pit with small stones in the way Remy had taught him when he was nine, and thought, *sex*.

He cooked the fish, wrapped in damp moss, in hot coals the way René had demonstrated when he was ten, and thought, *sex*.

But he was no longer a boy, and Celine Arseneaux was more trouble than this Cajun could handle at this time in his life. So he tried to ignore his raging libido, served the food on St. Jude paper plates, and thought, *sex*.

He listened to a song on a mix Charmaine had made up and left at René's cabin, along with a small CD player. It was appropriately named, "Hot Hot Hot" by Buster Poindexter, and he thought, *hot sex*.

He was lying on a blanket, drinking a paper cup of Tante Lulu's rhubarb wine while Celine bustled around cleaning up, attempting to pretend she hadn't said what she'd said. Maybe he could get so drunk that he would pass out and not do something stupid, which was not likely, considering his aunt's wine was weak as piss...about one-percent alcohol.

He had to think of something to dampen the fire. *I know. Her kid.* Jumping up, he went over to his backpack and pulled out a satellite phone. "Give me the number where your son is staying, and I'll dial it for you."

She brightened immediately. "You didn't tell me you had a satellite phone. You rat! Give it to me. I can dial myself."

He shook his head. "No. I'll dial. This phone is only for emergencies. This call is a one-time deal."

"A direct line with my grandfather *is* an emergency."

He narrowed his eyes at her. "You are not to mention anything that might link you with me...or LeDeuxs in general."

"But—"

He put up a halting hand. "This is a deal breaker. I know how your grandfather feels about us LeDeuxs, but this has nothing to do with that. I can't have any possible link between you, me, and the upcoming trial."

"Oh," she said, realizing what he meant.

"You can give your grandfather the chief's number. If he deems it an emergency, he'll patch you through."

She didn't like it, but she accepted, giving him the telephone number. He dialed and a small boy answered, "Hello. This is Etienne Arseneaux. Who's this?"

For some reason, the hairs stood out on the back of his neck. Confused, he handed the phone to Celine, but not before whispering a caution, "It's your son. Remember. No mention of me."

Listening to the one-sided conversation, he poured himself another cup of wine and lay back on the blanket, head braced on an elbow.

"Ah, sweetie, I miss you, too. You did? A big horse, huh? Oh, a pony. Did Uncle Samuel ride with you? Well, yes, he's your uncle, sort of; he's grandpa's brother. I see. No, honey, I can't join you there. I have a job assignment. Uh-huh. Maybe next time. I miss 'You and Me time,' too. Save up all your news for me 'til you get back, and we'll have an extra long 'You and Me time' with popcorn and slushes. Okay, ice cream, too. No, you cannot bring a pony back to Houma. Gramps's backyard is too small. No, I said. You can pretty please all you want. The answer is still no." She laughed out loud. "No, that does not mean you can get a dog when you get back."

John could see . . . or rather hear . . . what a good mother Celine was. For some reason, he had trouble reconciling his having the hots for a mother.

She continued to chatter as John watched her face, which was animated in a way which lit her up from within. Was this what parenthood did to a person? It must be. Luc and Remy and René reacted the same way when they were around their kids. It almost made him want to have a kid of his own. Almost being the key word.

The grandfather must be on the phone now. "I know, Gramps, but I can't tell you where I am . . . or give you a phone number." She held the phone away from her ear for a moment. Even from across the blanket, he could hear the sound of yelling. "I'm on a super secret assignment. Use the number I gave you, but only if it's urgent. I'll call you again tomorrow night . . ." She glanced over at him, and he shrugged. ". . . if I'm able. I love you, too. Give Etienne a hug for me. Bye."

She clicked the phone off and handed it to him. Meantime, her face went bleak.

"What's the matter?" he asked, refilling her cup of wine.

"I miss my son. I'm almost never away from him overnight . . . let alone a week." She took a long swallow of her drink.

John stared at her, remembering the Celine he'd met for the first time in high school. She hadn't been bad-looking then, but she'd been a little chunky and worn geeky clothes and had an attitude. Oh, she thought he was the one with an attitude, but it was the reverse. At least, it had been back then. She'd been so frickin' smart. Not that he was a dummy, but she and her crowd had looked at him and his friends as if they were low-level cretins. Okay, maybe they had behaved that way at times.

But look at her now. Holy sac-à-lait! Even without makeup or hot clothes, she was stunning. Not beautiful, but very, very attractive. The blue eyes with the dark brown hair were especially compelling. And she had a nice figure, showcased by tight jeans and an abdomen-hugging white tank top, covered with an unbuttoned, faded blue denim shirt that matched her eyes. Her hair was held off her face with barrettes on either side of her face.

He wanted her.

Which was insanity.

Tante Lulu had told him earlier about Celine's father having committed suicide soon after her mother died of cancer. Thinking back, he realized that it must have been just before she'd come back to Houma to live with her grandfather, just before starting high school. Had he been unconsciously unkind to her? At the least, he hadn't been sensitive to what a troubled kid she must have been. No wonder she had been so aloof...not stuck-up, like he'd thought at the time.

All this insight, combined with this new appreciation for her physically, was giving him the hard-on from hell. He searched his brain to think of something to break the thread of irresistible attraction.

"It just occurred to me, Celine. When you were all upset about being cut off from your family, you never once mentioned Derrick being able to contact you."

"Derrick? Oh, right. Derrick."

In that moment, as pink stained her cheeks, he knew. There was no fiancé.

And like a virtual video in his head, he saw a huge window of opportunity open. The question was: Did he care?

Hell, yes!
Would it be a dumb move?
Hell, yes!
Would he dare to jump through?
Hmmm!

Who said dancing is a form of foreplay?...

It was only eight P.M. Another hour of daylight before they would be forced to their beds by the hordes of mosquitoes practically salivating at the prospect of virgin skin.

Virgin? Hah, skin was the only thing virgin around here. John for sure had been around the block a time or two or hundred. She, on the other hand, was hardly promiscuous or even very experienced, but she could not claim to be lily white. So why was sex between two consenting adults, meaning her and John, so wrong?

Well, duh! How about how different we are? How about us being in conflicting professions? How about him practically kidnapping me? How about him being my son's father... and not knowing it?

John had erected his small tent with mosquito netting over to the side of the equipment tent where they had been working ever since dinner and where a sleeping bag had been laid down for her, covered with netting, of course. Now he was fiddling with a tape player and a mixture of songs. Patti LaBelle started to belt out "Lady Marmalade." Definitely Charmaine's kind of song.

Well, John's, too, if the swing of his hips was any

indication. And, oh, my, he was swinging his hips her way.

She backed up a few steps. "What are you doing?"

"Checkin' out your window, *chère.*" Meantime, he was dancing closer, and she was backing up more. Pretty soon she would be landing in the mud pudding again, but, no, she did a backward left turn.

He laughed and snapped his fingers in tandem with the beat of his hips and the music. "I love to dance. Do you like to dance, Celine?"

There was no right or wrong answer to that question. If she said yes, she would be bee-bopping with the Bayou Lord of the Dance. If she said no, he would be offering to teach her to dance. But maybe it was one of those loaded question thingees, where he was saying "dancing" but really meant something else. *Oh, Lord, why am I double thinking everything?*

"I like to dance, but I'm no expert, like you."

"There's no such thing as an expert when two people dance together. C'mon." He held both hands out to her, beckoning.

Taking her hesitation for assent, he swooped in, lifting her up and swinging her around in his arms, spinning like a top. When he set her on her feet, a little bit dizzy, he started to dance around her, urging, "C'mon, Celine, show me your moves."

He probably expected her to protest that she didn't have moves, but she did. Oh, nothing like his, but moves nonetheless, and she was tired of being thought of as a sexless geek.

And so, she shimmied up his front. She undulated against his back. She rolled her shoulders, swung her hips, and shook her bootie. He matched every one of her moves and showed her some new ones. All to the drumming beat of "Lady Marmalade," then James Brown's "I Feel Good," Brooks and Dunn's "Boot Scootin' Boogie," and Bob Seger's "Old Time Rock 'n Roll." That Charmaine sure had an eclectic taste in music.

They were laughing so hard they fell against each other by the time the music went slower. Now it was BeauSoleil's Cajun ballad, "La Fleche D'amour." They stilled abruptly, as if zapped with a Taser, when her breasts hit his chest. Without pulling apart...his hands were on her waist, hers were on his shoulders...they stared at each other, the air thick with a tension that was clearly sexual. With an unspoken question in the air, he finally made a decision for both of them by hauling her into his embrace. The slow dancing they engaged in then was foreplay as sensual as an intimate touch.

Again they danced from one song to another, but with each progressive song, their embrace got closer, their dance moves slower. Still BeauSoleil, but now "Les Blues de Chaleur," or "Hot Blues," and that classic "C'est un Peche de Dire un Menterie," better known as "It's a Sin to Tell a Lie."

At what point they had stopped dancing, she had no idea. All she knew was that John's eyes were closed, the beautiful black lashes fanned out on his tanned cheeks, and his mouth was moving toward hers. She couldn't turn away, being still in his tight embrace, but she didn't want to.

All of her senses were heightened. She smelled his minty breath; he'd been chewing gum earlier. She heard his breathing, even though it wasn't heavy. She felt his body pressed against hers; they were thigh to thigh, belly to belly, breasts to chest, despite his being four or five inches taller. Well, no wonder! His hands had somehow managed to be cupping her buttocks, lifting her up onto her toes. And now she was going to taste him.

"Celine," he whispered against her lips. "Open for me, darlin'."

At least he knew who he was kissing. But she wasn't about to be a submissive here. "You, too. Open for me, darlin'."

He smiled against her lips, then nipped her bottom lip for mimicking him. It was a lazy kiss that followed, a long leisurely exploration that went on forever. The kiss was gentle, but wet. Very wet. The boy could kiss, she'd give him that. In fact, if she wasn't careful, he would make her come, just with a kiss. On a groan, she pulled away, staring at him with dismay. To her embarrassment, she was panting.

And he appeared totally unruffled. Well, no, that wasn't true. His eyes were half-hooded with arousal, his lips parted and moist, his breath hot, and yep there was something long and hard making its presence known down yonder.

"Oh, baby," he murmured, hauling her back into another kiss.

She was too weak and confused to protest.

This time, he let her have the full arsenal of his renowned expertise. His lips demanded, his tongue plunged, his teeth nipped. Without words, he coaxed her to mirror his actions. They soon had an incredible rhythm going with their tongues, hers going into his mouth, and his following its retreat into her mouth with his own tongue, over and over in a smooth, unbroken exercise in the most delicious torment. If he hadn't been holding her up, her legs probably would have given out by now.

But suddenly he jerked back and started slapping the back of his neck and bare arms. Belatedly, she realized that dusk had fallen, and they were being eaten alive by giant kamikaze mosquitoes.

"C'mon, honey, let's get out of here." John grabbed her hand, dragging her toward his tent. He shoved her in, then ran back to the equipment tent, picking up a few items, then zipping them in when he returned. "I brought some calamine lotion," he said. "Take off your clothes."

Whaaat? she squealed mentally.

Her surprise must have shown on her face because John rose from where he'd just turned on a small battery-operated lantern to cast a soft glow, and said in a gravelly voice, "Or do you want me to take them off?" The tent was so small his head brushed the top of the canvas. Without waiting for a reply, he stepped closer and walked his fingers from her shoulders to her knuckles, turned her hands over, and kissed both palms and wrists. An extremely erotic thing for him to do!

She sighed.

He smiled.

Celine had that out-of-body feeling, as if she were standing above, watching, not a real participant. It was odd, really. She and John didn't even like each other, but here they were, about to have wild monkey sex, and that's what it would be, too, no doubt about that. In that blip of a second while her mind had wandered, John was down on his knees, and he'd managed to slip off her shoes, socks, and jeans, slicker than a cat burglar. A remarkable feat when you considered that she usually had to lie down to get into this particular pair of jeans.

"Spread, baby."

She did, a little bit.

And now...*oh, my God!*... he was kissing his way up her legs, slowly, instep to knee to thigh, bypassing her bikini-brief clad groin, then down the other side. Before she could say, "Do that again," he was behind her, doing strange things to the back of her knees...licking, blowing, nipping, kissing. Over and over 'til her knees started to buckle. A gurgling, incoherent sound came from her mouth.

Chuckling, he rose and yanked her T-shirt up and over her head. Then he stepped back and studied her body.

Her underwear was nothing fancy. Just white silk with an edge of lace. But he looked at her as if she were a Victoria's Secret model.

Her bra and panties joined her other clothes on the ground under his deft fingers. He let the backs of his fingers brush over her breasts 'til the nipples pearled, then he stepped back again. "I want to make love to you so bad my bones hurt. If I touch you again, I won't be able to stop." He tilted his head in question at her.

She tried to laugh, but it came out a gurgle. "John, I think we crossed that line back with the slow dancing."

The smile he gave her then was so sexy it was her bones that ached.

"Undress me," he urged.

Oh, boy! "I'm not sure I can maintain my composure that long."

She hadn't realized that she'd spoken aloud 'til he said, "Oh, darlin', composure is the last thing I want from you."

With a lack of inhibition she'd never shown before, Celine removed John's clothing in the same way he had hers, starting at the bottom, kissing his legs, even the back of his knees, encouraged by soft compliments and words of advice. By the time she'd removed his boxer briefs, his erection was something to behold, and she told him so.

Laughing with pure delight, he fell back onto the blanket, pulling her with him. Then he rolled so that she was under him. "Are you as excited as I am?"

"I don't know. Let me check." She pretended to be glancing down at his body.

That was the last time she joked for a while.

She reached up to caress his chest, and he swatted her hands away, instead arranging her arms above her head. "Not yet. Let me go first."

Any notion she'd had earlier of an out-of-body experience evaporated then. She'd already accepted that John LeDeux kissing her had been quite an experience. John LeDeux suckling her breasts was beyond bliss. But John LeDeux going down on her was a Holy Moly!-screaming-hell-pounding-body-arching-two-orgasm experience.

"Are you ready, sweetheart?"

Her eyes shot open from where she lay splatted out like a spread-eagled pancake. "For what?"

"The main event, baby. The fuckin' main event."

Her eyes probably rolled back in her head. She hoped she wasn't drooling. She for sure was having trouble concentrating through the erotic haze that surrounded her. Did he just use the F-word to her? During foreplay? Did she care?

But then he knelt between her legs, slipped on a condom, and pulled her up and on him. On...*him*! Celine was being bombarded with so many sensations, she felt as if she was in the midst of an erotic whirlpool. Totally out of control.

"Don't move," she ordered him as he filled her and then some. "I need to concentrate."

"Concentrate all you want."

He didn't exactly move. But the brute did flex inside her.

And Big O number four slam-dunked through her, or was it five?

He started slow by rocking her. Then he pushed her onto her back again and began long, long, long strokes.

Celine had read a sex study a few years ago that said in the average sexual encounter the man thrusts one hundred and ten strokes. She'd pooh-poohed the idea at the time as mere male delusion, but now she wasn't so sure.

He stopped suddenly, embedded in her farther than any man had ever been. "Tell me how you feel," he husked out. "Tell me what you like."

She put both hands to her hot cheeks. She'd never been into verbal sex play, but...but suddenly the idea excited her...a lot.

"C'mon. Show your wild side."

Like I have a wild side! "Okay," she agreed, wetting her lips nervously. "I like...I like how you fill me so much I stretch."

He put a forefinger under her chin and lifted so that she was looking at him. As a reward for her honesty, he drew back, then slammed into her.

She gasped and rippled around him.

"I like the way you clasp me so tightly," he told her.

She squirmed from side to side to show how much she appreciated his compliment. To her immense satisfaction, he trembled with the tight rein he was attempting to hold on his arousal. When he got himself under control, he said, "Continue."

"I like your stamina."

He choked out a laugh. "I'm not feeling much stamina right now."

"Really? Believe me, your staying power is phenomenal. I haven't had that many experiences, but I've never had sex last this long."

"Me neither."

Was he trying to say that they made a good combination? Or they were a fluke? Or maybe he just hadn't had sex for a while. But, no, he would probably not be able to hold out very long in that case. She had no chance to ask those questions because John said, "Brace yourself, Celine," and they were off to the races. Or rather the finish line.

Soon John strained his shoulders back, the cords standing out on his neck, and he released a long, loud masculine howl of satisfaction. She joined him in the end.

Sated, he fell asleep on her, his face nuzzling her neck, his penis still half-erect inside of her.

She was stunned. Nothing like this had ever happened to her before. The amazing sex had to be an anomaly. She wasn't sure what it meant, if anything, and her brain was too fuzzy, her body too exhausted, to think right then. One thing was certain, and it was not good: she was starting to care for the lout.

John's weight was heavy on her, but it was a pleasant heaviness. She could take it...for a short time.

There was something important she needed to discuss with John. They were not going to engage in an affair. This was a one-time thing. No regrets, but no return events, either. She would wake him in a minute and set the record straight.

But first...she fell asleep.

Chapter
12

Get along, little cowboy...uh, cowgirl...

John was so embarrassed.

He'd never conked out on a woman after sex before. But Celine Arseneaux had knocked him for a loop, in more ways than one. Every cell in his body felt satisfied. The endorphins in his body must have gone haywire, but he was supremely relaxed now. Like a wet noodle.

Well, not entirely relaxed or not entirely a wet noodle, he realized in amazement as his dick sort of raised its head...the dick that was still inside Celine, for the love of *Dieu!*...and gave him a silent high five, with the message, "Rev up the engine, big boy! Time for the next lap."

Carefully, he raised his eyelids to see if Celine was laughing at him for falling asleep...or too crushed by his weight to speak. But, no, she was thank-you-God asleep.

He smiled to himself, inordinately pleased that he

could have knocked her out like this. Forget about the fact that he had been knocked out, too.

Man, I am good! With that brain-dead thought in mind, he let Mr. Happy go to town. Just a twitch and some swelling...damn, he loved the swelling.

Celine's eyes shot open, disoriented at first. But it didn't take long for her to realize one of her least favorite men was on top of her with his cock practically up to her tonsils, ready to party again.

It was like a slideshow, watching the changing expressions on her face. First, surprise...to see him. Then, shock...at what she had just done...done well, if he did say so himself. Then, embarrassment...at what she had just done. Pretty soon she would be phasing into the "What was I thinking?" mode. Preempting her, he leaned down and kissed her lightly on the lips. *Holy shit! I don't want to be around when she gets a look at her kiss-swollen lips. Or the bite mark on her shoulder. Or the fingerprints on her breasts.*

"You were amazing," he told her.

She looked doubtful. "You're the one who's amazing."

He liked that; so he wiggled his hips a little, just to show her he still had a little more "amazing" on tap.

Her eyes widened and she gulped. "Listen, John, this was great, but we can't—"

"You have the neatest breasts," he remarked. "They're all puffy areolas with hardly any nipples showing...until you get excited, then they rise like small, pink peas." He started to play with her nipples to demonstrate.

A full-body shiver ripped through her, and he could swear he saw the goose bumps rising in slow motion. Shaking her head to clear it...not a good thing, according to his man dictionary . . . she tried again, "Seriously, John, I don't have the strength to do this again."

"That's all right, baby. Just lie back and let me do you." *Man's eternal last words! Adam probably said it to Eve a time or two.*

"You said the same thing last time."

"Okay, if you insist." He rolled over on his back, holding onto her waist so he didn't slip out. By now, his half-hard-on was full-blown and anchoring Celine to his body by nicely straddling his hips. She sat up straighter, realized the position she was in, then groaned with another full-body shiver which even he felt, inside. Shiver-sex, that was a new one for him.

"Why are you smiling?"

"I'm happy. We are good together, Celine. Really good."

"That doesn't mean . . . yikes! What are you doing?"

He was strumming her in a really important place . . . important for her, anyway. And him, too, truth to tell. "Wanna play a game, darlin'?"

"You can't be serious."

"Mais oui, chère."

"And that game would be?"

"Cajun cowgirl?"

"I can pretty much guess who the cowgirl would be in this game. What would you be?"

"The horse, of course."

At one point, Celine, to her later embarrassment, might have said, "Giddiup!"

At another point, John, with no embarrassment, might have said, "How do you like my saddle?"

They were both laughing by then.

And then they were not laughing . . . for a long time.

Later...much later...as Celine slept with her face against his chest and his arms around her, he could swear he heard thunder in the distance. Hmmmm, the weather forecast hadn't called for rain.

An alarming thought occurred to him. It couldn't be...no, it couldn't be Tante Lulu's thunderbolt of love. No way! Impossible! He was too young...not ready. He and Celine were practically enemies.

The strangest laughter echoed in his head then, and he had a really creepy feeling it was St. Jude.

Mirror, mirror, where art thou...

By 8 A.M. the next morning, they had a quick washup in the stream, a not so quick dirty swim, a quick pot of coffee, and a quick test to see how much weight the folding table in the kitchen tent could take. Who knew you could do that with cane syrup!

The rest of the Pirate Project team should be here any minute.

As a result, Celine was sitting sedately before the computer, uploading all the digital pictures she'd taken the day before.

John was sedately reading the manual for the magnetometer which had been acting up.

"Don't give me any of your looks when they get back," she ordered. "I don't want anyone to know about...you know."

"What look? I don't have a look."

"Hah! You have a look all right. And it goes without saying, you won't be discussing...you know."

"No, I don't know. Me, I'm just a dumb ol' Cajun. Do you mean the fact that we made love four times...five, if you count your attacking me when I was pretending to be asleep. Man, you were on me like a hobo on a hot dog. Or..." He drew his lips in thoughtfully. "Ah, now I know. You mean your thirteen orgasms."

"Oh, oh, oh..." she sputtered. "I never attacked you."

He arched his brows at her.

"And I never had that many...oh, what's the use!"

He was outright laughing at her now.

She threw a notebook at him.

He ducked and said, "Tsk, tsk, tsk. One would think you were trying to provoke me to toss you over my shoulder and have a little caveman sex with you."

"Caveman sex? What the hell is caveman sex? No, don't tell me. Listen, you idiot, last night was great, but—"

"This morning was great, too."

"—but my brain freeze is over. No. More. Sex. Is that understood?"

"What? You don't want a little lagniappe later...a matinee, maybe?"

"Get real! Read my lips, you—"

"Very nice lips, too, I must say. Yep, you've got a hootchie mama mouth."

She growled. "No. More. Sex."

"Define sex."

"Aaarrgh!" She pulled at her own hair.

"Don't worry, hon. I'm out of condoms anyhow. Of course, I could always ask Tante Lulu for some. Believe it or not, she carries them in her tote bag...for emergencies, she says. Do you think this is an emergency?"

"Don't you dare! You are not taking this seriously."

"Yeah, I am. To tell the truth, I agree. We are not a couple. We never will be. You are high maintenance and not just because you have a kid. I suspect that affairs aren't your idea of a relationship. I'm too young for responsibility. End of story."

She nodded, though, perversely, now she was disappointed. "We had to know from the get-go that this train wreck of an attraction between us was doomed."

"Easy to say, sugar, but the train has already left the station. Five times."

"Yoo hoo!" someone yelled.

They both looked over to the stream where two pirogues pulled up, one carrying Adam and Tante Lulu, the other carrying Caleb and René. No Brenda.

They got up and walked toward the stream.

"Brenda got morning sickness real bad and went back home. René come to take her place, temporary like," Tante Lulu said, even as she was bending over to pick up a bag of greens. The sight of her little butt in red stretch jeans was something to behold, especially when it was topped by a scooped neck shirt that had the logo, "Born to be Wild." The woman must be registered at Kids Klothes.

Caleb and Adam were "beaching" the two pirogues, and René, cursing under his breath, had just picked up five grocery bags full of Tante Lulu's supplies. Then the four of them glanced up at her and John. As one, their jaws dropped.

Tante Lulu was the first to speak. "Hot diggety damn! You two are cuter'n speckled pups with all those bug bites. But, Lordy, Lordy, how'd yer mouths get so bit up?"

Adam grinned. "If I had known there was going to be a party, I would have stayed behind."

René was shaking his head at John and laughing. "I am so gonna enjoy your pain as you get pushed and shoved down that thunderbolt road." He rolled his eyes toward Tante Lulu in some meaningful way.

"Guess yer gonna hafta call off the engagement," Tante Lulu said to her.

Oh, God! What is it they say about lies coming back to bite you in the butt?

"No, no, no," John protested. "No thunderbolts. We're just...friends."

"Friends with benefits?" Adam inquired in his usual oily manner.

"Lots of benefits," René agreed.

All Caleb said was, "Hoo-yah!"

"I cain't wait to call Luc and Remy and Charmaine. Payback is gonna be so sweet, little brother." René was already pulling out a satellite phone.

"I don't know what you all mean," Celine tried to say.

But John cut her off. "Chill, Celine. It's best to ignore them."

With feet dragging, she followed Tante Lulu up to the food tent and asked, "Do you have a mirror?"

Without speaking, the old lady dug into a huge tote bag and handed her a small cosmetic mirror.

It took only one glance in the mirror for Celine to see what everyone else had seen, and this was only her face and neck. Her lips were pink and puffy. There were whisker burns everywhere. God only knew what she would discover under her shirt and pants.

She handed the mirror back to Tante Lulu, then

stomped out to confront John. He was talking to his brother. Right off, she shoved him in the chest. "You rat! Why didn't you tell me how I looked?"

He studied her for an extended moment, head to toe. "Ah, well, me, I think you look great." Then he had the nerve to wink at her.

She shoved him again, then warned, "You are so screwed." She immediately regretted her choice of words, but it was too late.

John smiled at her and said in an undertone, for her ears only, "And very well, thank you very much."

Celine flung her hands out with disgust, spun on her heels, about to go to the equipment tent to prepare the camera and tape recorder for today's activities.

"Do you think she's upset with me?" John asked his brother, who was laughing like a stupid hyena.

Meanwhile Tante Lulu, who was cooking up a batch of couche-couche, a form of Cajun fried cornmeal, for breakfast, stepped outside and yelled, "Holy catfish! What happened to all the cane syrup?"

At first, there was silence, then everyone turned to look at her and John.

Did life get any better than this?

She thought she was unshockable...

Tante Lulu was alone, all the others having gone to the work site. Everything was going according to plan. If she had her druthers, there would be a wedding before Christmas.

When they'd returned this morning to the project site,

she'd been delighted to see that Tee-John and Celine had made a love connection. She could practically see the thunderbolts snapping between the two of them.

Deep in thought, she stirred the pot of spicy red beans and rice on the camp stove, which she would add to white rice at the last minute. The red beans and rice, a recipe of her mother's, had been a traditional Monday morning meal on the bayou because Monday was wash day, and this particular dish could cook unattended all day. Plus, it utilized the leftover ham bone from Sunday's dinner. No one ever said the Cajuns weren't practical.

Would her mother approve of the way she'd lived her life? Not many people knew it, but Louise Rivard had once been engaged to a young soldier from Lafayette...Phillipe Prudhomme. He died on D-Day on a Normandy beach. Oh, how she had loved that handsome brown-eyed boy!

Her mother had urged her to move on after a year or two of mourning, but her life had taken a different path, especially after Adèle married Valcour LeDeux, bore him three sons, then died when she was barely twenty-five. Tante Lulu had stepped in to help care for the children and shield them from their alcoholic father.

Yes, a different life path, but no regrets.

She checked the cooler then. It held six big muffulettas, a New Orleans version of the Italian sub. She'd prepared them early this morning, before dawn. They were best served at room temperature, but she would wait to take them out when she saw the team returning from upstream. It was only eleven o'clock now. The key to a good muffuletta was the olive salad dressing which she would let everyone put on themselves, to avoid the crisp bread getting soggy.

Having a little time to rest, she sat on a folding lawn chair and sipped at a mug of strong chicory coffee. The caffeine would probably keep her up tonight, but that didn't matter. When you were two years older than dirt, there would be plenty of time for sleeping way too soon...the eternal sleep.

This would be one of her last big projects, she reckoned. Not the Pirate Project, though that would be fun enough. No, it was the Tee-John Project. She had to get him settled before she went to her final rest.

Celine Arseneaux wasn't the one she would have chosen for Tee-John. All along she had thought the rascal would one day marry a really beautiful woman. Oh, Celine was pretty enough, just not flashy. But that was okay. Tante Lulu was more bothered by her uptightness. The girl needed to loosen up. And she needed to flesh out her Cajun roots, add a little *joie de vivre* to her blood. Then, too, there was the fact that she was already a mother, not what Tante Lulu would have expected for her wild boy...becoming an instant father.

But then, if Celine was the one St. Jude had picked for her nephew, well, there was no arguing with *that*.

All this thinking was giving her a headache. Rising from the chair, her bones creaking like an old rocker, she went to rummage through her big purse. Placing it on the folding table, she began to pull things out. An extra bottle of Tabasco sauce she carried everywhere; everyone knew "Cajun lightning" was needed on just about any dish. Five boxes of Snazzy Lady hair dyes: Witchy Black, Nutty Brown, Hot Mama Red, Blonde Bomb, and Pink Fizz. Three tubes of lipstick. Her favorite romance novel: *The Red-Hot Cajun*; she'd read it five times. Two boxes of condoms, in the event someone had an emergency case of the hornies; she shook one of the boxes, which, oddly, seemed to be empty; she tossed it into the trash. A prescription bottle of Viagra; she had no idea where that came from . . . well, yes, she did . . . whoo-boy! A little mini-vibrator shaped like a butterfly that Charmaine had given her as a joke on her ninetieth birthday. Some joke! She hadn't yet been able to figure it out. A flashlight, matches, tissues, antacid, wallet, Bible, pistol, rosary beads, a stack of St. Jude prayer cards, house keys, and five pens later, she found her pill box that usually held aspirin. But it was empty. She recalled belatedly that she'd used them all after seeing those newspaper articles about the Hot Cop, and forgot to buy refills.

"Horsefeathers!" she muttered, went to find the first aid kit, and dug around. They had enough stuff to do brain surgery, but no painkillers.

Glancing around the tent, she spotted Celine's purse. She hesitated for only a second at what would be an invasion of privacy. This was a crisis. Sort of.

Celine's purse was all neat and organized. Son of a mud bug, she hated organized people. It was a wonder Celine didn't have one of those accordion-pleated, filing case kind of bags.

She took the items out one at a time and laid them on the table. There were tissues, keys, a small notebook, and pen in one side flap, and in the other, birth control pills, a wallet, a clear pouch with liquid makeup, mascara, and lipstick, a fold-up brush, an emery board, a wallet, and . . . ta da . . . a little plastic travel case of Tylenol. She popped two in her mouth, downing them with a swig of sweet tea. Then she began to return the items where they had been.

The last thing to go back was the wallet. She stared at it for a long moment. There was a lot you could learn about someone if you checked out the contents of their wallet, just like she'd learned that Celine was that anal retentive thingee by looking in her purse.

It really would be nosy, one part of her brain said . . . the St. Jude side, no doubt.

But the other side said, *Nosy ain't all bad.*

Back and forth, she argued with herself, then snorted with disgust and dropped the darn thing on the ground, causing it to snap open. "Oops, I guess I better pick it up."

Celine had about fifty dollars and change, a driver's license that said she was twenty-six and lived on Crawfish Lane in Houma, two credit cards, a blood donor card, and pictures in clear plastic, which she flipped through quick-like. There were only six of them.

She frowned. Not even one photograph of Dillon, the fiancé. How strange! There was one picture of her grandfather, James Arseneaux, and the rest of a little boy.

She glanced closer. And almost had a heart attack, her blood was pumping so fast.

It was Tee-John. As a baby being held by a younger Celine, then maybe two years old, then three at a birthday party with three candles on a pirate-themed cake, then finally studio portraits in two different poses at about four years old.

What would Celine be doing with baby photos of Tee-John?

Her mind moved sluggishly as she pondered the puzzle. Celine hadn't moved to Houma 'til she was in high school; so, she wouldn't have even been around then.

Slowly, her mind came to the only conclusion it

could. This must be Celine's son Etienne. But why did he look like—

She gasped and put a hand over her heart.

Surely... oh, please, God, no... this little chile cain't be Tee-John's son. She studied all the pictures closer, especially the last ones. The little boy had the same hair as Tee-John, same devilish eyes, and same smile showing two missing front teeth. It could have been a copy of Tee-John's kindergarten picture.

It must be a coincidence.

Then she checked the date stamp on the back of the birthday pictures. Frowning, she realized that Celine's boy must be five, not four as she'd told them. But why would she lie? Or was it a lie?

She would take one of the more recent photos back home with her and compare it to those in her picture album. Then, she would do a little research with some friends who knew stuff about public records.

If it was Tee-John's son, did he know about it? If he did, Tante Lulu was going to be very disappointed in the boy. Even more disappointed than the time he got arrested for leading a no-underwear day at Our Lady of the Bayou School when he was eleven. Or the time he got caught at a rainbow party when he was fifteen; Charmaine had had to explain to her what a rainbow party was.

Tante Lulu did some mental calculations in her head. If Etienne was five, Tee-John must have been a senior at Tulane, about to graduate. And Celine... well, she would have been two years behind him. So, that was when the mite had been hatched, *if* it was Tee-John's son.

Could he possibly have a son and not acknowledge him?

No, that was impossible. He might be Valcour Le-Deux's son, but he wasn't bad. He would never ignore a child of his blood.

The other possibility was even more horrendous. Could Celine have had Tee-John's baby and never told him? If so, why?

Some of Celine's behavior began to make sense. The way she bristled every time Tee-John approached. The way she avoided talking about her family. Her whole secretive nature.

Oh, my heavens, I have to lie down. Her headache was pounding like a swamp woodpecker. She replaced the wallet, turned off the camp stove, then went over to Tee-John's tent, where she crawled in and made herself a pallet with a rolled-up sleeping bag for a pillow.

Only then did she pull the photo out again.

"Etienne LeDeux," she murmured. Then louder, "Etienne LeDeux."

She smiled.

It had a nice sound.

Chapter
13

The Motley Crew just got motlier...

Veronica looked at the ever-increasing pile of paperwork on the desk of her Jinx, Inc. office in Barnegat, New Jersey, and said, "To think I left corporate law to avoid this crap."

The two people sitting in front of her desk just laughed.

"I know what you mean. When I was a nun, teaching at St. Anne's College, I spent half my time filling out church documents. Believe me, the church is as bad as the government when it comes to red tape. And rules! There were so many 'Do Nots' it sounded like a Motown song." This from Grace O'Brien, a professional poker playing buddy of Jake's; she'd left the convent years ago, for reasons unknown.

"Honey, you must have been the hottest nun. *Playboy* would have loved you," said Angel Sabato, another poker playing buddy of Jake's. Angel ought to know about the nude modeling; he'd once bared it all for *Playgirl* under the heading, "His Poker Is Hot."

Grace's lime green eyes flashed with a temper befitting her fiery red hair. "I am tired of you always making jokes about my being a nun. There's nothing wrong with a religious calling."

"Whoa, whoa, whoa!" Angel held his hands up in surrender, laughing. "Pull in your prickles, Miz Thorny."

"You are such a child."

"And don't you just love it?" He tugged on one of her red curls playfully.

"You wish!" She slapped his hand away.

The two of them had got knocked out early in the World Poker Tournament in AC, where Jake was still in the game. The talent was intense, Jake had told her when he called this morning. That must account for the snippy moods these two were in. She and Jake had both planned a getaway to a boardwalk hotel, but her grandfather had been unable to babysit at the last minute.

"Listen, Mr. Studmuffin. You've got your tail in a knot just because the redneck from Alabama kept making fun of your earring, and then beat the stuffing out of you in the last round. Don't take it out on me. Good thing you got rid of that long hair, though, or Leroy would have really been on your case. Either that, or he might have asked you for a date." Grace grinned as she ragged on Angel.

Until recently, Angel had worn his long black hair in a ponytail and his body in leather...lots of leather. For some reason, he'd gone conservative lately...well, conservative for Angel. Today he wore a muscle shirt that showed off a barbed wire tattoo, boot-cut jeans, and motorcycle boots. And his hair was short...almost military short.

"Sweet cheeks, my tail is just fine," Angel drawled. "Your problem is frustration, pure and simple. Celibacy will do that. Nothing a little hot sex won't remedy. When was the last time you got laid, by the way...pre–Vatican One, or, could it be...never?"

"And you'd like to be the one to remedy that situation? Too little, too late."

"No one has ever called me little." He paused and grinned. "Did you hear about the nun who went to her first confession and told the priest she had a terrible secret...she never wore panties under her habit. Well, that priest was no dummy. He told her to say five Hail Marys and do five cartwheels on the way out of church."

"Very funny," Grace said, not laughing.

"What I was wondering, sweetheart, was..." Angel paused for drama, "Do you wear panties?"

"Grow up!"

"Ahem! Back to the reason for your visit," Veronica interrupted. "I don't understand why you want to join Jinx. What about poker?"

Angel shrugged. "It's lost its zing for me."

"Me, too," Grace said. "We've both won more than we've lost. Money is no longer an issue."

"Plus there are all these young Turks with calculator minds, figuring all the angles. What's the fun in that?"

"Okay, but why treasure hunting?" Veronica asked.

"I'm a born gambler and adventurer. Searching for treasure has to be as risky as gambling. And one of the last bastions for adventure," Angel explained.

"And maybe I might find a hunk to un-bore me." Grace waggled her eyebrows.

"Hey, I'm a hunk."

Veronica was puzzled by their behavior. "Are you two a couple?"

"No!" they both said.

"But you're applying for a job here as a package deal?"

"Yep," Angel said.

"We're friends," Grace added.

"With benefits?" Angel asked Grace with mock hopefulness.

"You wish!"

"Do you have any experience?" Veronica asked.

"I did some diving in the Navy," Angel told her.

"I mountain climb as a hobby." Grace stood and began looking at the framed photographs on the wall. Mostly they were pictures and newspaper clippings of her grandfather on some of his more famous expeditions.

Angel confessed, "Actually, Jake recommended that we come talk to you. He made it sound really exciting and implied it was learn-as-you-go type work."

"And this subject came up in what context?"

"We were talking about how poker was no longer a challenge, and—"

"Jake, too?" Veronica was a little surprised and a lot hopeful. She'd wanted Jake to quit for a long time.

"Well, yeah, I mean..." Angel was embarrassed at having let slip something that he hadn't known was a secret.

"What do you do for an encore, big mouth?" Grace inquired sweetly of Angel.

Veronica was going to kill Jake when he got home... after she kissed him about thirty-seven times.

"Here's the deal, guys. I have a small team down in Louisiana now, looking for pirate treasure."

"Oooh, I love pirates," Grace cooed.

"Correction. She loves Johnny Depp," Angel explained to Veronica.

"Same thing," Grace contended.

"It sounds more glamorous than it is. We're talking swamps, digging, heat, bugs, and snakes. If you're still interested, one of my team members dropped out, Brenda Caslow, and I could send you down there as sort of apprentices. Or you could wait 'til the next project. I have several on the calendar. A lost show cat. A collection of Victorian erotic pictures. An Incan treasure. A sunken Viking ship. A vial of bull semen. One of Cleopatra's wigs."

With each item she mentioned, their jaws dropped further.

"Bull semen?" Angel choked out.

"Erotic pictures?" Grace's green eyes shone with unnun-like interest.

"So, are you in?" Veronica asked.

"Like Flynn." Angel smiled at her.

She called Adam then; he was the manager on the Pirate Project. The satellite phone on the other end rang seven times before Adam picked up. "Famosa here."

"Hi, Adam. How's the project going?"

He strung out about seven foul words. "Nothing so far. Peachey and LeDeux are diving now with a metal detector and camera. We did eight dives yesterday and four so far today. No friggin' treasure in sight."

"Are you saying we should scrap the project?"

He exhaled with a whoosh. "No. It's just been a bad day. Mud. Bugs. Snakes. Gators. Tante Lulu."

"What's the old lady done now?"

"Everything." He paused. "She wants to make me a hope chest."

"Uh-oh. Matchmakers R Us. I thought she was concentrating on John."

"That's another thing. While we were gone overnight, LeDeux and that newspaper reporter had wild monkey sex. Lots of it, by the looks of them."

"Does it affect his work?"

"Well, no, but—"

"A little jealous, are you, Adam?"

"I don't give a rat's ass what the Cajun Casanova does. We're going to continue with the dives for the rest of today, but if we don't hit pay dirt or anything even close, we're moving our search onto land tomorrow."

"Don't be discouraged, Adam. Treasure hunts rarely produce results the first day or two. Remember that Panama hunt; it took us a month to find the lost documents."

"When are you coming back?"

"I don't know. Jake's still alive in the tournament."

"That's good."

"Listen, the reason I called is to ask whether you could use two more hands on the project."

"Can they shovel?"

Veronica looked at Angel and Grace, who were both studying the photographs now and carrying on a low conversation. "Yes, I think they know one end of a shovel from another."

"Is Grace the hot nun?"

"The hot ex-nun."

"Hubba-hubba!"

Adam had been hanging around with Tante Lulu for

too long. Veronica hadn't heard that expression in ages, probably from her grandfather the last time he saw his girlfriend Flossie in stilettos and fishnet stockings.

An hour later, after the two of them filled out a number of work papers and she gave them the directions to Tante Lulu's cottage, where they would be picked up tomorrow, they headed toward the door.

And Angel needled Grace some more. "Did you hear about the two nuns cycling down a cobbled street?"

"No, and I don't want to."

He continued anyway, "The first nun says she's never come this way before, and the second nun says it must be the cobbles. C'mon, Gracie, lighten up. You have to admit that one was funny."

"I am no longer a nun. Get that? Nun jokes don't work on a non-nun, idiot."

"Wanna take a ride on my Harley, honey? Over some cobbled streets?"

"Aaarrgh!"

"Good luck, guys," Veronica said, then muttered to herself. "Tante Lulu is going to be in matchmaker's heaven when she gets a gander at these two."

Oops, they did it again...

"That's it for this section. Ready to give it up?" John inquired inside his mouthpiece, which was wired to Caleb's ear mike. They were swimming underwater, beside each other, after another unsuccessful dive...the fourth of the morning.

"Roger," Caleb replied. "Time for a lunch break anyhow."

"Go ahead without me. I'm going to swim a bit. Here, take the camera with you."

"Is it safe...to swim alone?"

"Please, this is the bayou...my home. Besides, I have a speargun on me."

"Whatever you say."

"Oh, Caleb..."

"Yeah?"

"Watch out for snakes."

Caleb gave him the finger, then swam to the surface, John's laughter rippling in his ears.

John swam away from the area where Caleb was splashing out. He had plenty of air left in his tank for a leisurely crawl near the bottom. This was the first opportunity he'd had to be really alone for days, the first chance to think about recent events and what to do about them, not the least of which was Celine-I-am-so-screwed!-Arseneaux.

His head lamp illuminated the tea-colored water, but only a few yards at a time.

Like his life, really.

He knew the direction he wanted to travel in his life, but that was about it. The final destination was up in question, the specifics all short-term...as far as his head lamp, or short-circuited brain, could reach.

He liked law enforcement and was good at it. He would have preferred the FBI, but the prospect of living in a city all the time put him off, big-time, especially DC. And he was too southern to park his carcass in Yankee land for any length of time.

As for his personal life, he'd thought he was cool.

Enjoy the single life for a few more years…or a dozen. Then settle down finally…maybe…with a babe hot enough to keep him from straying. Pamela Anderson with a brain. Yeah, he laughed to himself, pure clueless male delusion fantasy.

And now…*and now*, there was Celine.

She meant nothing to him.

And she meant everything to him. When did that happen?

How could he have made love with Celine Arseneaux?

How could he have resisted?

His life was becoming one colossal SNAFU…situation normal, all fucked up. Everyone thought he was a screwup, but he'd done a good job the last few years, at least on the outside, of living a pretty normal life.

Making love with Celine Arseneaux was not normal; it was insane. A FUBAR factor of about a thousand percent. A disaster in the making. But, man oh man, it had been the best sex he had ever had. And that was remarkable.

Which made it all the harder to keep his resolution not to go looking for a repeat.

A dark cloud passed overhead, almost like a celestial warning, but he soon realized it was just a raft of duckweed passing by. Yep, he was going off the deep end when he started getting celestial messages in duckweed. But he figured it was time to hightail it out of Dodge before he became gator lunch. Next the duckweed shadow might really be a gator.

When he was up on dry ground again, he saw that everyone had gone back to the headquarters site to eat lunch. He tugged off his diving suit and equipment, thought about hanging out here, but then realized he hadn't eaten any breakfast after Tante Lulu's cane syrup remark.

Cane syrup. That brought an involuntary smile of remembrance to his lips. One of the biggest surprises about making love with Celine... and there had been hot damn more than a few... had been how uninhibited and inventive she had been once she'd passed over that line between "Should I?" and "Oh, baby!"

It was going to be hard not making love with her again. *Hard* being the operative word.

He had just shrugged out of his wet suit when all his best intentions went to hell. Celine had come back.

They were alone.

He already knew what turned her on.

She already knew what turned him on.

They could take care of business and still return for lunch.

He gave her his best "come hither" smile.

She snorted her opinion of his smile. "Get real! I came back to tell you about your aunt."

Okay, so Celine hadn't returned for a nooner... dammit!

"Something strange is going on with your aunt."

"Something strange is always going on with my aunt."

"This is different. First of all, she was lying down when we got back. Your brother went up to her right away, but she said she was just resting."

John was concerned. His aunt never rested during the day. He was about to pull on his jeans and rush back to see what was up, but Celine put a hand on his arm.

Big mistake, that.

His dick interpreted her touch in a way Celine surely hadn't intended.

"Just a second. There's more. She's acting really strange toward me...hostile, even." Her hand still remained on his arm.

He frowned. "Because of last night?" *I am not looking at her shirt. I am not imagining how her breasts look. I am not thinking sex against that tree over there.*

"I don't know."

Huh? He'd lost the thread of her conversation.

"She didn't seem upset earlier, but something serious is going on now. Something had to have happened while we were gone. And you should be forewarned..."

"Yeah?"

"She told René that she wanted to go back to her home tonight and stay for a couple of days."

He shrugged. "Nothing wrong with that."

"She said she wanted to go back before she strangled you."

"Me? She loves me. I'm her favorite."

But then something remarkable happened. Celine no longer had a hand on his arm. In fact, she'd stepped back a few steps. But she was staring at his body, below the Mason-Dixon line.

He glanced down to see if you-know-who was misbehaving. He wasn't, or not much. But he realized that his swimming trunks had been shoved down by his wet suit. The waistband barely hugged his hips, exposing his waist, his navel, and a lot of his belly.

Celine still stared at him, but then she licked her lips.

"That does it," he said, pulling a foil packet from his jeans pocket, then picking her up by the waist and walk-

ing the few feet to the tree. He lifted her under the knees
so that her legs wrapped around him and his love boat
was riding its favorite channel.

They were wildly kissing each other while she rocked
her hips against him. His eyes were probably rolling
back in their sockets.

Suddenly, she took him by the ears and held him away
from her. "We can't. No condom," she gasped out.

He smiled and waggled his eyebrows at her. "Surprise, surprise!" He pulled the condom from his swimming trunks' pocket, tore it open with his teeth, and was
sheathed, all in a nanosecond.

"Where?" she choked out.

"Tante Lulu's purse."

She groaned.

"Don't worry. She'll never know."

They made love then. Against a tree, with his suit
down at his ankles and her shorts and panties tossed over
his shoulder, they risked embarrassment if any of the
team returned early. It was short and sweet, but unbelievably hot.

At first, they were both silent as they dressed, both
regretting their having sex *again*. Both were puzzled by
this wild chemistry between them.

As they began to walk back to the cabin, she glared
at him.

"What? It wasn't my fault," he protested.

"Well, it sure as hell wasn't mine."

"You started it."

"Earth to alien! I can't stand you."

"Coulda fooled me. Honey, you were looking at my
belly button like it was the Holy Grail of sex."

"You had a condom with you. Talk about premeditation."

"Now you're complaining because I was sensitive and considerate enough to think of protection."

"Mister, you are the Howard Stern of sensitivity."

Now, she'd gone too far. She thought he was insensitive. Well, he'd show her insensitive. "Have I told you lately how much I like your breasts? You have what guys call Pepto nips."

"Drop. Dead."

"Besides, I'm not the one who's engaged here. Tsk, tsk, tsk. Poor Delbert!"

That shut her up, but she looked as if her head might explode.

They returned to René's cabin a half hour later, together. And everyone noticed. Even though they arrived about five feet apart, which should have announced, loud and clear, that they were not enamored with each other.

René just shook his head at him.

Famosa said something about redneck screwups, or maybe it was redneck screwing.

He went right up to his aunt where she was dishing out food. "I'm back, Auntie. What's for lunch?"

A stricken expression passed over her wrinkled face before she turned and walked away from him. She looked every one of her ninety-two years.

What could have happened in the four hours since he'd been gone?

✦

The father of the year is ... WHO? ...

Luc had come with Remy in his hydroplane to pick up Tante Lulu later that day. René had alerted him to the fact that their aunt was upset about something.

And, whoo-boy, she was definitely upset, and most of it seemed to be directed at Tee-John. Despite everyone's pleas, she wouldn't explain. Instead, she told Tee-John before they'd left, "I jist have some things ta work out. I'll talk to ya when I figger the answers. You'll be the first ta know, guar-an-teed. Dontcha be worryin' none."

Yeah, like they weren't all worried after that mysterious statement.

Remy landed the hydroplane in the stream in front of Remy's house. While Remy jumped out to secure the plane, Luc turned to his aunt, who had been unusually quiet on the return trip. He was the oldest of the brothers, the one who'd been engaged for the longest time in helping Tante Lulu fight Valcour LeDeux. Usually, she confided in him, but now she was shutting him out.

"Are you gonna tell me now?"

"I cain't, Luc."

"Yes, you can."

"It's jist a suspicion."

"About what?"

She shook her head sadly.

"Maybe I can help."

"Not this time."

"Auntie, you know what you always say. There's no problem too big for St. Jude."

Her eyes brightened. "Yer right. How could I have fergot that?"

"So, can I help you?"

"Wouldja?"

"You know I would do anything for you, Auntie."

"Even if I swore ya ta secrecy?"

"Even then."

"It's about Tee-John."

"What's the Sex Cop done now?"

"Thass not funny."

He made a show of zipping his lips.

"Tee-John is a daddy, thass what."

He laughed.

"Ya ain't got no call ta be laughin' at me. It's the truth."

Tante Lulu had stunned him many times over the years, but this one took the cake. He had to have heard wrong. He shook his head as if to get rid of the wax in his ears. "Pass that by me again. I had to have heard you wrong."

"Ya heard right." She took a photograph out of her purse and handed it to him.

He tilted his head at his aunt.

"Celine Arseneaux's little boy, Etienne," said Tante Lulu.

He looked at the picture. "Un-be-liev-able!"

Chapter
14

I know how to de-stress you, baby...

"We're comin' home."

"Oh, Gramps, I don't think that's a good idea," Celine said into the satellite phone John had handed her a few moments ago after a convoluted procedure of circuiting the call through his police chief. In her opinion, they were over-obsessing on the danger.

"All this hay and grass is givin' me asthma, *chère*. And Etienne is gettin' bored with ridin' that pony. He wants ta ride a stallion, and you know, girl, if I don't watch him good, he'll be ridin' off like a Kentucky Derby jockey."

"Has he been behaving?"

"What do you think?"

She laughed.

"Actually, he's been pretty good, 'ceptin' for the time he tol' one ranch hand's little girl where babies come from."

"That little bugger! Did you tell him about...you know? I never told him."

Her grandfather laughed. "According to Professor Etienne, a guy spits in a girl's belly button, and a baby starts to grow underneath."

She laughed, too.

"How much longer you gonna be gone on this assignment?"

"I'm not sure...it might be as much as a week."

"Why can't you tell me where you are?"

"I'll explain when I'm done here."

"You've never been away from the boy for this long."

"I know," she said a bit tearfully. "Can I talk to him?"

There was a brief shuffle, followed by, "Hey, Mom. I got a new tooth t'day. Didja know girls cain't pee standin' up? Kin I have a pig?"

"A pig! I thought you wanted a dog."

"I do, but pigs stink real good. And they fart real loud."

What was it about boys and body humor? Little girls got great pleasure out of Barbie's new hairdo; little boys would rather hear Ken fart.

"If I can't have a pig, a goat would be nice."

"Oh, Etienne!" She smiled into the phone. "Maybe we'll look for a puppy once I get home."

His jubilant yells were so loud she held the phone away from her ear. She was still smiling when she clicked off the phone.

John was standing there waiting for her to return it to him.

"Do you have to eavesdrop?"

He shrugged. "Can't have you divulging any secrets."

"To a five-year-old child?"

"I thought he was four."

"He is. I misspoke."

He frowned and was about to argue with her, about how mothers never misspoke their children's ages, no doubt, especially when they only had one. "Listen, this assignment is not working out for me. I'm thinking I should call my editor and bow out."

"What you really mean is that you're scared about us?"

"I'm not afraid of you."

"I never thought you were. I 'spect you're afraid *you'll* jump *my* bones again."

"You...you...you," she sputtered, following after him as he walked away from her toward the cabin. Caleb and Adam were laying out the equipment they would be using for tomorrow's move to a land dig. René was inside the cabin cooking, or rather heating up various dishes Tante Lulu had left, enough to last them for several days. René intended to stay only one more day 'til two new Jinx team members would arrive. It was like a revolving door of people here. Except for her. They were making her stay put. "You are a delusional slimebucket, John LeDeux."

"Flattery will get you everywhere, darlin'." He went inside and let the screen door slam in her face.

She yanked it open and hurried after him. "Killing is a legal defense in some parts of Loo-zee-anna, you know? I want to go home."

René glanced up at her words, then glanced at his brother.

"Not an option," John declared while picking up a mini carrot off the counter and popping it into his mouth.

"You can't make me stay here."

"Wanna bet?" *Crunch, crunch, crunch!*

"I'm gonna let you two lovebirds settle this. Why don't you make a salad to go with this jambalaya, Tee-John? Call us when dinner's ready." He was chuckling as he walked off.

"He didn't have to leave."

"He's probably off to call my brothers."

"Why?"

"To blab about what you just said."

"Why?"

"Because everyone in my family is a busybody."

"I'm sure you give them plenty to busybody about."

"I try. You know what your problem is, Celine?"

"I'm sure you're going to tell me."

"You have a perpetual grouch problem. Comes from not enough oxytocin hormones in your body."

She almost laughed. "I've never heard of oxytocin."

"It's better known as the cuddle hormone."

She did laugh then. "Are you for real?"

"It takes only twenty seconds of hugging to produce oxytocin, which in turn counteracts stress. And, baby, you are loaded with stress."

"You're making this all up."

"Cross my heart. I read about it in *Men's Health* magazine."

"And you honestly think a hug from you is going to solve all my problems?"

"I'm just sayin'."

"Pass that salad bowl over here. You're mushing up the tomatoes when you slice like that."

He shoved the bowl and all the ingredients over to her while he turned to check on the jambalaya. The table had already been set by René and a loaf of leftover bread set out along with a stick of butter, a bottle of wine, and a bottle of Tabasco sauce.

"So, what were you laughing about when you talked to your grandfather on the phone?"

"My son. He told a little girl on the ranch that babies are made when the guy spits in the girl's belly button."

"Hey, I told Sally Sue Benoit the same thing when we were in kindergarten."

"And did she let you spit in her belly button?"

He grinned at her. "Yeah, when we were sixteen. But no babies, thank the Lord."

The sound of a guitar could be heard from the porch then. It was René, an accomplished musician, who was strumming and singing softly in French. A famous Cajun ballad called "*Jolie Blon.*"

During one of the pauses, she asked John, "You don't want children?"

"Hell, no! My brothers are doin' more than enough to overpopulate the world, and I won't even talk about my father...the bayou sperm donor to the masses. Besides, can you imagine me as a father?"

No. "Not ever?"

"Oh, maybe someday...when I'm forty or so." He waggled his eyebrows at her.

Somehow those waggling eyebrows didn't touch any funny bones in her body.

Sensing her bad mood's return, John said, "Are you sure you don't want a hug?"

How'd you like to mud wrestle?...

Mud, mud, mud.

Every one of them was covered with mud, smelled like mud, and was eating mud by ten-thirty the next morning, except for René, who'd stayed back at the cabin to fix a pump.

John was the only one who wasn't surprised about the mud. "What did you expect, ya dingbats?"

"Shut up!" Peachey said as he leaned against the handle of his shovel and swiped an arm over his forehead, which resulted in more smearing of mud.

"He's right," Celine said...probably the first time she'd ever agreed with him. "Louisiana's land is below sea level. All you have to do is dig a few feet and you'll hit water, anywhere. Why do you think we have our cemeteries above ground?"

"I thought you rednecks just dropped your dead in the bayous to feed the gators," Famosa added. To John's immense satisfaction, the Cuban wore more mud than any of them.

"Only some of them. Usually Yankees that have the misfortune to drop dead here in the South." Famosa was gonna have a tag on his toe by the end of this project if he kept needling him, John swore to himself.

"You guys ought to do a TV documentary about this project...not just finding a treasure, but the process of searching. It's fascinating." Celine spoke even as she moved the video camera around the site.

"Yeah, we could call it *Creatures from the Bayou Black Lagoon*," John quipped.

"It's not a bad idea." Peachey tapped his closed lips thoughtfully...lips that now wore mud lipstick. "We have all that footage left over from the pink diamond project and the cave pearls."

"Count me out," Famosa said. "No way am I gonna let you guys make a fool of me in public."

"As compared to making a fool of yourself in private?" Peachey inquired.

"I know, we could throw in a little male/female mud wrestling, and it would be a big hit," John offered.

"Get a life!" Celine offered back.

Man, she had no sense of humor at all.

"Uh-oh!" Caleb leaned down into the hole they had been digging for the past hour and pulled out the remnants of a hoe. "Guess this is what the metal detector picked up."

There were more than a few swear words blueing up the air then, including a choice one from Celine, to his surprise.

"What? You thought I didn't know any swear words?" She stuck her tongue out at him.

"You do not want to show me your tongue, darlin'. To a Cajun man, that is a pure, one hundred proof invitation."

"Would you two stop with the verbal foreplay?" Famosa griped. "You're turning me on."

"Yeech!" he and Celine said at the same time.

"I think I've landed in Alice in Wonderland's bayou hole." Peachey shook his head at all of them.

Famosa pulled a copy of the map out of his back pocket. "Okay, let's start on the next tract, north of here.

I'll run the magnetometer. LeDeux and Peachey can start diving on opposite sides of the grid."

"I'll record the data about this dig," Celine offered. "Do you want me to continue videotaping?"

"Yes, to both," Famosa agreed. "Thanks."

What a suck-up! "Thanks," John mimicked silently to Celine.

She ignored him, which was almost more of a red cape challenge to him than the tongue thing.

He walked up behind her and said in a low enough voice that only she could hear, "When I bathed this morning, I noticed I had whisker burns on my butt. You might want to shave your legs."

She turned slowly, inch by inch. The look she gave him then practically shouted, "Come a little closer, baby, so I can cut your jugular with my teeth."

"Okay, okay, I'm sorry. I crossed the line with that one." He put up his hands in surrender. "But you have to know...what Famosa said about foreplay...well, I'm the one who gets turned on. By you. All the time. Dammit."

For once she was speechless.

And maybe a little bit turned on. He could hope. Or not hope.

Hell, he was screwed either way.

When three people know a secret, is it still a secret?

It seemed to John that something really strange was going on.

Remy had brought Grace O'Brien and Angel Sabato to René's cabin, a short time ago, just after the lunch break. They'd all met these poker friends of Jake's before, except for René and Celine.

Grace was talking animatedly to Celine, and Sabato was getting the rundown from Famosa and Peachey on the project work, which would resume shortly. His aunt hadn't returned, but sent a message that she had work to do.

The thing that was strange was the way that Remy and René were acting. Remy was telling René something which clearly shocked him, and every couple seconds the two of them glanced his way, with expressions that alternated between horror and sympathy.

What am I being accused of now?

He ambled over, and his brothers stopped talking suddenly. "What's goin' on?"

"What makes you think somethin's goin' on?" Remy shifted from foot to foot.

"The way you two are actin' like old biddy gossips at Our Lady of the Bayou bingo night. If you have somethin' to say to me or about me, just spit it out."

René made the mistake of glancing Celine's way and then back to him.

"Oh, shit! Is this about me and Celine?"

Both his brothers went a bit red-faced.

"I know what's up."

"You do?" his brothers said as one.

"Tante Lulu is on her bandwagon again. Well, I'll tell you right now, I'm not going to marry Celine Arseneaux."

"I wouldn't be so sure about that, bro," Remy said, and he wasn't smiling.

"She better not be plannin' a surprise wedding."

"There'll only ever be one of those, and I got the honors," René said. He wasn't smiling either.

"What's goin' on, then?"

"I promised I wouldn't say anything."

"You told René."

"I'm not supposed to tell *you* ... yet."

René patted him on the arm. "Don't worry ... 'til Tante Lulu is done investigating."

"Oh, that makes me feel better." *Tante Lulu investigating? This is not good.* An idea came to him. "Hey, if this is about Celine not having a fiancé, I already know that."

"Celine has a fiancé? You didn't tell me that," Remy chastised René.

"It better not be one of those dorky Village People events either." His family had a habit of performing these outrageous Village People musical extravaganzas when one of them was close to the altar. Which he wasn't.

"No Village People act," René promised. "At least not yet."

"You better watch the competition, though," Remy warned, motioning his head toward the other side of the clearing where Sabato was talking to Celine, who was leaning against a tupelo tree.

For some reason, he felt proprietary about Celine being against a tree like that. Too much of a reminder of what they had done against a tree yesterday. And Sabato for damn sure was looking at her as if he'd like to pluck a few peaches off of *her* tree.

He hated feeling like this.

Maybe there was something to Tante Lulu's thunderbolt crap.

Scary thought, that.

No way!

He decided then and there to begin his own novena to St. Jude, asking for a thunderbolt antidote.

Who are they kidding?...

Angel leaned backward, hands at his waist, and groaned as he worked out the kinks.

He noticed Grace watching him. She did a lot of that lately. He winked.

She snorted.

"I haven't done this much physical labor since I was on a reform school chain gang."

She snorted again. Honestly, she had the cutest snort. "They haven't had chain gangs for ages."

LeDeux raised a finger in the air. "Correction. Some prisons in the South still do chain gangs."

"Well, for teenagers, then," Grace amended.

"Okay, so it was a reform school farm," Angel said, walking over to tug on one of her red curls. She hated when he did that.

"I can attest to that," Peachey interjected. "I grew up on a farm. Ugh! Chain gang, for sure."

"Did you hear about the Mother Superior who ordered one hundred and twenty bananas for the convent?"

Grace groaned.

"When the grocer said he could give her a discount if she took one hundred forty-four, the Mother said she supposed they could *eat* the other twenty-four."

"You are weird, do you know that, Angel? Weird."

"And dontcha just love it?"

"Break's over, people," Famosa said. He was project leader and a pain in the ass. The Cuban dirtbag had taken a special interest in Grace. And Grace was returning the interest, dammit. Apparently, Grace had visited Cuba one time in her nun capacity.

He had known Grace for about ten years, and she had already left the convent by then. As close as they were, as friends, even he was in the dark about what had happened. But then, he didn't talk about his younger days either. All those years of friendship had caused him to be protective of Grace when men were putting the moves on her.

Who was he kidding? He had been in love with her for so long he ached with it. She didn't suspect a thing, and he didn't intend to ever tell her. She'd been a nun, for the love of a Harley. He, on the other hand, had been things he never wanted her, or anyone else, to know about. A buried past, which would hopefully stay that way.

"Got it bad, do you?" LeDeux remarked, coming up to shovel next to him.

That jarred him a bit...that he'd been so obvious. He must be slipping.

"No one else noticed," LeDeux assured him, as if that was any assurance. One word to LeDeux's wacky aunt, and he would have the Cajun matchmaker riding his tail.

"You should talk," he countered. "You watch Celine like she's private property."

LeDeux's face got red.

Who knew the bayou stud could blush?

"You're wrong. I was just watchin' you hittin' on her, and—"

"Whoa, whoa, whoa! I was not hitting on her. We were just talking about a newspaper series she did on Hells Angels."

"Stay away from Celine."

He chuckled. "Likewise on Grace."

"Not that we're a couple or anything."

"Same here."

"I feel a responsibility for her."

"Ditto."

The two of them glared at each other, then burst out laughing.

Chapter
15

Rogue to the bone...

They were sitting around on the porch of the cabin that evening, except for Caleb who'd volunteered to stay behind at the work site. No way was Celine going to risk alone time with John again.

Speaking of whom...

John sank down into an Adirondack chair next to her, propping his booted feet on the porch rail. She was safe, though; Adam, Grace, and Angel were at the other end of the porch playing poker. Grace had agreed to play on the condition Angel wouldn't tell any nun jokes. A Cajun radio station played softly in the background. René had gone back to Houma with Remy.

"Are you gettin' enough information for your story?" he asked, taking a slow sip from a longneck bottle of Dixie beer.

"Absolutely." She had her laptop propped on her knees, her feet also up on the low rail. She noticed John noticing her legs and the fact that she had shaved them after dinner in the small bathroom. Not that they'd really needed it!

Before dinner, they'd all bathed in one way or another... the interior shower or the bayou stream. The massive amounts of mud and sweat made it a necessity.

The boy did clean up good. *Mentally fanning myself here.* It wasn't just his even features, his being tall and lean, it was more his personality showcased by his dark Cajun dancing eyes.

Like Etienne.

Oh, God!

"In fact, I have material for several newspaper features once this project is completed, and none of the subjects is dependent on finding a treasure."

He raised his eyebrows at her.

"Not about you. Get over yourself. That line was crossed and crossed out."

He nodded. "So tell me, what do you find so interesting here?"

"Your aunt in herself would make an outstanding human interest feature. Good grief! Her *traiteur* work for more than six decades is fascinating. Historically important, actually."

"You're right. You oughta read her journals sometime. The people she's met and healed. Unusual remedies out the kazoo."

"Do you think she'd agree to an interview?"

"Are you kiddin'? My aunt, she loves to talk... and she loves bein' the center of attention."

She nodded. "Then there's Adam. He's fascinating, too."

John didn't like that assessment at all, as evidenced by the tightening of his jaw.

"You disagree? How well do you know him?"

"Well enough. I've been on two previous Jinx projects. You could say we have a personality conflict."

"Adam gives the impression of being a slimy womanizer, but after talking with him, I see lots more. There has to be a story in how he got to this country. And no denying, he's a well-respected professor of oceanography, an accomplished diver and treasure hunter, and a philanthropist...did you know he volunteers for Make-A-Wish?"

"I didn't know about the volunteer work. So, you gonna hook up with him?"

"Please! Must you be uncouth? Does everything have to be about sex with you?"

"With you, it seems to be."

She stared at him. What did you do with a guy who came out with stuff like this? And what did you do with yourself when you got goose bumps over his words?

He rubbed a hand over his day-old whiskers, staring back at her.

She ought to make a snide remark about his needing to shave and her own whisker burns, but she wasn't going to step into that minefield, knowing full well that he would speculate on which intimate body parts were affected.

"Sorry, Celine, I promised myself not to harass you anymore."

"Oh, really?"

"Keep goin'." He waved his bottle toward her. "Who else rocks your boat?"

She frowned at him.

"Picky, picky! Who do you think is newsworthy?"

"Caleb, the ex-Amish Navy SEAL treasure hunter, of course, though I doubt he would want any publicity."

"Didn't stop you with me."

"Are you ever going to forgive me for that?"

"I don't know. Whatcha got to offer?"

"I thought you weren't going to sexually harass me anymore."

"That wasn't sexual harassment."

"Besides, I think I've given you more than enough."

"Now who's bringin' up sex?"

She ignored his comment. "Then there are the two arrivals today. An ex-nun poker playing treasure hunter... gotta be a huge story there. And Angel Sabato spells human interest out the wing wang."

"Bet you're gonna go back to your office and pull up the picture of him in *Playgirl* magazine. Just to see his wing wang."

"Of course."

They smiled at each other then, and an open smile from John LeDeux, without any sexual motivation, was still a potent thing.

"Tell me about yourself, John. Oh, don't get your hackles up. I'm not going to write about you again."

"What do you wanna know?"

"Have you ever been engaged or married?" She paused. "Any kids?"

"No, no, and thank God, no."

She winced, which he thankfully didn't notice.

"What did you study in college? What did you do after you graduated?"

"Man, this *is* an interrogation," he said with a grin. "Criminal justice. I really wanted to work for the FBI and even started training classes, but I hated living up north. So, I came home, went to the police academy, and became an officer."

"Why police work?"

He seemed to hesitate, then said, "This is gonna sound hokey."

"I love hokey."

"Finally something she loves about me." He inhaled, then exhaled. "My father would never be voted Father of the Year. One time when I was about seven, I had a broken arm, and, well, some other stuff. Tante Lulu called the police, and I can still remember how it felt when that cop arrived. It was like one of those historical romance novels where the hero comes riding in on his white charger to save the heroine. A superhero to a little kid, I guess."

Celine's heart ached at his words, and those he didn't say. Valcour LeDeux had a reputation as a mean alcoholic, but she hadn't realized he abused his kids, too. "You could have become a teacher."

"I like guns." He waggled his eyebrows at her. "Plus, women love guys in uniform."

She could have pointed out that he no longer wore a uniform, as a detective, but she knew he deliberately veered her away from his revealing words.

"Your turn. What have you been doin' since we last…met? See how couth I can be, *chère?* I didn't even say…since we last did the dirty. Anyhow, why journalism?" He leaned over and flicked her chin playfully.

"I'm good with computers…have a double major in computer arts and journalism…but I've loved writing since I was a kid. And, despite your opinion of journalists, I think I can do good."

He nodded. "And your personal life, Lois Lane?"

"Hey, you didn't give me the scoop on your personal life."

He set his beer down and threw his hands out. "Ask me anything."

"How many women have you...uh, made love with?"

"You don't beat around the bush, do you? Not as many as you would think. And never married women."

"Oh, yeah? How about engaged women?" she countered, pointing to herself.

"You're not engaged."

"No, I'm not." She surprised herself with the admission. "How did you know?"

"His name kept changing. When you asked to make a phone call, you never asked to phone him. You don't act like a woman in love."

"And how does a woman in love act?"

"Same way as a man in love, I guess."

She cocked her head at him. When he didn't answer, she went on, "You're sugarcoating yourself. You have to know you have a reputation for being wild."

"That was in my younger days. My wild gene, she is gone rusty."

"You are so full of it."

He grinned at her. "Wanna play strip poker?"

A nun and a Cajun yenta: a heavenly match...

The next afternoon, they found the treasure. Actually, the first of the treasures.

John could barely restrain himself from getting on

the phone and calling his family...hell, everyone he knew. But the team members had decided to keep the find to themselves for now...mainly because, amazingly, it appeared that the pirate treasure was buried all over the place in small lots. Well, small lots was a relative assessment. The small box of doubloons they found today could easily be worth a half mil on the rare coin market.

A decision had been made to put off a public announcement 'til they were done with the project. So, Tante Lulu and Ronnie were the only ones who had been informed, and his aunt had sworn on a stack of Bibles not to tell anyone.

In the meantime, smiles and dandelion wine toasts were in abundance. To say the team members were jubilant would be a vast understatement. Sabato and Grace were claiming to be good luck charms. Celine even initiated a happy hug with John, and only pulled away when he put a hand on her butt.

He handed his satellite phone, already predialed through the chief, to Celine, who was sitting on the living room sofa. Then he went over to check out the gold coins soaking in pans on the kitchen table. Unlike silver and other metals, solid gold did not tarnish or corrode, even after a hundred and fifty years, give or take; so, all these needed was a good cleaning.

"Pretty exciting for a first day, huh?" he said to Grace, who was using a soft brush to clean off the dirt.

"Pretty exciting for *any* day, I would think." She smiled at him companionably. Grace was a petite redhead with pretty green eyes. About thirty-five, he would think. "I've been wanting to talk with you, John."

He tilted his head in question, even as he picked up

another brush and started to help her. Rusty and Doug Kershaw were waxing poetic musically about Louisiana men on one of René's CDs. Unlike Charmaine, René's tastes were pure Cajun.

"Now that I've quit poker, I need a new profession."

"Treasure hunting?"

"No, I don't think so...at least not long term. I have a PhD in alternative medicine and I've taught on the subject. What I was wondering is, well, do you think your aunt would take me on as an apprentice?"

Now, this floored him. He put down his brush and stared at Grace. She was serious. John didn't think he'd ever met anyone, other than family, that voluntarily spent a long stretch of time with his aunt. She would drive most people insane.

"I don't know," he answered. "She *is* ninety-two."

"All the more reason for me to glean all the herbal wisdom from her that I can before...well, before it's too late."

"Funny that you should bring this up now. Celine was telling me just this afternoon that my aunt would make a great subject for a feature story on her long history as a *traiteur*. I even mentioned the record books of herbal recipes that my aunt has collected over the past fifty years."

"She has written records?" Grace practically swooned. Then, something else he'd said must have struck her. "You and Celine...are you a couple?"

"*Mon Dieu!* No!"

She looked skeptical. "Look how she watches you. She's jealous. She thinks you're hitting on me."

"No shit! I mean, no kiddin'?" He glanced toward

Celine, who had shut off the phone and was, indeed, staring at them.

He gave her a little wave.

She bared her teeth at him.

He was pleased in a perverse sort of way that Celine might have some feelings for him.

"Don't be gloating, big shot," Grace said with a laugh. "You look at her the same way."

"I do not," he said indignantly.

Do I?

When secrets come back to bite you in the butt...

The next day, Tante Lulu and Luc stood outside the door of the house on Crawfish Lane. Luc couldn't remember ever seeing his aunt so nervous.

She'd just heard this afternoon that the Pirate Project had made a hit, and that it might be the first of many. She was going to be a rich old lady. And none of it mattered more than the kid.

"Let me handle this," he said.

"I jist have a bad feelin'."

The door swung open suddenly, and a little boy stared up at them.

The kid was the spitting image of Tee-John when he was that age. What were the chances of this just being a coincidence? About a million to one, he suspected.

"Grampa!" the boy yelled. "We got company!"

An old man...presumably James Arseneaux...came rushing forward from the kitchen, wiping his hands on a dish towel. "Dint I tell ya to never open that door ta—" His words broke off. "You!" he said, glaring at Tante Lulu.

"James," she said with a dignity that would befit the queen of England. Without an invitation, she sailed past the guy and the kid and entered the living room.

"Ya got some nerve...," Arseneaux sputtered.

"I'll tell ya who's got nerve," his aunt said, looking pointedly at the kid. Her voice softened then and she hunkered down. There were tears in her eyes. "Hello, Etienne."

"How 'bout you take Etienne out to the backyard," Luc suggested to his aunt. "I think I saw some swings there. Mr. Arseneaux and I need to have a talk."

The minute they were gone, Arseneaux pointed a finger at him. "You have no right!"

"Actually, I do have a right...or at least my brother does. Now, we can talk amicably here, or we can do it in court. Which would you prefer?"

Arseneaux put his face in his hands. "This is gonna kill Celine."

"Tell me what happened," Luc encouraged.

When he was done, one thing was abundantly clear. James Arseneaux hated the LeDeux family.

"You're tellin' me that the reason Celine never told my brother is because you insisted on it as a condition for your help when she was pregnant...and when she came to stay here with you?"

The old man's face flushed. "It weren't 'zackly like that."

"What do you have against my family? Oh, wait, my father, right?"

"Damn right! He screwed around with my cousin's

girl one time, promised ta marry up with her, then skedaddled off to marry yer mother. She committed suicide."

Tante Lulu had told him earlier today about Celine's father...James Arseneaux's son...committing suicide. That must have been a double whammy for the old guy.

"I'm so sorry. I really am. I had no idea. But why blame the rest of us for what my father did?"

"Blood tells."

"Etienne has that blood, too, and it's obvious you love the boy."

Arseneaux's bristly chin raised a notch. "What a mess! Yer gonna try ta take the boy away from us, ain't ya? All yer fancy pancy lawyerin', I heard 'bout yer antics in court. Well, I won' let ya."

"Let's not get ahead of ourselves here. First things first. My brother has to be told, and it's best that Celine be the one to tell him."

The old man was about to argue, then nodded, reluctantly. "She's outta town, but I'll tell her next time she phones."

"And that would be?"

"T'night."

The old man had aged twenty years in the last half hour, and he was old to begin with. Luc felt sorry for him, despite how wrongful his actions had been.

"Mr. Arseneaux...James, this doesn't have to be a tragedy. We're good people. Don't judge us by my father."

Again, he nodded reluctantly, but then he groaned. "Is that crazy old bag out there gotta be in the picture?"

"Front and center," Luc said with a laugh.

Chapter
16

She dropped the daddy bomb...

Celine was having fun.

They'd dug up four more chests of gold today, and flagged ten other spots that indicated metal beneath the surface. Ronnie and Jake would be coming in tomorrow to help with the work.

Everyone was in a festive mood and decided to quit work early. John was attempting to teach Grace and Angel how to dirty dance to a Cajun song, although Angel already had some good moves of his own. Grace kept slapping his hands away from inappropriate spots on her body.

"Did you hear about the nun and two priests?" Angel asked Grace.

Grace put a hand over his mouth for silence.

Caleb was cooking freshly caught fish over an open fire while Adam dropped live crawfish into a boiling pot of spiced water. The beer flowed.

Just then, John's satellite phone rang. He looked over at Celine and indicated it was her grandfather.

"Celine, they know," he said right off.

"Know what?"

"The LeDeuxs know about Etienne."

"No! Oh, please, no!"

Everyone in the clearing turned to look at her where she stood off to the side, clearly distressed.

"Are you saying that John knows?" How could that be? Surely he would have told her.

"No, but that crazy old lady and that lawyer nephew of hers were here t'day. Ya gotta tell John yerself, or they will."

"How did they find out...never mind, that doesn't matter now."

"They dint come here threatenin' or nothin'. Still, I doan trust that LeDeux lawyer."

"They didn't tell Etienne, did they?"

"No. 'Course not."

Her grandfather was clearly shaken, and stress was the last thing he needed with his blood pressure. Therefore, she assured him that everything would work out, even though she had no clear idea how.

They spoke some more, then she hung up, stunned.

"Is everything all right?" Grace came up to her and put a hand on her arm.

She was shell-shocked, but she managed to say, "I need to take a walk...to think a little. Make my excuses, please."

Though concerned, Grace nodded. Celine deliberately avoided eye contact with John.

She walked along the bayou for about ten minutes, unable to get her thoughts together. *How am I going to*

*be able to tell John? Will he care? Of course he'll care.
He's going to kill me.*

Ten minutes later, she was sitting on a stretch of grass
near the stream when John showed up. She should have
known that he would follow her.

"You best be careful, *chère*. There might be snakes or
red ants around."

"I checked."

He sank down beside her. "What's wrong? Is there a
problem at home?"

"You could say that."

"Your son?"

"Oh, yeah."

"What's he done?"

"It's not what he's done. It's what I've done."

"Huh?"

"You are going to be so angry."

"*Me?* Why should *I* be angry?"

"John, there's no easy way to say this. You have a
son."

He recoiled as if she'd punched him in the chin. "Pass
that by me again."

"Etienne is your son."

His eyes went huge. "Impossible! I couldn't be the
father of your four-year-old kid."

"I lied. He's five."

"Un-be-fucking-lievable!" He stood abruptly, combed
his fingers through his hair, and turned to study the
stream. A blue heron swooped down and caught a fish,
but John probably didn't even notice. Spinning on his
heels, he inquired in an icy voice, "I have a five-year-
old son?"

She nodded.

"And you chose not to tell me?"

She nodded again.

"You bitch!" He stormed off in the other direction, farther away from the cabin.

She just sat there, miserable and confused about what to do next. She didn't blame him for his fury.

A short time later, he returned, still obviously angry, but he sat down beside her again. "I'll want DNA tests."

She bristled.

"I have to be sure."

"Go to hell, John." She swiped at the tears brimming over. The stress of this past hour was finally getting to her.

John didn't look the least bit sympathetic.

"Why tell me now? What did your grandfather say on the phone?"

"Your aunt and your brother Luc paid a visit today."

"*What?* They know? How long have they known?"

"When your aunt was here the other day, she rooted through my purse for an aspirin and saw a picture of Etienne. She knew immediately...or strongly suspected...that he was yours."

"He...he looks that much like me?" He gulped, visibly touched, fighting all the roiling emotions inside him.

"Yes, and apparently his mischief gene was inherited from you. A hell-raiser in the making."

He didn't smile. "Well, this explains a lot."

"Like what?"

"Your skittishness around me. Your secretiveness. And, holy crawfish, that must be why Tante Lulu wouldn't talk to me before she left. She must have thought I knew I had a child and just abandoned it. Tells you a lot about her opinion of my character."

"I don't think she ever really believed that." She put a hand on his arm in assurance.

He shoved her hand away. "Don't touch me."

She told him then why she had kept the secret, trying to explain her grandfather's feelings toward the LeDeuxs.

John looked at her with disgust.

It sounded lame even to her own ears. There was no way she could lay the blame at her grandfather's feet. If anyone was to blame, it was she.

"Were you ever going to tell me?"

"Honestly, I don't know. Maybe someday if Etienne wanted or needed...I just don't know."

"Do you have any idea how immoral that is?"

"I wasn't sure if you would be interested."

"Bullshit!"

"I was probably wrong not to tell you."

"Damn right! No probably about it."

"Your brother has a reputation as a shark lawyer. My grandfather is afraid."

"He should be afraid. You should be, too."

"Don't threaten me."

"My brother isn't going to do anything I don't want him to, but I can tell you right now, you're gonna pay for this outrage, one way or another, whether it turns out Etienne is mine or not."

"Are you talking about a lawsuit?"

"That and lots more," he said with ice in his voice.

"Do I need a lawyer?"

He stared at her for a long moment. "Maybe... probably."

"This is a shock. I know it is, but Etienne is your child. I wouldn't lie about that."

"No? You would just lie by omission." He exhaled whooshily and asked, "Do you have any pictures of him?"

She nodded. "In my wallet, back at the cabin."

"Go get them."

She could hardly balk at his domineering orders. As she walked away, she glanced back over her shoulder.

John was sitting with his elbows braced on spread knees, hands covering his face. The image of abject misery.

The war begins...

Heart aching, hours later, John was still transfixed by the pictures, and he still found it hard to believe.

My son, my son, my son kept reverberating through his dulled brain.

His satellite phone had been ringing all night...the caller ID identifying them, in turn, as Tante Lulu, Luc, Remy, René, and Charmaine...but he'd not answered any of them yet. He knew they meant well, family being everything to them, but this was something he had to work through himself first.

He was a cute kid, and, yeah, Etienne did resemble himself when he was that age. DNA or not, the evidence was staring him in the face.

Do I want to be a father?

Yes.

And no.

He pictured himself teaching Etienne how to bait a hook and cast a rod. Could he swim? If not, he could show him how. Did he like football or baseball or computers? Was he smart? Hell, he didn't even know if he was in school.

On the other hand, John considered himself too young to bite the dust. He had lots more wild oats to be sown. In fact, he had a date with Eve Estrada when she got back next month from Paris, where she was exhibiting her paintings. Sex and paella were sure to be on the menu. Then, too, he and three buddies were planning to spend Christmas in the Bahamas with Tank's oldest sister and her friends. Tina owned a beachfront villa, thanks to a very generous ex-husband. Up 'til now, he would have expected to celebrate the holidays in a wild fashion. Maybe he still would.

John felt like he was being pulled in five different directions. He was so confused.

I have a son.

Celine had mentioned something about Etienne wanting a dog the other day. He for damn sure would be getting a dog.

Oh, my God! I have a son.

So many questions.

Everyone else was asleep in the cabin. Grace and Celine in one bedroom. Famosa, Peachey, and Sabato in another. He would sleep down here on the pullout sofa. It was expected to rain later, which would make the tent uncomfortable.

His phone rang again, and this time he picked it up, not wanting to awaken anyone.

"Etienne, he is a beautiful boy," Tante Lulu blurted out.

"Tell me."

"He's little, no higher 'n yer thigh, I 'spect. Dark hair like yers and blue eyes like his mommy. He's missin' two front teeth right now. He talks a mile a minute. A happy boy.

"He likes pirates and has a collection of ships and pirate figures. He collects Hot Wheels cars, too. And, whoo-boy, he is full of mischief! While we were there, a little neighbor boy came over, and they put a firecracker in the toilet jist ta see what would happen."

He smiled. "What happened?"

"It made a loud noise, then fizzled."

"Does he . . . did he mention a father?"

"No. We dint stay long enough fer that. His paw-paw sez he's been askin' questions lately. There was some kinda Father Night at his play school."

He gritted his teeth, angry once again.

"Celine done a good job raisin' the boy, Tee-John. Ya gotta give her that."

"That's about all I'll give her. I really want to see him, Auntie, but I talked to the boss. Even for this, he won't allow me to set foot in Houma. Not yet."

"Well, now, would he allow us, me and Remy, ta bring the boy and his paw-paw there fer a visit?"

He was suddenly hopeful. "I don't know. Maybe. If we're careful, he might."

"Good. You let me know in the mornin'. Now lissen up. We gots lots of stuff ta plan. When do ya wanna get married? I guess ya gotta wait 'til this trial thing is over, but—"

His system could take only so many shocks in one day. He exploded, "There is not going to be a frickin' wedding."

"But you and Celine have a chile. An', watch yer mouth, boy, there ain't no need fer swearin'."

Boy? I have a son, and she's calling me "boy." "No wedding!"

"Ya want time ta court her some, I s'pose."

No, I want time to beat her head in. "No wedding, no courting, no nothing. Right now the last thing I want is Celine Arseneaux for a bride."

"I gave Etienne a St. Jude statue t'day," she said, as if he hadn't even spoken. Then she went on to tell him lots of other stuff...how the house looked, what was in his son's bedroom, what was in Celine's bedroom, the ailments James suffered. Her usual prattle, bless her heart. She even told him what kind of toilet paper she saw in the bathroom...some kind of wasteful, overly expensive product. Who knew there was expensive toilet paper? *Designer toilet paper?* he joked to himself. *Damn! My brain is melting here.*

"Tell Luc I'll be calling him first thing tomorrow morning."

"Why?"

"I need to know my legal rights."

"Legal-smegal. Yer the father. What's ta know?"

"I'm considerin' a lawsuit."

"Fer custody?"

"Maybe. All I know is, she's gonna pay."

Just before hanging up, she said, "Tee-John, I was angry at first, too, but ya gotta accept that God works in his own ways. If this is the way he wants ya ta become a daddy, thass the way it has ta be."

"There's an old military adage, Tante Lulu. 'Pray to God but pass the ammunition.'"

"Whass that mean?"

"It means that Celine better duck. The next round is mine."

You could call it pirate humor...

The next morning was a zoo, which was a good thing for Celine. It kept her mind occupied with something other than the crisis in her personal life.

There were red flags scattered all over an area the size of a city block to indicate places where the metal detector had sensed something. And they were still scanning. No digging yet.

Grace had taken over the photography and audio recording while Celine was keying in site info to a high-tech laptop computer. Suddenly, she began to see a pattern. "Oh, good heavens! Adam!" she screamed. "Come quick!"

Adam was soon leaning over her shoulder.

"Look at this. Could it be as simple as a skull and crossbones? Did that wily old pirate actually bury his gold in such a goofball way?"

"It would certainly be a joke on all the people who've been searching for it, like, forever."

They grinned at each other, then did a high five.

Adam went over to tell the others about her discovery.

"It's at least worth a try," Caleb said. "If it turns out to be true, it will save us days of wasted digging."

"See, I told you that Grace and I were good luck," Angel bragged. "Angel and Grace, the holy charms."

Grace made a scoffing sound, but she smiled at Angel.

John was the only one who didn't come over to congratulate her. He was avoiding her like the bloody plague. Which was fine with her. She was done apologizing. And she'd be damned if she would buckle under his threats.

It took them more than three hours to continue running the metal detector and the magnetometers on land and underwater. It appeared that the four tips of the X, or crossbones, were going to be under the bayou stream. Some distance upstream from their original work site, the water had separated into sort of a wide island, which may or may not have been underwater in Lafitte's day. In any case, the X with its circle or skull around the center lay on land, but the tips underwater. There were days', maybe even weeks', worth of work ahead of them, unearthing the loot.

They broke for lunch and a lengthy planning session. Adam was on the phone constantly with Ronnie, who'd asked them, as a courtesy, to wait 'til she and Jake arrived later that day before doing any more digging. Ronnie, as owner of Jinx, Inc., wanted to share in the excitement, which Celine could understand. They were leaving their little girl behind with the grandfather.

She and Grace had set out cold sandwiches and a giant thermos of sweet tea when John's satellite phone rang. All of the phones had been ringing throughout last evening and this morning.

John went off to the side to take his call. Celine noticed his face go white, and his body stiffened. "Yes. Yes. Yes. Okay. Of course. I know. I'll tell her."

He replaced his phone in the pouch attached to his belt. Then he looked over, pointed a finger at her, and said, "You. Follow me." He turned and walked along the pathway toward the cabin.

"Huh?" She glanced behind her, then all around.

Everyone was watching, mostly with amusement.

"Was he talking to me?" she asked Grace.

"I think so." Grace laughed.

"The nerve of the bum! Does he actually think he can order me around like that?"

"Apparently so. That's called redneck charm." Adam loved when John did something stupid.

But then, John turned, walking backward, and said in a steely voice, "Get your butt in gear and follow me, Arseneaux, or you'll be riding my shoulder, ass high, like a sack of wheat."

"Does he talk to her like that all the time?" Angel asked Caleb.

"Only when he wants to get laid," Caleb joked.

"I think he's in love," Grace opined.

"I think you're all nuts," Angel remarked.

But all the comments just washed over Celine, who was totally confused. But then she realized that this must have something to do with Etienne. So, with red face, she ran to catch up. But she gave him the finger to his back, just to get the last word in, so to speak.

Laughter echoed behind her.

From the mouths of babes . . .

John was more excited than he'd ever been in all his life, even more than the adrenaline rush before a huge drug bust.

On the other hand, he was more frightened than he'd ever been, even more than the time Tante Lulu got knocked out by a flying squirrel. Everyone had thought she was dead.

And Celine wasn't making things any better.

"Will you stop the damn pacing?" he snarled.

"Oh, now you're going to talk to me? Shove it!"

"Whoa! I get first dibs on anger. I'm the injured party here."

"Please! You can only play victim so long before you start to sound like a whiner. You remind me of your son when he's sulking."

"Lady, you are so close to—" His words halted on hearing a plane engine approaching.

Now Celine was the one who looked terrified. She was about to introduce her son to his father for the first time. Under normal circumstances, he would have felt sorry for her, but he was still too fuming mad to be sympathetic.

Tante Lulu had called him an hour ago to say Remy was bringing her and James Arseneaux and Etienne for a visit...just for the afternoon. She'd known how much he wanted to meet the boy in person and might not be able to leave this remote region for days, or weeks. Luc would be coming, too, at his request. He needed legal advice.

Remy landed the hydroplane neatly with a splash in front of the cabin. John sat on the steps, waiting. Normally, he would go down and help the passengers alight, but he needed these extra few minutes to observe his son before talking to him.

Remy was helping James Arseneaux and then Tante

Lulu get onto dry land. Celine waded into the edge of the stream and held out her arms for the boy.

His heart skipped a beat, then thundered against his chest walls. He could barely breathe.

Damn, he was cute. His dark hair was going every which way. He wore socks with athletic shoes that lit up with each bouncing step, red shorts, and a black *Pirates of the Caribbean* T-shirt. He was chattering like a magpie to his mother, mostly about the plane ride and how Remy had let him sit on his lap one time and steer the plane. Then, squirming out of his mother's arms, he began imitating an airplane by running around in figure eights, arms outspread, making a whirring sound. He stopped suddenly to lean over and examine a doodlebug, fascinated at the way it rolled into a ball when touched. Then he swirled around to look at the cabin. That's when he noticed him.

Everyone was watching him watch his son. He frowned at Remy as his brother guided Tante Lulu and James inside the cabin, all of them carrying bags filled with groceries. Luc soon followed, nodding to him with the silent message that they would talk later.

Celine remained, plopping down to the grass to sit cross-legged. She looked so frickin' scared. What? Did she think he was going to blurt out his paternity? Or was it his lawyer brother that had her biting her bottom lip?

Etienne stood on the first step and stared up at him. "Who are you?"

"John LeDeux," he said. "And you?"

"Etienne Arseneaux."

Shit! That was one thing that was going to change, and soon. His son would carry his surname, guaranteed.

He was still sitting on the top step, legs spread, hands clasped together between his knees.

Etienne sat down next to him, spread his legs, and clasped his little hands together, mimicking his posture.

John smiled and felt his heart expand like that Grinch at the end of "How the Grinch Stole Christmas." Speaking of which...rather, thinking of which...he wondered if Etienne liked Dr. Seuss, or was that too young for him?

"I know who you are." Etienne was craning his neck to look up at him.

"You do?" John's thundering heart jumped up another notch. He glanced over to Celine, who could hear everything they were saying. She had a hand over her heart, wondering, like him, who had told the boy.

"Yep. Yer a cop."

He let out a whooshy exhale, just realizing he'd been holding his breath. "And how do you know that, tiger?"

"My grampa tol' me there would be a cop here t'day. I kin spell cop. C-O-P."

"Wow! You must be really smart."

"I'm gonna be a cop someday."

"Oh, yeah. Why's that?"

"My daddy's a cop."

His eyes darted to Celine.

She shrugged.

"Really?"

"Uh-huh. And he's brave and big and likes ta go fishin'."

"Your mom tell you that, too?"

"Nope. I jist know. He's a pirate, too. He's gonna take me on his ship someday."

"A pirate and a cop, huh?"

"Mommy's friend David took us on a boat one time, but it weren't a pirate ship. Jist a motor boat. But David's cool. He bought me sparklers las' Fourth of July."

John reminded himself to ask Celine about this David guy later. There might not be a fiancé, but Celine had left out the skinny on a boyfriend. Big surprise! Not the first time she'd neglected to tell him something. He put that concern aside for now and asked hesitantly, "You ever met your dad?"

He shook his head, glancing sheepishly at his mother. "Mom doesn't like me ta ask 'bout him," he whispered as if it was their secret.

His jaw tightened before he gritted out, "Did she tell you that?"

"Nope. I jist know. She gets tears when I ask. Do you have a dog?"

"No, but I'm thinkin' 'bout gettin' one."

"Big or little?"

He pondered what would be the correct answer. "Big. Definitely big."

"Ya hafta clean up the poop if ya get a dog. Betcha a big dog makes big poop."

He reached over and ruffled the kid's hair. "That's some haircut you've got there, Etienne."

"I cut it myself."

"No kiddin'."

Etienne leaned over and whispered, "Don't tell Mom."

"I won't. She'll never know."

Tante Lulu came to the screen door and said, "I'm makin' a little lunch. It won't be ready fer a half hour or so."

"I've gotta get outta here," Remy added, coming out

onto the porch. "I'm picking up Ronnie and Jake at the airport as soon as I get back, then bringing them here."

He stood, and Remy came up, pulling him into a bear hug. "Take things slow, Tee-John," he husked into John's ear. "It'll all work out."

Luc came up to him next. "You want me to stay?"

He thought about it and said, "No, but do some preliminary work for me. Find out what my rights are ... that kind of thing."

Luc nodded. He, too, gave him a hug and promised that this whole mess would iron itself out.

John didn't see how.

They all waved Remy and Luc off.

By now Etienne had climbed a fig tree and was shaking the fruit out of one limb.

"Would you like to go fishin' for a while?" he asked, looking up.

"Yeees! Catch me."

Before John could even register that the boy was taking a flying leap, he held him in his arms. For a second, John allowed himself the luxury of holding his son tightly, breathing in the skin of his neck with its little boy scent.

Almost instantly, he was squirming to be let down. "Can Mom go fishin' with us?"

John's eyes connected with Celine's. He wanted to say no, couldn't in the circumstances. "Sure."

Thus it was that John found himself fishing with his son a short time later ... a son he hadn't even known existed more than a day ago. And they had fun, even Celine, who laughed when she reeled in a fish the size of a minnow. Etienne was ecstatic when he caught an eel, especially when he kept waving it in his cringing mother's face. A little devil, for sure. Etienne had been disappointed to know he couldn't take the eel home for a pet, to go with his worm collection.

James Arseneaux even came down to fish with them for a while, casting black looks John's way every once in a while. John, black-looking him right back, would have liked to tell the old man what he could do with his attitude, but Arseneaux probably reacted out of fear...that he was going to take the boy away from them. As well he might. After a while, James went back to the cabin, where he could be seen rocking on the porch, watching them like an eagle, drinking a glass of Tante Lulu's sweet tea.

"Thank you," Celine mouthed silently at one point.

"For what?"

"Making this easier than it could have been."

"I'm not done with you yet."

"You ever met a pirate?" Etienne asked him. He had a habit of blurting stuff out of the blue.

"Not lately...although we are working on a pirate project here. The pirate Lafitte."

Etienne's eyes and mouth both went wide. He couldn't have impressed the boy more, unless he'd announced he was Johnny Depp. "Kin I help?"

"Maybe later...or...," He looked at Celine, "maybe you could come back tomorrow or the next day and stay for a while."

"Ya mean overnight?"

"Uh-huh."

"Yippee!"

Celine glowered at him.

John probably should have asked her first before

mentioning it to Etienne. Big deal! He had a lot to learn about being a father, but that was her fault.

"Who was The Feet?" Etienne wanted to know when he calmed down a bit.

At first, John didn't understand, but then he smiled. "You mean Lafitte. Well, he was a hero and a scoundrel. He helped the Americans during the War of 1812. But he also stole from people, although it's been said that he only robbed the rich, and he gave lots to the poor. Besides that, he was a very handsome man, and the ladies loved him."

"Like Johnny Depp?"

"Just like."

The kid was adorable. Smart and funny and cute as hell.

"I was a pirate fer Halloween."

"Really? I was a pirate one year, too, when I was just about your size. Bet your costume was better than mine, though."

"It was cool, but I only had a fake sword. Mom wouldn't let me have a real one." He slanted his eyes at John, as if he could cajole him into buying him one.

"Not a chance," John said.

Etienne's little shoulders slumped.

"Come eat," Tante Lulu yelled from inside the screen door.

Her yelling caused James to jerk up with surprise and spill some of his drink. He must have dozed off.

The three of them were walking up the incline toward the cabin when Etienne put his hand in John's and said, "I wish you was my daddy."

Chapter
17

A chip off the ol' block, for sure...

Tante Lulu sat quietly, listening to the chatter around the table. James was also quiet, but that was probably because she'd given him a piece of her mind about keeping Etienne from his daddy and judging all the LeDeuxs by that bastard Valcour.

Etienne did most of the talking, happy as a pig in a mud puddle. He was a carbon copy of his daddy, just the way Tee-John had been at that age, except for those times Valcour had gone on a rampage. Tee-John wouldn't describe himself this way, but he was a survivor. All of them were...Luc, Remy, and René. Not so much Charmaine, since she was raised by her mother, though living with a stripper hadn't been much of a life, either.

"Why do ya call him Tee-John?" Etienne asked her.

" 'Cause he was such a little mite, like you," she answered. "That means Little-John in Cajun French."

Etienne craned his neck to look up at Tee-John, who sat on his right. "Ya ain't little no more."

"Nope." Tee-John looked pole-axed at all he'd been hit with today, but he also seemed pleased to have a son. Tante Lulu had expected no less.

"Do ya pee standin' up?" Etienne asked Tee-John all of a sudden.

Everyone about choked on their tongues, but Tee-John, bless his heart, answered straight-faced, "Mostly. How 'bout you?"

"Me, too."

The things chillen came out with sometimes.

"I want a dog."

"You already told me that," Tee-John said with a smile.

Etienne gave him that slant-eyed look again, and his mother scolded, "You'll get a dog when *I'm* ready. Stop asking people for a dog." She gave Tee-John a look that warned, *Don't you dare buy him a dog.*

Tee-John gave her a look right back that said, *I will if I want to.*

"I dint ask," Etienne argued with his mother.

"You implied."

"Did not." He looked indignant, or as indignant as a five-year-old could. "What's implied mean anyways?"

They all laughed.

"Ya cain't get a dog 'til ya learn ta treat 'em right," James added, his rheumy eyes twinkling.

"Graaampa, I tol' ya, Wiener is one ugly cat. I wuz jist doin' him a favor, paintin' him purple." He looked to Tante Lulu for sympathy. "Dontcha think purple is a good color fer an ugly cat?"

"Absolutely."

"Wiener is another name fer a too-too," he elaborated.

Tante Lulu's lips twitched with humor. "I know."

"I would never name my dog after a too-too."

"I would hope not, chile."

Tee-John made a low choking sound, trying to stifle his laughter.

"When's yer birthday, honey?" Tante Lulu asked.

"November 11. Wanna come ta my party?"

"Are ya havin' a party, sweetie?"

"Prob'ly." He eyed his mother as if daring her to disagree. "Betcha I get a dog fer my birthday."

They all groaned at his persistence.

You could say he was kinda horsey...

Things had gone better than Celine had expected.

Oh, it was still a catastrophe, having John find out about Etienne, especially in this manner. But even her grandfather had told her that maybe John wasn't too bad, even if he was Valcour LeDeux's "stinkin' whelp." Now, if only the threat of a lawsuit weren't hanging over her.

Remy was going to bring Etienne back day after tomorrow for an overnight stay. John had promised to let him help on the Pirate Project. Celine had voiced concern that Etienne would get in the way, but Ronnie assured her it would be okay, as long as Celine or John kept an eye on him. After all, her own little girl had been on projects with her and Jake many times. They were a family-oriented bunch.

Of course John still wasn't talking to her, unless he had to.

The project was going extremely well, though. Ronnie and Jake had brought back sturdy two-gallon plastic boxes to hold the gold coins...seven of them filled so far with antique gold coins, mostly Spanish doubloons, probably made at the end of the seventeenth century. The value had to exceed a million dollars, but their historical provenance might double that amount.

To everyone's surprise, Angel had been involved in construction at one time, and his talents were put to use, sketching the arena, and documenting what was found where, in what position. His drafting skills gave the drawings a precision none of them would have been able to accomplish, even with computers.

"I heard your little boy was here today," Grace said, taking a brief rest from the photography work she'd taken over.

Celine saved the data she'd been inputting into the laptop, then turned to Grace.

"Yes, and he's John's son, too," she admitted, knowing they all probably knew by now anyway.

"So I heard. How's John taking it?"

"As far as Etienne is concerned, great. As far as I'm concerned, not so well."

They both glanced over at John, who had been digging ever since they came back to the site this afternoon, probably to work off his anger. It wasn't working. He pointedly ignored Celine, but gave Grace a little wave.

They all looked like mud babies. What a mess! Except for John, who managed to appear handsome in mud.

"I'll tell you something that I told John a little while ago," Grace said, drawing Celine out of her reverie. "When I was fifteen, before I entered the convent, I had an abortion. No, no, don't say anything. I forgave myself a long time ago. But what John needs to know is that lots of women today, in your situation, would have had an abortion. But you didn't. And it had to be hard."

More than you could imagine. Tears welled in Celine's eyes. "What did he say to that?"

Grace laughed. "What you'd expect. Four letters, and it didn't spell 'good.' Honey, it's the failure to tell him that has him so upset, not Etienne himself. He'll get over it."

"Ya think?"

Grace laughed again. "Eventually."

It was Ronnie who commiserated with her then. Squeezing her shoulder, she sat down beside her on a folding camp chair. "Been able to get anything done with all you've been hit with today?"

"Actually, work helps to get my mind off...things."

"You're right."

"Even though it's not accepted procedure, I've decided to pass my articles by you before publication. For accuracy and respect for privacy issues. I want you to be able to trust me." Since trust seemed to be lacking from another quarter.

"I'll tell the gang. I know they've felt uncomfortable about what you might disclose about their private lives."

"Especially John."

"Especially John," Ronnie agreed. "Keep this in mind, John is a good guy. He'll do the right thing."

That's what scared Celine. "What is the right thing?"

Ronnie shrugged. "I just meant that he's not going to do anything that would hurt you or your son."

"Maybe not Etienne, but..."

"Take it from someone who's been married and divorced to the same man four times. This is only a speed bump in your love life."

"Oh, we aren't in love, or anything even close. In fact, look closely, and you'll see pure hundred proof hatred shooting out of John's eyes right now."

"You know what they say about that fine line between love and hate."

"You're beginning to sound like Tante Lulu."

Ronnie laughed. "Bet she's planning the wedding already."

"She would like to, but I told her, and John told her, that it isn't going to happen."

"That's not going to stop her."

Celine groaned.

Jake, Angel, Adam, and even Caleb came up to offer their opinions and advice to her, too. All of it pretty much the same thing. Hold on, things would work out.

The question was: What did things "working out" mean?

Finally, John strode up to her and demanded, "So, is everyone tellin' you that you're Mother Teresa and I'm a horse's ass?"

She blinked with surprise. *"Whaaat?"*

"You heard me. I've seen everyone comin' up to you, all sweet-like, pattin' your shoulder, givin' you hugs, then turnin' to glare at me."

"That's ridiculous. You're the one who's glaring."

He was standing, hands on hips, while she sat...a domineering position. "Meet me downstream from the cabin after dinner. We need to talk."

"About what?"

"You can't be that dumb." With those insulting words,

he turned away from her and was heading back to dig some more.

"By the way, John," she called to his back. "You *are* a horse's ass."

He wasn't ready to make nice...

John wished he'd been able to go off by himself after his son left this afternoon, but work had called, especially when Ronnie and Jake arrived.

As a result, he'd felt as if he were walking a gauntlet of questions, congratulations, sympathy, advice, and all around intrusiveness from the project members. And he hadn't had a chance to vent his spleen with Celine yet...not fully.

If he had his druthers...a Tante Lulu word, for sure...he would be off drinking himself into a knee-walking stupor. Unfortunately, there was no strong booze here. And he'd never been that much into drinking his pain away.

Famosa had shocked the hell out of him by confiding, "I had a kid once."

"What?" he'd practically squawked. "What do you mean...*had?*"

"I got this girl pregnant when I was in college...like you. But unlike you, Molly told me right away."

"Oh, please, don't start bein' nice to me, Famosa. I don't think I could take it."

Ignoring him, although he'd probably have liked to flick him the bird, Famosa had continued, "Know what I did?"

"I don't want to know. Go away."

"I slapped five hundred dollars in her hand and said it wasn't my problem."

"Is this supposed to have some relevance to me?"

"Shut up, redneck, and listen for once. I assumed she had gotten rid of the kid. Hell, I probably just didn't want to know. A few years ago, I ran into Molly...a heart surgeon now at Johns Hopkins. Turns out she had the baby...a girl...with spina bifida."

"Oh, my God!"

"She only lived three months, but Molly stayed by her side in the hospital twenty-four/seven. Where was I? Probably on summer break...skin diving in the Bahamas."

"Oh, my God!" he'd said again.

"The message here, LeDeux: I never got a chance to correct my mistake. You have a living, breathing, healthy son. There were mistakes all around. Grow the hell up."

Now John was waiting for Celine to finish dinner and meet him for a heart-to-heart. He hadn't been able to eat himself, too agitated by the day's events.

He was sitting on a dead cypress tree. There were lots of fallen tress in the bayou, always replenished by new ones. And, yes, he'd checked for snakes before sitting down. They'd come across at least a dozen today while digging for the gold, only one of which had been poisonous, but Peachey had taken to popping antacids after the first three.

The moss hanging from the live oaks lining the banks swayed in a slight breeze. Creepy. Like a dead woman's hair. Any other time, he would see the beauty in this swamp land, but this evening it just seemed gloomy and gray.

Celine came up on him without warning. Usually he was more alert. She studied the log for a moment, then must have figured it had to be safe if he was sitting. She plopped down next to him.

"Tell me about Etienne. From the beginning. And I mean before he was born. Did you give birth in a hospital? Which one? Was it a long labor? How much did he weigh? Did you nurse him? Does he have a middle name?"

She stared at him steadily, unsure if he really wanted all the details.

He did.

"I found out I was pregnant when I was three months along. You had used a condom, in case you thought you hadn't."

"I wasn't that blitzed."

"Whatever. We both had too much to drink."

"Did you ever consider telling me?"

"I did. I wrote a note and left it in your apartment mailbox, asking you to call me. You never did."

He frowned. "When was that?"

"Early June. Finals week, actually."

"Celine! I'd already left for Jersey. All my class work and tests were taken early. I didn't even bother to come back for graduation."

"Surely someone would have passed the message on to you."

"Are you kidding? You expect that kind of reliability from college guys? During the chaotic tail end of the school year? I never got your message." He stared at her incredulously. "And that was your only attempt?"

"A couple months later, Gramps sent me a local newspaper photo of you winning some dance contest at Swampy's Tavern. You had your arm around a woman...it seemed telling to me."

He furrowed his brow, trying to remember, then exclaimed, "Ferchrissake! It was Charmaine, my sister."

"How was I to know that? You looked so carefree, so wild, so you. I figured there was no room for a baby in your life...especially a baby born of a one-night stand."

"Don't even freakin' try to say you were doin' me a favor."

"I wasn't. It was my baby I was doing a favor."

"You had no right—"

She stood and was about to walk away. "Look, this is accomplishing nothing. You want a blame fest...write me a letter."

"I'm sorry." He motioned for her to sit back down. "Did you ever consider an abortion?"

"I did. I won't lie about it. I was scared, and I had no money. No clue how to care for a baby." She shrugged.

There was a story there. John just knew it. But that could wait 'til later. "And?"

"I couldn't do it."

"Why?"

"Dammit! Give me a break here, John. I had your baby. That's all you need to know."

"I don't think so. What happened after that?"

"I had to tell my grandfather."

"Oh, boy, that must have been fun, especially with his opinion of the LeDeuxs."

"You have no idea!" She laughed in remembrance. "I had lived with my grandfather since I was in tenth grade, after my parents died."

John recalled that Celine's dad had committed suicide

and wondered how that had played into all the decisions she'd made later. A fifteen-year-old girl had to have felt abandoned. Was that one of the reasons she'd chosen to keep Etienne?

"I knew my grandfather's opinion of the LeDeuxs, and my having sex with one of them spelled betrayal of the highest order. But once he calmed down, he offered to take care of me and the baby, let me go back to finish college, give me all the support I needed, financial and otherwise. Provided I never involved you or any of the LeDeuxs in Etienne's life."

He wanted to rail at her for agreeing to such an immoral act, but stopped himself.

"I was in labor for twelve hours, but it was a natural childbirth, not caesarian. And his middle name is John."

He nodded his thanks for that small favor.

"His favorite movie is *Pirates of the Caribbean*."

"Isn't that a bit adult for a kid his age? Oh, don't get your mouth all pruned up. I wasn't questioning your parental choices."

"Pruned up?" She fought a smile. "He watches the bleeped-over version. Seventeen times so far."

"To show how far removed I am from kid-dom, I didn't even known there were curse-deleted DVDs. This I've gotta see, though. Johnny Depp saying 'darn.'" There was a lot he was going to have to learn about being a parent, and quickly, he realized. That was assuming he was going to be involved. "I guess that means I need to clean up my language around him."

"Yep. He's like a parrot. Repeats everything he hears, especially if he thinks they might be bad words. His favorite kind."

"My father swore like a sailor. Still does. Every sentence has to have a foul word. And he never gave a rat's ass if I was around or not. In fact, I think he taught me the F-word when I was Etienne's age." He hadn't meant to reveal all that and glanced quickly to Celine to see if she was maybe thinking he didn't have the genes to be a good father. Or that he was engaging in a pity party.

"I have to watch my language, too," she said. "We all slip sometimes."

"Stop being gracious, dammit."

"And that's a problem...why?"

"I don't want you bein' nice to me, because then I would have to be nice, and I'm still too upset to be nice."

"You think you don't know much about...uh, what did you call it?...kid-dom, but that was pure kid-speak nonsense."

"Maybe that's not such a bad thing...that I still have some kid in me."

"You're right. Etienne will love having a father who's still a kid."

Was she insulting him?

She put a hand on his forearm and squeezed.

He shoved her hand away.

They sat in silence for a few long moments, surrounded by the heady smells of lush flowers, trees, and the stream itself. They watched as the evening rituals of the bayou started up. The nighttime animals were beginning to come out. Bats, of course. Dozens of varieties of frogs, each with its own distinctive sound; René could probably identify them just by their vocal cords. There were other nocturnal creatures: flying squirrels, owls, foxes, skunks, opossums, raccoons. They would have to go back to the cabin soon, before the mosquitoes were out in full force.

"This all comes at the piss-poor worst time for me. See what I mean about my language? I said that without thinkin'. Anyhow, I can't plan anything until this trial is over. Even if the chief allowed me to come back now, I wouldn't be able to be around you and Etienne or my family 'til the Dixie Mafia guys are no longer a threat to any of you. They'd like nothin' better than to get at me through someone I cared about. Afterward, though, I'll need to be around Etienne."

"I'm more than willing to have you visit, or even have him come to stay with you occasionally on weekends or vacations."

"What planet are you livin' on, babe? I meant live with me. You can visit him, not the other way around."

"You can't be serious. I wouldn't give up custody of Etienne, and don't even think of threatening me with legal action. No court is going to take a child from its mother just because she didn't inform the father of paternity."

"Don't be so sure about that. Fathers have rights, too."

"You don't know the first thing about raising a child."

"I'll learn. Besides, I have a good lawyer."

"Would you be so cruel as to separate a child from its mother?"

"Would you be so cruel as to separate a child from its father?"

"John, you're not thinking straight."

"No kidding. You drop a bomb and expect me to be clear-headed and logical." His voice rose to a falsetto as he continued, mimicking her now, "By the way, John. You have a son. Now, be nicey-nice. I'll let you come over for a play date sometime if you're good," followed by, "Shiiit!"

She inhaled and exhaled several times, clearly trying to tamp down her temper. Well, la de da, he was in a temper, too.

"Listen, I haven't thought this through yet, but why can't Etienne move into my cottage? You could see him whenever you want. Hell, you can stay overnight sometimes if you want."

She laughed. She actually laughed at him. "That's big of you. Bet your girlfriends will love that."

"Stop bein' so sarcastic."

"Who's going to watch Etienne when you're working?"

"I'll get someone."

"That's just great. His father's a stranger, and he'll hire strangers to stay with him."

"Okay, Ms. Know-it-all. Let's compromise. What are you willin' to give up?"

Her chin went up, and her jaw jutted out.

"Okay, maybe that was a bit drastic. How 'bout he lives with you weekdays, but he lives with me all other times, when I don't have to work. Weekends, holidays, summer vacation." He congratulated himself on how generous he was being, considering his fury.

"Never! Even if I were willing, it would be too disruptive to Etienne's routine. No way!"

"Even I know how resilient kids are."

"He wouldn't understand."

Okay, I tried. Enough with the generosity. "Bullshit!

He's a smart kid. He halfway suspects by now that I'm his dad."

"This is ridiculous. You've only just met your son and you're making all these plans. What about the DNA tests?"

"I still want the tests done, but I'd have to be blind not to see the resemblance."

Now that she was going to have to dump her idea of winning by default...as in his not claiming his son...she tried a different tack. "Have you considered how this would change your life, or even if you want it to change? Slow down, for heaven's sake."

"How can I slow down? I've already lost five years."

Her face went mulish. Well, he could be mulish, too.

John stood. He'd had enough of this crap. Before he walked away, he told her, "I would suggest you hire a lawyer."

Chapter
18

They wanted him to testify, and, boy, did he testify!...

John's personal life was put on hold the next day with the order to return to town immediately, incognito, and report to the courthouse in Baton Rouge. The trial had been sped up and was about to begin.

He wasn't the only one required to go to all these convoluted lengths in order to testify. There were at least a dozen others, including the police, ATF, and FBI. They would be without disguises once on the stand, but coming to and leaving the courthouse, they were sitting ducks for Mafia snipers.

At this point, it was the upper hierarchy that were on trial: the club manager who was considered a "soldier," a counselor or consiglieri, an accountant, and two sons of the "godfather," who acted as "lieutenants." They were being charged with prostitution, narcotics (one kilo of coke found on the premises), gambling (a slot machine in the back), blackmail, extortion, bribery, racketeering, possession of illegal firearms, and various other sundry crimes, like resisting arrest and disorderly conduct, the hope being that at least some of the charges would stick. Ten "soldiers" had already been tried and sentenced for lesser crimes, which meant they would probably be out of jail in a year.

The cases against customers of the club and lower level employees had already been adjudicated in lower courts, most of whom only got a bullet, or one year, negotiated down to probation and hefty fines. A night in the holding pen had been enough to scare the bejesus out of most of them. Prostitutes...those who hadn't copped a deal with the prosecution...had been fined or given summary jail sentences.

Celine was pissed, to say the least, that she hadn't been able to contact a lawyer yet and that she wasn't being permitted to attend the trial as a reporter. It had been her story to begin with, she'd complained endlessly last night. As a concession, the chief was giving her an exclusive background story every day for the next week to call in to the newspaper, provided she didn't tell her boss where she was getting the confidential info, or that she'd been in hiding with Police Detective John LeDeux.

If it had been up to him, he would have told her to go fly a kite.

John got prepped in one of the side rooms before being called to the stand late that afternoon. Tank had gone just before him. As they passed in the hall, Tank rolled his eyes, indicating that John was in for it.

John's role in the investigation and bust had been minimal, but the defense lawyers were gunning for him, probably considering him an easy mark because of his reputation. Although cameras were not permitted inside, John could see that an artist was sketching him. God only knows what label they would put on him today, even though he was dressed respectably in a navy blue jacket, khaki pants, a button shirt, and a tie. He even wore wire-rimmed reading glasses, for effect. A regular *GQ* geek cop.

The prosecutor, Dean Avery, led him through the easy questions to set forth his part in the case. Then one of the defense lawyers...there were six...laid into him. The cross-examination was brutal, led by Rita Nicastro, Esquire, from New York City, a plump thirty-something woman with a mustache, poured into a no-nonsense gray suit.

"Is it true, Detective LeDeux, that you were once a stripper in Atlantic City?"

Whoa! This one went for the element of surprise. "Yes, ma'am." He put special emphasis on the "ma'am." He could tell that annoyed her. "For two weeks, *ma'am*."

She arched her bushy eyebrows, mostly for the benefit of the jurors. "Got fired, did you?"

"No, *ma'am*. I quit."

"Oh, why was that? Too shy?" A titter of laughter passed through the courtroom.

"Your honor," the prosector objected. "What does his shyness have to do with this case?"

The judge waved the objection aside.

"Hardly shy. Nope, I only did it on a bet."

"A bet? So, you're a gambling man. No, don't answer that. Were you in the Playpen on a bet, too?"

"No, *ma'am*. That was my job."

"Your job was to be a prostitute?"

"To *pretend* to be a prostitute."

"Are you saying you never had sex for hire?"

"Never."

"And if I were to say there were several women who would testify that you did?"

"They would be liars...*ma'am*. Or paid to testify to that effect."

"Your honor, I object!" Ms. Nicastro and five other lawyers shouted.

"Sustained," the judge said. "None of your lip, Detective LeDeux. Stick to answering the questions."

He'd known Judge Lightley for ages. In fact, he and his son Fred, better known as Zippo, had been friends in high school.

"Yes, sir."

"You testified earlier that you witnessed both men and women paying for sexual favors. Could you be more explicit?"

He raised his eyebrows and looked at the judge.

Judge Lightley sighed and said, "Go ahead...within reason. Keep in mind, there are ladies in the room."

John had been prepared for this question, and he wrung his hands virtually with anticipated pleasure. "I saw Mimi Delacroix, one of the prostitutes—"

"I object!" said six lawyers. Ms. Nicastro added, "Miss Delacroix has not been proven to be a prostitute."

"Beggin' your pardon, *ma'am,* but Miss Delacroix has a rap sheet a mile long."

The judge put up a halting hand before the defense lawyers could object again. "Detective LeDeux, this is a second warning. Answer the questions. No opinions. Jurors, you will disregard that characterization."

He nodded. "I saw Miss Delacroix go down on six men for fifty bucks a pop. She did a figure eight on another man and a corkscrew on yet another, both for a hundred bucks each."

There was a collective gasp throughout the courtroom.

"Then, there was Suzy Foo. For twenty bucks, she sucked the toes of a woman lawyer from Biloxi. Don't get your knickers in a twist, Ms. Nicastro; I didn't name the female lawyer.

"Elaine Hebert engaged in a *ménage à trois* with two men, but declined to do their dog. It was a German Shepherd. The going price for threesomes was three hundred dollars.

"Then there were the men. Jasper Wilson was the most popular. Whoo-boy, that man could get mondo erections. Women didn't mind payin' the two hundred dollars for a half hour of his time, if their smiles on exiting were any indication.

"Jules Sebastian was in the process of havin' a sex change operation. So, those with a taste for acey/deucy got him for a bargain fifty bucks.

"Jon Paul Savonne spoke French while doin' the deed, and got some uptown ladies to pay a hundred dollars for the lagniappe.

"Evan Sinclair had a tongue like that guy from Kiss. Need I say more? He was almost as popular as Jasper."

The courtroom was going wild with laughter and talking while he blathered on, ignoring the pounding of the gavel, the objections of the lawyers, and the prosecutor's staff putting their faces in their hands. Newspaper reporters were grinning from ear to ear, taking notes frenetically.

When the judge and the bailiff finally brought the courtroom back to order, Judge Lightley glared at him.

"Are you aware that you are this close—" He held a thumb and forefinger about one inch apart. "—to sitting in the lockup for contempt? And I don't just mean for the day."

"Sorry, your honor."

"Lawyers, up here *now* for a sidebar. Detective LeDeux, do you think you could manage to keep your mouth shut 'til we're done?"

"Yes, sir."

After the consultation, the prosecutor gave John a silent message to behave himself, and all six defense lawyers gave him a pointed glower.

He was still sitting in the witness chair when the judge turned back to him. "Detective LeDeux, this trial is not a joke. You will limit your remarks to direct answers to questions." He turned to the jury then and said, "Jurors, you are to disregard the inflammatory nature of Detective LeDeux's testimony." Hah! Like they were ever going to forget those descriptions!

After that, John was grilled on how he had witnessed these activities. "Through a peephole."

"Are you a voyeur?"

"No. Except…" He glanced at the judge for permission to elaborate.

"Go ahead," Judge Lightley said on a long sigh.

"Except I like the occasional X-rated movie."

Ms. Nicastro named the five defendants in the case and asked if he had ever witnessed any illegal activities in which they had been directly involved.

He gave specific dates, times, and what he had seen.

At the end, she got him to say that he was temporarily off duty with the police force, the implication being he had done something wrong.

"Where do you reside at the present time?"

John hesitated and gave his father's address in Houma. He'd like to see some Mafia thug try to take his dad down.

Ms. Nicastro frowned. "Are you saying that you have been living there for the past three weeks?"

"Not exactly. I'm...uh, on vacation."

"Where are you vacationing?"

"Here and there."

"Your honor," Ms. Nicastro complained to the judge. The judge glanced at him. "Well?"

"I've been fishin'." That was at least partially true, and here in southern Louisiana, "gone fishin'" was a legitimate excuse for just about anything.

"With Detective Woodrow?"

"Nah. His here and there for fishin' is different from my here and there."

The judge declared that would be a sufficient answer, knowing full well why the Mafia wanted to know where he was hiding.

"You're excused, Detective LeDeux." Under his breath, the judge added, "God help us all."

That night, the evening newspapers headlined him: "Cajun Cop Adds Sizzle to Trial."

The things kids say...

It took another day before John was able to leave Baton Rouge, what with all the meetings with his department, as well as the prosecutor's. Once the prosecutor, Dean Avery, had reamed him out, they had a good laugh together over his testimony.

Now, he was sitting in Remy's helicopter at a small Dallas private airport with his son at his side. They would be flying to Remy's home heliport and from there taking the hydroplane to the cabin. For him, 'til the trial was over and the bad guys were in jail. For Etienne, just an overnight visit.

The kid was so excited as the copter took off, it was a good thing he was belted in or he would have been bouncing up and down. No fear at all. Just talk, talk, talk.

"I have a toy helicopter. David gave it to me. Wanna play with it sometime?"

"Do you have a gun? Didja ever shoot any bad guys?"

"I want a dog."

"I'm hungry."

"I'm thirsty."

"I hafta pee."

"Where's my mom?"

"Kin I sleep with you t'night in a tent?"

"Betcha I kin catch five fishes next time. My friend Pete dint believe I caught an eel. Maybe we could take some pictures."

"I want a dog."

"My grampa has a big bubble by his too-too...a her-knee-yah."

"David has a big too-too. I saw it when we peed against a tree at the campsite."

"Wanna piece of bubble gum?"

"Do you have any tattoos? I really wanna get a tattoo. A pirate one. Or else I wanna get a peg leg."

"My mom has curly hair over her pee-pee."

"Do girls fart? My mom says only boys fart, but Pete sez his sister Glory Ann cuts the cheese in her sleep."

"I want a dog."

By the time they arrived back at the cabin, about noon, John was wondering if the kid ever shut up, and where did he come up with some of this stuff? Remy, on the other hand, could barely control his laughter...not at Etienne, but at him having a son who was going to be as wild and outrageous as he ever was.

Celine and Tante Lulu were waiting for them. The rest of the team was working at the site.

Wading to the plane, Celine lifted out her son. Then she kissed him and hugged him as if she hadn't seen him or talked to him for years, instead of days.

The boy skipped—he never just walked—up to the cabin alongside Tante Lulu, who tempted him with the offer of beignets and chocolate milk. Remy went off to see the progress of the Pirate Project. Leaving John alone with Celine.

"I heard you were your usual charming self at the trial."

And he, charming devil that he was, snarled out, "Who the hell is David?"

Talking to the Cajun brick wall...

Celine stayed back at the cabin with Tante Lulu while John took Etienne to the work site, with the promise of lots of mud and pirate gold.

She soon realized what a mistake that was when Tante Lulu started in on her.

The two of them were washing up, drying, and packing the morning stash of gold coins into storage containers. Not as much as the first finds, yesterday and the day before, but still impressive. There were also a few necklaces and rings in this last batch. Nothing spectacular, and all of it gold. No precious stones. Still, a nice change.

"Ya gonna marry up with this David fella?"

She rolled her eyes. *Here we go again.* "No. He's just a friend."

"Etienne talks about him a lot."

That little stinker. "He talks about the garbage man a lot, too."

"So, what kinda friend is he? The sleepin' over kind?"

"I am not going to answer that question. We date occasionally. He's a reporter on assignment in Afghanistan right now."

"Well then, ya gonna marry up with Tee-John?"

Good grief, she's persistent. "No."

"Why not?"

Aaarrgh! Because he hates me, for one thing. "I'm not in love with him," she blurted out, as if it had anything to do with anything.

"You will be."

Is that a fate worse than death, or a fate to be desired? "You can't know that."

"The thunderbolt has already struck, honey."

Celine would like to tell her what she could do with that darn thunderbolt.

"Besides, St. Jude is already a-workin'. You Catholic, hon?"

"I was baptized Catholic, but I've lapsed."

"Once a Catholic, always a Catholic."

There was no sense arguing with the old lady.

"A mommy and daddy should be together with their chile."

"Lots of single parents raise children today."

"Not in my fam'ly."

"You can't force things just because you want them a certain way."

"Won't be no forcin' necessary when the thunderbolt and St. Jude are at yer back. I already started on yer bride quilt. Since ya doan have a mama, I figger Charmaine kin give ya advice, be the mother of the bride, that kinda thing."

Charmaine, the quintessential bimbo? "That's nice."

"That Tee-John is gonna make the prettiest groom. Whoo-ee, the gals from here ta Texas gonna be cryin' when he walks down the aisle."

"I thought it was the bride who walked down the aisle, and she's the one supposed to be pretty."

"That goes without sayin'. I gots an antique weddin' gown that was never used iffen ya might be interested."

Tante Lulu made that offer in an offhand manner, but Celine could tell it was important to her. Was it possible . . . ? "Yours?"

Tante Lulu nodded.

"Me 'n Phillipe was gonna be married when he got home from the war, but he died on D-day."

"If I were going to be married—and I'm not—I would be honored to wear your gown. However, you're a lot smaller than me."

"I usta be taller. I had boobs and a butt at one time, too. Anyways, gowns can be altered ta fit. I'll show it to ya next time yer back at my place."

This conversation was making her way too uncomfortable. "Listen, Tante Lulu, you should know that John is talking about a lawsuit."

Tante Lulu waved a hand dismissively. "He's jist upset. He'll come around."

Celine wasn't so sure about that. "I think I'll go see how Etienne is doing at the work site."

"One more thing," Tante Lulu said. "Thank you."

"For what?"

"Etienne. He's the bestest gift I've had in a long while."

It was with tears in her eyes that Celine left.

The joys of parenthood, oh, my!...

Fatherhood was wearing a bit thin for John.

Picking up the little snot by the belt at the back of his shorts, he carried him over to the stream and dropped him in to wash off about ten pounds of mud.

Sputtering and laughing, Etienne stood in the shallow water and said, "Do it again."

"No. That's enough. You've gotta settle down, Etienne. You don't throw mud. You don't say bad words when someone corrects you. You don't put gold coins in your mouth. And the next time I say, 'Come here!' I mean *now*."

"Yer mean." His bottom lip quivered, and he burst out bawling.

"Oh, God! Now what?" He picked him up, sopping wet, and began to carry him the short distance to the work site camp. Halfway there, Etienne stopped crying and struggling, laid his head on his shoulder, and went limp. Totally asleep. Just like that. Tantrum to zonkers in one second flat. Meanwhile, the whole front of John was wet.

He'd just laid Etienne down on a pallet inside one of the tents and sunk to the ground outside with exhaustion, when Celine showed up.

"What's wrong?" she asked, her voice shrill with concern.

"Shhhh. He's asleep."

She peered inside. Then, satisfied that her son was all right, she sank down to the ground next to him. "So? What happened?"

"Nothing. He just had a meltdown after two hours of Energizer Bunny nonstop activity."

"In other words, the usual."

"How does your grandfather handle him?"

"He has help, and Etienne goes to play school three mornings a week. In the fall, he starts kindergarten. But, yeah, by the time I get home, my grandfather is beat. You have to understand, though, Etienne is being well cared for. I'm lucky to have my grandfather's help."

"I wasn't criticizing."

"I've been thinking about what you suggested yesterday. Maybe, instead of lawyers, we should be talking to a mediator."

"In order to mediate, you have to be willing to compromise. So far, all I've heard is how I need to go slow and be nice. I've been nice for twenty-eight freakin' years. Time for some bad." Even he realized how juvenile that last sounded, but like his son, he was having a meltdown, too, except his couldn't be corrected with a nap.

"I am not going to let Etienne live with you; that is totally off the table. Furthermore, I can't let him stay with you for any extended period of time, either, not 'til I see how...well, how things go."

"Why don't you say what you really mean?"

"I mean, I can't be sure you'll even want to be a real father, once the novelty wears off. And I can't have him exposed to your lifestyle."

"Now you've gone too far. What do you think I do in my spare time? Engage in orgies? Oh, God, you do, don't you?"

Her face pinkened with embarrassment. "Not orgies, precisely, but a steady parade of women."

"Unbelievable...that's what you are. Celine, I hadn't had carnal knowledge with a woman for a month before we did the deed."

"A whole month? Poor deprived boy!"

He gritted his teeth before speaking again. "Be careful of that corner you're backin' yourself into, *chère*."

"I won't be threatened by you."

"That wasn't a threat. Just a bit of friendly advice."

"John, be reasonable—"

"I'm tired of being reasonable, too."

"A couple hours in his company and you're already wiped out."

"I'll get better." Then he muttered under his breath, "I better."

She smiled at him.

She had a really nice smile. And he hated that he

couldn't allow himself to like her smile. "You know, I was startin' to like you before you pulled this crap."

"Same here."

They were both quiet for a while.

"What do you mean, 'same here'?" Man, he was pitiful. She'd just about gut punched him with the news of his son, betrayed him essentially, and made him so mad he had to clench his fists to keep from shaking her, and here he was asking if she liked him.

"I mean the same thing you did. I was starting to like you. It might have led to something more. No, it wouldn't have. But still, my opinion of you was changing a bit."

"Was there a compliment in there somewhere?"

She glanced at him, and smiled again.

Which caused his little ol' heart to go all fluttery. Jeesh! "I'm still angry at you, and I'm still gonna make you pay, and you're gonna wish you never met me."

"Actually, that would never happen, John." Her face was all serious and misty-eyed now. "Because if I'd never met you, there would never have been an Etienne, and, like your aunt said, he's a gift."

He hated to admit it to himself, but John was touched. With a cough to clear his throat, he said, "I think our gift is stirring."

Chapter
19

They could all become pirates...or not!...

After dinner, Celine sat at the table talking with all the adults, while Etienne played a video game on a minuscule black-and-white TV set over in the corner. Everyone was pretending to ignore the glaring tension between her and John.

"Exactly how much gold have we recovered so far?" Ronnie asked Adam.

"Roughly a thousand gold coins, an equal amount of silver, and a half dozen items of jewelry," Adam answered. "Mostly Spanish doubloons, but some silver reales, and coins from a few other countries. Dutch, French, Portuguese."

"A cursory search on the Internet," piped in Celine, who had been able to put her computer geek skills to good use, "estimates the value in the range of two to three million."

"It'll be even higher if we can establish the provenance to Lafitte through one of those unusual neck-laces," Caleb pointed out.

"I have a jewelry expert friend of mine working on that right now," Adam said.

"Celine, some of us have been talking," Jake began, "and we don't think you should run your story 'til there's a verdict in the trial and the bad guys are in jail." She was about to object...that could take weeks, but Jake continued, "You gotta know that once we announce this treasure and where it was located, reporters and every looney bird Harrison Ford wannabe is gonna flock to Bayou Black. The Mafia thugs might deduce, just by proximity to René LeDeux's cabin, that John has been hiding out here."

"Won't there always be that threat to John?" she asked, not looking at him, suddenly realizing that she had ammunition against his custody threats. She and Etienne would always be at risk, just by association with him.

"No, there won't," John insisted. "No more than a lawyer who prosecutes a criminal, or a stockbroker who loses a pigload of money for a client through no fault of his own, or a newspaper reporter who offends just about every breathing body in the universe." He cast her a "So there!" smirk.

Celine wasn't convinced of his logic, but she would save that argument for later.

"We've come to trust you, Celine," Ronnie added. "Therefore, I see no reason why you can't return to your home, *provided* that you assure us there will be no story 'til we give the go-ahead...and, of course, don't men-tion John's involvement. John's boss called a little bit ago and gave his okay, reluctantly."

She nodded, although she wasn't sure her editor would agree to the delay. In fact, she could lose her job over the issue.

"René is gonna have a bird tryin' to keep them amateur treasure hunters from trampin' around his precious bayou," John pointed out.

"We'll try our best not to be specific about the discovery site, and we'll alert the state to set up 'No Trespassing' signs all along Bayou Black," Ronnie said. "That won't eliminate the problem, but it should alleviate it."

"I think we should have a big party, Cajun style, to announce the Pirate Project treasures," Tante Lulu interjected, changing the subject, as usual. "A reg'lar *fais do-do*, a party down on the bayou." She was walking around the table, refilling glasses of lemonade, sweet tea, or rhubarb wine.

"If it's anything like the one we did for the cave pearl project, we can work it to our advantage. Great press for Jinx, Inc., and control of how the story is presented to the media." Caleb glanced sheepishly at Celine. "In fact, maybe our resident newshound could help us with that."

"Maybe," she hedged. She'd already crossed the line between objectivity and bias long ago on this story.

"Hey, I have a great idea," Angel said. "I have some Hells Angels pals—"

"Angel is big into motorcycles," Grace interjected, as if Angel needed her backup.

"Some of these bikers are heavily involved in pirate crap. I mean, they have their own reenactment events, and Web sites on how to talk pirate and how to hook up with other pirates. This whole phenomenon is called pirattitude," Angel explained. "They probably figure that bikers are modern-day pirates."

"It could be great fun." Tante Lulu was practically dancing with glee. "In fact, we could all dress up like pirates."

There were some groans around the table, Adam and Caleb both demurring on their actually donning such hokey costumes... although Tante Lulu would probably talk them into it.

"And you could get an exclusive," Ronnie told her, the message being, you rub our back, we rub yours.

Just then the bleeping of the video game stopped and Etienne sidled up to Angel, apparently having heard the word *pirate*. "Do you know Johnny Depp?"

Angel laughed and said, "No."

Finding Angel no longer interesting, he walked over to Celine and climbed up onto her lap. In one of the brief silences, Etienne announced, "John was makin' googly eyes at my mom t'day when she wasn't lookin'. Pete says boys and girls make googly eyes when they wanna make babies." He made loud kissing noises for those who didn't get the whole picture, which was no one.

Laughter erupted around the table.

Encouraged by this show of appreciation, Etienne elaborated, "Girls give boys cooties when they kiss."

"This from Pete again, I suppose," John said.

"Yep. Did you ever get cooties?" the bundle of big-mouth joy in her lap asked John.

"Lots of times."

"Eeeh! *My* mom never kissed a boy."

"Is that a fact?" John remarked, glancing her way.

"Uh-huh. She tol' me."

She sat there, her face turning five shades of red, she suspected.

Everyone was laughing, which made Etienne think he had done something wonderful. He grinned from ear to ear. "John tol' me that boys kin—" he started to say.

She slapped a hand against his mouth.

Now John was blushing. She could only imagine what he'd told Etienne.

Tante Lulu pretty well summed up the situation: "Tee-John, this is payback fer all the years ya did jist the same thing ta yer brothers and Charmaine. Remember the time ya asked Luc about penile rings, right out in public?"

Into the stunned silence, Etienne asked, "What's a pee-nail ring?"

And the thunder rolled...

John had been at René's cabin by himself for five days, waiting for a verdict. Everyone else had left.

He cleaned up the work site, packed tents, folded tables and chairs, stored pirogues, and, throughout it all, was generally thinking, thinking, thinking. It was lonely here, but not bad lonely. He needed solitary time to consider everything that had happened and what he wanted for the future.

It was a life-defining moment, and not to be taken lightly. His head needed to be on straight before he made any final decisions.

At one moment, the burning rage would take over, and he vowed to fight Celine in court for full custody of Etienne. He'd even talked it over several times with Luc, who kept trying to discourage such drastic action. It didn't seem drastic to him. Drastic was keeping a father ignorant of his son's existence for five years.

In saner moments, he admitted to himself that he was incapable at the present time of caring for a kid. First of all, he had to work, sometimes up to eighty hours a week. It would be unfair to leave Etienne alone all that time, even if his family would help out. Still, it rankled that Celine would win, and that's how it felt. A juvenile opinion, he knew, but there it was.

Then, too, having a kid forced a man to become responsible... mature even. And John resisted growing up. Yeah, at twenty-eight he should be past all the wildness, but that choice should have been his, dammit.

Then that insane fury would return, and he didn't care about the consequences. He wanted his son, and he would have him, no matter the collateral damage.

He was trying to catch some crawfish for his dinner, using a green leafy branch and a long-handled net, when he heard the sound of an engine. Soon Remy's hydroplane had landed in the stream, churning up the waters, thus putting an end to his crawfishing for the day.

"Surprise!" someone yelled.

And his entire friggin' family converged on his alone time.

Luc, Sylvie, Remy, Rachel, René, Val, Charmaine, Rusty, and Tante Lulu. The only saving grace was that they'd left their kids behind.

"We come ta give ya an intervention," Tante Lulu said right off.

"For what?" Horrified, he took the bag she handed

him and her purse that felt as if she was carting around a dozen bricks.

"Yer wild ways. Bein' a good daddy. Fightin' the thunderbolt. Lookin' fer love in all the wrong places. Marryin' up with yer baby's mother. Take yer pick." Tante Lulu was already huffing and puffing toward the porch.

He looked at his brothers for help. They just shrugged, as they, too, lugged bags of what he assumed were groceries. Were they planning an extended stay?

"We just wanna give you advice, sugah," Charmaine said. Her husband Rusty was having a good time watching her ass, which had been poured into a pair of skintight white jeans, as she walked up the incline in a pair of red cowboy boots. Typical Charmaine!

It was also typical of Rusty to be so obsessed with his wife.

"What kind of advice?" John rushed after her.

"Luuuvvve advice," René said, catching up and waggling his eyebrows at him.

"I am not in love. Celine is not in love. Forget the frickin' love."

"You *made* love, John, and you *made* a child." Sylvie, Luc's wife, leaned over to give him a quick kiss on the cheek. "Everything would be a lot easier if you could fall in love with Celine. In fact, I have a jelly bean I could give you."

"Don't you dare give me any dumbass love potion jelly bean. Whatever I decide to do, it will be about Etienne and what's best for him, not his lying mother."

"Couples don't get together or stay together for the sake of a child today," Val, ever the feminist lawyer, said to Sylvie, then advised him, "Don't let anyone guilt you into hasty action... even if I do think a merger between you and Celine would be a good idea."

"Mer-merger?" he sputtered out. "*Mon Dieu!*"

"Court should be a last resort, as I've told you at least a dozen times this week," Luc addressed him. To the others, Luc explained, "Tee-John has a skull as thick as a hundred-year-old bayou turtle."

"I want to get to know my son; I have five years to make up for. And I can't do that on the occasional weekend or a few weeks of summer vacation. Celine won't agree. So, I sue her butt off. End of story."

"I hope you didn't tell her like that," Rachel said.

His face heated up.

"He did!" Sylvie hooted.

"No wonder she's stopped talking to him," Val remarked.

"Dumber 'n dirt," Tante Lulu proclaimed. "Thass what men are when it comes ta wooin' a woman."

"Hey, I'm a good wooer. Not that I'm wooin' Celine."

"You need another St. Jude statue," Tante Lulu concluded.

He rolled his eyes. "Don't you think you guys are takin' a risk comin' here en masse like this? What if you're bein' followed?"

"Hah! You wouldn't believe the maze Luc made us follow to get to Remy's plane in Lafayette," René complained. "We all had to go separately. Then we set up these sort of dummy figures in each of our houses to appear as if we're home. All for you, bro."

"Thanks a bunch."

An hour later they were sitting at the newspaper-covered table expertly devouring crawfish; he'd added the two dozen he caught to the bushel they'd brought. In between, they ate buttered sweet corn on the cob, and thick slices of garden tomatoes covered with olive oil and vinegar and liberally dusted with salt and pepper. All of it washed down with Dixie beer. Another Cajun feast.

"Okay, we gotta come up with a plan," Charmaine said, licking the butter off her fingers, while Rusty watched, fascinated. When a southern belle caught a man, she caught him good, John observed silently. "A Tee-John Plan."

"Huh?" He choked on a mixture of beer and crawfish spices. By the time he cleared his throat, the gang was going full guns ahead.

"I don't think we can do the usual Village People routine," Sylvie said. In the past, his family had pulled off these hokey Village People entertainment events, dressed as sexy cowboys, construction workers, Indians, and, yes, cops, all to convince either one of their own, or their love-to-be, that it was a match made in heaven... Cajun heaven.

John had participated in every single one of them, enjoying immensely the target of their song/dance revues. He would not enjoy being the target. Before he could say so, not that it would deter anyone, Tante Lulu mused, "Well, Celine is a newspaper reporter... like that Lois Lane gal, and—"

Everyone, except him, got all excited as ideas popped into their dingy heads.

"Whoa, whoa, whoa!" Once he got them quieted down, he said, "Listen, I think it's time we retired the Village People nutcase spectacles."

"Says he who instigated many of them," Remy remarked.

He ignored Remy. "Seriously, we LeDeuxs have a reputation now for being flaming goofballs."

"And that's a bad thing?" Charmaine demanded to know.

"Especially after the last one...the secret wedding for René."

"Now ya gone too far, Tee-John," Tante Lulu said, smacking him on the arm with a wooden spoon. "That was one of my best St. Jude plans."

"I liked it," Val said in a soft voice. She and René exchanged one of those I-love-you-baby looks.

"You didn't at the time," John pointed out.

"Back to Lois Lane," Charmaine said. "I think it has possibilities."

"If you think for one damn minute that I'm gonna wear tights and a Superman cape, you've got another thing comin'. Jeesh! Next you'll be askin' me to jump off some tall New Orleans building."

"Mebbe jist a small buildin', sweetie." Tante Lulu was now patting the same arm she'd just whacked with her spoon.

"You could probably get Etienne to play Robin," Luc offered.

Traitor! he mouthed at him.

Luc just smirked.

"Well, I get to be Catwoman." This from Charmaine, of course.

"Hey, I wanted to be Catwoman," Rachel whined.

"How about we're all Catwomen," Sylvie said.

"Me, too," Tante Lulu said.

Everyone looked at her. It boggled the mind to picture their elderly aunt in a catwoman outfit.

"What?" She looked offended. "I kin allus wear those fake butt cheeks in my panties and the falsies in my bra. Remember, Charmaine, ya gave them ta me fer my ninetieth birthday?"

They all had to smile.

He kept protesting and protesting and protesting after that, but no one paid him a bit of attention. They just barreled ahead, discussing him and his future as if he had no say.

Later, when they were climbing back into Remy's hydroplane for the return trip, he told Tante Lulu, "I know you want to see me settled down, Auntie, but it's not gonna happen the way you want. I am not in love with Celine Arseneaux."

"You will be," his aunt said with her usual overconfidence. "I give ya two weeks ta be fallin' over dizzy with love."

He gaped at her and blurted out with the worst choice of words, "That would take a miracle."

She gave him one of those little Mona Lisa I-know-something-you-don't smiles.

In his head, he thought he heard a voice say, "You called?"

And off in the distance, there was the faint sound of . . . yep, thunder.

✦

Whaddaya think of men in tights, honey?...

"I want that treasure hunting story, and I want it *now*."

"Can't give it to you now," Celine told her boss as she sat in front of his desk. Bruce had been on vacation when she'd returned to work; so, this was their first face-to-face since she'd left on the Pirate Project assignment.

"Did they discover a treasure?"

"Yes."

"What? Is it worth a lot?"

"Yes, it's worth a lot, and I can't tell you what... yet."

"Why?"

"Security reasons."

"Whose security?" His face went beet red.

"Look, I'll have the story for you soon. It will be a great story... a stupendous story. And it will be a scoop. No one will get the story before me."

"You've thrown a hell of a lot of promises out there. Sure you can fulfill them?"

"Yes." *I'm pretty sure.*

"Since when is it our responsibility to protect the security of the entire friggin' world?"

"I'm not going to argue with you, Bruce. I'm not giving you the story yet."

"That's some line in the sand you're drawing, Celine."

"This doesn't have to be a fight. I've continued to give you good stories on the trial."

"That's another thing. Who's your source?"

"You know better than to ask me that."

A knock on the door interrupted what was probably going to be a volley of swear words from her boss. Bruce's secretary stuck her head inside. "There's a Louise Rivard here to see you, Celine."

"Here?" Celine was surprised. She hadn't talked to Tante Lulu since she'd left Bayou Black a week ago, although her grandfather said she called every day and had been to visit Etienne twice.

"Isn't that the dingbat relative of John LeDeux? Is he your source?"

"Yes, and no. John is not my news source related to the Mafia trial. And, yes, Tante Lulu is the great-aunt of the LeDeux brothers. But the reason she must be seeking me is that I plan on doing a feature story on her fifty years of work as a *traiteur,* a bayou healer."

"You're just full of little gems, aren't you?"

"Don't be snide."

"She's a notorious certified crazy."

"Who's a crazy?" Tante Lulu pushed her way into Bruce's office, apparently choosing not to wait for Celine to come to her. "Are ya callin' me crazy, Mister Cavanaugh?"

She stood there carrying an enormous purse. Her hair was purplish gray today, and tightly curled. She wore a lavender and aqua and white flowered dress. On her feet were white orthopedic shoes and anklet socks with pink lace trim.

Nope, no one would ever think crazy on meeting her.

Bruce gaped.

"Wait 'til I tell yer grandaddy ya call old folks crazy. I 'member when you was a teenager and got yerself arrested fer—"

"Celine!" A red-faced Bruce stood. "Take Ms. Rivard

into your office where you'll be more comfortable. Please. Oh, and it was nice meeting you, Ms. Rivard. I can't wait to read about your wonderful folk healing. Bye." The only thing he didn't say was, "Don't let the door hit you in the butt."

On the way to Celine's office, Tante Lulu winked at her. "Pompous ass, ain't he?"

"Oh, yeah." Something occurred to Celine. "Do you really know Bruce's grandfather?"

"Goodness sakes, no. Whatever gave ya that idea?"

Celine laughed, then motioned for Tante Lulu to sit in front of her desk while she sank down to the chair behind it. "So what can I do for you?"

"I was jist wonderin', honey," she said.

The hair stood out on the back of her neck, red flags waving before her eyes.

"Whaddaya think of Superman?"

Chapter
20

Annie Oakley had nothing on Tante Lulu...

"Do you want the good news or the bad news?" Luc asked him right off when he answered his satellite phone.

"Bad news first," John said.

"Celine was at Tante Lulu's—"

"That *is* bad news."

"No, that's not the bad news. Celine was there to interview her for some feature she's gonna do on bayou folk medicine."

"Okaaay."

"The bad news is that two of Lorenzo's goons showed up at Tante Lulu's, figuring they might be able to coerce her into telling them where you are."

"Sonofabitch! Is Celine all right?" He began to pace, frustration oozing out of his pores. He hate, hate, hated being isolated out here, unable to help.

"Celine and Tante Lulu are fine. The goons aren't so fine."

He stopped pacing. "Can I assume this is the good news part?"

"Yep. Tante Lulu blew the kneecap out of the one guy—"

He had to smile. "Finally, that pistol she carries in her purse must have come in handy."

"Yep. She says she was aimin' for his heart."

Good Lord! "And the other goon?"

"Oh, Useless took care of him. Chased him around the cottage a few times, then took a chomp out of his shoe. In fact, that ol' gator held on 'til the police arrived."

He laughed so hard then, he had to sit down. Finally, he wiped his eyes. "Why does all the good stuff happen when I'm not around?" But then, something else occurred to him. "Are they safe there anymore?"

"Celine is fine. Back at her home. She wasn't recognized, and she left before the reporters arrived. Tante Lulu is stayin' with Charmaine for the time bein'. I think they're workin' on a bride quilt."

"Whose? Never mind, I don't want to know."

After Luc hung up, he tried Celine's number. No answer.

No sooner did John get word the next day that the Mafia dudes had been sentenced than he was on the horn to Remy. "Get me out of here!"

The first thing he did when he got back to his cottage was take a shower, listen to the gazillion messages on his answering machine, read the newspaper account about Wild Bill Rivard, aka Tante Lulu, and her encounter with the mob, arrange to have his cleaning lady resume her twice-monthly routine, and call his family members to tell them he was back home. The chief had told him he didn't have to return to work 'til Monday...five days away.

An hour later, he hopped into his red Impala convertible and drove to Houma. Once he found James Arseneaux's house—a modest, 1950s style cottage—he didn't hesitate to go up onto the porch and knock on the door.

"What are you doin' here?" Arseneaux greeted him.

"Some welcome! I've come to see Etienne."

"Ya shoulda called first."

"I did. Three times. Then I left a message on the answering machine."

"I hate answering machines."

"Where's Celine?"

"Workin'."

"Is Etienne here?"

He scrooched his wrinkled face up, probably considering a lie, but just then, he heard Etienne yell from upstairs, "Grampa, is my quiet time up?"

"Quiet time?" He glanced in question to Arseneaux.

"He whacked down all the dahlias in the backyard with his spear."

"Spear?"

"Broom handle."

"Hey, I dint know you was here." Etienne was standing at the top of the stairs. The ear to ear, toothless smile on his face was enough to make any father's heart skip a beat.

"Hey, tiger, how'd you like to take a ride in my convertible?"

Before the kid could answer, Arseneaux asked, "Ya got a car seat?"

"No. Do I need a car seat?"

"It's the law. Jeesh! What kinda cop are ya?"

One who knows zip about kids. "Okay, how 'bout we

walk down to that ice cream shop. I see it every time I go to Luc's office."

"Ice cream! Yippee! I like praline."

"Me, too."

"Ice cream at one o'clock in the afternoon?" Arseneaux griped, but he knew that he couldn't keep John from his son, so he just shuffled off.

Three hours later, John was ready to go take a nap. Or swig down a few oyster shooters. His kid could sap the energy out of a battery. They'd had ice cream, half of which ended up on Etienne's face and shirt. A lady sitting next to them in the ice cream shop handed him a wet wipe. Was he supposed to carry stuff like that around with him? Then they went to the park—named Houma Lilypond Park, although there wasn't a pond or lily in sight—where Etienne insisted he climb the monkey bars with him, ride the merry-go-round, go on the big slide, and race him around the field six times.

After that, they fed the ducks down on the bayou, and there were plenty of bayous here in Houma, which was a really interesting town. With numerous bridges and bayous stemming out like spokes on a wheel, some called it the Venice of America.

When they got back to the house, Etienne showed him his bedroom, then insisted he sit on the floor and play pirates and Vikings with him. When he'd asked him if he was a good pirate, Etienne had given him a look of disgust, as if he knew nothing. "A baaad pirate."

And questions! *Mon Dieu!* The kid asked a million questions.

"Do ya like kids?"

"Do ya have any kids?"

"Do ya like girls?"

"Kin I buy some firecrackers?"

"Kin I buy a tittie magazine?"

"Kin I borrow yer handcuffs?"

And everything was followed up with the question: "Why?"

And some of his questions were downright alarming.

"Didja ever pull down yer pants and flash yer hiney at the nuns?"

"Didja ever climb ta the tippytop of a tree higher than a house?"

"Didja ever pet an ally-gator?"

Then he provided some useful information, like, "Are you ticklish?"

"Yes."

"Where?"

"The bottom of my feet."

"Oh. My mom's ticklish behind her knees."

"Oh, really?"

John practically staggered up the porch steps at the end of the afternoon. When Arseneaux told him that Celine had called and would be home late due to a last-minute assignment, he decided not to hang around. "Tell Celine I'll call her later," he told Arseneaux.

Arseneaux just grinned maliciously at him, and John knew his message would land in the virtual circular file.

War of the Almost-Roses...

Two weeks later, after twenty unanswered phone calls, on top of convenient absences by Celine every time he went to visit Etienne, John had had it up to his flaring nostrils. He felt like one of those hamsters running on an ever-spinning wheel.

"File the papers," he ordered Luc as he stormed into his Houma office.

"What's up now?" Luc, who'd just come back from the courthouse, put his bulging briefcase on his desk and told his secretary to hold all calls. Closing his inner office door, he plopped down into the chair behind his desk and steepled his fingers in front of his mouth.

"Same old crap. You told me to try to work it out with Celine. Well, I've tried, hit a gazillion brick walls, and she's not interested. End of story."

"The way I hear it, every time you call her, you end up making threats. What kind of bullshit diplomacy is that?"

"She's the one who should be contacting me, making concessions, trying to make nice," he insisted. "I want to sue for custody. I'm gonna put an addition on my cabin. Hire a live-in sitter. Go to Disneyland. Be a freakin' great Brady Bunch father...except with one kid. To hell with Celine!"

"Tee-John," he sighed, "take my advice, please. This is not the route to follow."

"It's the only route I'm seein' right now. Yeah, I know it'll be hard. In fact, how do you do it with three kids? I spend a few hours with one kid, and I'm beat."

Luc smiled. "You need a wife."

"I'm tryin'. Not to get a wife, ferchrissake, but I've been tryin' to have some kind of relationship with Celine, but she's avoidin' me like somethin' smelly."

Luc grinned.

"What?"

"I've never known you to be the pursuer."

"This is different."

"Why? Do you love her?"

"Pfff! I hardly know her."

"So?"

"Until a few weeks ago, I hadn't thought about Celine in more than five years. Even then, there wasn't much thought that went into our one-night stand."

"Tee-John, I knew Sylvie since we were in grade school. Never thought much about her 'til one day I walked into her lab, and zing, I was a goner. It happened that quick."

"I do lust her," he conceded.

"That's a start."

"If you keep grinnin' like that, I might have to punch your lights out."

"You could try, little brother. You know, it just occurred to me... when I called you a couple weeks back to tell you about the Mafia thugs... normally, you would have asked about Tante Lulu first, but the first person you were worried about was Celine."

John frowned. He hadn't realized. Hmmm. Maybe that *was* telling.

"Seriously, why not just try dating for a while? See where it goes?"

"Dating?" He laughed. "What, you think I'm still a teenager, and I'm gonna take her to the prom?"

"Give me a break, Tee-John. What do I know about couples today? I've been married more than fifteen years. If not dating, then be lovers for a while."

"I wish! She's shut down the love factory on me."

"Is this Tee-John LeDeux speaking? The guy whose scoring average is about one hundred percent... the guy who once claimed he'd never met a woman he couldn't seduce?"

He winced. "You're right. I've been acting pathetic. Time to be proactive. Time to charm the pants off Celine Arseneaux."

"I presume you mean that literally."

"Damn straight!"

"I'll forewarn you, buddy, if you get custody of Etienne, Tante Lulu will be movin' in with you faster than you can say, 'Oh, my God!'"

"Oh, my God! Okay, I'll give it one more try, but then it's time to do your Perry Mason routine."

"Perry Mason was a criminal lawyer."

"Whatever."

So it was that he arrived, unannounced, at Celine's house that Saturday afternoon. He knocked, but didn't wait for an answer. Instead, he walked in.

And saw a man.

A man who was sitting on the couch, holding Celine's hand. In the background, probably the kitchen, he heard Etienne talking to his grandfather.

"Who the hell are you?" he asked. *Just call me Mr. Diplomat. Not!*

The guy arched his eyebrows and stood. "David McLean."

Oh. David of the big too-too. His eyes shot to the guy's crotch. Nothing spectacular that he could see.

Celine knew where he was staring and why and could barely suppress a smile.

"I assume you're John LeDeux," McLean said, stretching out his hand for a shake.

Reluctantly, he shook the guy's hand.

"Back from Afghanistan?"

McLean nodded.

"How long you gonna be stateside?"

A tiny smirk appeared on McLean's mouth. He knew exactly why John had asked and was enjoying his discomfort. "A few weeks."

"Did you want something?" Celine asked, standing now, too. Next to McLean. Dammit!

Matching John in height, McLean was wearing khakis and a golf shirt. His short blond hair framed a suntanned face which some might call handsome. Personally, he thought he was too girly-looking.

Celine was wearing a red and white striped sundress with sandals and...*Holy shit!*...crimson-painted toenails. Her hair was piled up on top of her head in some kind of sexy knot with tendrils escaping around her face. She had makeup on; for some reason, that bothered him.

"I came over on the suggestion of my lawyer...to talk," he blurted out.

"Now is not a good time," Celine said.

Right away, his blood pressure rose, but for once he restrained himself from saying something he might regret. "Well, you let me know when would be a good time, then, sweetie." With that, he stalked out, leaving the two of them stunned.

He needed a drink...or five.

Mi casa es su casa...

Next day, a Sunday, she showed up with Etienne at his cabin. It was barely nine A.M., and he was in the kitchen making a cup of instant coffee to go with his leftover cold pizza from the night before.

He was barefooted, but decently covered in boxers and a T-shirt, although the shirt did have the crawfish imprint, "Shuck Me, Suck Me, Eat Me Raw." Luckily, Etienne couldn't read that well yet; nor would he understand...he hoped.

"See, Mom, I tol' you he'd be home."

John's eyes connected with hers, in question.

"You said you wanted to talk." Her face was pink with embarrassment. He would imagine she didn't show up at men's houses, unannounced, very often.

"Good morning, then," he husked out.

She wore navy blue Bermuda shorts, a lighter blue tank top...the kind with a built-in bra...white sandals with the red toenails peeping out, and a high ponytail. No makeup.

She looked better to him than she had the day before, and she'd looked damn good then.

"Good morning," she replied, and her voice was husky, too.

"See, Mom, John has a house on stilts right in the water, and ya kin fish off his back porch and see gators and egg...egg...egrets and snakes and stuff."

"Oh, that's just what I want to do on my day off. Look at snakes."

"Oh, Mom!"

"Are you here because Etienne insisted, or was it your idea?"

She hesitated, then admitted, "I wanted to come."

He grinned.

"That's not what I meant."

"I know what you meant." He stretched out a hand and tugged on her ponytail, causing more strands of hair to come loose. "I'd like you to see my house. I can run over to Boudreaux's General Store and pick up some stuff for lunch. We could fish a little. Swim. Take a nap." He waggled his eyebrows at that last.

"A nap! I doan take naps. I'm a big boy."

"So am I," he said meaningfully to Celine. "C'mon, sugar, it'll be fun."

Despite what he said, he wasn't sure how much fun he could take from this bit of pure temptation. And forget about naps. He knew exactly what nap meant in his man-dictionary, and so did she. But she wasn't bolting.

Interesting.

"Why do you call my mom sugar?"

"Because she's so sweet."

Etienne giggled at the idea of his mother being sweet.

So it was that Celine, the unsuspecting chick, entered the fox's lair that day.

Then trouble came knocking on his door...

John was as nervous as a cat in a room full of rocking chairs, and all because his son and Celine were in his home, together, for the first time.

Etienne, of course, loved it. What kid wouldn't want

to live in a home on stilts over water? First, Etienne had been fascinated by the huge black and orange Monarch butterflies that flitted about the area. Then a moving hump-shaped rock got his attention...an armadillo.

The bayou could be a paradise for a little boy. Right now, he was leaning over the porch railing, fishing or spitting into the water, or both.

But what did Celine think?

Really, it was just a glorified cabin. Yeah, it had modern appliances in the little kitchen, and the bathroom had been remodeled last year. But it was small and had only one bedroom. Still, it was prime waterfront property, and the dwelling could always be expanded, or torn down for that matter, and a new house put up.

Later, they were in the kitchen, having fished and swum to Etienne's heart's content.

"So, what do you think of the place?" He and Celine were setting out already prepared po'-boys with side salads on his kitchen table.

"It's great. Can't beat the view."

"Before I forget, there's been an ominous silence from my family lately...regarding you and Etienne. That has every alarm bell in my head going off. I suspect they're plannin' something."

"Like what?"

"You don't want to know."

"Not one of those embarrassing LeDeux events?"

"They better not."

She picked up one of the St. Jude salt shakers on his table and laughed. She'd already remarked on the large number of St. Jude items around his house. "Maybe I should pray to St. Jude...to counteract whatever they're planning."

"Won't work," he told her. "Tante Lulu's got the dibs on St. Jude."

They spent the rest of the day together, hiking and re-laxing on the porch which fronted the bayou. John found himself watching Celine. A lot.

She was great with Etienne. Patient...like not los-ing her cool when he spilt grape juice on her shorts. Loving...the way she hugged him so much, and often for the smallest things, like catching a fish the size of a minnow. Stern...like refusing to budge when he begged for a dog. Smart...like having a knack for teaching him lessons without him knowing it, like making him count the number of different butterflies he saw.

And she was damn attractive. He already knew what those spectacular breasts looked like under the bra and T-shirt. So, of course, that's all his sexually charged X-ray eyes saw. Her hair was a pretty dark brown color, but there were red and gold highlights here in the sun-shine. Her pale blue eyes were one of her most interest-ing...even startling...features. When she bent over to examine a squeaking frog with Etienne, he noticed her butt—not fat but a nice handful for a man's hands...his hands, to be precise. He also homed in on the back of her knees, which he'd like to lick some more.

Now that she wasn't so pole-up-the-ass stiff with him and inclined to make sarcastic remarks to counter every little thing he said or did, he liked her personality, too. Quick to laughter. Really intelligent. Caring. Sexy. Oh, yeah, sexy, without being blatant about it.

Mon Dieu! I sound like one of those catalogues for a dating agency.

Not that he didn't see Celine's faults, too, but, hell,

he had plenty of his own. Like standing here, gawking at her like a pimple-faced adolescent dork.

The thing was, the more he watched Celine and the more he listened, the easier he found it to say, in his head, *I love you.*

No, no, no, I don't love her. I'm just thinkin' about lovin' her.

Celine glanced up at him then from the living room, where she was now setting up a DVD of *The Incredibles.* "Time for a bit of quiet time for a tired boy," she told Etienne. Then to him, "Did you say something?"

"Uh, did you hear thunder?"

Sure enough, off in the distance, thunder rumbled.

"It's probably just a summer storm somewhere," she said. "I doubt if it will reach us."

A voice in his head said, "Wanna bet?"

Chapter
21

He needed her knees...

Celine was in big, big trouble, and she was having too much fun to put a halt to the disaster headed her way...the disaster being in the form of one great big love bug.

Yep, she was falling in love with the worst possible man. No way would a guy like him be satisfied for long with a woman like her, even though he *was* giving her "the look," now that Etienne had fallen asleep in the middle of his movie. His head was resting on folded arms on the rug, his little butt up in the air.

Her heart constricted as she watched John lay a St. Jude afghan over him with loving care. *Oh, God! How could I resist loving a man who loves my son? Or a man who loves his aging aunt so much he actually uses a St. Jude afghan?*

"You're good with Etienne," she remarked from the lounge chair where she was sitting, sipping at a glass of white wine. In a St. Jude glass, of course.

"It's not hard bein' good with him. He's a great kid." He walked over and took the wine from her, setting the glass on a nearby table. "I have to ask, did you make love with McLean last night?"

At first, her face froze up and he could tell she was going to refuse to answer, but then she disclosed, "No."

"Good." Pulling her to her feet and into his arms, he murmured against her mouth, "I've been a good boy all day. Gimme a little sugar for a reward."

She did, looping her arms around his neck and kissing him warmly. "How was that?" she asked afterward.

"Hmmm. Okay."

She swatted his shoulder and squirmed out of his embrace.

But he held on to one hand, raised it to his mouth for a wet, open-mouthed kiss on the palm, then said, "Come with me, *chère*," and started leading her toward his bedroom.

When she dug in her heels, he looked back at her.

"Why?" Dumb question, she knew before the words were out of her mouth.

"Because I want to check out the back of your knees, babe."

"This is so not a good idea."

"I know."

"We have issues coming out the kazoo."

"I know."

"Making love isn't going to solve anything."

"I don't know about that. We get along better with body language than actual words. I want you, babe."

She hesitated. "God help me, but I want you, too."

So it was that she spent a long, lazy hour in John Le-Deux's bed, and it wasn't just her knees he checked out.

By the end of the day, she was even closer to falling in love with the baddest boy on the bayou.

Disaster, disaster, disaster.

Especially when there was a knock on the door which awakened Etienne, which prompted him to start crying. He was always cranky when his sleep was interrupted abruptly.

Celine dressed quickly, not bothering to put her hair back in its ponytail, but rushing out to lift Etienne onto her lap, where he whimpered and fell back asleep.

Meanwhile, John, wearing boxers and nothing else, went to the screen door. There stood the most gorgeous woman Celine had ever seen.

She was model slim and tall, about five-ten, with a long swath of coal-black hair hanging straight to her waist and sharply defined olive skin, probably Hispanic. She wore a gauzy, calf-length, multicolored skirt, a lavender silk blouse, and high-heeled purple slingbacks.

"John!" she crooned the second he appeared and opened the screen door. Launching herself at him, she wrapped her arms around his neck and kissed him warmly. Celine was pretty sure there was tongue involved, though probably only on the woman's part. But John sure as hell wasn't resisting. When the woman leaned her head back, still holding onto his shoulders with her belly pressed against his waist, she inquired in a sultry voice, "Did you miss me, honey?"

"Uh, sure, I mean...Eve, I have company."

"Oh." Releasing him, she stepped back and regarded Celine, then disregarded her as unimportant...probably not pretty or hot enough for the bayou stud, in her opinion. But then she noticed Etienne, who was now awake but shy—staying in Celine's lap. The woman studied Etienne more closely and probably saw the resemblance.

"This is Celine Arseneaux and her son Etienne. Celine, this is Eve Estrada. She's an artist who's been exhibiting her work in Paris this summer."

Celine nodded, knowing perfectly well who Eve Estrada was. The *Times-Tribune* had done several features on her. In fact, a gallery down the street from the newspaper office showed her paintings in a front display window. Now that she thought about it, that was an Estrada bayou landscape hanging on John's living room wall.

"We should go," Celine said, standing.

"You don't have to go," John said.

She glanced between him and Eve. "Yes, I do."

Etienne started to cry, not wanting to leave.

John hunkered down on his haunches, trying to appease his now-howling son.

Celine was embarrassed beyond belief as Eve surveyed the homey scene. No doubt Celine's recent sexual activity was apparent as well.

"I'll walk you to your car," John said then, after picking up Etienne and quieting him with pats on his back and shushing sounds.

Celine remained silent, both furious and humiliated.

"It's not what you think," he said, once he'd buckled Etienne into his car seat, and she was belted in the driver's seat.

"You have no idea what I'm thinking."

"Yeah, I do. You think I'm about to do two women in one afternoon."

She shrugged. "Your reputation precedes you."

"Fuck my reputation." Immediately, he glanced at

Etienne to see if he'd heard. He probably had. "I didn't know she was coming here today."

"Is she your girlfriend?"

"No."

"Your lover?"

He didn't answer right away, which was answer enough.

"Forget about it," she said. "It's none of my business."

"The hell you say. Eve and I are not lovers *now*."

She arched her brows. "You used to be?"

"Used to be, occasionally, but not for a long time."

"How long?"

"If I asked you these kinds of questions, you'd spit in my face," John complained.

"I'm thinking about it."

"Three months."

"Just before she went to Paris," Celine deduced, then exhaled with disgust. "And now she's here to pick up where you left off."

"I thought we were doing well today," John said with a tiredness she shared.

"I did, too. All the fool, me."

He bristled, but that's all. He should beg her not to go. He should tell he that he would get rid of Eve and they could talk. He should tell her that he hadn't been with another woman in months. He should yank her into his arms and kiss her hurt away. But his pride reared its head, and he replied in kind, "That makes two fools, babe. You and me both."

With that, she spun clam shell gravel as she exited his drive.

And they were right back to step one.

Invasion of the LeDeuxs...

There were LeDeuxs overrunning John's home the next weekend, helping him put on an addition. With all these fingers in the pie, so to speak, his house would probably end up looking like one of those Rube Goldberg contraptions.

He'd always planned to enlarge his house, which had started out as a fishing camp. Now seemed like a perfect time.

Luc and Sylvie came with their three teenage daughters: Jeanette, Camille, and Blanche, with her boyfriend, eighteen-year-old Slick Eddie Comier, a hotshot Lafayette baseball player. Needless to say, Luc was keeping a sharp eye on Comier.

Then, there was Remy and Rachel with their horde of six children, five adopted and one biological, none of them married. Why Tante Lulu concentrated her matchmaking efforts on him, rather than some of them, was beyond him. One of Remy and Rachel's kids, Maggie, who was born with Down syndrome, died four years ago. Rashid was studying music in New York City; the twins Evan and Stephan were in medical school; and Andy was a benchwarmer for the Saints football team. Still at home were Suzanne, a Cajun beauty, who would probably end up being Miss Louisiana one day, like her Aunt Charmaine, and their natural born son Michael, or Mike.

René and Val came with their preteens Jude and Louise, named after Tante Lulu.

Charmaine and Rusty brought three-year-old Mary

Lou, who was having a great time running around with Etienne. His son had already told Mary Lou how babies were made...the spitting in the belly button business. Mary Lou had turned him green with envy because she lived on a ranch with real live horses. As a result, Etienne now wanted a horse, instead of a dog. Like that was ever going to happen. *A horse on the bayou? I don't think so.*

Angel and Grace showed up, too, which was a godsend. Although John and his brothers had limited carpentry experience, Angel's construction skills came in handy when they were trying to manage two new bedrooms, a second bathroom, and an expansion of the living room. Grace had finally managed to corral the younger kids into the front yard, where they were playing games.

Tante Lulu was, of course, directing the whole enterprise.

The only one missing was Celine, who'd declined to come. In fact, she was avoiding him, again, when he was not avoiding her.

It was a contest over who could be more immature.

Luc came up and sat beside him during one of the breaks. "How does Celine feel about this addition?"

He shrugged. "She considers it a threat. One more step in my trying to get custody."

"Is it?"

"Maybe."

"Tee-John, I had an informal talk with Judge Ainsley in family court. He says if you land in his case file, he'll order mediation before he'll even consider a custody petition."

"Damn!"

"Should I try to set something up?"

"I suppose, but Celine will have to agree to come. Right now I'm not on her favorite people list."

"Well, it has to be voluntary, on both parts. Can't you convince her?"

At first, he frowned with pessimism.

But then, he had an idea. Grinning, he told his brother, "Hell, yes."

He was John LeDeux. Celine was a woman. Enough said.

"Ha, ha, ha, ha!" the voice in his head echoed.

The pirate takes a wench...

"She's not so hot fer Superman," Tante Lulu told the ladies sitting on rockers on her back porch the next day, sipping tall glasses of iced sweet tea. "I found that out when I went to her office."

The ladies—Charmaine, Sylvie, Rachel, and Val—craned their necks to look at her at the end of the row of rockers. Hers was smaller so her short legs could meet the floor.

It was a gray, misty day on the bayou. No animals or birds about. Not even Useless. But the sun would no doubt come out soon, like always, and dry everything up in minutes.

"Well, so much for that idea!" Charmaine was disgusted, the Lois Lane/Superman idea having been her brainchild.

"We were never going to get Tee-John in tights anyway," Val remarked.

"We need a new plan," Rachel said.

Val disagreed. "I don't know about our interfering like this, guys. It was different when two people were clearly in love, but just didn't admit their feelings yet. Or at least only one of them was reluctant. Tee-John and Celine both claim *not* to be in love."

"It ain't interfering if it's good works," Tante Lulu asserted.

"I have a theory," Sylvie mused. "I believe that Celine has always had a crush on Tee-John. Even drunk, she's the type who wouldn't hop into bed with a guy she didn't care about, for a one-night stand anyhow. Then, having his child, I suspect caring has developed into something more. She may or may not admit it to herself, but that girl is in love."

They all pondered that possibility, then nodded. Maybe they were just hopeful optimists, but Tante Lulu didn't think so.

"How about Tee-John?" Rachel asked. "That is one wild boy. Roping him would not be easy for any woman."

Tante Lulu waved a hand dismissively. "The love bolt'll whack him good. In fact, he's halfway there, iffen I'm readin' the signs right."

"So, we need a new plan then." Rachel again.

Tante Lulu put on her thinking cap. "There is that pirate party we were talkin' about havin'."

"That's it! Tee-John will be a pirate, and Celine will be the pirate wench that he kidnaps." Sylvie had had a problem with severe shyness at one time. Luc sure had cured her of that if she got ideas like this.

"I kin jist see Tee-John with one of those scarves on his head, and a mustache and a gold hoop in his ear and those knee-high boots with flaps." Tante Lulu sighed. "He'll look way better than Johnny Depp."

"Where would he kidnap her to?" the ever logical Val wanted to know. "There aren't any pirate ships about that I know of."

"How about René's old shrimp boat?" Charmaine suggested.

"Does that old rust bucket still float?" Tante Lulu asked.

"Yes, he took it out last year, but it's kind of smelly. And it doesn't look much like a pirate's love lair." Val grinned at that last.

"Puhleeze!" Rachel exclaimed. "I'm a decorator. There isn't anything we can't make into a pirate ship. Some sails, a pirate flag, some swaths of silk and braziers for the bedroom. Piece of cake!"

"And don't forget those biker friends of Angel's," Val reminded them. "We ought to meet with them. Bet they'll have lots of ideas."

"Oooh, boy! What do you think our husbands are going to say about us meeting with Hells Angels?" This from Sylvie.

As one, they grinned, not at all worried. In fact, they looked downright gleeful.

"You know . . ." Val tapped her chin thoughtfully. "We might even be able to rent one of those longships that are on the Hudson River every year. It would have to be a small one, of course, but—"

"Wouldn't that be expensive?" Rachel worried.

"It'd be worth any amount of money ta me iffen it got Tee-John ta the altar," Tante Lulu said.

"Are we sure about this? Before we go any farther, we need to be sure pirates are the way to go." Sylvie looked at each of them in turn. "Maybe Celine doesn't even like pirates."

"Honey, there ain't a gal alive that doan get wet in her panties when she sees Johnny Depp," Tante Lulu told them.

None of them disagreed with her.

It wasn't the Olympics, but there were games...

Her late afternoon appointment had run 'til six. It had taken another hour to return to the office and write the article. By the time she got home around ten, Etienne and her grandfather were already asleep. She ate lukewarm leftover jambalaya and the heel of a loaf of French bread, standing at the kitchen counter.

She barely had the energy to shower and brush her teeth before donning a sleeveless pajama top that hit her mid-thigh. Not that her attire mattered. She would have worn a hair shirt if it had been hanging on the bathroom door.

Walking into the dark bedroom, she flicked on the ceiling fan, started to set her alarm for six, but then stopped herself, remembering that tomorrow was Saturday. With a loud yawn, she crawled into bed and was almost instantly asleep. *Zonked out by eleven,* she observed sleepily. *Some life for a single girl!*

It couldn't have been more than an hour later that she heard an odd rustling sort of sound. Her eyes fluttered open. Seeing nothing in the moonlit room, she figured it must be the overhead fan. It had needed oiling for days now. She went back to sleep.

After awakening a second time, she stretched her arms overhead and wondered dimly what had disturbed her now. She should get up and turn the stupid fan off.

That's when she realized that she couldn't get up.

Her eyes shot open.

Her arms were restrained above her head in a pair of handcuffs attached to the wooden rods in her headboard.

And the noise which must have awakened her was the soft sound of a man shrugging out of his clothes. She was about to scream...'til she saw who it was.

"John LeDeux! What are you doing here?"

John stopped in the middle of taking his clothes off and looked at Celine. Luckily, she'd slept through his cuffing her. "You're awake. Good."

"How did you get in here?"

"I didn't come up the drainpipe, that's for sure." He'd tried and almost killed himself. "Nope, I came right through the front door."

"I locked the front door."

"I unlocked it."

"Where did you get the key?"

"No key. Just my trusty lock picker."

"Good grief! That's breaking and entering."

"Not technically."

"You're a police officer. That's probably a double crime of some sort. And using handcuffs for non-police work, that has to be practically a felony. Whoa, whoa, whoa! What do you think you're doing?"

Man, she talked a lot. Just like her son. But maybe

that was a good thing. Keep her talking 'til he was in position to give her mouth something better to do. He was down to his briefs. That's probably what prompted the whoas.

"Luc says you and I need to go into mediation before I can file a lawsuit. I'm here to get your okay."

"And you couldn't call me for that?"

"You never answer my calls."

"That's because you always threaten me."

"I'm not threatening you now. I'm here to plead my case."

She tried to laugh, but it came out as a gurgle. He took that as a good sign. "You have a strange way of pleading your case. Is this a joke?"

He shook his head. "I've tried being polite...well, semi-polite. I've tried threats. This time I'll try to convince you with my old tried and true methods."

"Handcuffs?"

"Nope. I figure it's time for you and me to have some fun, sugar. And by the end of it, we'll be in mediation, or I'll have died trying."

"You and I have already had all the fun we're going to have."

"Hardly."

"Just for the record, have you been having any 'fun' with Eve lately?"

"Not at all."

She looked skeptical, but pleased.

"Have you been having 'fun' with David?"

"Not of the sexual kind."

He was definitely pleased.

"Release me, John."

"Not a chance."

"Why?"

"Why haven't I been getting it on with Eve? Because I don't want to."

"That's not what I meant. God, your ego is enormous. I meant, why not release me? I'm not opposed to mediation... provided certain conditions are laid down first."

"Too late for conditions, baby. And I don't want to hear any more about Eve. Or David. Or any other freakin' person in the world. Just you and me. We're gonna duke it out, my way."

She turned her head as he shimmied out of the briefs. Then she yelped when he flipped the sheet off the bottom of the bed and began to crawl under the sheet up and over her body, like a cat. A lusty tomcat. When he got up to eye level, he tossed the sheet off both of them, looked down, and said, "Hi."

"Hi yourself. Get out of here."

"Not a chance." He wiggled his hips against hers to show her why not. The "why not" was pressing against the vee between her legs.

"I could scream."

"You will eventually."

"Your ego is remarkable."

"You're repeating yourself, honey. Sexual arousal will do that to a person."

She sputtered.

He rolled over to his side and began to unbutton her pajama top. Every time he undid a button, he looked down at her and grinned.

She bit her bottom lip in an attempt to resist him.

A losing battle, he could have told her. The mood he was in, a block of ice wouldn't be able to resist his efforts, and Celine's skin felt far from cold.

"Etienne could walk in here any minute."

Oh, so now she's trying the kid ploy. "I locked the door."

She groaned. "Why are you doing this?"

"Are you kidding? Because I want to." He separated the sides of her pajama top and stared down at her breasts. His cock did a little happy dance at the mind-blowing view. "Have I told you how much I like your breasts?"

"Only about a dozen times."

He touched the tip of one with a forefinger. She jerked up so violently she would have flown off the bed if the handcuffs weren't restraining her. She whimpered then, which was almost his undoing; he loved how sensitive her breasts were. He loved her whimpering. He loved…

"Unlock these damn handcuffs. Now."

"Why?"

"So I can hit you."

He chuckled. "Maybe later. Gotta keep those cuffs on 'til I'm done."

"Done what?"

He gave her an incredulous look. "I'm not sure what, to tell the truth." *Believe that, and I've got a bayou bridge to sell you.*

"Is this about my not answering your phone calls?"

"No. Not entirely. This is about provin' somethin' to myself."

"Like?"

Talk, talk, talk. "Hell if I know. Just lie back and enjoy, darlin'. I'll figure it out eventually." He laid a palm on her belly, which retracted instinctively, and it felt so frickin' good, he did it again.

"You're acting crazy," she gritted out.

Tell me about it.

"Why the handcuffs?" she asked breathily, probably because he was tracing an imaginary X with his finger from the bottom of one breast to opposite hip, then doing the same with the other side of the X. She gasped at the end when he blew into the center of the X, aka her belly button. "Surely a smoothie like you doesn't need coercion."

"A smoothie like me is smart enough to know you're not going to let me do all the things I want without a little...uh, light bondage."

What things? she probably wanted to ask.

He'd like to know himself.

"Here's the deal. We're gonna play the park game." He leaned down and pressed a light back-and-forth kiss on her lips. Then he grazed her chin with his mouth and moved on up to her ear, where he wet the whorls with his tongue, blew them dry, then inserted the tip of his tongue. A couple of those exercises and she was keening her pleasure. Only then did he explain, "I spent an afternoon with Etienne at the Lilypond Park, as you know. We did ice cream cones, the merry-go-round—you know, the kind where you push it 'til it goes faster, then jump on—then the sliding board and the monkey bars and exploring the woods. Over and over."

"You want to play a kid game with me? Oooh, you're torturing my ears."

Of course I'm torturing your ears. That's the point. Later you can torture me, if you're good. Hell, even if you're not good. "Sugar, there are kids' games, and there are kids' games."

"Huh?" She was still reeling from the ear sex.

"First, let's try the merry-go-round." He traced increasingly small circles on first one breast, then the other, starting at the base, up to the areola, but never any higher. And the circling got faster on the up curve, slower down below.

At the beginning, she was giggling, despite her best intentions. But then, she wasn't giggling anymore.

"I'm hungry now. How about you? A little ice cream? Oops, you're dripping. With wide sweeps of his tongue he again made paths from the base to the areola of her breasts, never higher. Her always puffy areolas were more swollen, and the small nipples stood up with neediness.

"John," she pleaded.

"Tell me."

She did, in a throaty whisper.

"Ah, you mean the cherries on those ice cream cones." He suckled her then, and a whole lot more. Teeth, tongue, lips, and fingers played her skillfully.

She was writhing from side to side. Her teeth were gritted, and she made a *shhh* sound of pleasure-torment.

"I could bring you to climax just by playing in this part of the...um, park, but, honey, there's lots more to show you."

"Then show me, dammit."

"Patience, patience, *chère*. Did I tell you that in between rides and climbing, Etienne showed me how to explore?"

"Okay, Marco Polo, show me your stuff. And forget the patience baloney."

He laughed. Meanwhile, his hands started exploring...her thighs, her hips, her flat belly and navel. "We even explored the forest around the park. It was a dark and mysterious place." With those words, he began to trail his fingers along a path through her "forest."

Arching her hips up off the bed, she silently urged him to enter her. If her hands had been free, she probably would have grabbed hold of him and made him do it.

"Ah, I see you're ready for the slide." When he plunged inside her hot, slick slide, her inner muscles contacted around him in a series of incredible spasms.

"I'm tired of games," she said.

"Me, too." He unlocked her cuffs and made love to her then, not with the expertise built up over years of experience, but with a passion engendered by her, and her alone. And if her response to him was any indication, she felt an equal passion.

It was incredible sex. The best. Each time he made love with Celine it got better. And that surprised the hell out of him.

Once their heartbeats had slowed down, and they were no longer panting, she rested with her head on his chest and one leg draped over his thigh, the knee pressing up against his defeated explorer.

He kissed the top of her hair, which was mussed in a dozen directions from the hard writhing. He kind of liked it. Sex hair. "So, are we gonna get into mediation?"

"I suppose, but, John, I've been a single mother for five years. It's hard for me to give up any control."

"It's gotta happen. And, by the way, don't you think it's time we told Etienne that I'm his father?"

"Not yet." She was panicking, he could tell. "He needs time."

"Bull! Etienne doesn't need time, you do."

"You're right."

"We get along, Celine. At least in bed. Maybe we

should…uhm…date and see where things go." *I can't believe I said that. Luc would laugh.*

"No."

Ouch! "You sure know how to hurt a guy."

"Puhleeze, you could care less."

"That's not true."

"I do like your games, though. In fact, I know a few games myself."

John knew she was trying to divert his attention away from the question of a possible relationship for them, outside of bed, but he'd gotten her agreement to mediation. That was a start.

She slanted her eyes up at him, meanwhile drawing little circles around his belly button. "Wanna play?"

You're asking a player if he wants to play? "Let the games begin!"

Later, John could swear he'd won the gold.

And he had to wonder if the key wasn't in seducing Celine, but in her seducing him. What a concept!

Chapter
22

Roommates with benefits?...

Late afternoon, the following Wednesday, he and Celine interviewed mediators in a conference room at Luc's office. They each got to eliminate two candidates before being forced to make a mutually agreeable choice.

He was gung ho for the first one, a psychologist sex therapist with minimal legal education. Celine was not.

When Dr. Epstein left the room, Celine turned on him. "I am not getting counseling from a woman who wears fishnet stockings."

"I didn't notice."

She laughed.

"I liked her tongue piercing, though."

He objected to the next one. A man. Dr. Samuel LeBlanc, Esquire. Yes, he'd actually used the word "esquire."

"I like him," Celine said.

"I don't. He looked at me funny."

"Funny?"

"Yeah, I think he was prejudging me for having abandoned you and Etienne all these years."

"He didn't say a word."

"He gave me a look."

The third one was gunning for John, as well. Turned out the guy was a geek computer friend of Celine's from high school, now a lawyer who supplemented his legal aid work with mediation services.

"He'll probably be calling you for a date later."

"You're delusional."

"Wanna have a quickie in Luc's storage room?"

"Really delusional."

Celine didn't like the fourth one, a blonde-haired recent law school graduate.

"All she did was smile at me. Jeesh!"

Finally, they settled on retired lawyer Judy DeWitt, who looked a little like Dr. Ruth, except she had short bobbed hair dyed an unnatural pitch black.

After an hour of questions, the mediator asked them to consider a possibility and report back to her at their next meeting the following Monday: "How would you feel about living together in a non-sexual sense, with Etienne?"

"Like roommates?" Celine asked.

"Exactly."

"Without benefits?" he asked.

"Exactly."

As he walked Celine back to her house where he'd parked his car, he said, "Well, that was a wasted couple hours."

"Do you think?"

"You can't seriously believe we could live together without sex."

"I could."

"Don't even dare to tempt me into proving you wrong."

"We could even date other people," she offered.

"Oh, that would be cool. I would sit there twiddling my thumbs, watching cartoons with Etienne, while you go off to boff David."

"That was so crude. Besides, you could always have Eve come over and entertain you."

He stopped walking and just stared at her. "You wouldn't mind my dating someone else? Because I sure as hell wouldn't like your in-my-face dating."

She stared back at him, then admitted, "Yeah, I would mind."

"Maybe...maybe we should consider living to-gether...really living together to see how that goes?" He'd never lived with a woman before. Too confining. Too serious. And he was having trouble breathing, just making the suggestion now.

She shook her head.

What? He'd actually made the offer of a lifetime, and she was turning him down?

She laughed, and he figured it was because his mouth was hanging open in incredulity. "It wouldn't be a good example for Etienne, and if it didn't work out, he would be devastated."

"There are no guarantees in life."

She blinked several times, then put a hand to his face. "John, I'm going to be honest with you. I'm a little bit in love with you. Probably always have been, even when I'm hating you. Oh, don't go all pale and nervous. I don't expect you to reciprocate. But that's why I'm not living with you. I am not going to open myself up to that kind of pain."

She walked off then, leaving him still standing, stunned and, yeah, a little bit scared.

She loves me. A little bit.

How do I feel? Am I in love? Even a little bit?

What is love?

I need some advice.

He pulled out his cell phone and punched in some numbers.

"Luc, I'm in trouble."

Can you say "Arg"?...

Charmaine was no prude.

In fact, she had been known to do some outrageous things in her bimbo life. But this stretched even her limits. Rusty was gonna kill her if he ever found out.

In fact, Luc, Remy, René, and Jake were going do a bit of killing, too, if they discovered what Sylvie, Rachel, Val, and Ronnie were up to. Which they were bound to do when this Pirate Ball was announced to the public.

Sitting in front of them, on Tante Lulu's back porch, were four Hells Angels pirate buffs who were going to help them pull off the LeDeux extravaganza to beat all others. And there had been some doozies.

First was Bull Latham, a scary-looking marine vet who ran outdoor adventure programs in Colorado; his hair was cut military short, and his face had an angry scar running from chin to right ear, half of which was gone. Mostly, he just scowled...or growled, which she interpreted to mean he agreed with something that was said.

Black Hawk Jones, an Arapaho lawyer, had gotten a divorce recently...his third, and he was looking for action, as evident in the fact that he'd hit on every woman here today, except for Tante Lulu. She might be next. He was forty-eight years old and still wearing leather pants. Enough said!

Izzie Silverstein, a short, half-bald accountant from Manhattan, had the cutest dimples. Everyone liked him and his great sense of humor. Any man who could laugh at his bald spot got her vote.

Sven Ericcson was a three-time finalist in the Mr. Universe contest. If he flicked his hair over his shoulder Fabio-style one more time, she was pulling out her salon shears.

Although none of them could be described as handsome, they were attractive in their own way, and they were all built like brick outhouses, as Tante Lulu had remarked to her in an undertone. In addition, they sported tattoos, lots of tattoos. Black Hawk and Sven had long hair that many women would envy...Charmaine knew that for a fact, being a hairstylist.

Souped-up Harleys were parked in the driveway. Anyone passing by would probably not be alarmed, though, thinking that Tante Lulu was up to her usual antics. Nothing she did surprised people down on the bayou.

Angel Sabato, the best looking of the bunch, had arrived yesterday. In fact, they were his friends from his old biking days. He still had a hog, which was what bikers called their bikes, and so did Grace O'Brien, the ex-nun, who was here studying *traiteur*ing with Tante Lulu.

Resting half his butt on the arm of Grace's rocking chair, Angel continually teased her with little whispers in her ear or suggestive remarks or one of his endless nun jokes. She gave back as good as she got, bless her heart. Actually, Angel appeared to be marking his territory, setting up invisible signs to the other guys that Grace was his. Grace might have something to say about that.

Sven sat on the porch swing next to Charmaine. Thigh to thigh. Good thing she was married to a handsome guy like Rusty. Otherwise, she might have been tempted. Then again, maybe not. Vanity in a man was rather off-putting.

"So, it's settled," said Ronnie, who was checking off a list on her clipboard. "We rent the Veterans Club hall. Have glass cases to display the treasure for the press and dignitaries who will be attending, by invitation only. Bull is hiring at least six security guards for inside, and another six outside." She looked to Bull, and he growled his assent.

"We'll let Jake set up a computer video presentation of the project as it progressed. Adam will handle the booth devoted to Jean Lafitte and his history. I'll take care of the Jinx, Inc. table. Gotta promote the company. And we'll have a special section of the arena for scheduled interviews with the project participants. René will have a PowerPoint presentation and brochures related to bayou environmental concerns. We're even going to allow a Katrina relief organization to take donations at the door, voluntary entry fees. Afterward, before the ball begins, a special Brinks truck will drive up and cart the treasure off for transport to New Jersey."

"Mebbe Caleb's sister Lizzie kin sing fer us," Tante Lulu suggested. "She's comin' ta Nawleans fer *American Idol* tryouts anyways."

The others nodded.

"Are we all going to be in pirate costumes?" Sylvie inquired.

"Yes," Ronnie said. "During the press event, we'll be in costume, along with some actors we've hired to act out the parts of famous pirates...Jack Sparrow, Blackbeard, Anne Bonny, and, of course, Jean Lafitte and his brother Pierre. Sven is going to handle this." She smiled at the Mr. Universe wannabe, and he nodded his head in acceptance of her presumed compliment. "Then at the nighttime ball, I think we should require *everyone* who attends to be in pirate or period costume. And Sven will get us additional celebrity impersonators in pirate costume for the evening festivities...Johnny Depp, Presidents Bush and Clinton, Pamela Anderson, Dolly Parton, and some surprises."

"Doan fergit Richard Simmons," Tante Lulu reminded Sven.

He gave her a little wave.

"I know a guy in New Orleans who does Mardi Gras costumes," Izzie said. "We can make sure he gets in an extra supply of costumes: pirates, British and American miliary uniforms, and colonist gear."

"There were Native Americans around at that time, too," Black Hawk pointed out. "The Houma Indians, I think. Anyhow, I'll be demonstrating an Arapaho dance, and we'll have representatives of the Houma nation here, as well."

"I'll take charge of the reenactors and the battle," Izzie said. "In the field behind the Veterans Club."

"And the four of us will be promoting the new Hells Pirates group forming as an offshoot of Hells Angels," Sven added. "We already have a Web site, and Izzie is gonna be the secretary."

It boggled Charmaine's mind, and no doubt the rest of the women, who thankfully had nothing to say.

"Do ya think we'll be able ta get that little longship fer Tee-John ta capture Celine?" Tante Lulu asked Val.

Val had connections in New York City. She nodded. "Believe it or not, my friend is looking forward to it. Of course, he insists on staying aboard as captain, but that shouldn't cramp Tee-John's style any, since most of his work will take place below decks."

The four bikers grinned at each other, probably thinking they were all looney birds, which they were. But then, they were a bit looney themselves. Hells Pirates, indeed!

"I'll handle the entertainment," Charmaine said. "Dress rehearsal next Friday."

"Is yer friend a real captain, like could he marry folks?" Tante Lulu asked Val.

"Maybe. I'll ask," Val said.

Oh, Lord! Here we go again with another surprise wedding. Actually, Luc had revealed to Remy who'd told Rachel who'd told Val who'd told Charmaine who'd told Tante Lulu that Tee-John had come to him several days ago about love advice. They were all feeling better about their plot now, knowing that Tee-John was beginning to suspect his true feelings. When a grown man asked "What is love?" he was already in love, in Charmaine's opinion.

So, it was full speed ahead on the Tee-John Project.

"You people are kind of crazy," Bull commented with a deep growly laugh, the first time he'd put more than two words together since they'd arrived.

"So? Any objections?" Tante Lulu put her hands on her tiny hips and confronted the big guy.

"Hell, no. We like crazy," Sven said. "And, by the way, make sure you invite some single wenches."

Just when he thought everything would work out ...

The disaster happened on Monday when John went in to work.

"Some items are missing from the evidence room," the chief told him, right off, without any preamble.

John was sitting at his desk, trying to catch up on the pile of paperwork that had accumulated in his absence. Glancing up at his boss, he detected a strange look of worry on his face.

"What? You don't think I took anything, do you?"

The chief shook his head. "It was the digital camera you used at the Playpen."

John frowned, still unsure of the significance of the chief coming to him with this problem.

"We think it was Congressman Martinez's people, trying to make sure the photos of his wife were destroyed. We'll get to the bottom of who did it, and who in the department allowed it to happen. That doesn't matter now. The damage is already done."

"Damage?"

"Whoever took the camera saw the photos in there of you and that reporter gal...Arseneaux, I think her name is. They got a little revenge for your part in the bust by, uh..."

John stood, now as alarmed as the chief seemed to be. "Spit it out."

"They were given to the *National Enquirer.* The tabloid plans on running a spread tomorrow, the angle being that you two are an item, and therefore the prosecution of some of Louisiana's finest...meaning Martinez's wife, along with Ted Warner and that whiny ass evangelist, was all a ploy concocted by you two."

"For what purpose?"

The chief shrugged. "An exclusive story for Lois Lane, and a coup in your career."

"That's stupid."

"Since when are the tabloids smart?"

"Well, I have no intention of talkin' with some yellow journalist to sell more of those rags."

"I wouldn't let you anyhow. Besides, we're safe. All the department has to do is issue a release claiming the photo was doctored and there is no relationship between you two. Yeah, it's embarrassing for the two of you, but not to worry. I'll handle it personally."

"Oh, shit!"

"Now what? No, please don't tell me you really are nailing her."

John explained the situation to his boss, including the bit about his secret child.

The chief sank down into the interviewee chair next to his desk and put his face in his hands, rubbing up and down. When he looked at him again, he said, "This is a disaster."

"Tell me about it. God only knows how Celine will react."

He soon found out.

When the ax falls, duck...

Celine felt blindsided when she entered the newspaper office building.

A *National Enquirer* reporter and a cameraman were waiting for her. They pounced as soon as she exited her car in the parking lot.

"Are you Celine Arseneaux? Can you comment on your relationship with the Sex Cop? Did you two conspire to create the story on the Playpen bust? Could there be a new trial based on your...um, relationship?"

"I have no idea what you're talking about."

The reporter waved the photo of John kissing her, the one he used as a screensaver on his computer. Celine felt crushed. The only way that photo could have gotten in the hands of the tabloid was via the traitor...the traitor she had been starting to love.

Oh, John might not have given the photo to the newspaper. In fact, she doubted that he had. But he was responsible for taking the photo, and she sure as hell had been under the impression that he'd deleted it from the camera, that the only copy was in his hands.

She shoved past the reporter and cameraman, declining to comment, except when asked, "Are you having an affair with John LeDeux?"

"No!" she answered unequivocally.

Once in the building, she found her problems were only beginning.

No sooner had she sat down at her desk than Bruce motioned her toward his office. "Arseneaux! In here. Now!" he barked.

His face was so red with anger, she feared he might bust a blood vessel.

He shoved a copy of the infamous photograph into her face. "Did you know about this?"

"Yes, but—"

"And you chose not to tell me?"

"I thought it was a dead issue. I didn't know there were copies around other than—"

"Other than the one LeDeux has?"

She could feel her face color. "Yes."

"Are you having an affair with LeDeux?"

"No. Well, sort of. Okay, sit down before you have a stroke."

He looked as if he'd like to leap over his desk and strangle her.

"I'll explain. John and I have some history. In fact, I hope this won't be repeated, but he's the father of my son Etienne."

Bruce let her relate the entire story before interrupting again. When she was finally silent, he said, "You wrote that hot cop story when you carried this kind of baggage?"

"You made me write it."

"Please, Celine, give me some credit. I wouldn't have done so if I'd known."

"No, you'd have just pulled me off a good story."

"Was LeDeux the source for your mob articles?"

"Not directly."

Her non-answer did not please him. He stared at her in stony silence before an idea seemed to occur to him. "The pirate treasure hunt story that you're about to give me...please, don't tell me that LeDeux is involved in this, too."

"He is, but that doesn't make it any less than a great exclusive. I'll show it to you now, if you want." She was about to stand and go back to her office for the hard copy.

He waved her back down. "I want that story, and the *traiteur* one, too. Damn! Why didn't I see the connection with that Rivard woman? But consider this a notice of dismissal. You have two weeks to find another job."

She inhaled sharply. "You can't do this."

"You've given me grounds out the wazoo."

"You've been looking for those grounds ever since I took this job."

"Maybe, but you sure as hell gave them to me, all tied up in a big pink bow. Ethical standards, baby. Ethical standards."

As she stormed out of his office, she told him in very graphic terms what he could do with his ethical standards.

Fired! She reeled as the word shot through her stunned brain.

Fired! All because of John LeDeux.

Fired! She couldn't afford to be without work. She would have to start a job search immediately.

And like hell she was going to give Bruce the treasure hunt or the *traiteur* stories. They would be going with her to her new employer, whoever that might be.

She stomped back to Bruce's office and leaned in. "Forget about giving me a notice. I quit."

Then, despite Bruce's sputtering and threats that she wouldn't be able to get unemployment compensation— *As if she had ever thought that far!*—she cleared out her desk, making two trips down to her car. On her final pass through, she ignored Bruce's glare and her co-workers' glances of sympathy. Finally, in her car, heading back home, just an hour after she'd arrived, Celine sighed deeply.

She'd lost more than a good job today. She'd lost what could have been the love of her life.

Chapter
23

Then the you-know-what hit the fan...

John had tried repeatedly to contact Celine before she heard about the *National Enquirer* article from someone else. No response, even to his voice mails that it was urgent that she call him back.

He was assuming she'd found out and was pissed. With good reason. But it wasn't his fault, and he needed to explain that to her.

So, he'd headed over to Houma, bringing with him a bike he'd bought for Etienne. It was the cutest thing. A two-wheeler with training wheels, painted black with red flames. He'd seen a bike in the backyard on previous visits, but it was smaller and a bit battered.

There was no sign of Celine or her car, but there was a reporter hanging around, hoping to trap either her or him into divulging something tantalizing, though facts weren't all that important to the tabloids. If they didn't get the info from the horse's mouth, they got it from their own horse's ass selves.

He threatened to beat the crap out of the reporter, a short twenty-something guy with a broken nose and an attitude. Not a great thing for a cop to do. Nothing like a lawsuit to cap off his day. No surprise on the broken nose, though. It had to be a job hazard, working for a tabloid.

After waiting like forever in his car, parked at the curb, he decided to show the bike to Etienne, who was as ecstatic as a five-year-old could be. John told James where they were going, then walked beside Etienne as he rode the bike to Lilypond Park. James hadn't been as hostile as usual. Maybe he was warming up to him. But then he probably hadn't heard about the tabloid yet.

Etienne's mouth was going nonstop, as usual, even as he was riding his new bike.

"Do you boink?"

"Huh?"

"Boink. Dontcha know what boinkin' is? It's when a guy—"

"Whoa, tiger. I know what boinkin' is. The question is, do you? No, don't answer that. Why do you want to know if I...um, boink?"

"Pete sez when a boy likes a girl and she likes him back, they boink."

"How old is this Pete?"

"Oh, he's lots older than me. He knows *stuff*."

"How old?"

"Seven."

Good Lord! The kid is actually wondering if I'm boinking his mother.

Then, there was the animal issue.

"I want a dog."

"I know you do."

"Do dogs boink?"

"Yes."

"And cats?"

"Yes."

"And—"

"All animals boink, Etienne." *I cannot believe I said that.*

"Yeech!"

Then they moved on to more important issues.

"I like to spit."

"That's just great."

"Do you like to spit?"

"I probably did when I was your age. Now, I just spit when I have a bad taste in my mouth." *Like a hangover.*

"Pete knows how to hawk a looey. That's a big spit."

I'm gonna have to meet this Pete.

Like lightning, or Tante Lulu, he changed subjects without warning.

"Pigs smell. Why do pigs smell?"

"Do you have a dad and a mom? I only gots a mom."

"Why do girls have pussies? Is there a kitty in there?"

Thank God, Celine was pulling into the driveway when they got back. Etienne's questions were giving him a rash.

Her eyes flashed fire at him, promising a fight. But then she noticed the bike. The fire in her eyes turned into a bonfire.

"Where did you get that bicycle?" she asked Etienne in an icy voice.

The kid didn't notice her tone and enthused happily, "John bought it fer me. Ain't it cool, Mom?"

She didn't answer, but instead told him, "Go in the house and tell your grandfather to give you some cookies and milk."

"But, Mom, I wanna stay here and—"

"Etienne. Go."

With a pout, the kid steered the bike up the sidewalk and around the side of the house.

Before she had a chance to launch into him, John took her by the elbow and said, "We are not having this conversation outside. There's a tabloid reporter hanging around."

She was shocked at that prospect and let him propel her up the steps and into the living room. He could hear Etienne chattering away in the kitchen to James.

"Celine, I had nothin' to do with this tabloid garbage."

"I beg to differ."

"The camera was stolen from the evidence vault. I didn't know about it 'til this mornin'."

"And why was the photo still in the camera?"

"What?"

"You heard me. You led me to believe that you had the only photo and that you were going to destroy it. And at no time did you tell me that there were so many different shots of the...kiss."

She said *kiss* as if it were a distasteful word.

"I never promised any of that. I said I wouldn't use the photo against you in any public way if you...well, I never intended to use it anyway."

"You just wanted to barter for a weekend of wild monkey sex."

He made the mistake of smiling.

She hissed.

"Celine, be honest. I never forced you to do anything. And you never made love with me because you felt threatened."

"No, I did it because I was stupid. But not anymore."

"C'mon, Celine, we have somethin' good goin' on between us. You can't let this ruin things."

"We *had* something good, John. No more."

"You're not being fair. I'm a cop. I can't ethically destroy evidence. I did manage to keep it out of the eyes of the other officers. Give me credit for that."

"Apparently you didn't keep it out of everyone's eyesight, because someone obviously sold it to an outside buyer."

"You're right about that." He sighed deeply. "Where do we go from here?"

"Nowhere. You can see Etienne as much as you want, within reason. I choose not to be here when you arrive or bring him back."

"I might love you. I think."

"Might? Be still my heart." She laughed then, and it was not a nice laugh. "Bull!"

"You don't believe me?"

"I wouldn't believe you if you had your tongue notarized."

"You're bein' unreasonable."

"Oh, yeah? I got fired today."

"Oh, no!" He reached to her in sympathy, but she ducked away from him. "Is there anything I can do?"

"You've done enough."

"You can't lay the blame on me for this."

"Can't I? One more thing. You had no right to buy Etienne that bicycle without my permission."

"His old one was too small for him, and I happened

to see the new one in the window of a shop near Luc's office." He shrugged.

"I repeat. Don't buy him stuff."

"Hey, he's my son, too."

Their voices had gotten increasingly loud; so, it was only belatedly that they realized that Etienne was standing in the doorway, looking with puzzlement from his mother to John.

"Are you my daddy?"

Celine moaned.

This emotional abyss was not something either of them was equipped to handle today. But it couldn't be avoided.

He walked over and hunkered down to Etienne's level. "Yes, I am, Etienne. And I'm very proud to be your father."

"Why weren't ya here before?"

"I didn't know about you 'til recently. How do you feel about havin' me for a dad?"

"Okay, I guess."

"Can I give you a hug?"

The little boy pondered the request as if it was a weighty subject. "All right."

John opened his arms and held his son tightly. Eyes closed, he savored the little boy smell of him...skin, milk, and chocolate from the cookies.

"Why is Mom cryin'?"

He turned and stood in one fluid motion, Etienne still in his arms. "Because she's so happy," he lied, tears in his eyes as well.

"Are you gonna live with us?"

His eyes held Celine's, which were still filled with hurt from his presumed betrayal. "I don't know."

"Can I have a dog?"

He had to laugh then.

But Celine wasn't laughing.

He soon left, with a promise to Etienne to return for a visit the next day. As for Celine, he saw nothing but a brick wall in their future.

Maybe they were never meant to be.

Oyster shooters: the all-purpose clueless Cajun remedy...

He was drowning his sorrows in oyster shooters at Swampy's Tavern with his three brothers.

It was the middle of the afternoon, and not many customers in the place. René's band, the Swamp Rats, often entertained here with rowdy Cajun and zydeco music.

"We should probably cut out the drinking and go over to the Veterans Club to help decorate for tomorrow's pirate do," Luc said.

Gator, the longtime bartender and part-owner, lined up four shot glasses, plopped a raw oyster in each, then doused them with one hundred proof bourbon and a dash of Tabasco. Only then did he raise his bushy eyebrows in question to them.

As one, they reached for the glasses and tossed them back and down their throats. Also, as one, they did full-body shivers and exclaimed, "Whoa!"

Gator shook his bald head at them, his lone loop earring flashing in the artificial light.

"Hey, Gator, it just occurred to me..." John was staring at the bartender. "You would make a great pirate. Wanna come tomorrow?"

"Me, I get enough pirate wannabes here in the bar. I doan need ta make a fool of myself thataway." Gator went off to wait on someone over by the jukebox, which was belting out country songs.

Looking at Gator's earring as he passed, John decided, "I think I'll get my ear pierced."

"Do you remember when you were a kid," Luc prodded him with a laugh, "you asked me how men went about piercin' their cocks. Apparently you had seen somethin' in the French Quarter."

"Well, I might be blitzed, but I'm not that blitzed." *My brothers know way too much about my past.*

"You could have 'Celine' tattooed over your heart," René suggested. "Or on your butt."

"Or not!"

"You know what they say," Luc offered. "A peacock who sits on his tail is just another turkey."

"Are you tryin' ta say I'm a turkey?"

"If the shoe...uh, feathers fit, and all that."

"I'm thinkin' about quittin' my job," he disclosed, after an unexpected belch escaped his lips.

That got his brothers serious in a nanosecond.

"Why?" Luc asked.

"I don't know, this whole Mafia case and the newspaper coverage has turned me sour. Not on law enforcement, but workin' for the Fontaine department, or anywhere within a hundred miles. And I won't go back to DC and the FBI. I'm thinkin' about openin' my own private detective agency."

They all pondered that possibility. Then René remarked, "You've got a head start, Tee-John. You're already a dick."

He jabbed René in the shoulder with a fist.

Remy picked up a stick pretzel and started to chomp. The oysters in the shooters were about all they'd had to eat today. "Remind me, why're we gettin' plastered?"

None of them were that far gone, although John wished he could escape to the numbness of a good ol' bender. It had been a hell of a week.

"We're drownin' my sorrows," he told Remy.

"What sorrows?"

"Unrequited love." *Oh, crap! I didn't mean to say that.*

All three of his brothers turned to gawk at him for his flowery words. Then all three of them grinned.

"I consider your amusement a totally inappropriate reaction to my pain," he complained. Celine was holding to her decision not to see or talk to him. After a week of trying, he'd stopped trying. Didn't mean he was giving up, just reconnoitering. He'd heard that she got a new job with one of the newspaper syndicates, but that was no reason for avoiding him.

He'd never been so miserable in all his life. If this was love, it was highly overrated.

René patted him on the shoulder. "We've all been there, buddy."

"Not to worry, though," Luc chuckled. "By tomorrow night your problems should be over."

Remy and René immediately said, "Shhh" to Luc.

Too late. The hairs on the back of John's neck were not only standing erect, but they were doing the hula. "Why?"

With a sigh of resignation, figuring he'd already said too much, Luc disclosed, "I'm pretty sure Tante Lulu has a plan."

John put his face in his hands and groaned. Then he lifted his head and ordered two more oyster shooters. Once he felt a bit more braced, he confronted his brothers. "Spill."

"Charmaine ordered us not to tell you," Luc said.

"So?" It's not like they hadn't disobeyed that order before.

"You're gonna ruin the surprise, Luc," René complained.

"Tell me, dammit."

"Okay, here's the deal, and we only know this through our women. Did you know there's a pirate longship anchored out on the Gulf?'

"What? You're kiddin'."

"No kiddin', little brother," Luc replied. "Apparently Val has some connection with those people who run that Tall Ships event on the Hudson River. And apparently there are these smaller reproduction Viking/pirate longships... and ta da, they brought one here."

"My wife has connections," René bragged.

"Okay, so there's a pirate ship out on the Gulf. What does that have to do with me?"

His brothers grinned.

He was beginning to hate his brothers' grins.

"They brought a longship here for me? Wow!" *This is not gonna be good.*

"You were aware that Celine would be there, right?" This from René.

He nodded. She had the exclusive story on the treasure hunt, as promised, and would be providing reports on the entire day's events for her new employer.

"Cut to the chase, you guys. Longship, Celine... what else?"

"You'll be dressed as a pirate, and I certainly hope you plan to put Johnny Depp to shame," Luc said.

"He could do no less, our Tee-John," Remy remarked.

"Aaarrgh!" he said.

"That should be 'Arg,'" René corrected.

"Aaarrgh!" he said again.

"You're gonna capture Celine in the middle of the ball and take her off to your pirate lair... i.e. pirate ship, and have your wicked way with her, married or unmarried, depends on you, but the minister aka ship's captain will be there, along with Father Boucher from Our Lady of the Bayou Church, just in case," Luc told him in one long sentence. "Oh, and I'm gonna be handy to be best man... just in case."

"Tante Lulu's gonna give you away." Remy grinned at him.

"Etienne's gonna give his mom away." René grinned, too.

Okay, he hadn't thought his family could surprise him... or grin so damn much. But, sonofabitch! "And how would I be takin' her off to my... um, lair, since I have no trusty steed?"

"Your hog." This little tidbit from Remy.

"Huh?"

"A souped-up Police Special Shovelhead Harley, to be precise." Remy again. He was probably responsible for that choice, having had a number of bikes over the years.

John's mouth gaped open for a few long seconds. Then he smiled.

"I like it!"

Did St. Jude have pirattitude?...

"Holy smokes!" Tante Lulu said when she reentered the empty Veterans Club hall that evening before the Pirate Ball.

"I'll second that. You outdid yourself this time, Auntie," Tee-John told her with a squeeze of her shoulders.

He'd picked her up and driven her over here, probably because he didn't trust her driving at night. If it were up to her family, she wouldn't be driving at all, but they couldn't stop her. Nosirree, she had work to do.

"Well, I dint do it myself. And I sure as tootin' ain't responsible fer all these decorations. Whooee, are those live parrots in those cages? Wonder if they know any dirty words."

"You were the drivin' force, *chère.*"

"Drivin' force? I like that."

The large hall was festooned with ship sails and fish netting all over the ceiling and walls. A theater company had lent them several fake ships that were stage props. In one corner, where food and drinks would be served, was a sign that read, "Angel's Grog Shop." Another corner proclaimed: "Grace's Tavern, Good Eats." Throughout the room were dozens of skull and crossbones motifs, fake anchors, parrots, peg legs, eye patches, swords, and flintlock pistols, not to mention blown-up movie posters from dozens of pirate movies. She hadn't realized there were so many. The three *Pirates of the Caribbean* ones, of course, but then there was *Treasure Island, The Buccaneer, Blackbeard's Ghost, Blackbeard the Pirate,* and three Errol Flynn pirate movies, including *Captain Blood.*

"Now there was a real man, that Errol Flynn." She sighed.

Tee-John laughed. "Do you know where that expression 'In like Flynn' comes from?"

"By the devilish gleam in yer eyes, mebbe I doan wanna know."

"It was a tribute to Errol Flynn's talent as a seducer, especially of two underage girls who accused him of statutory rape. He was found innocent, but still the expression stuck."

She smacked him on the shoulder. "Where do ya get this nonsense? Errol Flynn was a hero."

"If you say so, Auntie."

"This is gonna be so much fun," she said, smiling at Tee-John, who hadn't been having much fun lately, thanks to Celine. Hopefully, that would change tonight. He was looking mighty fine in his pirate outfit: a white musketeer shirt tucked into black tights leading to knee-high, cuffed boots. A red sash belted his waist, where a sword hung from a sheath. He wore one gold loop earring and a patterned red handkerchief tied around his head. Johnny Depp never looked this good.

She was dressed pretty much the same, except she wore a vest over her shirt and one of those head rags over a long blonde wig, the one she'd lent to Tee-John for his disguise. A bra with falsies inside and padded-cheek panties took twenty years off her...she hoped.

Tee-John had said she looked hot when he first saw her, but then he said that all the time.

"Ya shoulda seen the crowd here this afternoon fer the media event...thass what Ronnie and Jake called the unveilin' of the Pirate Project. People was on this place like Hurricane drinks at Mardi Gras. In fact, they was chuggin' down that 'grog' like it was liquid gold."

"Where *is* the gold anyway?" John had chosen to stay away this afternoon, not wanting any more publicity than he already had, with that kiss picture floating around.

"They had it in glass cases with security guards durin' the media event. The guards, men and women, were in costumes depictin' real pirates. Afterwards, them Brinks trucks came in and carted it away. The gold is goin' ta some vault 'til they decide which coins ta sell and where."

"You're gonna be rich."

"I'm already rich, and I doan mean money."

He nodded, knowing that she referred to family. Always family.

"There was newspaper and magazine reporters and TV cameras from around the country, and a few from over the ocean. Even a Hollywood director who wants ta produce a documentary. And the usual local and state hoity toities. Ronnie sez three hundred people showed up, a hundred more than expected. A wallopin' big success, fer certain. And another three hundred'll be here t'night fer the ball. Celine was here."

"I figured she would be."

The boy looked like the tail end of hard times, and it almost broke her heart.

"She's comin' t'night with her grandad and Etienne."

"Etienne told me." He laughed. "I bought him a cute

pirate outfit off the Internet at dresslikeapirate.com. He'll probably be tryin' to climb that keel pole in the center of the room. What a little imp!"

"Jist like you."

It felt as if a fist was squeezing his heart. "Did you know there are thousands of Web sites devoted to pirates? Even ones that teach you how to talk like a pirate? Yep, talklikeapirate.com."

"Yer changin' the subject."

"I know."

"Celine still givin' ya a hard time?"

"She isn't givin' me any time at all."

"I hope she doesn't bring a date."

"Whaaat? Why did you say that? I thought David returned to Afghanistan. Is she datin' someone else? Do you know somethin' I don't?"

"I'm jist sayin'. Thass all." She could see her words had shocked the dickens out of him. Good. He needed something to jump-start his engines. "Best ya be doin' somethin' ta reel in the gal."

"Reelin'-in presumes the 'fish' has already been caught." He eyed her suspiciously. "I know about your plan, you know."

"Poo-ey!" she said with disgust. "Who tol' ya?"

"Everyone. Luc, Remy, René."

"Blabbermouths."

He arched his eyebrows at her.

"What? I ain't a blabbermouth."

He continued with the eyebrow arching business.

"Okay, a little bit of a blabbermouth. Ya doan mind our plan?"

"I'm skeptical."

"Do ya love her, Tee-John?"

He gave her a soulful look. "I'm miserable all the time. I think about her constantly. I've made a fool of myself trying to get her back. Not that I really had her to begin with."

"Thass love."

"This pirate capture thing is probably going to be a royal FUBAR. And I'll be the royal fool."

"Whass a fooey-bar?"

He laughed. "A mess. I'll tell you one thing, I'm not doin' this unless I get some cue from Celine that she...uh, feels the same."

"Ya know what ya gots ta do, dontcha?"

"St. Jude," he guessed.

"Darn tootin'."

"Hey, I'll try anything."

Chapter
24

And then she stepped into the LeDeux trap...

Celine was late when she entered the Veterans Club hall that evening, having had to finish up the treasure hunting story and upload today's photos, which took longer than she'd expected.

Etienne, and his friend Pete who'd come along, were like regular jumping beans, so excited to be involved in an actual pirate event. The two would probably get kicked out of the place if they shot the wrong person with rubber bands from their fake flintlock pistols. Gramps had already confiscated them three times while they'd waited for her to get ready. But they looked adorable in their pirate outfits, especially Etienne, who'd been wearing his ever since John brought it over yesterday. Not that she'd been there at the time. Nope, she'd made sure to avoid the louse all week.

And she missed him so much it hurt. She was beginning to wonder if she'd been too harsh with him. Cutting off her nose to spite her face.

Love hurt, she was finding that out big-time.

The two boys ran off to look at a parrot in a cage, and her grandfather, who'd dressed as what he called "an old sea dog," scooted after them. Or as much of a scoot as he could manage at his age. But then she saw an outlandishly dressed Tante Lulu, with her arm linked with a Richard Simmons pirate, grab hold of Etienne by the back of his vest. And Celine knew that between her grandfather and Tante Lulu, Etienne would be safe.

So, she relaxed and looked around.

The Jinx folks, with no small credit to those crazy LeDeuxs, sure knew how to throw a party. She'd been impressed this afternoon when she'd come to report on the pirate treasure's unveiling, but this ball tonight was something else! There had to be several hundred people here, all dressed in colorful and creative pirate and period costumes, at least a hundred of which were out on the dance floor, getting it on to "The Monster Mash," music provided by a well-known New Orleans DJ.

There was Edward Teach, better known as Blackbeard, Captain Hook from *Peter Pan*, Francis Drake, the gentleman pirate, Anne Bonny and her lover, Calico Jack Rackham, Mary Read, the fictitious Bluebeard, and of course Johnny Depp's character Jack Sparrow from *Pirates of the Caribbean*. In addition there were wenches—dockside, tavern, and just plain loose women; anonymous pirates, male and female; soldiers of that time period, both British and American; cabin boys and sailors; landlubbers, as in peasants and merchants; and everything imaginable. Some of the costumes were highly creative. She also noticed celebrity impersonators in pirate costumes. The Johnny Depp, Dolly Parton, and Pamela Anderson ones were signing autographs.

Noticing a sign announcing "Angel's Grog Shop," she walked over to talk with Angel Sabato.

"Ahoy, there, babe," he said, looking up from the tap where he was pouring a beer for a customer. "Lookin' good."

She did a little pirouette to show off her costume, which was a little more revealing than was her norm, but she wasn't feeling normal these days. It was what the costume shop called a wench dress. A peasant-style blouse, tucked into a jagged edged, knee-high skirt, cinched in by a lace-up corset thingee that made her waist appear tiny and her breasts appear voluptuous. She'd even teased her hair into a big mass of curls, sort of like the Texas 'do that Charmaine LeDeux-Lanier always wore.

"Hey, Celine, this matey here is Sven Ericcson," he said, introducing her to the guy working the booth with him.

They exchanged hellos, or rather ahoys.

He was a good-looking guy with long blond hair and muscles enough to . . . yep, a placard on the table identified him as a three-time Mr. Universe finalist. He seemed interested in her but then was called to the other end of the booth by a customer. Another sign proclaimed that all money would go for Katrina relief.

"How's business?" she asked Angel.

"Unbelievable. Sven there, along with three of his biker buddies, helped set up this event. Great guys. They're Hells Angels that I've known for years, soon to be Hells Pirates."

"Okaaay."

He just grinned.

"And you know Luc, don't you?"

She nodded at Luc, handsome as all get-out in his frock coat, lace jabot, and plumed tricorn hat. He gave her a little bow and a wink as he continued to draw "grog" from a keg.

Not wanting to take Angel away from the customers lined up behind her, she took the beer he handed her, then turned.

And wished she hadn't.

About ten feet away from her, John was dancing with a pretty young thing...a petite blonde, dressed as a barefooted cabin boy in britches and a shirt of such a thin fabric her bare breasts were clearly visible. So much for the cabin *boy* costume! They were doing some kind of jitterbug, a mixture of slow and fast dancing.

Her heart constricted painfully at seeing him with a woman. Not Eve, yet another woman. Then his eyes connected with hers in surprise. She turned quickly back to Angel. "Would you like to dance?" she asked hurriedly.

To her credit, he didn't seem surprised by her taking the lead. He was about to take off his apron when she felt John standing behind her.

"Celine, me lass," she heard as well as felt on the back of her neck.

"Go away."

"Let's dance, ye saucy minx."

She would give him a saucy minx, the scurvy dog. "Go dance with your...your..."

Without waiting for her to finish her sentence, he put an arm around her waist and pulled her out onto the dance floor. Angel, the traitor, didn't intervene.

When she was in his arms, trapped by his fingers locked behind her waist, he smiled down at her, taking in every bit of her sexy outfit. It was almost as if he were undressing her. And, fool that she was, she didn't even mind. In fact, she liked it.

"Hello, wench. I've missed you."

She had all these mean things she wanted to say, but she felt tears welling in her eyes.

He saw, and tugged her close, her face resting on his shoulder. "I know, I know," he kept saying as he ran soothing hands up and down her back. She felt him kiss the top of her head.

"That was Tank's younger sister," he said.

As if that meant anything.

"I was jealous when I saw you talkin' to Angel. Don't do it again."

She choked on a laugh. As if he had any right to tell her what to do!

"Oh, good Lord!" he said suddenly and rushed off to the center of the room, where Etienne was halfway up the keel pole and was shooting rubber bands at the people below.

She hurried after him.

Her grandfather and Tante Lulu were both there, trying to talk him down, but the little scamp just ignored them. He didn't ignore John, though.

"Etienne! Come down here right now."

Her son glanced down and grinned.

"I mean it. I won't hesitate to use the broad side of this sword to paddle your behind." He probably wouldn't, but the threat proved effective, as the grumbling boy descended slowly. Folks around them resumed dancing, and after John had hunkered down and given Etienne and his friend Pete, who had been egging him on, a good talking-to, the kids went off with her grandfather, Tante Lulu, and Remy's teenage son

Mike, who promised to show them how to sword fight with little plastic swords.

"C'mere," John said, leading her off to a side that wasn't so crowded. "I need to tell you somethin' before I go help my family with their act." He backed her up against the wall and propped both his hands over her head, leaning in so they could hear each other over the sound of the band.

"Their act? Oh, you mean the Cajun Village People thing. You're doing that tonight?" Her voice was a little breathy, and he knew it was because they were so close.

He felt a bit breathless himself. This was so important, and he needed to get it right. "Not exactly, but, yeah, there's some half-assed routine Charmaine has worked up. That's not what I want to talk about, though."

"Yo, Tee-John. Time to set up." Charmaine slapped him on the butt as she paused before passing by. "Hi, Celine." She looked from Celine to him, then winked at him in encouragement.

"Hi, Charmaine," Celine said.

"Wanna join us on stage, honey? Great outfit, by the way."

"Oh, I couldn't." Celine's face heated up at the prospect of appearing in one of their squirrely song-and-dance numbers.

Charmaine shrugged and went on.

"I love you, Celine. I honest-to-God love you. I know, this isn't the most romantic place to tell you. Why are you crying?" He could tell he'd startled her, but he didn't have much time. "Do you love me, Celine?" *Please, God, don't let her say no.*

"Yes, but—"

"No buts." He put a fingertip to her lips, then his

mouth. Gently. Just a whisper of a kiss. He didn't want to scare her off.

"There is a but, John. The misery of the past week has convinced me that I don't need this kind of stress in my life."

"Were you happier before?" *Besides, misery loves company.*

"Not happier. But calmer."

Whew! "Oh, sugar, surely you don't want to settle for calm. Listen, I have to go. Stay right here. And remember, I love you, no matter what happens." *Even if I make a fool of you and myself. Even if I drag you out of here by your hair. Even if I screw things up so bad. Even if—*

"You're acting really odd."

"You have no idea."

It was a piratical affair...

Celine laughed, she clapped, she sang along just like everyone else in the crowded hall. These LeDeuxs were something else!

They were all dressed like pirates, fancy to not-so-fancy, some with head rags and eye patches, others with frock coats. And the ladies...Tante Lulu, Sylvie, Rachel, Val, and Charmaine...were either lady pirates or pirate wenches. That Charmaine, in a low-cut peasant blouse and breeches, would tempt any pirate worth his salt.

They sang pirate songs, like "Row Me Hearties" and "Yo, Ho, Ho (and a Bottle of Rum)" with their own racy lyrics. They danced. They had the audience in stitches. At one point, Blackbeard (Tee-John) was trying to teach a pirate with a peg leg (René) how to dance. Hilarious. And John dirty dancing with Charmaine was something to behold. They gave new meaning to pirattitude.

A routine they did with famous pirate pick-up lines had the audience howling. Clearly attributing the "jokes" to a Web site called talklikeapirate.com, Rusty started out by saying to his wife, "Do you know what the top pirate pick-up lines are?"

"No, honey, what?"

Red-faced, he went on to tell her, "Wanna know why my Roger is so jolly?"

The other men, one by one, mentioned their favorites:

"I'd love to drop anchor in yer lagoon."

"How'd ya like ta scrape the barnacles off me rudder?"

"Ya know, darlin', I'm ninety-nine percent chum free."

"Prepare to be boarded!"

"They don't call me Long John because me head is so big."

"Let's get together and haul some keel."

"That's some treasure chest ye've got."

"Well, blow me down!"

Not to be outdone, Charmaine announced the top pick-up lines for lady pirates, starting with, "So, tell me, why do they call ye Cap'n Feathersword?"

And the other lady pirates followed up with:

"I've crushed ten men's skulls between me thighs."

"That's quite a cutlass ye've got there, lad. What ye need is a good scabbard."

"Wanna shiver me timbers?"

After the laughter died down, they announced a special final skit called "Blackbeard in Love."

Tante Lulu started it out by stepping up to the microphone, "Avast, me hearties! There once was a pirate named Blackbeard who loved a nice pirate lady named ... Tiffany."

Val continued, "But Tiffany didn't want to have anything to do with the blackguard," and rolled her eyes.

"He was so sad," Tante Lulu continued.

John, presumably Blackbeard, now with mustache and goatee, swaggered up and gave a woeful look at his aunt.

"The poor pirate," Tante Lulu related. "He picked posies fer her when on land. He robbed ships ta get her fine gold necklaces. He kissed her 'til her knees wobbled and her juices boiled."

Rachel stepped up and pretended to swoon.

The audience laughed at this.

"Still Tiffany resisted his efforts. Does ya wanna know what happened?"

The audience yelled, "Yes!"

"Well, Blackbeard's buddies, Jack Sparrow ..."

Luc stepped forward.

"And Bluebeard ..."

Remy now.

"And Peg-leg Pete ..."

René, of course.

"All of them, and that Jack Sparrow, came up with an idea. Blackbeard would capture Tiffany and whisk her off on his trusty steed."

"Where would he take her?" everyone else on the stage chimed. John had disappeared.

"Well, blimey," Luc declared, "to his lair aboard the good ship *Skull 'n Bones,* of course."

"But...but...did Blackbeard have a trusty steed?" Val asked the audience.

Suddenly the roar of a motorcycle erupted outside the hall, and the audience laughed again.

"But, by jingo, where is Tiffany?" Remy inquired into the mike.

Silence came over the audience as everyone looked around, then parted into a wide corridor in the direction of security guard pirates in the crowd. And suddenly Celine realized that the corridor led to...*her*.

She no sooner thought *Yikes!* than the motorcycle came roaring through the front door, right into the hall and up to her. To no one's surprise, it was Blackbeard on the souped-up cycle, better known as that rascal John LeDeux. With the motorcycle idling in front of her, he smiled and said, "Hop on."

"No way!" She tried to back up but realized she was already up against the wall.

"Either hop on, or I put you on. Your choice."

"You're crazy."

"What else is new?" Realizing that everyone was watching, he jumped off, walked over, and lifted her up by the waist and onto the seat, her skirt riding up her thighs.

While she was busy pulling the hem down, he hopped on behind her, whispering in her ear, "I hope you've got panties on, darlin'. Then again, no, I don't." With that he revved the engine and they were off, her holding on to the seat for dear life, and John's genitals prodding her behind.

They zoomed out the door and up to the highway. Soon they were riding off toward the Gulf.

At first, she was too stunned to protest. Then she half-turned to tell him to turn the damn bike around, when she noticed...rather heard...a loud noise behind them. "What is that?"

"The weddin' party."

"No!" she said. But, yes, they were being followed by a train of motorcycles.

"Unfortunately, yes," he said.

He stepped on the accelerator then, and she could no longer speak. And John, who could have spoken in her ear, remained oddly silent.

Just as suddenly as he'd speeded up, he slowed down, then began a series of maneuvers, in one street and down another, clearly trying to evade their followers. When it became apparent that he'd lost the other cyclists, he pulled into a park. To her surprise, it was Lilypond Park near her home.

He shut off the ignition and jumped off, walking away from her.

Celine just sat there, stunned. What had just happened? First, he'd embarrassed the life out of her by making her a spectacle at the Pirate Ball, claiming to be taking her to some pirate lair. And did someone mention a wedding? Then he came here to a park and just left her.

Slowly, she got off, then walked up to him where he stood with his forehead against the monkey bars.

"John, what's happening?"

"My family...my dingbat family...planned the whole thing, and I was actually going along with it. I would capture you at the ball, take you off to my pirate ship out on the Gulf...and, yes, unbelievably, they've got a real brig there. There is a ship's captain and a priest waiting there, too, in case we wanted to get married. Talk about! Typical LeDeux crap!"

Celine didn't understand. "If you were going along with it, why did you stop? Not that I wanted you to continue."

He turned and smiled...a sad smile. "I decided I didn't want you like that."

Her heart sank. It shouldn't matter, but, oh, it hurt so bad to hear him say he didn't want her.

"Don't look like that, Celine." He put a hand to her face, and she could have wept at the sheer joy of his touch.

"You decided you don't want me?" Her voice wobbled with emotion.

He laughed. "Just the opposite. I want you too much."

"I don't understand." She couldn't help herself; she turned her face slightly and kissed the palm that still held her face.

Inhaling sharply on a hiss, he explained, "I want us to be married. But not in a heated rush, or a crazy-assed spectacle. I want to be married in a church, with me in a tuxedo and you in a gown, and Etienne there, and my family, and...I don't know. I just don't want to do it like this."

"Oh, John!" She was so choked up she could barely speak.

John dropped down to one knee in front of her, looking absolutely ridiculous in his pirate outfit, still sporting the mustache and goatee. He took one of her hands in his and asked, "Celine Arseneaux, will you marry me?"

She couldn't speak.

"I sure as hell hope those are tears of joy."

She nodded, practically bawling, then dropped to her knees in front of him. "Yes." She kissed him, over and over and over, between sobs. "Yes, yes, yes, yes, yes."

He shifted back slightly and looked down. "Have I told you how much I like...laces?"

She looked down as well, and grinned at the bulge between them. "Have I told you how much I like...tights?"

When they finally came up for a breather, after they'd made love on the monkey bars of Houma Lilypond Park, he quipped, "I take that as a 'yes.'"

His family didn't find them 'til next morning at his cabin, where they'd celebrated a pre-wedding honeymoon.

Tante Lulu was ecstatic. And no one was surprised to hear her say, "Thank you, St. Jude."

Chapter
25

Another LeDeux bites the dust...

One month later, John LeDeux and Celine Arseneaux were married at Our Lady of the Bayou Church in Houma.

He wore a tuxedo, the bride wore a flowing white gown that once belonged to Tante Lulu. Luc was the best man, and Charmaine was the maid of honor. Ushers were Remy, René, Jake, Angel, Caleb, and Adam. Bridesmaids in sleek peach sheath dresses were Ronnie, Grace, Rachel, Sylvie, and Val. James Arseneaux gave the bride away. Tante Lulu, tears streaming down her face, gave Tee-John away. Even Tante Lulu looked classy today, her gray hair neatly coifed in a curly cap topped by a red straw hat to match her red silk, calf-length gown. Etienne, in a mini tux, was the ring bearer, and Charmaine's Mary Lou was the flower girl.

Everyone expressed surprise that the wildest of the LeDeux brothers would insist on such a traditional wedding attended by five hundred of Louisiana's best... and not so best. Even the reception was a sedate affair at the country club. Well, not so sedate. There was a huge blown-up photo behind the wedding party's table of John and Celine kissing, the infamous one from the Playpen. And, once the sumptuous Cajun dinner was over and they got past the praline peach-tiered cake-cutting and bridal bouquet-tossing and garter nonsense—Angel took the honors of putting Celine's garter on Grace's leg in an exercise so sexy it would go down in Louisiana wedding history—then the music started. And John Le-Deux showed everyone that he still had a lot of wild left in him.

Lizzie, who would be trying out for *American Idol* again next week, sang "Oh, Promise Me," then a bunch of other hokey love songs, to the enthusiastic clapping of a horde of new fans.

He dirty danced his bride around that dance floor. They chicken-danced and did the Hokey Pokey with everyone, including Etienne, who it turned out was quite a good dancer. Well, no wonder, considering who his daddy was.

Since Ronnie's grandfather Frank Jinkowsky and his girlfriend Flossie were there, the band had to play a few polkas. Watching Cajuns polka was not pretty.

Valcour LeDeux and his wife Jolie, John's mother, were invited, but did not come. John had no desire to see his father and barely tolerated his mother. Still, he'd felt the need to invite them, but was thankful they hadn't accepted.

John kissed his bride so many times that evening, the partygoers lost count. He smacked her on the butt. She pinched his butt in return. He chugged down oyster shooters, and taught his bride how to appreciate the delicacy, too.

The couple planned to make their home at his enlarged stilted cabin on Bayou Black. Celine would continue to work for the newspaper syndicate, and John would continue as a cop, though he still harbored ideas about going off on his own as a detective. His friend Tank Woodrow might even join him, a decision to be made after the wedding.

The only surprise came at the end of the evening when two strangers arrived.

Tante Lulu took one look at them, slapped a hand over her heart, and said, "Oh, my God!"

The two men, early thirties, were twins, clearly not invited guests since they were not dressed for a wedding. One wore jeans and a T-shirt that said, "Alaska Air Shipping." The other wore khakis and a button-down shirt.

They were tall and tanned and good-looking. And they were clearly LeDeuxs, more of that Valcour LeDeux's illegitimate offspring. Aaron and Dr. Daniel LeDeux had come to Louisiana to confront their miscreant father, whom they'd only heard about recently on the death of their mother.

Tante Lulu tried to make them feel welcome, though they were brooding sorts, unused to the open hospitality of Cajuns, she supposed. Must be all that cold up North, she conjectured to Tee-John.

"Do ya s'pose that Valcour was doin' it with an Eskimo?" she whispered to Tee-John just before he left for his honeymoon to parts unknown, though a pirate ship was rumored to be involved.

The twins overheard, and Daniel told her in a cold voice, "My mother was a Cajun, born in Lafayette."

The other twin, equally cold, though why they felt the need to be cold to her was something she would address and soon, guaranteed, added, "And a physician, like Dan here...though not back then."

"Are you two married?"

"No!" they both said, as if she'd asked them if they were two-headed aliens. Talk about!

Tee-John, laughing, leaned over and whispered in her ear. "Maybe you have two more candidates for the thunderbolt."

Tante Lulu brightened. "Does you two have hope chests?"

Gaping at her, and she wasn't even in her usual outrageous attire, Aaron shook his head and said, "Are you crazy?"

Everyone around them answered for her, "Yes!"

Tante Lulu just smiled and said, "Does anyone hear thunder?"

TANTE LULU'S PEACHY PRALINE COBBLER CAKE

The cake:
white cake mix
3 whole eggs
1/3 cup oil
1 cup water

The streusel:
½ cup brown sugar (more or less, depending on taste)
2 pkgs (1.23 oz each) peaches-and-cream instant oatmeal
3 oz pecan pralines, chopped (reserve 2 tbsp for garnish)
¼ cup (½ stick) butter, melted

Fruit:
1 medium peach, sliced thin, or 1 small can peaches, thoroughly drained

The frosting:
1 cup milk
4 tbsp cornstarch
1 cup Crisco (half butter, if desired)
2 cups granulated sugar
pinch of salt
2 tsp vanilla

The cake: Preheat oven to 350 degrees. Make cake batter and put into two round, greased and floured, cake pans. Mix streusel, and sprinkle over top of both cakes. Bake 35 minutes or until toothpick inserted in center comes out clean. Let cakes cool.

The frosting: Cook milk and cornstarch until thick, stirring often. Cool. Cream all remaining ingredients, adding the cornstarch mixture gradually. It should be fluffy and not overly sweet.

Place one of the cooled layers, streusel side up, on a cake platter. Frost, topping with half the sliced peaches. Cover with the second cake, streusel side up. Frost top and sides. Garnish with sliced peaches in a pinwheel pattern, finishing with sprinkle of remaining chopped pralines.

Note:
♦ This is a very rich cake because of the streusel and instant oatmeal. If using plain oatmeal, the amount of brown sugar can be altered, to taste.
♦ Peach juice, if available, can be substituted for some or all of the water in the cake.
♦ Any white frosting can be used, keeping in mind how sweet the cake already is. A Crisco frosting will be less sweet.
♦ Of course the white cake can be made from scratch.

Last bit of instructions from Tante Lulu: "Set out a pitcher of iced sweet tea, *chère*. Invite over your friends and family. Then, *Laissez les bons temps rouler!* Let the good times roll!"

Dear Reader:

Well, finally, that Cajun rogue Tee-John LeDeux got his own story. Hope it was wild enough for you.

And Tante Lulu certainly was in her usual rare form, if I do say so myself. I love the one description of her in this book: Grandma Moses with cleavage! Yep, that says it all.

You will notice that I have left the door open for several other books. Angel Sabato and Grace O'Brien, for example. Or the twins from Alaska: Aaron and Daniel LeDeux. Whatever future books may be on the horizon, please know this: Tante Lulu will never die in any of my books. And besides, she still has a few more hope chests to make and St. Jude statues to pass out.

I have said it before and will say it again, I love the Cajun country: its beauty, its music, its language, its food, and its culture. With that in mind, after hundreds of requests, I have included Tante Lulu's recipe for Peachy Praline Cobbler Cake in this book, and there will be more free Cajun recipes on my Web site. In fact, send me some of your favorites to share.

I try to be as accurate as possible in my books, but sometimes it's the little facts that we mess up on. Yes, I now know that you don't peel okra. Yes, I now know that John Deere tractors are only ever green and yellow. And, holy crawfish, who knew there were no big rocks in southern Louisiana? You readers sure do keep me on my toes, and I love you for it.

There really are numerous Web sites on the Internet dealing with pirates, as mentioned in this book. The one I especially like is www.talklikeapirate.com, from which I have shamelessly borrowed humor—with attribution, of course.

Please visit my Web site for lots of free goodies: original novellas, genealogy charts, books, videos, recipes, and promotional materials. As always, I thank you for your support and wish you smiles in your reading.

Sandra Hill
www.sandrahill.net
email: shill733@aol.com

About the Author

Sandra Hill is the best-selling author of more than twenty novels and the recipient of numerous awards.

Readers love the trademark humor in her books, whether the heroes are Vikings, Cajuns, Navy SEALs, or treasure hunters, and they tell her so often, sometimes with letters that are laugh-out-loud funny. In addition, her fans feel as if they know the characters in her books on a personal basis, especially the outrageous Tante Lulu.

At home in central Pennsylvania with her husband, four sons, and a dog the size of a horse, Sandra is always looking for new sources of humor. It's not hard to find.

Two of her sons have Domino's Pizza franchises, and one of the two plays in poker competitions. They swear they are going to write a humor book entitled *The Pizza Guys' Guide to Poker*.

Her husband, a stockbroker, is very supportive of her work. He tells everyone he is a cover model. In fact, he made that claim one time when she did a radio interview and swears the traffic around their home was heavy for a while as people tried to get a gander at the handsome model. Then there was the time he made a blow-up of one of her early clinch covers with a hunk and a half-naked woman and hung it in his office. He put a placard under it saying, "She lost her shirt in the stock market . . . but does she look like she cares?"

So be careful if you run into Sandra. What you say or do may end up in a book. If you want to take the chance, you can contact her through her Web site at www.sandrahill.net.

Want to know more about romances at Grand Central Publishing and Forever? Get the scoop online!

GRAND CENTRAL PUBLISHING'S ROMANCE HOMEPAGE

Visit us at www.hachettebookgroupusa.com/romance for all the latest news, reviews, and chapter excerpts!

NEW AND UPCOMING TITLES

Each month we feature our new titles and reader favorites.

CONTESTS AND GIVEAWAYS

We give away galleys, autographed copies, and all kinds of fun stuff.

AUTHOR INFO

You'll find bios, articles, and links to personal websites for all your favorite authors—and so much more!

THE BUZZ

Sign up for our monthly romance newsletter, and be the first to read all about it!